IN THAT SLEEP OF DEATH

AN ADAM LAPID MYSTERY

JONATHAN DUNSKY

In That Sleep of Death

Jonathan Dunsky

Copyright © 2024 by Jonathan Dunsky

Cover designed by Deranged Doctor Design (DerangedDoctorDesign.com)

Cover Photographs © Malivan_Iuliia/Shutterstock (man); inLite studio/Shutterstock (man); Marina Litvinova/Shutterstock (street); ZoranKrstic/Shutterstock (storm)

Published by Lion Cub Publishing.

ISBN: 978-965-7795-47-7

Visit JonathanDunsky.com for news and information.

BOOKS BY JONATHAN DUNSKY

To Stacey Levy

1

The first time I saw him was on a night with bad dreams. I woke up screaming, my body drenched in sweat, my heart thumping in terror. I'd kicked the winter blanket to the floor, and my violent tossing and turning had twisted the sheet off the bottom of the mattress.

My room was stifling, the air stale and heavy. It felt like a prison cell. I couldn't bear to stay there a second longer.

I threw on some clothes and exited the apartment without bothering to wash my face or dry the sweat off my skin. My shirt clung to my back like a parasite. Outside, not a soul stirred. Hamaccabi Street was empty and silent. No lights shone in any of the apartments. Everyone was asleep. My watch said it was a little after three.

It was March 19, 1952, and the air had a cold bite. I buttoned up my coat, raised the collar, and blew hot air on my palms.

On the corner of Hamaccabi and King George, I stopped to light a cigarette, and that was when I saw him. A tall, slender figure walking on the opposite side of King George. He wore dark slacks and a black jacket and... it couldn't be. I had to blink twice to make sure, but there was no mistake. The man was wearing army boots. The cuffs of his slacks were tucked into them.

He walked at an unhurried, plodding pace. His arms swung like slow metronomes at his sides. His head was lowered, his back slightly stooped, his eyes aimed at the sidewalk in front of him. As though he were carrying a heavy burden or was weary to the bone.

And why wouldn't he be? It was the middle of the night. He should be in his bed, tucked under the covers, dreaming of better times. Yet here he was, just like me, a solitary walker on the nighttime streets of Tel Aviv.

Was he also driven from his bed by nightmares? Did his bedroom feel as suffocating as mine?

I did not know his name, had never seen him before, yet I felt a strange kinship toward him, this night wanderer. For an instant, I was about to call out, to announce my presence, but something held my tongue.

Would he want my companionship? Was I even sure I wanted his? Wasn't our presence, mine and his separately, on the street at this ungodly hour proof that we were lonely creatures by habit or circumstance? It would be rude to impose myself upon him.

So as he trod the sidewalk north, I took the opposite south. And so, with each step, the distance between us widened, so that when I turned to gaze behind me a minute or so later, I could see no sign of him.

———

The following night, rousted out of bed by another savage nightmare, I walked toward the sea. Gradually, as I approached, the slap of incoming waves grew from a whisper to a roar. I stood on the promenade and gazed westward at the Mediterranean, a roiling endless surface silvered by the full moon.

I thought about the home I'd once had. The country that had expelled me to a near certain death. Hungary was a wound that could never heal, a betrayal that could never be forgiven. And a lesson on what it meant to be a Jew in a foreign land.

A movement down on the beach broke my reverie. I squinted, unsure if what I was seeing was real or merely a trick of moonlight and shadow. But no. I wasn't mistaken. There he was. The solitary walker I had seen the previous night.

His black hair and dark clothes blended with the night. If not for the paleness of his face and the swinging of his arms, I would not have been able to make him out. From where I stood, I couldn't tell whether he was wearing army boots or regular black shoes.

He strode right on the waterline. Sea foam licked at his feet. He didn't seem to notice or care. He did not gaze up at the moon, did not pause to appreciate the untamed beauty of the sea. He simply trudged onward, toward what I could not imagine.

There was an intentness to his gait. A grim, laborious purposefulness. As though his walking was not a means to an end but an end in and of itself. Again, I had the urge to call out to him, to perhaps share with him the reason for my nightly sojourn, and inquire as to his. But as on the previous night, I held my peace and did not disturb his. Though looking at him, I was far from sure that peace was the state he was in.

But the real reason I kept my silence was that the man, or the manner of his walk, prodded at a memory that lay buried just beneath my consciousness. Whatever the elusive memory was, my reaction to its proximity was unmistakable. My throat constricted, and a vise tightened around my heart. Breathing through my mouth to ease the anxiety that coursed through me, I kept my eyes on the man as he slogged north on the damp sand, leaving footprints that were soon claimed by the sea.

———

Three nights later, I was once more banished from my apartment in the middle of the night. My sleep was often plagued by night terrors, but the past week, my dreams had been particularly horrific. Part reality, part imagination, the images I saw, the voices that howled in my head, were intensely brutal. I could feel them chasing me down the stairs and into the dark street below.

The night was cold and damp. It had rained earlier, and the sidewalks were slick and glistening. A sharp wind curled around me, probing the defenses of my clothes, nipping at my skin through every crevice and opening.

Allenby Street, normally bustling and loud, stretched empty and forlorn, as though Tel Aviv were a ghost town and not a lively new city in a vibrant new country.

I walked past Moghrabi Theater, looming like an abandoned pagan temple, past shuttered storefronts and vacant bus stops, pausing for a moment to peek into Greta's Café, now dark and empty. The thudding of my shoes on the sidewalk was the only sound. I moved from darkness to light and back again as I entered and exited the pools of illumination cast by streetlights. My thoughts made a similar dance, waltzing from the mundane to the dejected. Mostly, I wondered what had brought on the increased venom of my nightmares and when they would return to a more manageable level of toxicity. I was at the corner of Allenby and Maze when I nearly ran into the man.

He had rounded the corner in total silence, or perhaps my ruminations had simply deafened me. I had to jump back to avoid colliding with him.

"Hey, I'm sorry," I said, heart stuttering due to the near collision. "I didn't see you."

The man gave no indication that he had heard me. He did not stop; his step did not falter. He simply walked on at that same steady, leaden pace. Each foot rose slowly, as though pulled against its will, before coming down with a dull thump. It was the walk of a man who was going nowhere.

Tonight the man's slacks were gray. But the boots were the same. I had been right: they were army boots. Black and scuffed and creased. I noticed the heels showed advanced signs of wear. These boots had seen many miles. Judging by the glimpse I had gotten of the man's face, it was clear the same could be said of him.

Was he sleepwalking? Or was he as enveloped in thought as I had been a moment ago? Was that the reason he hadn't heard or seen me? Or maybe he had and simply chose not to display any awareness of my presence. A man walking alone at this hour might resent any attempt to intrude upon his solitude.

He smelled of old and fresh sweat, which made me think he had been walking for a long while. His clothes were simple but did not look old, not like his boots. I stood for a while watching him put one foot in front of the other as he continued up Allenby Street. Not once did the rhythm of his march shift. Not once did the angle of his head change. There was a mindlessness to his gait, as though he were an automaton, driven by gears and cogs instead of human emotions and desires.

As I watched his back recede, I couldn't shake off the image of his face. It clung to the forefront of my mind like an indelible memory. Long and lean and pale, with sharp cheekbones and furrows across his forehead too deep for a man in his late twenties. But it was his mouth and eyes that imprinted his features upon my brain. His mouth with his lips pulled back and his teeth tightly clenched, as though he were barring a scream. His eyes haunted and tortured yet strangely flat and distant. They were the eyes and mouth of a man not merely gripped by a nightmare but living one.

I stared at him until he turned a corner and disappeared from view. Only then did I notice the cold that had seeped into my bones.

———

I looked for him the next night, scouring the streets near my apartment—Allenby, King George, Sheinkin, Balfour—but did not see him. Finally, I went home, chiding myself for my foolishness. Why was I sacrificing hours of sleep seeking this man whom I did not know? This did not stop me from repeating the exercise the following night. This time I headed to the beach, where I had seen him the second time. I stood and gazed at the sand being pummeled by the waves, huddled in my coat against the salty wind that whipped around me. I stayed there for a long time, an hour at least, but the man did not show.

The third night, I widened my search, going all the way to the

Yarkon River to the north and Jaffa Road to the south. I walked for over three hours, increasingly questioning my sanity, but propelled onward by an undefined need to see the man again. As I walked, I imagined our meeting. Questions I would ask him, the conversation we would have, the sound of his voice, his accent. I had a suspicion that I would be disappointed when such an encounter actually took place, but I could not say why I felt so.

As the eastern sky grayed with the onset of dawn, I gave up and headed home. I crashed on my bed and slept fitfully in my clothes until noon.

After midnight that night, I went in search of him again, this time venturing deep into Jaffa. I walked empty roads lined with crumbling buildings, past alleyways where the shadows were thick and menacing, down shabby streets where the sidewalks were as narrow as an afterthought. These could be dangerous streets at night, so I kept a hand in my pocket where my knife nestled, but this precaution did not prevent me from berating myself for my recklessness.

As I pounded the pavement, I imagined the man was at this moment traversing another part of the city, his army boots beating a somber rhythm that harmonized with mine. Did he feel that I was seeking him out? Did he sense that he was not alone? Or was he as oblivious of my existence as he'd seemed the time we'd almost collided? Would our paths cross again, or were we now two moons orbiting the same planet but never sharing the same space? Was our chance meeting a onetime occurrence? And why did this possibility sadden me so?

At three o'clock, my back throbbing and feet aching, I ended my search and started for home. I was angry at myself for the time and energy I'd expended on this inexplicable quest. I vowed that this was the last time, that I would not sacrifice another minute of sleep looking for this stranger.

Yet, when I got to the corner of Allenby and Maze, where I had nearly run into the man, I veered from my intended route and hooked a right. I knew what I was doing. I was hoping against hope that on this final attempt I would stumble upon him again, even as I was going home. From Maze, I turned north to Yohanan Hasandlar and decided to cut through Sheinkin Garden on the way back to King George.

The boots protruded from behind a hedgerow. From their position, I could tell that their owner was lying flat on his back.

I ran forward, and there he lay. His head tilted leftward, his washed-out green eyes gazing directly at me with an eerie blankness. His mouth hung open and slack, his face strangely serene. He appeared to be genuinely at peace.

As long as you disregarded his caved-in skull and the halo of blood surrounding his head.

————

I swore under my breath, then cast a quick look around.

Nothing stirred. The murderer was gone. Crouching next to the dead man in the army boots, I ran my eyes over his body. There did not seem to be any injuries apart from the massive one to his head. Not that there needed to be. The one to the head was all it took.

I touched my fingers to the man's throat and felt no pulse. Not that I expected any. Only dead men don't blink.

Using my handkerchief, I reached into the dead man's pocket and retrieved his identification card. Now I finally had his name, Emmanuel Feldbaum, and an address in the northern town of Afula, quite a distance from Tel Aviv. I committed both to memory before returning the identification card to its place, wondering what Feldbaum had been doing here, so far from home.

I searched the other pockets and found no wallet, which suggested a robbery. A robbery might also explain the positioning of the body. Hit a man on the back of the head and he will usually fall forward on his face. But Feldbaum's body was supine, not prone. Why the discrepancy? Because the mugger had turned him over to gain easier access to his pockets. But why would a mugger lurk here, in Sheinkin Garden, in the middle of the night?

In hopes of catching the odd night owl alone with no witnesses around, that's why. I smiled at my own foolishness. What was I doing, going through this man's pockets? His death was a police matter now. It was no business of mine.

And yet...

My eyes landed on Feldbaum's face. An oddly personal sadness came over me, and I couldn't tell why. This man was a stranger to me. He and I had no connection to one another apart from our nocturnal excursions. But here I was, with an acute sense of grief as though he and I had shared some fate.

I rose to my feet and did a quick grid search around the body. Nothing but dry leaves and crumpled cigarette butts and blood. It hadn't rained in a couple of days, and the earth here was hard and dry, not conducive to footprints. However, two shallow drag marks trailed a meter or so from Feldbaum's boots, indicating that the killer had dragged the body to better hide it behind the hedgerow.

But there was nothing that pointed to the killer's identity. Nothing to indicate where he had gone after the crime. At least nothing that I could see in the dim glow of moonlight.

There was nothing I could do for Emmanuel Feldbaum. I hoped the police would find justice for him.

I walked to the nearest pay phone, thumbed a coin into the machine, and called the police. I told them that I had come upon the body of a man in Sheinkin Garden and that it appeared the man had been murdered. When the officer asked for my name, I cradled the receiver.

The civic thing to do would have been to give my identity, wait for the police where I'd found the body, and tell them everything I knew about Emmanuel Feldbaum. But what did I really know? Nothing that could shed light on who killed him. And I knew that anyone who finds a body is treated as a suspect. And in these circumstances, me crossing a gloomy public garden in the wee hours of the morning, the initial suspicion would be even greater. I had some contacts in the police, including a few detectives, but I did not think that would help me much. Especially if I told the police that I had seen Feldbaum several times over the past week, always late at night. In that case, I would become the subject of an intense investigation. My life would be scrutinized, and I did not want that. Some of the things I did, including how I made a part of my living, were not entirely within the boundaries of the law. Inviting the police to examine my affairs could have highly negative consequences.

So after I ended the call, I made my way home. I removed my shoes and clothes and got into the shower. I closed my eyes and leaned my head against the wall and let the hot spray sting my shoulders and back. The water sluiced the sweat off my skin and the tension out of my body, but it did not remove the image of Emmanuel Feldbaum from my mind. Feldbaum with his eyes dead and open, his skull breached, and his worn-out boots in which he would never walk another step.

2

The story came too late for the morning papers, but the evening papers picked it up. There it was, near the bottom of the front page, wedged between a short piece on a diplomatic scuffle in the United Nations and an advertisement for Dubek cigarettes. The headline screamed "Man Found Murdered in Sheinkin Garden."

A little after three o'clock this morning, police were alerted to Sheinkin Garden by an anonymous phone call. Upon arrival, police officers discovered the body of a man who had been bludgeoned to death. The motive for the murder remains unclear. The police are pursuing several leads. The name of the victim is withheld until the next of kin can be notified.

I wondered who that next of kin might be. I doubted the police would be able to tell them very much. I ran a weary hand over my tired face and wondered for the thousandth time since I had come upon the body who had murdered Emmanuel Feldbaum and why.

It's none of your business, Adam, I told myself. *It's a police matter. You didn't even know the man. Don't waste your time brooding over things that aren't your concern.*

During that evening and the days that followed, I endeavored to do just that. But every morning, I found myself scouring the papers for additional news about the murder.

There was none.

Like a stone tossed into a pond, the story had made a small splash and then sank out of sight, relinquishing its hold on the news with shameful alacrity, as though the slaying of a man warranted but the briefest spell of public attention.

Two months passed with no news of the killing. As life dragged me onward, the way it invariably does, I found myself thinking less and less of Emmanuel Feldbaum. In a little more time, there's no doubt he would have slipped from my mind entirely.

But then something happened that stopped this process cold.

————

The man who entered Greta's Café was stocky, about five ten, with a thick neck and curly black hair that was in full-blown retreat at the temples. Brown eyes, wide face, big nose, large lips. Hair peeking over the collar of his shirt; more of it tufting his forearms. Late thirties, I estimated, but I might have been shortchanging him a little.

He wore a short-sleeved white shirt tucked into black trousers and a workman's cap, which he removed upon entering the café. He kept turning it in his large hands as he walked up to the serving counter and spoke to Greta. She flicked her eyes my way, and the man's gaze followed. I watched him approach with heavy, tentative steps.

"Mr. Lapid?"

I was in the middle of a chess game. The man seemed to notice the board for the first time and hastily said, "I'm sorry. I didn't mean to interrupt. I'll—"

"No. That's all right." I pushed the board aside. "Why don't you take a seat, Mister...?"

"Rapoport," he said. "Ami Rapoport." Instead of sitting, he glanced at the empty chair across from me and then around, searching for my opponent. There was none to be found. I'd been playing a lightning game against myself. A way to take my mind off... well, everything, but now the moment was spoiled.

"Don't worry, Mr. Rapoport. No one is coming."

He frowned slightly, turned his cap another full revolution, and finally sat. He put the cap near the edge of the table, then pulled his hands onto his lap. He licked his lips, a picture of indecision. I didn't prompt or encourage him. A man comes to a private detective, you give him all the time he needs.

"I hope you can help me, Mr. Lapid," he said at length.

"That depends on the sort of help you need."

"What I need is a detective. I understand you are one."

"Who told you that?"

"A policeman over at the station on Yehuda Halevi Street. A nice officer named Tzanani."

"Ah, Reuben. Yes, he is nice."

"He said you're good. That you used to be a police detective. He said if anyone could help me, it would be you. I'm not sure what you can do that the police couldn't, but..." He turned up his hands.

"But here you are," I said.

"Yes. Here I am." His eyes betrayed his uncertainty in my abilities. I wasn't offended. I was one guy working alone, with nowhere near the resources of the Israeli police. Why shouldn't he be dubious of my chances of helping him?

"In truth, Mr. Rapoport, I can't guarantee results. What I can say is that if I take on your case, I'll give it a damn good try."

His eyes went down and then up again. "I don't have much money."

"We can talk about that later. First, how about telling me why you need a detective?"

He rubbed his hand over his mouth and jaw, then gave an almost imperceptible nod. He had made up his mind.

"A man was murdered two months ago," he said. "His name was Emmanuel Feldbaum. What is it?"

"Oh, eh, nothing." I wiped the surprise off my face. "I'm just familiar with the name, I think. I may have read about him in the newspaper."

"Yes, there were some reports."

"Let me see if I remember," I said, feigning an attempt to seize an elusive memory, though all the details stood out in sharp relief before my mind's eye. "The body was found in Sheinkin Garden, right?"

"You have a very good memory."

I shrugged, kicking myself for being too much on the money. If I weren't careful, Rapoport might begin to wonder how I knew so much about an obscure homicide that had not been mentioned in the press for over a month.

Trying to undo the damage, I said, "If I recall correctly, he was stabbed, wasn't he?"

"No, that's not what happened. Emmanuel was hit on the head. The police say it could have been a hammer or a pipe, something like that." Rapoport's throat shifted as he worked hard at swallowing the gruesome image.

"I take it the police have not made much progress."

"None whatsoever, far as I can tell. One of the detectives explained to me that this sort of crime can be tricky to solve. A middle-of-the-night robbery. No witnesses. A random victim. Nothing much to go on."

"He's right. Such cases can be difficult. Was anything of value taken?"

"Why do you ask?"

"If a certain item was stolen—a watch, a ring, something like that —the police will ask around to see if it was pawned off or fenced. Often, you can get a lead that way."

"I got the impression the police were mostly waiting for evidence to fall into their laps. That they weren't actively seeking it."

I explained why that might be so. A police force juggles many cases, with fresh ones coming in all the time. As any detective knows, the fresher the case, the easier it is to solve it. Evidence and leads, like produce or bread, grow stale quickly. That's why cases that don't yield quick breakthroughs are often relegated to the back of the line. Not closed and sometimes not forgotten either, but starved of attention and resources while detectives move on to more recent crimes.

Rapoport absorbed all this in somber silence, a slight pressing of the lips his only sign of anger at this unjust reality. I got the sense that he was a man used to the disappointments of life. Yet here he was, unwilling to surrender to another one.

"Is that also how it is with you?" he asked. "You work a case only until a new one comes along?"

"Not at all. That's because I don't have superiors to report to or paperwork to fill out, and I can always turn a prospective client down. I work a case until I feel I can't do anything more about it. Or until the client tells me to stop."

"Why would a client do that?"

"Usually because they don't want to pay to have me continue, not when the chances of success are so slim."

"I see," he said, shifting in his seat. "Like I said, I don't have much money."

"We can work something out, Mr. Rapoport. Don't worry about that for now. Let's talk about Emmanuel Feldbaum. What was he to you? What can you tell me about him?"

3

"We met in a concentration camp called Sachsenhausen in April 1945," Rapoport said. "A few weeks before Germany surrendered to the Allies. I'd been in different camps beforehand. I was in Gross-Rosen and later in Mittelbau-Dora. You heard of these camps?"

"A little," I said. "I don't know much about them."

"All were concentration camps in Germany. Gross-Rosen and Mittelbau-Dora were horrible, and from what I understand, Sachsen-hausen wasn't any better. Though all of them must have been better than those awful places in Poland, like Sobibor or Auschwitz or"—he paused, and I saw his gaze flit from the number tattoo on my forearm to my eyes and then away—"or Treblinka. That's where the Nazi scum sent my family. Treblinka. And there..." Rapoport's voice trailed off.

"Did any of them survive?"

He opened his mouth to speak, but no words emerged. He buried his face in his hands, and I caught Greta's eyes and signaled her to bring us two coffees. A moment later, Rapoport heaved a loud breath. "I'm sorry, Mr. Lapid."

"No need to be. I understand fully."

Greta set the coffee cups before us, and Rapoport's head rose with the steam. His nostrils flared as he drew in the wonderful, bracing scent. "Thank you," he said to Greta, sounding oddly incredulous that glorious things like this coffee could share a world with the horrors that had befallen him and his family.

She smiled. "Don't mention it. There's more where that came from if you want."

Rapoport took a sip and sighed. We were alone again; Greta had gone to the kitchen.

He said, "With the Allies' advances in the final months of the war, Germany began evacuating some of the concentration camps and moving the prisoners to other ones away from the front. Why they bothered, why they didn't simply murder us all, I don't know. Maybe they thought they could use us somehow, get us to do more slave labor. I was first evacuated from Gross-Rosen to Mittelbau-Dora and then in April to Sachsenhausen. And there I met Emmanuel."

A crushing weight settled on my shoulders and chest as I remembered the evacuation of Auschwitz in January 1945. The freezing march west through miles of snow. The indescribable effort taking just one more shuffling step required. The slapping reports of rifle shots as German guards killed those prisoners whose strength had run out. The constant battle between the longing for life and the temptation for the release of death.

I felt a flash of anger at Rapoport for making me think of that horrible time. I drank some coffee and told myself to calm down. Rapoport wasn't to blame. Neither of us was. We were both victims of the same wretched evil. An evil that still plagued us years after its demise.

"I was in a horrible state when I got to Sachsenhausen," Rapoport continued. "To this day, I'm not sure how I survived long enough to get there. I was so tired and hungry and weak, it's a wonder I could stand. So when the Germans decided to evacuate Sachsenhausen shortly after I got there, I was sure I was done for. But Emmanuel saved my life."

"How?"

"I'm not sure why he chose to waste any energy on me. We didn't know each other, and he was nothing but skin and bones himself. But throughout that dreadful march, he must have seen I was struggling. He grabbed me under one arm and pulled me along with him. The guards shot anyone who faltered, anyone who stopped or fell, and there were plenty who did. If not for Emmanuel, I'd have been shot too. Why he chose to help me and not one of the others, I cannot say. What I can say is that he saved my life. We were liberated by the Red Army not long after."

Now I knew what it was about Feldbaum's plodding walk that had seemed familiar to me. He reminded me of how prisoners walked during the death marches. Weary to their marrow. In constant pain. Walking without a destination. Their only goal, the sole focus of their meager energy, was to take the next step. To keep the executioners at bay.

I tamped down the memory and asked, "What happened then?"

"I went to a displaced persons camp near Hamburg and got to Israel in 1949. Emmanuel went back to Poland to look for his family. We had no contact until three months ago, when we ran into each other on the street."

"When did he come to Israel?"

"A couple of weeks before we met."

"Where had he been since the end of the war?"

"Poland. Like I said, he went back there to see if any of his family survived and returned to their home. None did. Like me, he was the only one of his family left. Then he got into trouble of some kind and did a stretch in jail."

"In Poland?"

"Yes."

"What sort of trouble?"

"I'm not sure. Emmanuel wasn't so easy to understand at times. But I think it had something to do with the family house. Probably some Poles took it over and wouldn't give it back. I gathered he had a rough time over there. It could have been worse, I suppose. I've heard stories of Poles killing returning Jews."

I did too, and it filled my veins with bubbling fury. Those poor

Jews had survived numerous circles of hell only to be butchered by their erstwhile neighbors upon returning to their old homes. And the murderers had suffered no consequences. Their crimes went unpunished.

"What happened after you met here in Israel?"

"Emmanuel had no money. The government had put him in a *ma'abara* in Afula, gave him some menial job, but he didn't like it there, so he left and came to Tel Aviv. He had nowhere to sleep, so I told him he could stay with us."

"Us?"

"Me and my wife. It was the least I could do, I figured. After all, I owed him my life."

I wondered why he felt the need to explain his hospitality to me.

"I wanted to help Emmanuel get off to a good start in Tel Aviv," Rapoport went on. "I found him a job with me—I work in construction. Doesn't pay much, but it's steady work, and there's plenty of it to be had these days, you know."

I did know. There was building going on all over Israel. With so many Jewish immigrants pouring into the country since Israel became independent in 1948, there was a massive shortage of housing. That was why so many indigent immigrants lived in *ma'abarot*, the name given to shanty immigrant camps that dotted the length and breadth of the country. The government promised that the *ma'abarot* were a short-term, necessary evil, an unavoidable stopgap until more housing could be built, but who knew how long that would take?

"I thought he'd stay with us a week or two until he found his feet," Rapoport said.

"But it didn't turn out that way?"

"No, it didn't." Rapoport paused, seeming to weigh his words. "He stayed with us until the day he died."

"Why so long?"

"He couldn't afford to leave."

"Why not? You said you got him a job."

"He didn't hold on to it for long."

"He got fired?"

"Yes."

"Why? What did he do?"

Rapoport drank more coffee, his cheeks rippling in discomfort. He didn't want to speak ill of his dead friend.

"Look, Mr. Rapoport," I said, "I'm not about to judge Emmanuel, but I need to know all I can about him if I'm going to take on this case."

Rapoport rubbed a hand over his face and gave a heavy nod. "Okay, I suppose you're right. The reason Emmanuel got fired was that he would get lost in his own head. One minute he was working, everything looking normal, and the next you'd see him standing like a statue, staring at empty air, his face all weird. Or he would start talking in this low, strange voice, in a mixture of Polish and Yiddish, to someone who wasn't there. A few times, he did some minor damage—spilled a bucket of paint, dropped some bricks. I talked to the foreman, explained what Emmanuel had gone through in the war, and he said he understood, that it would be all right. But then he fired him. Nothing I said could make him change his mind. He said a building site was no place for daydreamers, that Emmanuel could hurt someone with his absentmindedness."

The memory of Emmanuel Feldbaum showing no reaction to the two of us nearly colliding on the street played in my head. That had been more than absentmindedness. On that night, and likely also while working, Emmanuel Feldbaum had been in another place and time entirely.

"Did you ask Emmanuel about these episodes?"

"He would look surprised by the question. He said he had no memory of them." Rapoport shrugged. "Look, Mr. Lapid, the truth is, I didn't know Emmanuel all that well. I don't know what he was like before the war. But you can imagine the sort of things he went through. I think they changed him. They changed all of us who were in those camps, but they changed Emmanuel more than most."

They had certainly changed me, I thought. In more ways than I was comfortable contemplating.

"After he got fired from the construction job, how did Emmanuel spend his days?" I asked.

"He would rise in the night and go out. I don't know when exactly. I'm a very deep sleeper, and he never woke me when he went out. What I can say is that by the time I got up, he was already gone. My wife said he would return in midmorning, when I was already at work, and crash on his cot. He would sleep until the afternoon. I asked him where he went, what he did, and his answers were vague, like he couldn't remember."

I knew what Emmanuel Feldbaum did. He would walk around all night and part of the morning, then return and pass out from exhaustion.

Rapoport said: "I know he was hoping to find people from his hometown in Poland, he asked the neighbors and the guys we worked with, but he never found anyone."

"What about another job?"

"I tried to get him another one at Soffer's Stationery and School Supplies, a store near my home. Nothing special. Shelving, loading, that sort of thing. But it's a start, you know? Mr. Soffer, the owner, has a reputation as a kind man, and he said he'd give Emmanuel a try, but he wanted to meet him first. Well, they met all right, but Emmanuel must have made a really lousy impression because Soffer told me later he wouldn't hire him." Rapoport sighed. "Truth is, Emmanuel showed little interest in working. It was like he didn't care about money or the realities of life."

"He wasn't paying you for room and board?"

"No. Nothing," Rapoport said, the corners of his mouth contracting in disappointment or annoyance.

"Was he seeing a woman?" I asked, and wasn't surprised when Rapoport said he hadn't been. "Did he have any friends?"

"If he did, I didn't know about them."

"Can you think of anyone who might want him dead?"

"Why do you ask? The police say it was a robbery."

"They may be right. But if they are, I must tell you that the chances of my catching the killer are next to none. You see, when someone commits murder as part of a random robbery, there are generally two, maybe three ways to catch them. First: someone sees them in the act or while they're leaving the scene, or maybe someone spots blood on their clothes when they get home and alerts the police. Two: they try to pawn something valuable they took off the victim."

"And the third way?"

I waited a beat before answering: "They're caught after they kill someone else."

Rapoport looked a bit nauseated. "You think whoever did this will kill again?"

"There's no way of knowing. What you need to understand is that all three ways are passive. Either there's a witness, or there isn't. Either the killer pawns something, or he doesn't. Either he kills again and gets caught, or not. Whichever of the three ends up being true, there's not much a private detective can do that the police haven't already done."

"So you're saying it's hopeless."

"Not at all. Sometimes the police miss something that I can pick up on, but that is unlikely to happen in the case of a random robbery. But if it wasn't random, that changes the picture fundamentally. Then what we have on our hands is a completely different case. A case in which someone targeted Emmanuel personally."

"I can't imagine someone who would. Emmanuel was strange, but he wasn't a bad guy. He was just unlucky, I think. Many of us were and still are, but he was even more so. Something happened to his mind in Europe. A part of it got wrecked, and whatever healing he'd been able to do wasn't enough. Maybe if he had more time, he..." His voice faltered, and he stared at his hands, a deep breath sending a tremor through his big shoulders. "I tried to help him, to repay him for saving my life, but I failed. The only thing that's left is to see that he gets justice. That's what I want. I want whoever killed Emmanuel to pay for his crime."

4

Then it was time to discuss money. I went easy on him. Twenty-five liras, with only ten up front. Rapoport handed me two crumpled five-lira notes, and I could tell how painful he found parting with them. Then he told me his address, and it confirmed my initial impression of him. It was in a poor part of town.

"I'd like to come by and see your home. I'll also need to talk to your wife."

"My wife? Why?"

"I need to ask her some questions."

"I don't want her involved. Any questions you have, you can ask me."

I studied his face. His mouth was clamped shut, and he held his gaze steady, but his dismay wafted off him like a bad smell.

"Look, Mr. Rapoport, if I'm going to work this case, I'll need to talk to people who knew Emmanuel. You and your wife shared your home with him for several weeks. Other than yourself, she must have seen more of Emmanuel than anyone else during the final weeks of his life."

"But if it was a robbery like the police say—"

"Then it may prove pointless to talk to her. But you came to me because you're unsatisfied with the way the police are handling this case. So I'll be keeping an open mind and investigate it with as few preconceptions as possible." I paused, considering for a second to reach into my pocket, take out the money he gave me, and slide it over to him, giving him the chance to unhire me, but I was scared the sight of the money would tempt him to do just that. Because the truth was, I wanted this case. I wanted it desperately. I felt a connection with poor, dead Emmanuel Feldbaum. I didn't know why. I couldn't explain it. But it was more than the mere coincidence of seeing him on the lonely nighttime streets of Tel Aviv and later finding his body. There was something about him that struck close to home in a horrible way that I did not wish to fully identify. But I knew it was there, and its pull was powerful and impossible to ignore.

I couldn't admit it to Rapoport without coming off as a lunatic, but my desire to find out who'd killed Feldbaum likely matched his own. I might have agreed to work the case for no payment at all, though I wasn't about to tell Rapoport this. I wasn't going to turn good money away. I could certainly find use for it.

"Do you understand me, Mr. Rapoport?" I asked.

He didn't answer right away. His thick fingers were busily revolving his cap. He screwed his eyes shut tight, like a spasm of pain had just sliced through him. When he opened them again, they were full of resignation. He let out a barely audible sigh and nodded. Decision made.

I hid my relief. I was still on the job. I could investigate the case even without being retained by Rapoport, but then I'd be hampered from the get-go. I thought about asking him why he was so averse to my talking to his wife, but I decided to let it go for now.

I asked him for anyone who'd had contact with Feldbaum, and he named several neighbors and co-workers, adding that he doubted any of them truly knew Feldbaum or could possibly have had anything to do with his death. I nodded my understanding as I jotted the names in my notebook.

He fell silent, but something about his inflection when he'd spoken his last few words told me that he'd planned on saying something more but had a change of heart. Glancing up from my note-book bolstered this impression: Rapoport's mouth was still open. Seeing me looking, he snapped it shut.

"Anything else?" I asked.

"No. Nothing."

"You sure?"

"Yes. Of course I am."

I waited a beat, but he said nothing else. Was he hiding some-thing, or was I imagining it? I thought about pressing him, but there would be time for that later, when I knew more, when the possibility of him not cooperating with me at all would matter less. I tapped the end of my pencil twice on my notebook before putting them both in my pocket.

"All right, Mr. Rapoport. That's good enough for now. I'll come by your home later today. When will you be there?"

He said he was going back to work, but he'd be home at five. We shook hands and he left. Greta came over to the table with a tray to clear our cups.

"There's something strange about that man," she said, looking toward the door through which Rapoport had exited onto Allenby Street.

"What?"

"He looks so strong physically, but his demeanor is anything but."

She was right, and I wondered what had made Rapoport so. Was it his time in the camps and the loss of his family, or was it due to his current circumstances?

"I take it he's a new client," Greta said.

"Yeah."

"Why do you seem so thoughtful? Is it a difficult case?"

"I think it might be. I don't know yet. For the time being, there are only questions and no answers."

"You don't think you'll be able to get to the bottom of it?"

"The police didn't, and they had the case when it was fresh." I paused, looking around. It was one thirty. Most of the lunchtime crowd had already gone, and it would be several hours before the after-work people flooded in. The two tables nearest mine were empty, but some of the others were not. "I'll tell you about it later, Greta. When we have some privacy."

She nodded and went off with the tray. I stepped over to the bar where the telephone was. I still remembered when Greta had it installed not too long ago. Some of the regulars had treated the device with vague suspicion, distrustful of any change to their favorite café. But time had passed, and the telephone had become a part of the place, like the chairs and tables, only sometimes noisier.

I called Reuben Tzanani at his office in the police station on Yehuda Halevi Street. He answered with an airy, almost cheerful hello. Most cops got jaded and cynical within a couple of years on the force, but not Reuben. This despite him taking his job as seriously as any man could. Not that this won Reuben any promotions. He was a lowly desk cop and would likely remain so.

Not for the first time, I wondered whether he was truly suited for his chosen profession, but as always, I kept these thoughts to myself. What did I know? Perhaps the police force could use more officers like Reuben. Maybe it would make people like cops more. After all, how many other cops would a run-of-the-mill civilian like Ami Rapoport describe as *nice*?

"Hello, Ant. It's Adam," I said, using Reuben's military nickname. Despite being slight of stature, Reuben had the ability to carry a lot of weight on his shoulders. I was alive because of it. When I had been injured during the War of Independence, it was slim, short Reuben Tzanani who hauled me to the rear lines for medical treatment.

"Adam, I was expecting your call."

"I appreciate the referral."

"Actually, I wasn't sure I was doing the right thing. The case isn't new, but it's not that cold either."

"But no one is working on it anymore, right? Or you wouldn't have given Rapoport my name."

Reuben let out a sigh. "You know how it is. The police are under-staffed and overworked. With the population doubling since 1948, you'd expect the number of police officers to grow at a similar rate, but it's not even close. I suppose there are budget constraints, like in everything else, but still..."

"There's a price for everything," I said. "You can't scrimp in one place without paying for it through the nose in another. So the case is on hold?"

"Basically, yes. And I can't fault the investigating officer for failing to crack it. I read the file. There's not a lot to go on. I'm not sure what you'll be able to do with it. It's a robbery that ended badly."

"Was there anything to rob? From what Rapoport told me, the victim had very little."

"That could explain the killing, couldn't it? The robber got enraged by how little there was to steal and took out his frustration on the victim."

"Why did he take the wallet, then?"

There was a pause, and I regretted asking the question. It made Reuben seem foolish for not thinking of it himself.

"To sell it, maybe?" Reuben suggested finally.

"Maybe. You're right; it's possible," I said, but I didn't believe it, and I suspected Reuben didn't either. Feldbaum's wallet couldn't have been an expensive model, and why would the killer risk having it on him when it would put the noose around his neck if the police caught him?

"Or maybe the killer went through the wallet and didn't want to leave it behind because it had his fingerprints on it?"

"Yeah, that's a good point, Reuben," I said, and it was. Though a smart killer would have just wiped the wallet clean and dropped it next to Feldbaum's body. But maybe the killer hadn't thought all of this through.

"Were there any defensive wounds?" I asked.

"No, none." Reuben sounded thoughtful, and for good reason. The lack of defensive wounds might indicate that the killer had caught the victim by surprise, before knowing how empty or full his pockets were.

"Maybe the victim had already handed over his wallet and was walking away when the killer struck," I said, mainly to spare Reuben's feelings, though there was a slim chance that it had indeed happened that way.

"Yeah, maybe so," Reuben said. All trace of his earlier airiness was gone. Maybe he was looking at the crime scene photos. Reuben often felt more keenly for victims than his more hard-bitten colleagues. Being jaded had its upsides.

"Can I come over and see the file, Reuben?"

"Sure. I knew you'd call, so I have it right here. Are you coming over now?"

5

I was there in under thirty minutes. As on previous visits, I couldn't help being struck by the contrast between the elegance of the building housing the police station at Yehuda Halevi 6 and the dreariness within its handsome walls. The fine arched windows and delicate stonework of the exterior gave way like a routed army to the gray drabness that characterized every police station I'd ever stepped into —in Israel and in Hungary and also in Germany after the war.

Reuben was in his cramped office on the second floor. A simple desk. Metal filing cabinets lining one wall. The window open, letting in air and city noise.

Reuben was reading a typed report, his brow furrowed in concentration, a pencil in his right hand. I rapped on the doorjamb.

"Adam," he said with a smile. "Come in, come in. Close the door, will you?"

There was a single chair in front of the desk, and I lowered myself onto it. The office smelled of dry paper and fresh ink and cheap police coffee.

"How've you been, Adam? It's been a while since I last saw you."

I told him I was fine, that I was sorry I hadn't dropped by. It was true; I was remorseful. I hadn't realized I had missed Reuben until that moment.

"I have news," he said, his eyes glittering. "Gila's pregnant."

"Again?" Gila was Reuben's industrious and ever-smiling wife. They had five children, the youngest of whom was still a baby.

Reuben laughed. "Yes. My father says that at this rate I might surpass him. You know, I have seven siblings."

I did know. Along with numerous uncles and aunts and nephews and nieces, and other relatives besides. Reuben was the offspring of Jews who'd made *aliyah* from Yemen in 1882. They had settled in Jewish neighborhoods north of Jaffa that had later been incorporated into Tel Aviv. His clan numbered over a hundred people. Mine comprised just me. That was the difference between Jews who had fallen under Nazi occupation and those who had not.

"Congratulations, Reuben," I said, and meant it, but not without a twinge of envy that made me both ashamed and angry. "How is Gila feeling?"

"As usual. She's happy and not about to take a moment's rest unless she absolutely has to. The children are excited, though I have no idea where we'll fit another bed." But Reuben's tone and expression showed not a hint of concern. A new baby was cause for nothing but joy. There was nothing to be worried or fearful about.

Innocent Reuben. He had never lost a child. He didn't know any better.

"Can I see the Feldbaum file?" I asked.

He handed me a folder. "I can't let you take it with you. You'll have to read it here."

I told him that would be fine. He asked if I'd like some coffee, but the smell from his own cup did not make the prospect appealing. He cleared a stack of files from his desk, giving me space to work, and returned to his own paperwork. I opened the folder and started to read.

———

29

Following my phone call to the police on the night of the murder, a patrol car had been sent to Sheinkin Garden. My call had been logged at 4:10 a.m. The cops found the body at 4:28. They had taken their time. Maybe they suspected the call was a prank. Or maybe they'd been busy with something else.

A detective was rousted and called to the scene. A Sergeant Bilenko. He brought a photographer with him. I examined the crime scene photos, the images sharpening my recollection of that night.

There was Emmanuel Feldbaum, lying on his back with his limbs spread unevenly around him, a dark stain around his head. The stain was black in the photographs, but in my memory it was the vibrant red of freshly spilled blood. I found the body not long after the killing took place. The murderer might have still been close by. I had just missed him.

Bilenko noted the freshness of the blood in his report and added a side note that made my guts cramp: *The guy who called?*

The implication was clear. Sergeant Bilenko thought it likely that the caller and the murderer were one and the same. It was a reasonable assumption. I had called late at night when the streets were nearly deserted, and I had refused to identify myself to the police officer who answered the phone.

There was no way I could see in which Bilenko would figure out I was the caller, but it still made me uneasy to be a suspect in a murder, though an unnamed one. What was I doing, involving myself in this case? I should be keeping my distance. I shot a quick glance at Reuben to see if he'd noticed my discomfort, but his nose was buried in a file of his own.

Like me, Bilenko had gone through Feldbaum's pockets, noting his identity and the absence of a wallet. *No watch*, Bilenko had written, followed by *Robbery?*

The body was taken to the morgue, where it was subjected to the added indignity of an autopsy. I lit a cigarette and started to read more slowly since up until now I had known practically everything. From this moment on, I was a stranger to the case.

The medical examiner wrote that the killer had struck Feldbaum three times on the head, all of them from behind. The first one must have brought Feldbaum down. The second and third had come when he was already prone. This gave me pause. My initial impression was that the killer had hit Feldbaum once to incapacitate him so he could rob him unopposed. But three blows seemed excessive and suggested a deadlier motive. But perhaps I was jumping to the wrong conclusion. Perhaps the robber had simply wanted to make sure Feldbaum was unable to resist, and did not mean to kill him at all. Or maybe, in the heat of the moment, he simply hadn't been counting.

I had told Rapoport that I'd have a greater chance of solving the murder if the killer had targeted Feldbaum personally. But that didn't mean I would close my eyes to what was still the most likely scenario, that Feldbaum's long run of bad luck had reached its highest, or rather lowest, and final point. That he'd simply been in the wrong place at the wrong time. Nothing more sinister than that.

All three blows had pierced the skull. All three could have been fatal on their own. The weapon had been a blunt object, likely made of metal. A hammer or maybe a pipe with a similar surface size along its curve. Given the power behind the blows, the medical examiner wrote that the perpetrator was likely male. As Reuben had told me, there were no defensive wounds on Feldbaum's hands or arms. It was possible that he literally had not known what hit him.

During his examination of the victim's head, the medical examiner found signs of an older injury. A few inches above the ear, there was a dent in Feldbaum's skull. Another trauma caused by a blunt object. The examiner estimated this injury to have occurred between three and five years ago.

After the war, then. During Feldbaum's time back in Poland? When he had been imprisoned? Rapoport's impression that Feldbaum had gone through a rough time there looked to be accurate.

The medical examiner listed Feldbaum's height, weight, build, and general physical condition. His teeth were in a deplorable state, but that had nothing to do with his death and was hardly surprising. Feldbaum had gone through years of concentration camps. It wouldn't have been out of the ordinary for him to have been missing some teeth.

Feldbaum's body was a chronicle of trials and tribulations, both old and new. His torso was extremely lean; his ribs showed through pale, nearly hairless skin. His fingertips held traces of old frostbite. His palms carried myriad small scars that hinted at hard physical labor. Wicked lash marks, about ten years old, slashed across his buttocks. The latter, I assumed, he'd gotten as punishment in a concentration camp. I had been similarly abused in Auschwitz, though my scars disfigured my back.

"You poor man," I mumbled.

"What was that, Adam?" Reuben asked, lifting his eyes from the report he was studying.

"Nothing," I said, and carried on reading.

The victim's calves were unusually developed, the muscles enlarged and bulging. The soles of his feet displayed signs of old and mistreated blisters. They were rife with corns and calluses, some of them as hard as wood. The toes were crooked, some overlapping or curling at unnatural angles. Some of this might have been hereditary, but the examiner detected signs of several toe fractures that had been badly set or not treated at all.

He could not determine the cause of these symptoms, but he hypothesized that they might have been the result of excessive walking in ill-fitting footwear, though he admitted to having never seen anything like it. He could not estimate how much walking the victim had to have done for these symptoms to develop, but it must have been an enormous amount. This was followed by three punctuation marks, a sharp departure from the otherwise dry style of writing, and I could imagine the medical examiner, going through the motions of yet another tedious autopsy, suddenly coming across something novel and strange. He must have gotten excited despite the morbid circumstances. His curiosity had been piqued.

But then his professionalism had reasserted itself, and he concluded his examination by stating the obvious: that the victim had died from blows to the head.

I put the autopsy report aside, leaned back in my chair, and lit another cigarette. I thought about Emmanuel Feldbaum's life and wondered when he'd last known happiness or peace. It might have been years, perhaps not since 1939, before Nazi Germany pounced on Poland and the life of Polish Jews turned to hell. Or maybe he'd experienced some joy when he was liberated by the Russians. But if he did, it didn't last long. He quickly lost his freedom again, was beaten again, and later found himself so haunted that he walked the streets of Tel Aviv in the dead of night, trapped in a nightmare of such tenacity that it did not release its grip on him even after it had chased him from his bed.

"Are you okay, Adam?" I heard a voice say, and I blinked and saw that it was Reuben.

"Yeah. It's just this guy." I gestured at the murder file on the desk. "He went through a lot."

"Yes, I saw," Reuben said, his eyes rounding in compassion and concern. "That was another reason I wasn't sure giving Rapoport your name was the right call. I feared it might... I didn't know how you'd—"

"Don't worry about it, Reuben," I said quickly, sucking a bracing drag off my cigarette and moving forward in my seat, eyes back on the murder file. "I'm fine."

I could sense Reuben's eyes still on me as I stared at the file, unable to continue reading while under his scrutiny. Perhaps he wanted to say something more, but luckily he didn't. I heard a rustle of paper and let out a breath. I did not want to talk about the similarities between Emmanuel Feldbaum and me. I was afraid Reuben might sense that there was something more that linked us.

Sergeant Bilenko had investigated the case much as I would have done, following two separate lines of inquiry. In the first, he reached out to informants in the criminal world, but none could supply any relevant information. In the second, he interviewed people who'd known Feldbaum, on the off chance that one of them had murdered him, but he uncovered no motive for anyone to have done so. Feldbaum was indigent, he had no family, and he did not seem to have any enemies. No one stood to benefit from his death.

The more Bilenko got to know the victim, the less he seemed to like him, and this dislike showed through in his report. Feldbaum was an odd duck. He could not hold a job. He had strange habits. He would roam during the night and sleep through much of the day. He would often say things that made little sense, talking about people long gone or imaginary. He seemed to live in his own head, detached from reality, and his memory was faulty and unstable. Here Bilenko wrote, *Old head injury?*

Feldbaum had lived off Mr. and Mrs. Rapoport, the former of whom had known Feldbaum during the Second World War. Rapoport had told Bilenko how Feldbaum had saved his life, and the sergeant had noted that Rapoport seemed deeply distraught by Feldbaum's death. Mrs. Rapoport did not appear to share her husband's grief. She said all the right words, but they rang hollow. Bilenko wrote that the couple were poor, and having to feed and house Feldbaum must have strained their tight budget. This could hardly be a motive for murder, though, since at any time they could have told Feldbaum to leave. In fact, Mrs. Rapoport had told Bilenko they'd been about to do just that. If Feldbaum hadn't died, he would have been thrown out.

I wondered if this was true, and if so, why had Rapoport kept it from me?

Bilenko concluded that Feldbaum had likely fallen victim to a random robbery that had escalated to an unpremeditated killing. There were no suspects at this time, but the sergeant made it clear he was still actively pursuing the case, attempting to develop new leads, and waiting for several additional lines of inquiry to run their course. What those inquiries were, Bilenko failed to specify.

The careful phrasing made me smile grimly. I'd been a detective myself. I could read between the lines. I could tell what Bilenko was doing. By that time, he had already written the case off and shifted his attention to another investigation. But just in case a superior happened to read his report, Bilenko wanted it to look like he hadn't given up, that he was still working the case hard.

I couldn't blame the sergeant. He must have had a heavy caseload.

Pushing against the wall of an unmoving investigation meant he had less time to close other, more promising cases. If this had been anything less than a murder, he might have made an even smaller effort.

As it stood, the killing of Emmanuel Feldbaum was a dead case. The police weren't working on it. It would stay open forever unless a piece of evidence miraculously presented itself.

Or unless I closed it myself.

6

"What do you think?" Reuben asked when I closed the murder file.

"I don't know. It might be pointless."

"I was afraid you'd say that."

"But I'll give it a good try nonetheless, and we'll see how it goes."

"I pray to God you succeed, Adam. Because no man should die that way. Especially not here in Israel."

It was a version of a common sentiment. An expression of both idealized hope and dismay at how reality chipped and cracked that vision. Many in Israel believed, or wanted to believe, that we were building a model society, a light among nations. There was no place for murder in such a country.

All cops knew this was nothing but a childish dream, that Israel, like all other countries, had its dark and seedy corners, its evil and greedy residents. Reuben knew this too, but he still clung to the hope. He still believed. Despite all he'd seen. Despite all the nastiness within the reports that came over his desk every day.

His gentle face wore a fragile expression of defiant hope. What was he doing in this office, in that uniform? Didn't he know that justice was like a short blanket, that it never covered everything, that it always left some part of the body naked and icy cold?

"You can't take these things too much to heart, Reuben," I said.

"So why do you, Adam?" he answered, and I knew that he'd sensed the unexplained connection I felt with Emmanuel Feldbaum. His eyes latched onto mine as he waited for my reply, and it felt as though he were peering into my brain, where I held the secret of my prior acquaintance with Feldbaum like a thief hiding a stolen gem under his shirt near his heart.

I pushed my chair back and stood, averting my eyes as I pocketed my notebook and pencil. "I'm still on the case, remember? I'm supposed to care."

And with that cowardly answer, I bid him goodbye and left.

It was now nearly four o'clock. I had a little time to burn. I bought a soda at a kiosk, along with a copy of *Ma'ariv,* and sat on a street bench, where I drank the former and perused the latter.

The main headline concerned the upcoming agreement between the three Western powers—the United States, Britain, France—and West Germany. According to the agreement, West Germany was to regain its sovereignty and its authority to conduct its own domestic and foreign affairs—rights that it had lost when Germany unconditionally surrendered in May 1945.

The agreement was to be signed the next day, May 26, 1952, a mere seven years after the end of the Second World War. A mere seven years after Germany killed millions of Jews, including my family.

The Soviets were fuming mad at the agreement, and their response to it was the subject of speculation. What was clear was that Germany, at least the western part of it, was to become once more an honored member of the community of nations. It made me want to scream or hit something. Or maybe shoot someone.

Adding insult to injury was news concerning the protracted and seemingly stalled negotiations between Israel and West Germany regarding reparations for the Holocaust. The Germans were in no hurry to conclude the matter. And why would they be? Their legitimacy was on the brink of being restored regardless.

In fact, the Germans were using the negotiations with Israel to ask their other creditors to settle for lower war reparations, claiming their inability to settle both their wartime debts and their yet undetermined obligations to Israel.

Another story quoted one of the editors of *Pravda*, a Jew, as saying that Soviet Jews had no desire to immigrate to Israel. Jews in the Soviet Union enjoyed the same freedoms and privileges as all other Soviet citizens, he claimed. None of them wanted to move to a capitalist country. Something told me that the esteemed editor was not being entirely truthful.

On page three, a column lamented the widespread black market operating in Tel Aviv. One could not board a taxi without being offered chocolate, the column stated, and black marketeering was being conducted in the open on the doorsteps of all the major cafés on Allenby Street. I made a mental note to ask Greta about it.

On Lilienblum Street, the column asserted, one could buy anything from dry prunes and tins of Nescafe to canned fish and sausage; while in Carmel Market, the selection was even bigger—including sugar, cocoa, margarine, and even soap. I decided to pay these two dens of iniquity a visit in the very near future, just to see for myself.

With my belly full of soda and bad news, I headed west toward the sea. The sun was bright, and the day was hot and humid. Soon, my shirt was damp against the scar tissue on my back. I thought about the lash marks on Emmanuel Feldbaum's body. Here was yet another thing we shared. Another link in the mysterious chain that connected us.

Crossing Hayarkon Street, I saw my miserable destination. The neighborhood called Mahlul.

Strewn like a drunk's discarded clothing, Mahlul sprawled messily across five hundred meters on the low sandstone ridge at the edge of the beach, with its westerly homes a few dozen meters from the water.

Mahlul was made up of hundreds of shacks built without plan or order. The shacks were made of driftwood or lumber lifted from building sites, where many of the neighborhood's men worked. The roofs consisted of either concrete shingles over slanted wood beams or scraps of metal weighted down by large stones to keep the metal in place during high winds.

The walls and some of the roofs were covered in thick tar paper as insulation against both the rain and the tempestuous sea. The first flooded the neighborhood nearly every winter; the second swelled on blustery days, swept across the narrow beach, and pummeled the nearest homes with its watery fists.

Mangy cats roamed among the shacks, looking like they owned the place. The residents not only tolerated their feline neighbors but welcomed them. The cats served an important function. They hunted for the rats that were said to proliferate in the inadequate sanitation in the neighborhood and that sometimes bit babies in their cribs.

Established in the early 1920s by impoverished immigrants and Jews who'd fled Jaffa following the 1921 Arab Riots, Mahlul had been birthed in desperation and clung to it over the next three decades. Destitute and miserable, the early residents had grabbed whatever land they could and erected haphazard structures from whatever material they could lay their hands on.

A symbol of the temporary turned permanent, Mahlul persisted like a wart on the modern face of the first Hebrew city. An ugly contrast to the stone residential buildings just across the street to its east. A place that should not have been yet continued to exist.

As I entered the neighborhood, it occurred to me that Emmanuel Feldbaum had fled the *ma'abara* at Afula only to live his final days in a neighborhood that was very much like a *ma'abara* itself. Almost like the way he had evaded murder in Europe only to fall victim to it in what should have been his sanctuary.

Sun-bronzed children thronged the crooked dirt paths that residents had plowed with their feet. They played hide-and-seek or chased each other among the shacks, whooping with joy or triumph or the anguish of capture. Their poverty showed in their ill-fitting, repeatedly patched clothes. Some wore shoes that were too small for them, so their parents had sliced open the tip, allowing the big toe to poke through. The hair of the boys was buzzed, that of the girls cut inexpertly by parents who needed to economize on everything.

I saw a woman beating dust out of a rug. Another hanging laundry on a drooping clothesline. A third tending to one of the many small vegetable gardens homeowners cultivated to enrich their diet.

Here was a man hammering a loose board into place. There was another mending a shoe. Everywhere was industry and diligence. Life was difficult here, and you had to work hard to keep it from becoming unendurable.

Rapoport had given me directions, but I soon got lost in the chaotic layout of Mahlul. I had to ask a local to point out the right shack.

It was a sorry thing. Smaller than most of its neighbors and listing a bit to the right. A peaked roof with a thin chimney pipe. Walls made of mismatched pieces of wood. A patch of weedy dirt where a garden must have grown once and then been abandoned due to lack of energy or a disappointing harvest.

I knocked on the door. Rapoport opened it, a hangdog expression on his wide face. Like a man resigned to a painful visit to the dentist. He moved aside to let me in, shutting the door behind me.

The shack was a single space, with a rear slice sectioned off by several sheets hanging off a bar attached to the ceiling. Through a gap between the sheets, I could see the rear section was a bedroom with a double bed and a dresser and little room for anything else. Not the sort of setup that would afford much privacy to a married couple with a grown man sharing their small home.

Rapoport, perhaps guessing my mind, said, "I'm going to install a door there soon. Just haven't had time for it."

The larger section of the shack served as kitchen, dining room, and living room, and it didn't look as though it did any of its jobs well. There was too much in it, and somehow too little as well. There was a small table, three chairs, and a beaten-up sofa. There was an oil heating stove, which the Rapoports must have also used for cooking. Next to it hunched a couple of large lidded pots that I suspected were full of water. A few pans, plates, glasses, and other kitchenware crowded a few shelves. The place smelled of tar, burnt oil, and wood polish. It was sweltering.

Poverty screamed from every wall and surface, but there were also signs of maintenance and care. The walls shone with a recent coat of polish. The chairs by the table all matched. Curtains made of swathes of sheeting with red flower stitching fluttered by the two open windows. Against one wall stood an empty baby crib, and I could tell it hadn't come from any store.

"You have a child?" I asked.

"No," Rapoport said, a timid smile encroaching on his forlorn cast. "But soon. Finally."

"Finally?"

"I was married before. In Europe. We tried to have children, but we never did. Which turned out to be lucky, didn't it, given what happened?"

I didn't answer. I wasn't sure what the answer was.

"Well, Gertrude, my first wife, died in the camps. Batya and I got married in 1948, and we've been trying ever since. I was starting to think I'd never have children, that I wasn't meant to, and then, finally, she got pregnant."

He sounded excited and happy. He was eager for fatherhood, thirsty for it.

"I used to hope for a boy," he said, "but now I'd be just as happy with a girl. I can't wait for the baby to come."

"I'm happy for you," I said, and pointed at the crib. "You made it yourself?"

He nodded, pride puffing his chest. "I'm pretty handy with wood. I do the occasional carpentry job after work."

He motioned to a wall on which various woodworking tools hung. It would have been easier to keep them in a box, so I guessed displaying them served a different purpose. Like ornaments, symbols of his skill and the promise of a better future.

I saw that the tools were old and had seen heavy use. All except one.

"You've got a new hammer," I said.

Rapoport looked at the wall and then back at me, a slight frown on his face. "Yeah. How did you know?"

"It looks newer than the rest. What happened to the old one?"

"It got lost."

"Oh? When?"

"About two months ago. Why?"

"I'm looking to buy one myself, is all. Where did you buy it?"

He named a store on Ben Yehuda Street whose name I made no effort to remember.

"Too bad about the old one," I said, looking around the small space. "I suppose that if it was lying around here somewhere, you'd have found it by now."

"I must have left it outside," Rapoport said, gesturing with his chin toward the door. "That's where I made the crib. I didn't want sawdust in the house. I must have left the hammer there, and someone took it."

It was plausible, but I didn't think it likely. Rapoport obviously took great pride in his carpentry, and from the way he kept his tools, I could tell he took good care of them. He wouldn't leave a hammer just lying around outside his home. Not for more than a few seconds.

I filed the matter away for a later examination, saying, "Can't be too careful these days," then added a shrug in an attempt to appear casual, though on the inside, I was anything but.

Feldbaum had been killed with a blunt object that could well have been a hammer. And now I learned that a hammer had gotten lost around the time he died, in the same place where he'd lived his final days. That was some coincidence.

"Where did Feldbaum sleep?" I asked.

"Right here." Rapoport pointed at an empty corner near the crib. "We borrowed a folding cot from a neighbor. We gave it back after the murder."

A cot would have made the cramped room fit to burst. Not to mention the man sleeping in it. Especially since, as Rapoport told me, Feldbaum had slept through much of the day. It would have made life difficult for Mrs. Rapoport as she went about her daily chores.

Which raised the question...

"Is your wife home?"

"No. I'm sorry. I was sure she'd be here." But his eyes dropped when he said this, so I figured he was lying.

Anger heated my face, and I was about to let him have it for wasting my time with this nonsense, but I managed to rein in the impulse. There was no point in picking a fight over this. Not at the moment. "Think she'll be home soon?"

His shoulders rose a little and then fell back into place. "I suppose so."

"All right. The police report said Feldbaum had a few belongings. Do you still have them?"

Rapoport nodded. "Yeah. I kept them. But I don't think they can help you. The police detective looked through them and didn't find anything useful to the investigation."

"I still want to see them for myself."

He nodded, crouched down, and pulled out a small battered suitcase from below the crib. He set it on the dining table and left it there for me to open. I flicked the tarnished clasps and lifted the lid.

Opening the suitcase let out smells of dry leather, old clothes, and lost dreams. Inside there was a comb, a shaving brush, a straight razor, a pair of trousers, a few pairs of socks, two shirts, some underwear, a Polish-Hebrew dictionary. Nothing new. Nothing that seemed of any value.

I riffled through the dictionary. Nothing was tucked among the pages. The margins were free of scribbles. I took out the clothes and felt through them. The pockets were as empty as the clothes themselves.

Underneath where the clothes had lain were a few pieces of paper. I examined each in turn.

One was a ticket stub with a departure date in February 1952 and the name of a ship. It had sailed from Rome to Haifa. This must have been how Feldbaum had gotten to Israel. The fact that he had kept the ticket stub told me he'd viewed his *aliyah* as an important step.

Perhaps as a new beginning. He'd had no idea that it was his end that he had been sailing toward instead.

There was a small piece of paper printed in Cyrillic script and stamped with faded red ink. It looked official. I showed it to Rapoport, who explained: "It's a pass issued by the Red Army, where we were camped soon after liberation. I can't believe Emmanuel kept it."

Neither could I. Nor could I imagine why he'd done so.

A bigger piece of paper folded into quarters turned out to be the front page of a newspaper. It was old and creased to within an inch of its life. Opening it as gently as I could, I was still surprised it didn't tear. There were no pictures, and the paper was in Polish. "Any idea what this is?"

Rapoport began shaking his head, but then peered more closely at the page. "I think it's from Emmanuel's birthplace. See here? It says *Gazeta Mastarnia*. Mastarnia was Emmanuel's hometown. I can't read it."

Neither could I. All apart from a smattering of words here and there. And the date at the top, near the paper's name: August 30, 1938. Nearly fourteen years ago. One year and two days before Nazi Germany invaded Poland and the world of Polish Jews was upended and set ablaze.

Holding it between my fingers, a slight tremor came over my hands. This was a relic from a world that was no more. A testament to a community of Jews that had been erased. This should have been in a museum or an archive, not at the bottom of a ratty suitcase in a shabby shack in a neighborhood prone to both floods and fires.

I wondered how many Jews from Feldbaum's town had survived the Holocaust. Maybe a handful. Maybe just Feldbaum himself. Perhaps the killer, by murdering Feldbaum, had wiped out the last remnant of that community.

"Why did he keep this?" I murmured to myself, still in the grip of both sadness and awe, turning the page over, the text on the thin paper as inscrutable as Feldbaum's motivation.

Rapoport, thinking I'd addressed him, said, "I have no idea. He never showed it to me. Never said he had it."

"I'd like to keep this," I said.

I wasn't really asking for permission, but Rapoport said, "Sure. By all means. You think it may hold a clue as to who killed him?" His tone overflowed with doubt, but I wasn't offended. He was sure it was a robbery, so naturally this page from a fourteen-year-old newspaper of a dead community on another continent couldn't possibly be useful.

He was probably right. But still...

"I'm going to show it to someone who can read it for me," I said, folding the page carefully and gently slipping it into my pocket. "I'd like to know what it says."

"All right," Rapoport said, and he was about to say more, but then the door creaked open, and a slice of early evening light poured into the room.

"Who's this, Ami?" A voice sounded from behind me.

7

I turned and saw a brown-haired woman in the doorway. She had a shopping bag in one hand; the other she pressed to her swollen belly. The mysterious Mrs. Rapoport.

She was five foot three and scrawny apart from her belly, giving her the appearance of a knotted piece of string. Her face was long and might have been pretty if not for her expression. Her eyes were narrowed in suspicion, her mouth was a straight slash across her face, and her jaw was set so tight that it banished all traces of softness from her features. It didn't help that sweat shined on her forehead and that her cheeks were flushed from the heat.

Beside me, Rapoport visibly deflated, like a defendant hearing a harsh sentence he had expected but still hoped against hope to evade.

"Hello, Batya," he said, hurrying to her. "Here, let me help you with that." He took the bag from her and carried it to the kitchen area. She moved deeper inside, looking from me to the open suitcase on the table and back again, her eyes narrowing further still. She lowered herself gingerly into the armchair, bracing her belly. She must have been six or seven months pregnant at least. Rapoport brought her a glass of water, which she took without a word of gratitude.

"Are you interested in buying the suitcase?" she asked me. Her tone was mellower than the one she'd used a moment ago to question her husband. "You can have it and everything in it for ten liras."

I almost smiled. It wasn't worth half that, which I was sure she knew full well.

"I'm not here to buy anything, Mrs. Rapoport."

Her lips tightened in irritation. "So why are you here?" She looked at the suitcase again and cocked her head. "You're not a policeman, are you?"

"No. But I would like to ask you a few questions about Emmanuel Feldbaum."

Batya Rapoport shot her husband a look. Her voice dropped to a lower, more ominous register. "What is going on here, Ami? Who is this man?"

"He is..." Rapoport began. "I, eh, well, you see, I..."

"My name is Adam Lapid," I said, coming to Rapoport's rescue— or perhaps pushing him closer to danger, I couldn't be sure. "I'm a private detective. I'm investigating the murder of Emmanuel Feldbaum."

Batya's eyes were now a pair of slits. "Who hired you to do this?" She didn't wait for me to answer. Her head jerked toward her husband, her eyes springing wide along with her mouth. "You did this, Ami? You hired him? You—*you paid him*?"

The last three words burst out as an incredulous accusation. As though Batya Rapoport had just learned that her husband had committed a murder, not engaged a detective to solve one.

"He saved my life, Batya," Rapoport said softly. "I'm indebted to him."

"You've already done enough. More than enough." And to me: "How much did my husband pay you?"

"Enough to buy that suitcase," I answered.

"Ten liras?" She gaped. Her cheeks, which had lost some of their flush, now reddened again, though this time it was due to temperament rather than temperature. "Is this true, Ami?"

Rapoport nodded stiffly. His stance was that of a chastised schoolboy awaiting the headmaster's ruler, but with a strain of defiance that I liked. "I owe Emmanuel as much. That and much more besides."

"Emmanuel is dead, remember? You can't repay him anymore." Batya's tone was shriller now. It reverberated in the small room like the whine of an injured cat. "And you owe him nothing after all we've done for him. What on earth possessed you to hire a detective? Are the police not good enough?"

"The police have given up," Rapoport said. His voice was quiet and even, a sharp contrast to his wife's. I realized I was witnessing a common dynamic. She berating him; he weathering the storm stoically like a breakwater.

On a theater stage, it might have been a comical scene, given their respective sizes. Batya was much shorter and skinnier than her powerfully built husband. But up close, it was sad and pathetic. Now I knew the cause of the discrepancy between Rapoport's looks and manner. I also knew why he hadn't wanted me to meet his wife.

"You don't know that," Batya said. "The police wouldn't have just come out and told you that. You simply decided to take matters into your own hands without discussing it with me first. Just like you invited that man to stay with us without getting my approval."

My approval, I thought, cringing on the inside. *That man.* She was obviously referring to Emmanuel Feldbaum. Not the way most women would describe a recently murdered houseguest. Especially not one who had single-handedly saved their husband's life. But clearly, Batya Rapoport had not liked having Feldbaum under her roof.

"Mister... what did you say your name was?" Batya said to me, and when I replied, she continued: "Mr. Lapid, when did my husband hire you? Today? Well, that's good. Because he made a mistake. A stupid, foolish mistake. We won't be needing your services after all. So I ask that you return the money he gave you. As you may have already guessed, we don't have much."

"I haven't made a mistake, Batya," Rapoport said, just the tiniest bit of iron penetrating his otherwise subdued voice.

"Yes, you have, Ami. Yes, you have. Just like you did when you invited Emmanuel to live here. A man who didn't even remember you, for heaven's sake."

"He didn't need to remember me," Rapoport said. "I remembered him and what he did."

"And it wasn't just his memory that was off. The man was insane," Batya said. "One moment, he was acting normal; the next he would be talking to thin air, staring off into nothing. No idea what switched him from one state to the next. He should have been living in an insane asylum instead of here with us."

"You have no idea what he went through."

"You had it just as bad as he did, and you're not crazy. Or at least I didn't think so until you hired a detective, paying him money we don't have to do a job the police are doing for free."

"Enough!" I said loudly. They had been glaring at each other, locked in their marital feud, but now their eyes snapped to me. Without giving it a second's worth of thought, I pulled out my wallet, extracted the banknotes Rapoport had given me earlier that day, and thrust them at Batya. "Here's your money. Take it. I don't want it."

Batya looked stunned at the sight of the money. Even though she'd asked for it back just a moment ago, she must have been expecting me not to agree, at least not fully. Then, with a blink, her paralysis broke, and she snatched the cash from my hand. "Thank you, Mr. Lapid. That's very decent of you." Some of her belligerence had drained away now that the money was safely in her grip. She looked and sounded almost chastened.

I nodded, a little shaky and trying not to show it. Had I lost my mind? What on earth possessed me to do that? It wasn't as though I was rolling in it. And did this mean I was really going to work this case for free?

"What did she mean, Feldbaum didn't remember you?" I asked Rapoport, thereby answering my own question in the affirmative.

Rapoport said, "When we ran into each other on the street, Emmanuel didn't recognize me. He didn't remember what he'd done for me. How he'd saved my life."

And you still took him in, I thought. *Without him asking you to repay him for his help in the war.* Rapoport might have looked weak under his wife's onslaught, but there was much to respect about his sense of gratitude and honor. And maybe he wasn't as weak as he looked. After all, he had still gone ahead and hired me, knowing full well how his wife would react if she found out.

I said, "You told me Emmanuel had memory problems. What else couldn't he remember?"

"All sorts of stuff. It seemed like his memory was shattered. All that was left were pieces floating around in his head. Nothing whole. For instance, he told me he got into trouble in Poland and was arrested. But he couldn't remember why he was locked up or what he went through in jail."

The old head injury, I thought. That blow on the head had robbed Feldbaum of much of his past; the ones inflicted by the killer had stolen his future.

"Didn't you say it had something to do with his family's house?" I asked.

"That's what I think. It's another example of Emmanuel's bad memory. He told me that when he returned to Poland, he tried to get his father's new house but couldn't."

"His new house? Are you sure that's what he said? How could the house be new in 1945? It had to have been built before the war."

Rapoport shrugged. "I figured he called it new because it was built right before the Nazis came and evicted Emmanuel and his family from their home and put them in a ghetto. Emmanuel wasn't too clear at times."

"At times." Batya snorted. She was still clutching the money I'd given her, her fingers tightly closed as though she were trying to strangle the life out of the banknotes. "Make that *all* the time. His brain was totally scrambled."

"Enough, Batya. Please," Rapoport said. And to me: "Emmanuel did not remember the house at all. When I asked him to describe it, he couldn't do it."

"Why are you asking all these questions, Mr. Lapid?" Batya asked, suspicious again.

"Because if I'm to find out who murdered Emmanuel, I need to know all I can about him."

Batya's eyebrows shot up. Rapoport said, "Are you serious, Mr. Lapid? You're still going to investigate the murder?"

I nodded, stifling a sigh. I shouldn't have been within a hundred kilometers of this case, and now I was going to work it for free? How did I allow this to happen? Was I the one with scrambled brains?

Batya said, "If you're expecting us to pay you later—"

"You don't have to worry about that, Mrs. Rapoport. I'm not going to charge you anything."

"Then why would you want to do this?"

Why indeed? Was it because, like me, Feldbaum had been a haunted man, scarred of body and bereft of family, exiled from his bed and roaming the desolate night streets of Tel Aviv? Because of the bond I felt with him? How strong was that bond really? What other foolish things would it lead me to do?

"Because no man should die the way Emmanuel did. Especially not here in Israel," I said, silently thanking Reuben for supplying me with this easy-to-rattle-off answer.

"Thank you, Mr. Lapid," Rapoport said, his voice husky with emotion. "Thank you so much."

Batya did not appear to share her husband's gratitude. "I still don't see the point. Why not let the police do it?"

"Don't you want to see Emmanuel's killer caught?" I asked.

"Of course. Of course I do." But just like Sergeant Bilenko wrote in his report, Batya was saying the right words, but they rang as hollow as a *muselmann's* stomach.

"So you won't mind answering a few questions, I'm sure."

"No. Of course not. Go ahead. Ask away." But she clearly didn't want to talk to me for one second longer.

"Thank you, Mrs. Rapoport. I appreciate it. Now, I understand that when Emmanuel was staying with you, by the time you and your husband woke up in the morning, he would already be out."

"Not just in the morning," Batya said. "If I got up in the middle of the night, say at one or two, I would find his cot empty. First couple of times it happened, I thought he went to relieve himself, but then one time I had trouble falling back asleep, and he didn't come back. That's when I realized he would go wandering off at night. I'm not sure at what hour. It was just another aspect of his lunacy. At least he did it quietly; I'll give him that. He never once woke me up when he went out."

"Any idea where he went?"

Both of them shook their heads.

"You never asked?"

"I did," Rapoport said. "But he never remembered having gone out at all. I know a few times he went to the beach. There was damp beach sand in the treads of his boots, and the cuffs of his trousers were wet."

I recalled the night I had seen Feldbaum walking at the water's edge, oblivious to the foam licking his feet.

"He slept with the wet trousers on," Batya added. "Didn't bother taking them off. It soiled the sheet, and guess who ended up cleaning it."

"He was walking in his sleep, I think," said Rapoport. "He wasn't aware of where he was going. I told him he needed to talk to a doctor to get something to help him stay in bed. How could he work, I told him, when he didn't get enough sleep at night? That may have caused some of the mistakes he made on the construction site."

"What did he care about work?" Batya said. "We were paying for everything. You wouldn't believe how much he ate. He was always hungry."

That's because he was walking for so many hours each day, I thought. He was burning a lot of energy. But there was no point telling Batya this. Why should she care? She was living in poverty, stretching every lira as far as it would go. Why wouldn't she feel resentful about having a houseguest who was costing her dear money she didn't have?

"Why did he walk in army boots?" I asked. "Where did he get them?"

"Who knows?" Batya said. "Who can say why he did anything?"

"He was wearing the boots when we ran into each other on the street," Rapoport said. "I don't know where he got them."

"Did anyone else know about Emmanuel's habit of going out at night?" I asked.

Rapoport shook his head, but Batya said, "I told some of the neighborhood women about it."

"Why'd you do that, Batya?" Rapoport asked her, protective of Feldbaum's reputation, maybe.

Batya raised her chin. "Why shouldn't I? That's what you do with friends, talk about your life, share your troubles."

I could imagine her blabbing to the other women, exaggerating her hardships. Angling for sympathy. Basking in their denunciations of both Feldbaum's peculiarity and laziness, and her husband's misplaced hospitality.

"Would any of your friends have told others about it?" I asked.

"They might have," Batya said, confirming my fear. It was the sort of gossip people like to spread, especially those who live hard lives. What better way to feel a bit more blessed in one's own lot than to cluck and shake one's head at another's misfortune?

This meant that Feldbaum's nightly sojourns were widely known among the people of Mahlul and perhaps outside the neighborhood too. So anyone who wished to do him harm might reason that the best time to strike would be at night, when Feldbaum was out walking alone and vulnerable, when no witnesses were about.

I repressed a sigh. My job, impossible as it had seemed before, had gotten harder still.

"You told me Emmanuel wanted to find people from his home-town in Poland," I said to Rapoport.

"Yes, he did." He was about to say something more but hesitated.

"He would bother the neighbors," Batya said, saying what her husband wouldn't and doing so with relish. "Ask them if they knew this or that person. He wouldn't remember whom he'd talked to already, so he would ask the same people again and again. It was another way he became a nuisance. I had to apologize on his behalf."

"Whom did he ask about?"

"His family," Rapoport said. "I could tell because they all had his surname. And then he would sort of snap back into reality and remember they were all dead and fall into a long silence. Other times, he asked about other names, probably friends and neighbors from his hometown."

"Remember anyone specific?"

"There was one name he asked about most often: Menashe Volkoff. I don't know why. I asked him about it, and all he would say was: 'Menashe is here. Menashe would know where it is.' He couldn't explain what *it* was."

"By *here*, he meant Israel?"

"I don't know. You would think so, but with how confused Emmanuel was, I can't be sure."

"I take it he never found this Menashe Volkoff."

"No."

"Did you try to help Emmanuel find him?"

"I told Emmanuel he should ask the police, but he never did. The idea of talking to the police frightened him, maybe because of his imprisonment in Poland. Maybe I should have done it for him, I don't know." Rapoport bit his lip in regret. "I thought about putting an ad in the papers..." He glanced at his wife.

"Thank God you had the sense to ask me about it first," Batya said. "Talk about throwing good money away on nonsense. Most likely, this Volkoff died in the war in Europe—if he ever existed at all. I wish, Ami, that you'd used the same good sense and consulted me before hiring Mr. Lapid."

"Any other names you remember Emmanuel asking about often?" I asked.

They shook their heads.

"What did Emmanuel do during the day?" I asked Batya. "I mean after he lost his job."

"Nothing much," she said, with a curl of the lip. "He would come back in midmorning and crash on the cot. Not a 'hello' or a 'how do you do?' or a word of explanation on where he'd been. Sometimes he would take off his boots, and sometimes he wouldn't, but he would always fall asleep in an instant. Sleep so deeply I was sure he was dead a couple of times."

The way she said it, I wasn't sure whether this was something that had worried her, or if she had wished that it would turn out to be true.

"He would help around the house sometimes, wouldn't he?" Rapoport said, again rising to Feldbaum's defense.

"Sometimes he would, yes. He swept the floor a few times, went grocery shopping for me. But then there were other times when he would sit on his cot and do nothing. And it was uncomfortable with him sleeping through the morning while I was cleaning and cooking. I had to be quiet so as not to wake him. I couldn't move things around to clean. I couldn't imagine raising a baby here with him."

"Well, now you don't have to," I said. "I'm sure it's a relief, isn't it?"

Batya was utterly still for a moment. Her hands, which had been moving about as she spoke, accentuating her words, now came to rest on her belly, as though to protect the child within, or perhaps simply herself. She gave me a look as cold as a Polish winter.

"What are you suggesting, Mr. Lapid?"

"I'm not suggesting anything, Mrs. Rapoport. All I'm saying is that it sounds like you didn't like Emmanuel much, and you didn't like him living here. So it must be a relief that he is out of your life for good."

A muscle jumped near her jawline. Her throat worked as she swallowed. "You don't actually think..." she began, then, turning to her husband, said: "Ami, are you going to let this man make these kinds of insinuations about me? In our home?"

Rapoport, his face hard, said, "You've gone over the line, Mr. Lapid. How dare you accuse my wife—"

"I wasn't accusing her of anything, I assure you," I said, trying my best to look horrified at being so misunderstood, while at the same time observing Batya closely to gauge her reaction. She was glaring at me with steaming anger. It might have been the natural anger of the wrongly accused or the bloodthirsty rage of the maniacal murderer. I couldn't tell which.

"I'm so sorry if it sounded as though I was," I continued. "I know full well your wife had no reason to kill Emmanuel Feldbaum." I paused, and the silence that fell upon the room was taut and tense. "After all, I read in the police report you were about to throw him out."

Rapoport flinched, his posture easing as a large breath leaked out of him. "I was going to ask him to leave, yes."

"Why didn't you tell me this when we first met?"

He shrugged his big shoulders. "I guess I forgot."

Or you were ashamed to admit it, I thought, with no trace of anger. Rapoport had done more for Feldbaum than most would have. He had tried to help him rebuild his life. Gotten him a job. Given him a place to sleep. Fed him more than his share. And he would have likely continued to do so if it weren't for his wife and the baby on the way.

This was probably what he'd been about to tell me at Greta's Café and decided not to. The fact that I didn't blame Rapoport for intending to ask Feldbaum to leave did not mean he did not blame himself.

"I'm sorry if I upset you, Mrs. Rapoport," I said to Batya, though of course I wasn't.

The curt nod she gave made it unclear whether she accepted my apology or simply pretended to.

"When is your baby due?" I asked.

"Ten weeks."

Which made her about six and a half months pregnant, as I'd previously estimated. I couldn't see her committing a violent murder with her belly so big, but what about two months ago? She would have been only four and a half months along when Feldbaum was killed. Her belly would have been much smaller. Could she have killed him then? I tried to remember how my wife had looked when she was four and a half months pregnant, and was dismayed to discover that I couldn't. My memories of her were fading. I was gradually losing my last connection to her.

I gritted my teeth and forced myself back to the present. Could Batya have killed Feldbaum? Did she, in a fit of murderous rage, grab her husband's old hammer, follow Feldbaum as he went out on one of his nightly walks, and whack him in the head three times? She was smaller than Feldbaum, not to mention pregnant, so normally, I would have said there was no chance she would risk getting into a physical altercation with him. But I knew full well that Feldbaum wasn't aware of his surroundings when he walked the streets at night. Batya might have known this too. She might have known Feldbaum would not resist an attack.

But what was her motive? As I'd learned, Feldbaum's days at the Rapoport household had been numbered.

Then my eyes fell to the two banknotes crumpled in Batya's tight fist, and I knew why it might not have been enough for her to have Feldbaum out of her home.

She knew her husband well. She knew how indebted he felt to Feldbaum. So indebted that he not only took him in but had intended to pay for ads in the newspapers on his behalf. Batya might have assumed that her husband would continue supporting Feldbaum after getting him to leave. His conscience would drive him to it. The only way he wouldn't was if Feldbaum was dead.

This might explain her acute surprise that her husband had hired me. She must have been shocked to learn that Feldbaum's murder hadn't been the end of it. Her husband had found a way to spend money on Feldbaum even after his death.

"The night Emmanuel died, did you see him go out?" I asked, watching her closely for any tells.

"No. I slept the whole night through."

"When did you learn that he died?"

"The next day, when the police came."

Nothing showed on her face. If she was lying, she hid it well.

"Can you think of anyone who might have wished to kill Emmanuel?" I asked her. I'd already asked her husband this question at Greta's Café.

"No, I can't. Emmanuel was crazy as a bat, but I don't see what anyone would gain from killing him. He was poor. Even poorer than us. He had nothing, absolutely nothing, as the man who killed him found out that night." She paused, and her eyes glinted with the same pure anger I had seen before. "I can tell that you think I'm a heartless woman, Mr. Lapid. I can see it in your eyes. You probably also think I'm a cheapskate. An ungrateful miser who didn't want to spend any money on the man who'd saved her husband's life. Well, I don't give a damn what you think. Let me guess, you live in an apartment, right?"

I didn't answer, which was answer enough.

"I thought so. Well, look around you. See how we live. In this miserable shack, which gets freezing in the winter and boiling in the summer. Which leaks whenever it rains, no matter how much work Ami does on the roof. Which is always at risk of flooding from the sea or burning to the ground from our stove. I want what you have. I want stone walls and a solid roof. I want to live in a place where rats don't scurry about as freely as in a sewer. I want it for me, for Ami, and for my baby.

"So you're right, Mr. Lapid. It is a relief to have Emmanuel out of my life—out of our lives. I didn't like him being around me. I didn't want to spend one more minute in the same room with him. He made my skin crawl. And he was costing us a lot of money we can't spare. Money we should be saving to one day move out of this dreadful place and into a real apartment. It may sound callous, given what happened, and I'm not happy he's dead, but I sure am glad that I'll never have to see him again. And if that makes you think badly of me, then you can go straight to hell. Now I'm tired, and I want you to leave. And I'd prefer it if you don't ever come back."

8

Outside, the heat had broken. A cool wind was blowing in from the west, filling my nose with the smell of the sea. The sun was heading toward the water, where it would sleep for the night.

I fired up a cigarette and headed toward the nearest shack. I talked to the couple inside. Both echoed what the Rapoports had told me about Feldbaum. He had been strange. He had an odd look in his eyes. There was something unnerving about him.

"Did he ask you if you knew certain people?" I asked.

"Yes," the man said. "Again and again. He forgot he'd already asked me before. At first I got angry; I thought he was playing some game. But then Ami told me he'd been in the camps in Europe, so I couldn't stay mad. After that, whenever Feldbaum asked me if I knew this or that person, I would listen patiently, then shake my head and wish him luck finding them. What else could I do?"

The story repeated itself in other neighboring shacks. A few people remembered Feldbaum asking about Menashe Volkoff but claimed he had never said why. Most likely, they hadn't bothered asking. They remembered no other names. I assumed they had stopped paying attention to what Feldbaum was saying.

In one shack, a ginger-haired boy of twelve admitted that some of the other children would make fun of Feldbaum when he was in one of his trances. "They'd follow him around, laughing and taunting him, mimicking how he would stop suddenly and stare into space."

"That wasn't very nice," his mother said. "They should be ashamed of themselves."

"I know, Mom," the boy told her. "I asked them to stop."

This, I thought, was a lie. The boy hadn't asked them to stop. By the way he averted his eyes, I could tell he had taken part in the taunting. But now, with Feldbaum dead, he felt guilty and ashamed.

"How did Feldbaum react?" I asked him.

"Usually, he didn't. Sometimes he would stop and ask us—eh, I mean the other kids I was telling you about—he would ask them if they knew some people. They didn't."

"Do you remember the names Feldbaum asked about?"

He didn't. Feldbaum had been a source of juvenile amusement, not someone to be taken seriously or listened to with even a modicum of concentration.

"He never told you—I mean the other kids—to quit bothering him?"

The boy shook his head, his eyes glittering with suppressed tears. What had seemed like harmless fun felt different now with Feldbaum dead. "It was like he didn't care."

A man smoking a pipe outside his home told me between puffs how Feldbaum had once helped him carry some furniture from a truck on Hayarkon Street to his shack.

"Thin as a string he was, but he was stronger than he looked," the man said. "Picked up way more weight than I could, but what was even more impressive was the way he walked with the weight on his back, so sure-footed, I was sure he'd been a stevedore or something back in Europe. I asked him what he did before coming to Israel, and he said his father had been a haberdasher, and he'd worked at his father's business before the goddamned Germans rolled into Poland. Not a line of work in which you haul heavy stuff around, I wouldn't think. I asked him how he got to be so strong, and a cloud went over his face, you know? Like I'd mentioned something awful that had happened to him. I started apologizing, but he cut me off, asking if I knew where his father's house was, that it was around here someplace. I understood then that there was something seriously messed up with him."

"Did he happen to say anything about this house? Describe it somehow?"

"No. Nothing. He looked crestfallen that I didn't know where it was. Crestfallen and a little confused, like he wasn't sure himself what he was talking about. The Germans probably destroyed the house. Or some Polish family lives there now. Either way, the house is lost."

A pudgy brunette and a short redhead were busy washing clothes in suds-filled basins when I interrupted their lively chatter to ask about Feldbaum. Both wore shapeless dresses and had the chafed and reddened fingers of women who worked long hours with their hands. They told me how Batya Rapoport had used to complain about Feldbaum. "I understood her completely," the brunette said. Her name was Bella. "I wouldn't want a man like that living in my home. And he wasn't working, wasn't bringing in a lira to help support himself. It all fell on Batya and her husband. I understand he and Ami met each other during the war in Europe, but still, there's a limit to hospitality, isn't there?"

Batya hadn't told them that Feldbaum had saved her husband's life. Probably because she knew it would make her look bad for wanting him gone.

"I understand he used to go walking around at night," I said.

The redhead nodded. She was called Ruthie. "I saw him once. I woke up from a bad dream, and there was a shadow of a man at the window. It gave me a start, coming out of the dream and seeing him there. I nearly screamed, convinced the man was looking into my home, right at me. But the shadow moved on, and I went to the window and peeked out and saw it was him. He was walking in this slow, heavy way. It gave me the shivers. Dead of night, it was. Batya told me later he would do this often."

"Did you ever talk to him?"

"A couple of times, soon after he moved in. He seemed okay at first. Quiet and reserved, but okay. But then it would seem like he wasn't listening to you. Maybe not seeing you either. That he was somewhere else. So I made sure to avoid him. He made me uneasy. He made all the women uneasy."

"Well, nearly all," Bella said, and the pair exchanged a significant look.

"Who was the exception?" I asked.

Another look, and a silent message passed between the two, culminating with Ruthie giving her friend a nod.

"Hannah Goldman," Bella said, the name fairly coated with disdain.

"Who's Hannah Goldman?"

"She lives in the neighborhood."

"Not that she's very neighborly," Ruthie added.

"Not to us women," Bella said.

"No. Not to us."

"But if you're a man, that's a different story." Both wrinkled their faces at this, as though Hannah Goldman gave off a bad odor and they could sniff it on the wind.

"She lives alone?" I asked.

"Yes. No husband," said Bella. "At least not hers. As for other women's husbands..."

Neither woman completed the sentence, but I got the idea. Not that it made a whit of difference to me how Hannah Goldman lived her life. All I wanted to know was the nature of her connection to Emmanuel Feldbaum.

"What makes you say Feldbaum did not make Hannah Goldman uneasy?" I asked.

"Because they used to talk together," Bella said. "I saw them twice, sitting inside her shack, looking as friendly as can be."

"And they might have done more," Ruthie said. Her tone hinted at lewd and unseemly activities best not put into words in polite society. "You can never tell with Hannah."

Both shook their heads at the scandalous nature of Hannah Goldman, their unneighborly neighbor.

"Did you tell Ami Rapoport any of this?" I asked. Because Rapoport hadn't told me about Hannah Goldman.

"No. But I did mention it to Batya," Ruthie said.

Who hadn't bothered to tell her husband about it. Nor did she mention it to Sergeant Bilenko, I thought, because she and Ami had spoken to the detective together.

"When you talked to the police detective," I said, "did you tell him about Miss Goldman?"

Both women nodded their heads. "But nothing came of it," Bella said, with more than a hint of petulance. She had probably dreamed the police would swoop down upon the immoral Hannah Goldman and cart her off to prison, and she was disappointed that nothing of the sort had happened.

In fact, there was no mention of a Hannah Goldman in the police report. Either Sergeant Bilenko hadn't spoken with her, or he had chosen to keep their conversation out of the official record.

Either way, I now had a new lead to pursue.

9

Hannah Goldman lived near the edge of Mahlul, close to the Muslim cemetery that bordered the neighborhood to its north.

She wasn't home. Neither was anyone else. Only a pair of chickens inside a wired enclosure flush against the right wall of the shack, pecking at seeds and clucking at each other.

Apart from the coop, there was a tiny handsome garden sprouting with leafy greens and vegetables. Not a weed in sight. Apparently, Hannah Goldman had a green thumb. The shack looked well-kept too—the wood painted, the roof in good condition. A peek inside through a slit between the curtains revealed a gloomy interior, but I could not make out any specifics apart from certain furniture.

I knocked on the door of the nearest shack, and a man in his fifties told me that Hannah Goldman taught languages at an evening school. "And she's one to keep odd hours, even on her days off."

The sky was darkening when I departed Mahlul, and when I inventoried what I'd accomplished in the time I'd spent there, I could not help but feel a dose of dejection.

I had spoken to a couple of dozen people and learned nothing useful that I could see. Only that Emmanuel Feldbaum had been strange and his mind had been broken. And that he'd mentioned the name Menashe Volkoff a lot. I doubted Volkoff was alive. He must have died in Poland during the war. It would likely prove a waste of time, but I could ask Reuben to see if he could find anything about him, on the off chance that Volkoff had made it to Israel.

I'd have to wait till tomorrow, though. It was too late to call Reuben now.

It was strange to leave the decrepit neighborhood, with its shabby shacks and dirt pathways, and, simply by crossing the road, enter the modern streets of Tel Aviv, with their paved sidewalks and white stone buildings.

I imagined Batya Rapoport, standing outside her home after sundown, staring east at the better parts of the city, her face set in grim determination, her heart stormy with anger and resentment and desperate longing.

No wonder she wanted out of her shack and into one of those apartments. Especially as she would soon be giving birth. Her maternal instincts had already kicked in. She wanted her child to grow up in a better home. I could understand why she had wanted Feldbaum gone. Similar to how an animal mother would protect her young against any intruder who breached their lair, Batya saw Feldbaum as a threat. By intruding into her current home, he'd reduced her chances of moving into a better one. Housing him delayed her dream of leaving Mahlul, her and her child.

But would she, like said animal mother, lash out in violent rage against the perceived threat? Her hatred of Feldbaum was fierce enough, but did she have it in her to commit murder? To bludgeon a man to death? I remembered how she had looked at me, the pure heat of her anger, and I thought she would be capable of it.

She would be taking quite a risk, though, getting up in the night from the bed she shared with her husband to follow Feldbaum and kill him. What if Rapoport woke to discover her gone?

But then I remembered Rapoport telling me he was a very deep sleeper. Batya would know this, of course. She might feel that the chances of her husband noticing her absence were slim to none.

What about her neighbors? What if one of them saw her out and about on the night of the killing?

Again, the chances were low. Mahlul was badly lit at night. Batya could move in the darkness with little fear of being spotted by an insomniac neighbor.

It would be different elsewhere in the city, including near Sheinkin Garden, but there she wasn't known. Someone might remember a woman walking about in the middle of the night, but Batya could have camouflaged her figure under heavy clothes and masked her face with a hat. At four and a half months along, she wouldn't be showing all that much. Anyone who saw her might not even realize she was a woman. There was little chance that she would be identified. Besides, if Batya did come across someone, she could simply put off the killing to the next night.

She might decide to risk it. Especially since she would guess that no one would suspect a woman, let alone a pregnant one, of such a brutal slaying.

Sergeant Bilenko didn't.

But I did.

My mind was roiling with these thoughts as I entered Greta's Café. It was almost eight and the place was nearly full. Greta was chatting with a customer at one of the tables, and I gave her a nod before curling my arm over the serving counter to grab the chessboard and pieces.

I played a quick game, trying to focus on the flow of the pieces instead of the case, but it was no use. Every time I moved a pawn, I remembered Emmanuel Feldbaum's ponderous, relentless walk. Every time a queen swept across the board to gobble up a piece, I imagined it was Batya Rapoport swooping in for the kill.

"Want something to eat, Adam?" Greta asked after I'd pushed the board aside.

The question made me aware of my hunger. I'd not eaten since Ami Rapoport hired me earlier that day.

"Yeah. Sure."

She glanced at the board. "A bad game?"

"Too much on my mind."

"The case? Is it looking to be as difficult as you thought?"

"Yeah. But maybe you could help me with that later on, once the place clears out."

"I'd be happy to."

She went away and returned with vegetables, bread, a pat of margarine, and a small bowl that I soon discovered contained a dark jam.

I raised an eyebrow.

"Blueberry jam," Greta said. "From England."

"Did you get it from a black marketeer selling his wares on your doorstep?"

"What?"

"According to a report in *Ma'ariv*, black-market dealings are happening in broad daylight on the doorsteps of major cafés on Allenby."

"It's good, then, that my little establishment could hardly be called *major*, or my customers would have to elbow their way through unscrupulous criminals every time they wanted to get in the place. Especially since it's been my experience that elbowing one's way has a dimming effect on one's thirst and appetite."

"Where did you get the jam, then?"

"A friend of a friend."

"And what did you give this friend of a friend in return?"

Greta feigned indignation. "I hope you're not suggesting I take part in the black market, Adam."

"Perish the thought."

"Because it's one thing to have people buying and selling things on the doorsteps of cafés, but for the proprietress of one such café to engage in such activities herself..."

"Unconscionable."

"Quite."

"Beyond the limits of both belief and imagination."

"It gladdens my heart that you say so."

"Nothing makes me gladder than to know I've gladdened your heart, Greta. Now, about this friend of a friend."

"Oh, yes. Well, let's just say this friend of a friend's omelets should prove less powdery for the coming two weeks."

Fresh eggs were rationed in Israel. In their place, the government allotted each citizen a certain quantity of powdered eggs, which only served to augment one's longing for the real thing.

"And the eggs? Where did they come from? Another friend of a friend?" I asked.

"More like an acquaintance of an acquaintance."

"And what was his compensation?"

"Her. It's a woman. All I can say is I hope her husband and children like chicken."

"If they don't, I'm sure they could find someone to take it off their hands, feathers and all. By the way, was it the same marvelous creature that laid the eggs the friend of a friend received for the jam?"

"Hmmm. I don't suppose that it was. But a distant cousin, perhaps? That's entirely possible."

"That would be nice. Like a crime family."

"Yes. A poultry mafia."

Greta and I smiled at each other.

"For fourteen eggs, I sure hope you got more than this tiny bowl," I said.

"I've been running this café for many years, Adam. Rest assured, I'm not one to make bad bargains." She paused, giving me a pointed look. "Though there have been one or two egregious exceptions."

"Really? Anyone I know?"

Again, we exchanged smiles.

I had begun frequenting Greta's Café shortly after my arrival in Israel in 1947. Sometime after that, a thug called on Greta, demanding protection money. Greta turned to me for help. I met the gentleman in question, and my fists and his face had a torrid, short-lived, and calamitous affair. After he'd staggered off, minus some teeth and a good deal of dignity, Greta and I came to an arrangement. In lieu of her paying my fee in cash, I would eat and drink the equivalent.

But Greta didn't keep a tab, so over the next couple of years, I must have consumed several times what she owed me. Eventually, I told her that I would start paying for my meals. But I knew she was undercharging me. She liked having me in her café as much as I liked being there.

"I've got a few jars in the kitchen," Greta said. "Give it a taste. Tell me what you think."

I scooped a spoonful of jam and put it in my mouth. I closed my eyes as my taste buds fired up like a happy chorus. The jam was tart, rich, tangy, and delicately sweet. People made jams in Israel, but I had tasted none so fine.

"Well?" Greta asked.

I opened my eyes. "That chicken did not die in vain."

Greta laughed. "Are you going to build a monument in her memory?"

"I just might. If I could persuade you to part with one of those jars you have stashed away."

Greta tapped her chin. "Hmmm. I'll be sure to take it into consideration. Enjoy your meal, Adam."

I did. I ate everything she'd brought me, finishing with a cup of her excellent coffee and the rest of the jam as dessert.

The meal was a welcome respite from all I'd learned that day. Only when the food was gone did my mind drift back to the case, and my mood soured.

I pictured Emmanuel Feldbaum treading the uneven paths of Mahlul with a gang of unruly children in his wake, hurling ridicule at his back. I imagined his wasted body hauling furniture with a strength he should not have possessed. I envisioned him rising from his cot in the corner of the shack that had been his last home to begin his nightly trek on his damaged feet.

And then I played in my head what his final walk must have been like. I could see it clearly. Feldbaum plodding along darkened streets. His feet moving according to the same desolate rhythm they had set on the nights I saw him. His eyes open but not fully seeing. His mind locked in a nightmarish prison of his past ordeals.

There was the turn into Sheinkin Garden. Feldbaum took it. Was this merely bad luck, a coincidental decision, or was this part of his regular route? Was the killer lurking among the trees for no particular victim or for Feldbaum personally?

Either way, Feldbaum headed deeper into the small garden. Trees loomed on both sides. Their leaves shattered the moonlight into fragments that mottled Feldbaum's face. Nocturnal insects whispered and buzzed. A faint breeze was blowing, caressing Feldbaum's cheek like a farewell kiss. Did the wind also carry a trace of the killer's odor? The acrid stink of nervous sweat, the pungent aroma of wicked excitement? If it did, and if Feldbaum's nose caught it, it did not pierce the shell of his detachment.

Step by trudging step, Feldbaum moved closer to his oblivion. What went through his mind in those last moments? Did he see visions of Sachsenhausen? Of emaciated prisoners? Of piles of corpses about to be loaded into crematoriums? Of his dead family?

Maybe he was searching for his father's lost house. Or for one of the many other things the Nazi storm had stolen from him. Perhaps he didn't fully know that the house was no more. That all the rest was gone as well. That nothing remained but himself, and that some of his former self was also lost beyond hope of recovery.

Either way, he was not aware of the danger that lurked in the shadows. His present doom had blinded him to his impending one. He was a captive of his memories and suffering.

His footfalls made dull thuds. Dust rose and fell back onto the dirt path. His steps left the shallowest of marks, soon to be erased. Just like himself.

His eyes stared both forward and inward. They saw enough to stop him from tripping over exposed tree roots, but they absorbed little else. If they did see the killer, or even the killer's shadow, they did not relay the information to Feldbaum's brain. Just like the night he and I nearly collided on the corner of Allenby and Maze.

Feldbaum passed by a gnarly tree with a bowed trunk. Then the killer pounced. There was no fight. No attempt at resistance or evasion. Feldbaum was oblivious to his last.

A hard object swooped through the air. It connected with the back of Feldbaum's head. A grisly crunching sound. A spatter of red in the air. Maybe the killer grunted in effort, or maybe he was silent. Maybe Feldbaum let out a groan of pain, or maybe he dropped without a sound. Either way, Feldbaum was now on the ground, at the killer's feet. Dead, or verging on it.

Maybe the killer knew this. Or maybe not. Either way, the violence was not over yet.

As a means of making sure, or maybe just for enjoyment's sake, the killer bent down and raised the weapon again.

Down it went. Once. And then once more. More sounds of bone breaking. More blood. Now it was clear. Feldbaum was dead.

The killer dragged Feldbaum behind a hedgerow, then flipped the body over and began going through Feldbaum's pockets. Whether the motive was greed or subterfuge, the hands moved quickly and eagerly. The work was nearly done. The killer was keen to get away.

Sitting in Greta's Café, I saw all this like a movie reel playing against the screen of my mind. Everything in deadly sharp relief. Everything but the killer.

The killer's face remained veiled. The hands holding the murder weapon, and the weapon itself, were blurry beyond recognition. There wasn't a single clue that could lead to an identification. As, of course, there couldn't be since I hadn't actually witnessed the killing. Knowing this did not alleviate my frustration one bit.

As my vision of Feldbaum's death came to an end, I became aware that my hands were clamped into fists, and my teeth were clenched so hard that my jaw had started to ache. I hissed out a low curse.

Emmanuel Feldbaum had survived years of suffering and pain and loss. A piece of him had died in Germany during the war. Another piece in Poland in the war's aftermath. In Israel he should have found solace and security. But what he found instead was his end.

Reuben had been right. Feldbaum should not have died like that.

10

It was eleven before Greta's Café cleared of customers.

All except me.

I helped Greta tidy up the place. I emptied ashtrays; I cleared the tables; I wiped them down, then piled them with overturned chairs. Only my table remained bare, with two chairs standing beside it.

Greta brought a pitcher of water with ice and poured each of us a glass. I drank from mine. She held hers to her cheek. She looked tired.

"You feeling okay, Greta?"

"I'm fine. It's been a long day, that's all. Thank you for helping me put everything in order."

"You don't have to thank me. Just take it off my tab."

She smiled and sipped from her glass. "Consider it done, Adam. Now tell me, what's going on with you? What's this new case you're working on?"

I told her. It took about forty-five minutes to get it all out. From the first time I saw Feldbaum on the street, through my finding him dead in Sheinkin Garden, to my being hired by Ami Rapoport and visiting Mahlul earlier that day.

Greta listened without comment, taking it all in. When I finished,

I asked, "You think I should have identified myself to the police when I called to report the murder?"

"Would it have helped them catch the killer?"

"I don't see how."

"Then it doesn't matter all that much, does it?"

"You're not disappointed?"

She shook her head. "It would have been the civic thing to do, but I understand why you didn't."

I felt instant relief. I did not wish Greta to think badly of me.

"But the wiser course of action would have been to turn the case down," she said.

"I know. But I can't. I don't know why, but that's the way it is."

Her eyes were full of compassion and worry. "You see a part of yourself in him?"

She meant Feldbaum. I didn't like the thought of my having anything in common with that shattered man, but there was much I shared with him. Both of us had languished in Nazi camps. Both of us had lost our families and former homes. And both of us had wandered the streets of Tel Aviv in the dead of night, exiled from our beds. Was a part of me also broken?

"All I know is I can't let it go," I said evasively. "By some fluke of chance or fate, I was hired to work this case, and I intend to give it my best. I don't know if I'll succeed—chances are I won't—but I'll do what I can so Emmanuel Feldbaum will get a small part of the justice he deserves."

Greta nodded. "All right, Adam. I understand. You said there was something I might be able to help you with?"

I took out the newspaper page I found in Feldbaum's suitcase. "Feldbaum had this. I can't read it."

Greta peered at the page. "What am I looking for?"

"I don't know. I have no idea how this page survived the war or how Feldbaum came to have it. But it must have meant something to him, or he wouldn't have kept it. It may be unrelated to his murder, but I have absolutely nothing else to go on."

"All right. Let's see what we have here."

Greta began, translating from Polish to Hebrew, and I got a snippet of life in Feldbaum's hometown in the summer of 1938.

The main story was about a trade fair scheduled for the following week. Merchants and farmers from that entire area of Poland were to attend. Most of them were probably dead now.

In other news, the local synagogue had received a donation of a new Torah scroll. Two families were happy to announce the betrothal of the son of the first and the daughter of the second. A Yiddish theater in a nearby town was putting on a show based on the writing of Sholem Aleichem, and tickets could be had for a low price. At the bottom, there was an ad for a stationery store. Another for a wainwright. A third for a haberdashery.

"Hold it," I told Greta. "Read that whole ad."

"Which one?"

"The one for the haberdashery."

She did. The haberdasher invited people to sample his new wares, including a recent shipment of fashionable clothes from Warsaw. His name was Feldbaum.

"A relative?" Greta asked.

"The victim's father," I said, angry at myself for not spotting the name when I first looked at the page in Rapoport's shack. In truth, I hadn't looked too closely once I realized it was in Polish.

"Maybe that's why Feldbaum had this," Greta said.

"Yeah. That's probably it." This fourteen-year-old newspaper page could have been Feldbaum's last connection to his father. To the entire family he lost. No wonder he kept it. Though why he had it lying at the bottom of his suitcase, where it ran the risk of getting ruined, I could not imagine. If it had been me, I'd have treated this page like the treasure it was.

"Want me to keep going?" Greta asked.

I nodded with a sigh. "Might as well, I suppose."

Greta turned the page over and read its opposite side. The news here was both local and from farther afield. A few small pieces about the Jewish Yishuv in Mandatory Palestine. One on tightening British restrictions on Jewish immigration to the region. A second about a series of Arab attacks that left a bunch of Jews dead. And a third about plans to build a new city between Netanya and Haifa and a local event in which one could buy land there. Between the Arab attacks and the British restrictions, I doubted that event had been a success.

There was an article about a training farm near the city of Lodz, the Borochov Kibbutz, where young socialist Jews trained in agriculture preparatory to making *aliyah*. Another article about an upcoming gathering of Beytar, the right-wing Zionist organization that had since evolved to the Israeli party Herut. *Aliyah* was the main topic on the agenda as well. Menachem Begin was to attend.

There was a piece about a couple of Polish destroyers undertaking a voyage to Copenhagen. An article on anti-German demonstrations across Polish Pomerania after Nazi activists from the Free City of Danzig had pushed a local man under a train. A report about the works on the Royal Canal in the Polish city of Kobryn.

There were more ads. A man was offering violin lessons. Another inquired after a lost bicycle. A woman was selling a used sewing machine. She made a point of stating it was a French model.

And that was it.

Nothing that helped shed any light on the murder of Emmanuel Feldbaum. I still had nothing to go on.

11

Ami Rapoport worked on a building site in the north of Tel Aviv. A sign at the entrance announced that the plan was to build three four-story buildings. Four apartments to a floor. Forty-eight apartments in total. I wondered what Rapoport thought of building apartments he could not afford. How Batya felt about it. Maybe it killed her on the inside. Maybe it had led her to kill Emmanuel Feldbaum.

The construction company was called Hebrew Builders. The name curled above a drawing of a shirtless muscular man shouldering a slab of stone. In the background was the outline of buildings. The man's face was stretched in a smile. Building the Jewish state was nothing but joy.

The contractor's name was printed in bold letters on the sign. Benjamin Caspi.

I passed through an opening in the fence. On the site were about fifteen men in dusty clothes. Some stood on scaffolding against the exterior of one partially built building. Others were on the ground chatting, not doing much of anything. There was one floor to go still, and then they'd need to spruce up the inside. The smell of stone dust, cement, and dug-up earth hung heavy in the air.

Ami Rapoport spotted me and hurried over. "Good morning," he said, moving his weight from one foot to the other. "I, eh, well, I feel like I should apologize for yesterday. Batya—"

"There's no need, Ami," I said, more sharply than I'd intended. Seeing his startled look, I added more softly, "I understand where she was coming from. Emmanuel was hard to live with."

He blew out a breath, and pain twisted his face. "I wish to God things had been different. Not just his death, but his time with us, too."

"You did what you could. Most wouldn't have done half as much. Okay?"

"Yeah," he said. "Yeah, I know."

He didn't sound convinced. Nothing I could say would make him so.

"What's going on with those guys?" I asked, gesturing toward the group of idle men.

"They're waiting for a truck to arrive with material. It's running late."

"Is your foreman around? I'd like to talk to him."

The foreman, Moshe Berman, was a plug of a man. Short, wide, hard-bodied. His head was bald, sweaty, and reddened by the sun. He had a square face with a thick black mustache and a big nose dotted with blackheads. He scowled at me as I began talking, annoyed by the presence of a stranger on his construction site. But his expression softened when I explained the reason for my visit.

"I remember reading about the murder," he said, shaking his head. "I felt terrible."

"I understand he used to work here under you."

"That's right."

"And that you fired him."

A muscle twitched near his mouth. His eyes jerked over my shoulder. I turned and saw he was looking at Rapoport.

Wishing to avoid any ill feelings on the part of Berman toward my client, I hastened to add, "Ami doesn't blame you for that, Mr. Berman. He just told me about it."

Berman gave a curt nod, whipping out a handkerchief and

mopping his damp scalp. "I gave Emmanuel a job because Ami's a good worker and he asked me to. Emmanuel had no construction skills, but he wasn't the first man to start out that way. You can learn everything by doing, as long as you work hard and your head's on straight."

"Was Emmanuel's head on straight?"

Berman shook his head. "There was something wrong with him. I don't know what you call it. I'm no doctor. Ami said it had to do with what Emmanuel went through in the Nazi camps."

"Did you notice it right away?"

"Not when I first met him, but soon after he started. He was by that fence there. I called to him, I needed him to bring over some tools, but he didn't react. I went over there and saw that he was staring off into space. I moved my hand in front of his eyes, and nothing. It was only when I grabbed him by the shoulder that he snapped out of it, whatever it was."

"Did he say something?"

"At first, he looked surprised to see me there. Then, when I asked him what the hell happened, he gave a shrug and asked me what I wanted. I didn't press it. I figured the man's mind had been wandering, that's all. I thought it was a onetime thing."

"But it wasn't."

"Not even close. The day after, Emmanuel was alone back there by that worktable. I wanted to show him something, and when I got close, I could hear him mumbling."

"What was he saying?"

"I don't know. It was in Polish, I think, and I don't speak that language. All I got was the words 'Tel Aviv,' and even that was sometimes garbled."

"Was he talking to himself or to someone in his imagination?"

Berman shrugged. "It could have been either one. But if I had to guess, he was talking to someone."

"Why do you think that?"

"Something about his tone. It was plaintive, desperate. I'm not in the habit of talking to myself, but it seems to me a man won't sound like that when he's doing it."

"Did you catch any names in what Emmanuel was saying?"

"Not that time."

"But other times, you did?"

"Yeah. And not just me. I think almost everyone who works here did."

"What were the names?"

"There were all sorts, but the most common was a guy called Volkoff."

"Menashe Volkoff?"

"Yeah. That's the one."

"Did Emmanuel say anything about him?"

"One time he said something like 'Need to find Menashe Volkoff. He knows where it is.'"

"Where what is?"

"No clue. I asked Emmanuel, but he looked dumbfounded by the question."

"Did he say anything else about Volkoff?"

"Not when I was around. When I asked him who Volkoff was, he looked perplexed, like it was the first time he'd heard the name. But maybe Ami or one of the others would know more."

But Ami didn't. And neither did any of the neighbors I'd spoken with. I said, "It sounds like Emmanuel wasn't a good worker."

Berman bunched his lips, then heaved a sigh. "No, I can't say that he was."

"Ami told me Emmanuel did some damage with his absent-mindedness."

"That's true."

"He also said you assured him Emmanuel wouldn't get fired despite that."

Berman's stance turned defensive: his back straightened, his shoulders pulled back. "Normally, Mr. Lapid, I'd have fired a worker like Emmanuel much sooner. But I took pity on him. I can't imagine what it was like being in one of those camps, having your family killed by those Nazi animals. I think we who were lucky enough to avoid that need to do what we can for people like Emmanuel who survived that hell. It's our duty as Jews."

"Yet you ended up firing him."

Berman lowered his eyes. "I had to. Emmanuel was too unreliable. I had no choice but to let him go."

His voice was thick with remorse and regret. Logically, he'd had more than enough cause to fire Feldbaum. But emotionally, it was tearing him up on the inside. Probably because of Feldbaum being dead. Or maybe it had started the moment he axed him.

"Can I talk to your workers?" I asked. "I want to talk to anyone who knew Emmanuel."

"Why don't you come back at the end of the day? These men are working."

I pointed at the group of men who were still idling about, doing nothing but chatting and drinking from tin cups. "They don't seem to be very busy."

"They're waiting for a truck," Berman said. "It should be here any minute."

"I'll tell you what, how about I go talk to them, and the minute the truck arrives, I'll leave?"

Berman chewed on his mustache. He checked his watch. "All right, but be quick. I'll give you ten minutes, and then you go, truck or no truck. Not a second more. Is that clear?"

I told him it was, and he repeated that I had just ten minutes, and didn't sound too happy about giving me that much.

I approached the group of idlers. They numbered half a dozen. They fell silent as I drew near. I introduced myself and started asking questions. I'd have preferred to speak with each of them alone, but with only ten minutes, I did not have that luxury. I was starting to think this was a stupid idea. I'd have to come back anyway to speak with the others. But I might as well make use of the ten minutes Berman had allowed me. Maybe I'd learn something.

The men began answering my questions willingly enough. But five minutes after I got started, their expressions turned wary, and their eyes lodged on something behind me. Before I could turn to see what it was, a strong hand grabbed my shoulder and spun me around.

"Now who the hell are you?" the man who'd grabbed me asked.

He had a deep voice and was in his mid-forties. Tall, well-built, with thick black hair cut expertly and parted on the side. Thick jaw, notched chin, and a manly nose dominating a broad, angular face. A large mouth set in an uncompromising line. Strong eyebrows over imperious eyes the color of charcoal. Those eyes were fastened on my face, and there was nothing soft about them.

I gave him my name, told him my profession, and explained why I was there, but the workers' reaction to this man's presence kept me from mentioning Rapoport's name. With each sentence, the man's lips pressed together more firmly, the muscles in his cheeks tensing gradually like rope tugged ever harder from opposite ends.

"Who gave you permission to enter my building site?" he asked.

I was about to answer when I saw Berman rushing over. He was panting a little. "Mr. Caspi, so nice to see you, sir. I wasn't expecting you till nine."

"I got a call saying a truck was delayed. I wanted to be here when the driver arrived, to give him a piece of my mind. But what I want to know now is why this man is here." Caspi leveled a finger at me like he was identifying a pickpocket in a lineup. "He's not a policeman. He has no authority. I don't want anyone on my building site who's not supposed to be here. You're responsible for this, Moshe."

Berman began to splutter. "I, well, I, eh—"

"I just walked in," I said. "I didn't think I needed special permission."

"Well, you do," Caspi said. "And you don't have it."

"I would have thought you'd be delighted to know that someone is investigating the murder of a former employee of yours, Mr. Caspi. Don't you want to know who killed him?"

Caspi's face darkened. His mouth jerked open, undoubtedly to say something cutting, but he was forestalled by another voice.

"Want me to throw him out, Mr. Caspi? It will be my pleasure."

The man who'd spoken was an intimidating specimen. Six two, thick shoulders, forearms like hairy cannon barrels, large hands bunched into fists of frightening size.

The man had been on the scaffolding when I'd arrived. Now he was at ground level, just two meters away, staring at me with contempt and vibrant hostility.

Caspi looked around us. The work noise had died down. We'd acquired an audience. All the workers were watching us. Both those on the ground in the front-row seats and those in the gallery on the scaffolding.

Caspi took a big breath and composed himself. "That won't be necessary, Boris. Mr. Lapid will be leaving of his own accord. Won't you, Mr. Lapid?"

"You haven't answered my question: don't you want to see Emmanuel Feldbaum's killer face justice?"

"Of course I do," he said in a tone that suggested he considered me nothing more than a fool and a nuisance. "But this is a workplace, and these men need to get on with their assignments. Any man here who wishes to talk to you can do so after the workday is done." He turned to the men and raised his voice. "But you're under no obligation to do so. Mr. Lapid is not with the police. They are the ones running the official investigation. Mr. Lapid is nothing but a private citizen with no authority whatsoever."

He took my arm and began ushering me toward the exit.

I held my ground. "What about you?"

"Me?"

"You can spare me a few minutes, can't you? Until that truck gets here."

Again Caspi looked around. Some of the men were stealing glances our way; others were watching us openly. I had spoken loudly enough so they all could hear me.

"I'd be happy to. But not here." Again, he led me toward the street, and this time, I did not resist.

He let go of my arm as soon as we exited the building site. He did not stop walking but continued a couple of dozen paces until we'd rounded a corner. Caspi didn't want any curious employee to spy on our talk.

We stopped in the shade of a tree. The ground was littered with tiny hard berries. The shifting leaves cast irregular shadows on Caspi's face, giving it the appearance of a distorted chessboard, all the squares misshapen and melting.

Caspi took out a cigarette case from his pocket and lit one of its occupants with a silver-plated lighter. He did not offer me one.

"Who's your client, Mr. Lapid?" he said in a casual tone. There was a trace of a Polish accent in his voice. He'd lived in Israel for some years, but he had not been born here.

"I'd rather not say."

"You wouldn't, huh? I don't suppose it's Ami Rapoport, is it?"

"No, it's not," I said, trying to spare Rapoport the wrath of his boss. "My client is a private person. I'm not at liberty to share her name."

"So it's a woman, is it?"

I made a face as though I was angry at myself for revealing that much. I hoped for Rapoport's sake that it was persuasive.

"As I explained, Mr. Caspi, I cannot reveal my client's identity."

He eyed me suspiciously with those dark eyes of his. "I find it hard to believe that someone actually paid a detective to investigate Feldbaum's death."

"Why is that?"

"He didn't strike me as a man who had deep relationships with other people. Perhaps with the exception of Rapoport."

"You knew Feldbaum well?"

"On the contrary. I knew next to nothing about the man. He didn't work for me for long. I don't think I exchanged a single word with him."

"Yet it was enough for you to be surprised by the fact that someone cared enough about him to hire me."

"From what I understand, Feldbaum was an oddball. The sort of man people shy away from. That's what I heard from my workers."

"They didn't like him?"

"I don't recall any of them claiming to be his friend. Again, with the exception of Rapoport. He's the only person I can think of who cared enough about Feldbaum to hire a detective to solve his murder."

He was eyeing me closely, trying to read my face. Clearly, he was not convinced that Rapoport was not my client. I would have to pass word to Rapoport somehow, to let him know that I'd protected him, before Caspi could speak to him and expose my lie.

"From what I could gather," I said, "Ami Rapoport does not have the means to hire my services, even if he wanted to. He's poor, and he has a baby on the way. What else did your men tell you about Feldbaum?"

Caspi pulled on his cigarette and made a vague little motion with his hand, but his gaze stayed riveted to my face. "That Feldbaum's mind was shot, his memory faulty. Was that not the case?"

"That's the impression I got. I'm surprised you hired such a man."

"I didn't. My foreman did. I don't involve myself with such petty decisions. Clearly, it was a mistake. Feldbaum was unfit for the job. My foreman is usually reliable and makes good decisions, but he has too soft a heart."

And you clearly don't, I thought.

"Not too soft," I said, "or he wouldn't have ended up firing Feldbaum."

Caspi took a long drag off his cigarette, blew out a stream of smoke, and watched it spread and thin out. "Eventually, everyone has to face reality."

"You don't think Feldbaum could have been given more time, considering his history?"

"You're talking about his imprisonment in Nazi camps?" Caspi asked, tapping ash off his smoke. "That's awful, of course. I feel terrible for the suffering Feldbaum experienced over there. But I run a business, not a charity. And a building site is no place for unstable minds. It's a risky workplace. What if he dropped a hammer on someone's head?"

"Interesting that you chose a hammer," I said.

Caspi's hand paused midway to his mouth. His cigarette had

burned to half its original length. Its fiery tip was like an evil, unblinking eye.

"What do you mean by that?" he asked.

"It's just that Feldbaum was bludgeoned to death, and the police believe it was done with a hammer." The police report had said no such thing. A hammer was but one of the possible murder weapons. But I wanted to see Caspi's reaction.

His face turned as hard as the concrete with which he built his buildings.

"Are you insinuating something?" he asked, in a low, thick voice.

"Not at all."

"Are you absolutely sure about that?"

"Indeed I am."

"That's good. That's very good," Caspi said, taking a final pull on his cigarette before letting it fall to the ground and grinding its life out with the toe of his shoe. "Because for a moment there, it sounded like you were suggesting I might have had something to do with Feldbaum's death."

"Oh," I said, adopting a tone of surprise but not doing much to make it persuasive. "I meant no such thing, I assure you. Why would I? What possible motive would you have?"

For a long moment, Caspi didn't answer. He just looked at me, his jaw locked, teeth clenched. His eyes simmered with barely suppressed fury—a fury, I thought, that went beyond that of the wrongfully accused. And in that moment, I sensed that there was a vicious side to him, a facet of his character that was cold and brutal and self-serving. I didn't know if it could lead him to murder, but I thought it was highly possible.

When Caspi spoke, his tone was measured and flat to an unnatural degree, a result of effort rather than his true state of mind. "You're right about that. I had no reason whatsoever to want Feldbaum dead. As I said, I barely knew him. And at the time of his death, his life and mine were no longer connected."

The loud rumble of an engine sounded then, and Caspi walked a few paces to the corner and looked around it.

"There's the truck," he said. "That's all the time I can give you, Mr. Lapid. I wish you all the best with your investigation."

And then he stomped off. I counted to twenty and followed. When I passed by the entrance to the building site, Caspi was by the truck, shouting at the driver.

I felt sorry for the poor fellow and a little guilty. A portion of the abuse now being heaped upon him was due to my needling Caspi.

Caspi didn't notice me walk by. I stopped by the fence, where there was a gap between two slats, and hissed a loud "Psst," at a passing worker, one of the guys I'd begun speaking with before Caspi interrupted. When he came over, I asked him to get Ami Rapoport for me. "And don't let anyone know I asked, okay?"

He grinned and nodded, and a minute later, Rapoport was on the other side of the fence. I explained the lie I told Caspi and warned him not to reveal that he was the one who'd hired me.

"Caspi might try to trick you, make it seem like I told him you're my client. Just play dumb. Say I paid a visit to your home, but you have no idea who hired me."

Rapoport gulped and nodded understanding. He looked a little pale, and I didn't blame him. Caspi seemed the kind of boss who had a twitchy finger on the firing trigger. And Rapoport needed his job.

"Just stick to the story, and you'll be fine," I said. "And grab a quick talk with Berman and tell him the story too. He's a good man. He won't blab. It's better for him that my client be someone not working for him. Now tell me, is there a place you and the others like to go to after work?"

"Some of the guys go to Café Silver on Gordon Street. But I rarely join them."

I could guess why. It would cost money. And heaven forbid if Batya found out.

"All right," I said. "Better get back to work now. I'll drop by when I have something to report."

I lit a cigarette and walked away. As I did, two thoughts kept niggling at me. The first was that Caspi had reacted too hotly to my presence. The second was that I had been straight with him when I told him I didn't think he had a motive to kill Feldbaum. That bit about the hammer was to get a rise out of him, only because I didn't like him. I hadn't really suspected him.

So why did I have the sense that he had been hiding something from me? And what could it possibly be?

12

Soffer's Stationery and School Supplies took up the ground floor of a narrow two-story building on Frishman Street. The store's name was painted in white letters on a black background. Below it was an awning that gave an inviting shade in whose cool sanctuary one might rest and examine the store's wares. I didn't. I just went through the open door.

There were no customers. The only other person was a tall, well-built man standing on a stepladder with his back to me, stacking products on a high shelf. He had black hair and wore gray slacks and a white shirt whose tail had escaped the confines of his belt.

He didn't hear me come in and only turned around when I said hello. He had a square face with a high forehead, a wide jaw, and a straight nose. There were two moles near the center of his left cheek, a dimple in his chin, and a pathetic dusting of dark hair over his upper lip, like a boy about to celebrate his *bar mitzvah*. But he was about nineteen.

"Are you Eli Soffer?" I asked.

He shook his head. There was a gap between his lips, and the bottom one glistened with moisture. More spittle collected at both corners of his mouth. He didn't seem to notice or be bothered about it. He had deep-set dark-gray eyes, and they should have looked powerful, but there was a vacantness to them that dissipated whatever impact they might have made. His expression was flat and shallow, like a lazy painting of a man who was thinking of nothing whatsoever.

"He's in the back," he said falteringly, as though he had to think hard before uttering each word, and I realized there was something wrong with him. Slow, some would say. Others would put it in more degrading terms.

"Can you get him for me?"

He didn't ask me why, nor did he inquire as to my name. He just climbed off the stepladder and, without saying a word, went behind the counter and through a door into a back room.

I heard voices, though I couldn't make out the words. A minute later, out stepped an older man, preceding the one I'd spoken with.

"Go back to work, Oded," the older man said, not unkindly. "I'll see about our customer."

He was a short, paunchy man with doleful, liquid eyes. He wore a black *kippah* over thinning brown hair and had the thick mustache and long, unruly beard common to religious men. His facial hair only served to emphasize the general softness of his features—the weak nose, the watery mud-colored eyes, the deep worry lines carved across his forehead. His body only added to the effect with his protruding belly, his slight stoop, and the way his head angled a little forward and down, reducing his effective height by an inch at least. His facial hair and his tired, sorrowful cast made it difficult to judge his age. He might have been in his early forties or a decade older.

He stood leaning on the counter, the shelves at his back filled with various small items—pencils, sharpeners, erasers. It was a neat little shop, and he was a neat little man—in his attire at least, which was ironed and clean. Only his beard and mustache ruined the effect —the mustache was long overdue for a trim, and the beard was a curling mess that reached halfway down his chest. I stepped over to him and offered my hand.

"Adam Lapid."

He shook it. He had a gentle grip and a dry hand. His tone was as soft as the rest of him but had a pleasant timbre. "I'm Eli Soffer. How may I help you?"

"I'm not a customer, I'm afraid. I'm a private detective. I'm working on a case related to a man you knew. Emmanuel Feldbaum."

Soffer's eyes widened, and the added size made them seem even wetter. Looking into them was like staring into a murky pond whose bottom had been disturbed, birthing whirlpools thick with particles of soil.

He shook his head while running his fingers through the curls of his beard. "Terrible. So terrible. What is this country coming to?" He put his hand back on the counter. A frown deepened the lines on his brow. "But why are you involved? Aren't the police investigating the case?"

"Ami Rapoport feels that they've given up. He's not ready to. He hired me to see if I could, somehow, get to the truth."

"I see. But I don't understand why you're here, Mr. Lapid. I didn't know Emmanuel Feldbaum."

"I understand he applied for a job here shortly before his death."

"That he did. But that was the only time I met him. I don't see how that single encounter could have any relation to his tragic death."

He was gazing at me quizzically, and I couldn't blame him. I didn't want to admit that I was simply flailing about half-blind, hoping to stumble on some clue that would point me in the right direction.

"I doubt that it does, Mr. Soffer. What I'm trying to do is get an idea of who Emmanuel Feldbaum was. I'm talking to whoever had contact with him in his final days."

There was a scraping sound behind me, followed by a handful of footfalls. The sensation of someone close to my back, and then a voice, hesitant and slow, "Anything else you want me to take care of now?"

It was Oded, the man I'd spoken with earlier. He was clutching the stepladder that he'd been standing on when I'd entered the store.

"No. Not right now, Oded. Please go to the back room and finish unpacking the new delivery."

Oded obeyed, slipping behind the counter and through the door silently.

Soffer closed the door to the back room and said, "I should have asked Oded to leave as soon as you told me why you're here. It might get him upset to hear about a murder. Oded is very sensitive."

"He's your son?"

"Not officially. But I guess you could say I've adopted him."

"That was nice of you. Rapoport told me you're a kind man."

"Did he now? Well, that's nice to hear." He gave a small shrug. "But I don't think it merits high praise. Oded needed a home, so I decided to give him one." He gestured upward with his hand, and his eyes flitted in the same direction, which I took to mean they lived above the shop.

I said, "I think it's one of the most precious gifts a person can receive: a home."

He appeared to give this some consideration and eventually signified his agreement with a slow nod. Perhaps he was thinking of an old home in a much colder country somewhere, a home that used to be his but no longer was. I was thinking of my old home in Hungary.

"And it's one of the most painful things to have taken from you," I added.

He tilted his head a notch, giving me a probing stare, perhaps sensing my frame of mind. "Yes. I suppose it is." He ran a hand through his beard and sighed. "Oded's a good boy. I've known him since he was little. I was a friend of his family, you might say. His mother was a good woman and one of my first customers here. Whenever she came here, she would bring Oded along. As you can imagine, a boy like Oded, she couldn't just let him wander about on his own. Even the army didn't want him. Before she died of cancer some years ago, his mother begged me to take him in, and so I did."

"You're a good man, Mr. Soffer."

Soffer cast his eyes down, apparently embarrassed by my praise. "You're wondering why I didn't hire Feldbaum, aren't you?"

"That was one of the questions I planned to ask. But in general, I just want to know as much as I can about him."

Soffer gnawed on his lip. It was as if he hadn't heard me. He had something he needed to say, a weight to get off his chest. "Ami Rapoport asked me to give Feldbaum a job. I guess he thought I have a soft heart because of Oded." He gave a small shrug. "I suppose that I do. Ami said Feldbaum was not ordinary, but he didn't go into much detail. Maybe he hoped that when I talked with Feldbaum, my compassion would overrule my good sense. I'm ashamed to admit that it didn't."

"Why should you be ashamed?"

"I suppose there's no logical reason. Maybe because Feldbaum is dead. Maybe because he truly was deeply damaged. I wish I could have helped, but I need someone I can trust. Someone dependable. Oded, for all his faults, is. I didn't feel that Feldbaum was the same."

"What made you think that?"

"The look in his eyes. The way he talked. He was... how shall I put it?"

"In a different place and time?" I suggested.

"A different place and time. That's it precisely. Very sad. I wish I could have helped, but I'm running a business, and times are not easy. I need good staff. You understand, I hope."

"I do," I said, thinking that just like Ami Rapoport, Soffer was a man who did more good than most people would, but still he was assailed by guilt. "You have nothing to feel bad about."

He inclined his head. "That's kind of you to say. But I still wish... well, it's too late now, of course. But maybe, with your help, poor Feldbaum can still get justice. Which is all that he can get now, I suppose. Are you making any progress in your investigation?"

"I only began yesterday," I said.

"Ah. I understand. Well, I wish I could have helped you more, but, as I said, I only met him once, and even that conversation was short."

I nodded, masking my disappointment. Nothing good had come of my visit to Mr. Soffer's store, and worse, something bad had. I'd made a good man feel the poisonous bite of guilt more acutely.

I was about to bid him good day, but then a new question occurred to me.

"When you and Feldbaum spoke, did he say anything about a house?"

"A house? What house?"

"His father's house." I started to explain that Feldbaum would ask people he met about his father's house in Poland—new in his memory, but old and probably gone in reality—but seeing Soffer's blank expression, I broke off in favor of a different question. "Did he mention the name Menashe Volkoff?"

"Menashe Volkoff?" Soffer repeated slowly. "I don't think so. Who's he?"

"I don't know. I think it was someone Feldbaum knew back in Poland. Someone he wanted to find. He asked a lot of people about him."

"Well, he didn't ask me," Soffer said. "Why did he want to find this man? Do you think he might have killed Feldbaum?"

"I doubt it. I believe Menashe Volkoff is long dead. He probably died in Europe during the war."

"Then why are you asking about him?"

"That's the way my work is. You dig even when there's little chance of unearthing anything worthwhile, but that process some-times leads you to a clue you wouldn't have found otherwise."

"Interesting," he said.

"You try ten things, and nine of them end up being a complete waste of time. But you can never know in advance which of the ten is going to be the exception. Like I said, I'm pretty sure Menashe Volkoff has been dead for some time. But if, by some miracle, he's alive and in Israel, I sure would like to talk to him."

Soffer studied my face. "I get the sense you care deeply about this case, Mr. Lapid."

Just like Reuben, I thought with a twinge, sensing things I'd rather no one did. "It's my job. It's what I was paid to do."

"I see," he said, but there was a doubtful tinge to his voice. I hadn't convinced him.

His insight made me uncomfortable. Was I that easy to read?

Again, I thought that I would have been wiser to have never taken this case.

Eager to get out of there, I said, "Thank you for talking to me, Mr. Soffer. Have a good day."

I was at the door when he stopped me. "Wait, Mr. Lapid! I just remembered something."

I turned. "What?"

"Something Feldbaum said during our talk. A man he asked me about. His name is on the tip of my tongue but just out of reach."

I stepped closer, my heart rate notching up. Perhaps my visit here would not be fruitless after all.

Soffer's eyes were screwed in concentration. He wore the agonized expression of a man reaching for an elusive memory that kept slipping away. Oddly, it made him look younger, more vital somehow.

"Clear your mind," I told him, keeping my voice calm and level so as to disturb his concentration as little as possible. "Breathe deeply and slowly, and stop trying to reach for the memory. Let it come to you."

Soffer's breathing was the only sound in the store. For a moment, it seemed as though Tel Aviv itself was holding its breath, waiting anxiously to see if the weary-looking shopkeeper would deliver the goods.

I was just as anxious. Silently, I urged Soffer to produce the name. I felt, and I could not say why, that without it, I would never be able to solve this murder. In my mind, this mysterious name took on the shape of a key. A key that fit the lock of the box that held the secrets of Emmanuel Feldbaum's murder. I prayed that Soffer would give it to me.

He opened his eyes. He said nothing, nor did he move, and in his stillness, I detected the signs of defeat. My heart gave a pang, and I cursed inwardly, tasting the bitterness of dashed hope.

But then Soffer parted his lips and murmured two words. He'd spoken so softly that I had to ask him to repeat himself.

"Yosef Rudinsky," he said.

"That's the name?"

He nodded.

"Are you sure?"

"One hundred percent." He examined my face, and, bit by bit, his lips curled in a tentative smile. The first time I'd seen him showing any levity whatsoever. Just like his earlier expression of concentration, the smile sheared years off his appearance. "This information might help you, right?"

"It might," I said, reciprocating his smile, though mine was broad and unbridled. I felt an exaggerated sense of triumph and had to caution myself not to get my hopes up. Despite my earlier imagining, the name Soffer had just given me might very well prove worthless.

But that didn't change my absolute certainty that I finally had a breakthrough in the case.

13

Before I left his store, I asked Eli Soffer a few more questions.

"Did Feldbaum say anything about Rudinsky? Apart from asking if you knew where he was?"

"Not that I remember, no," Soffer said.

"Don't answer right away. Take a moment, and maybe the memory will come to you like before. Did he say or suggest that Rudinsky and he came from the same town in Poland?"

Soffer shook his head.

"Did Feldbaum say when he last met Rudinsky?"

Again the answer was no. Soffer's smile had vanished by then. His face had reverted to his formerly morose, worry-burdened cast. He had felt a spark of satisfaction at remembering Rudinsky's name, but that feeling had perished under the barrage of my further questions, to which he could not supply a helpful answer.

I shook his hand and thanked him for his help. I asked him to contact me if he remembered anything else, and gave him the address and telephone number of Greta's Café. "I'm there most days. If I'm not, you can leave a message for me. I'll get it soon enough."

He nodded, bid me a warm goodbye, and wished me luck in my investigation. I thanked him again and left.

Out on the street, the heat was nearly palpable. There was no wind, and the humidity was such that the air had weight and substance. With hot, moist hands, it pressed upon me from all sides.

I stopped at a café, ordered a cold drink, and telephoned Reuben Tzanani.

"I have two names I'd like you to check for me," I said. "Would that be all right?"

"Do they have something to do with the murder in Sheinkin Garden?"

"I'd be surprised if they did, but they came up in the investigation." I explained about Emmanuel Feldbaum's habit of asking about people from his past, trying to determine their current whereabouts. "The first name came up in the original investigation, but I don't think the investigating officer followed up on it. The name is Menashe Volkoff. You got that?"

Reuben read the name back to me. "You think Sergeant Bilenko should have checked this Volkoff guy?"

"He probably didn't see the point. If Feldbaum fell victim to a robbery-turned-murder, why bother? Besides, Bilenko must have assumed Volkoff is long dead. That's what I believe, too."

"Then why do you want me to check his name?"

"I've got nothing else to go on. And I'm working on the assumption that someone targeted Feldbaum. I don't know that I believe that's what happened, but it's what I have to do. I'd check the names myself, but I don't have access to government files. The police do."

"All right. I'll do it. But it might take a while to find something. If there's anything to find at all."

"I know, Reuben. Thank you."

"Don't mention it. What's the second name?"

"Yosef Rudinsky."

"Got it. Is there anything you know about these men? Any detail that might help me search?"

"Nothing, really. But I'm assuming they lived in the same town as Feldbaum did in Poland." I told Reuben the name and spelled it out to him in the original Latin letters, just in case something turned up in the records of the British Mandate that preceded the establishment of Israel.

"Okay, Adam. I'll see what I can do. Anything else?"

"No. That's it."

"Good. Now there's something you can do for me."

"What?"

"Shoshana's birthday is on Wednesday. She asked me to invite you."

Shoshana was Reuben's eldest. A slender, happy child, with curly black hair and large, intelligent eyes.

I hesitated. My instinctive response was not to go. Family events at Reuben's were boisterous, crowded affairs, full of lively, joyous relatives basking in the happy comfort of their large family.

Which contrasted painfully with my not having a family of my own.

"You don't have to stay for long, Adam," Reuben said, and the tenderness in his voice, the realization that he understood more than I'd ever given him credit for, cracked something deep inside me. My hand tightened around the receiver, and I had to stifle a moan that was clawing its way up my throat. I shut my eyes and breathed deeply until I'd regained my equilibrium.

I wanted to decline, but Reuben had agreed to do a favor for me. And there was Shoshana, whom I recalled fondly, despite not having seen her in a long while.

"What time should I be there?" I finally asked.

"Five o'clock," Reuben said, and I could hear the smile in his voice. "You don't have to bring anything. Just yourself."

I finished my drink, then browsed the shelves of a nearby bookstore. All the books were either the sort of highbrow literature I found tiresome or non-fiction volumes I had no interest in. No Westerns or adventure novels that were easy on the mind and eyes. I left without buying anything.

I ate lunch at Greta's Café. I played chess. I caught snatches of conversation from nearby tables. A woman moaned about her mother-in-law. A man groused about his boss. A couple debated which movie they were going to see that night. No one talked about crime. No one had murder on their minds.

Except me.

The place was full, and Greta was busy. Yet she still managed to find the time to stop at my table for a minute.

"Is everything okay, Adam?"

"Yes. Why do you ask?"

"You look a bit troubled."

"I have to go to a girl's birthday party on Wednesday."

"From your face, I'd have guessed you were heading to a funeral."

"I don't know what to get her. What do you buy a girl of nine?" I felt a stab near my heart as the question left my lips. My own two daughters would have been past that age if they'd lived.

Greta furrowed her brow, but then a customer called to her from across the café. "I'm sorry, Adam. I have to go see what he wants. Don't worry. You'll figure it out. You've solved greater mysteries before."

It was one forty when I got to Mahlul. The shacks looked to be baking in the early afternoon heat. The sea was a dazzling sheet of rippling glass to the west, beautiful and vast and powerful in its spring tranquility.

Hannah Goldman was working in her garden when I arrived. She was crouching on her heels, digging into the soil, a watering can at her side.

She wore a white shirt and short khaki pants, like a kibbutznik. Sandals on her feet, a wide-brimmed hat on her head. Her arms were suntanned, as were her calves, and she was humming a tune I didn't recognize.

For some reason, I did not make my presence known straight-away. Instead, I watched her as she dug and sprinkled and weeded her small garden. There was something entrancing about the fluidity of her actions. She'd done this activity many times before, and it showed in the smooth economy of her movements.

In their coop, the pair of chickens ceased their pecking and eyed me with an unbending fixation. I couldn't guess what was going through their tiny brains, and for some reason, I found that unnerving. Which prompted me to break my silence.

"Miss Goldman?"

Hannah Goldman stopped her humming and looked over her shoulder. Her eyes were two narrow brushstrokes behind a pair of glasses, their color impossible to make out due to the way her hat shadowed her face.

"Yes," she said, clearly peeved at being interrupted. "That's me. Who are you?"

"My name is Adam Lapid. I'm wondering if you could spare me a few minutes. I want to talk to you about Emmanuel Feldbaum."

Her left eyebrow twitched up. Putting down her trowel, she stood. She was tall and slim, with shapely calves and knees. She brushed dirt off her hands and tilted her head questioningly, and I could see her eyes were a light and startling clear blue. "Why are you asking about him? You're not a policeman, are you?"

"A private detective. Ami Rapoport hired me. I understand you knew Emmanuel. That you two had some sort of connection."

Her mouth gave a little twist at that, but I couldn't tell whether it was from annoyance or humor. I followed her eyes as she glanced past me, and saw a frumpy woman staring at us from the doorway of her neighboring shack. The woman's expression lacked any redeeming qualities—it was one hundred percent naked, judgmental, and possibly prurient snoopiness. Hannah Goldman removed her hat and flashed the woman a wide smile that was anything but neighborly. She gave her a breezy wave and called out, "More grist for the gossip mill, eh, Zelda?"

Zelda crimped her thin lips and shook her head reproachfully.

"Be sure to give the other ladies my regards," Hannah Goldman said with exaggerated cheer. "Don't forget now, you hear?"

Zelda muttered something under her breath, retreated into her shack, and shut the door decisively, as though to keep out an evil spirit. Hannah Goldman smacked her hat on her thigh and laughed. It was a hearty laugh, ringing and full, and when she was done, her blue eyes were sparkling. She said to me, "Seems like I owe you one,

Mr. Lapid. Your visit sure got dear Zelda there all riled up. She'll be running to her friends any minute now, bursting at the seams with innuendo and moral indignation."

"Glad to have been of service," I said, with a curt bow, though I couldn't say why Hannah Goldman was so cheerful about the whole business.

"And he's polite too," she said. "My, my, you don't see that every day around here. Come on inside. That will give Zelda more ammunition for that machine gun masquerading as her mouth. Bring in that watering can, will you?"

I followed her inside, watering can in hand, unsure of what to make of Hannah Goldman but curious to learn more.

14

Hannah Goldman stuck her hat on a peg by the door. Then she went to the window, parted the curtains an inch, and peeked out. Her lips curved in a wide grin, dimpling her cheeks.

"Ha! There she goes, the stupid sow. Dependable as a Swiss clock. Off to report my immorality to the rest of her uptight, self-righteous friends."

"Zelda?" I asked.

"Who else?" She looked at me. Sunlight reflected off her glasses, masking her eyes. "You know what she thinks, don't you? That you and I are lovers."

Heat invaded my cheeks, and I hoped they weren't coloring. Still, my face must have shown my shock because she laughed.

"I'm sorry. Do I embarrass you?"

"Are you always this direct?"

"Of course not. Most places, I can't be. But here, in my home, I get to act as I please. And whoever doesn't like it can put my door to good use and never bother coming back."

With that, she yanked the curtains aside, and sunlight splashed into the shack. It was neat as a pin, nothing out of place, everything spotless and tidy. A small table with one chair and a stool. A two-seater of faded color and indeterminate age. A padded armchair by the window, with a thick book lying open on an armrest with a footstool nearby. More books crowding a tall bookcase, thick volumes in several languages.

A bunch of photos of Hannah Goldman hung on the walls. Some alone; some with company. And at the far end, a double bed. A married woman's bed. But there was no ring on Hannah Goldman's finger, and on the bed itself were two pillows piled at the center. *She lives alone*, I reminded myself.

The shack was about the same size as the one the Rapoports lived in, and it should have felt as cramped, but it didn't. In fact, it felt downright airy, maybe because the walls had been painted white, giving the illusion of more space. Or maybe because desperation is stifling. There was plenty of it in the Rapoport home, but no trace of it here.

Overall, Hannah Goldman kept her household in order, and her garden was thriving. This had to be the result of hard work and determination.

"You look hot," she said. "Want some cold water?"

I said I did, and she opened the icebox and got out a full pitcher. She poured each of us a tall glass, and we sipped from them, still standing. I used the opportunity to examine her surreptitiously.

She had raven hair that was coiled at the back of her head. Her face was oval, with elegant lines and high cheekbones. Her eyes were a stark blue and set wide apart, flanking a perfectly straight nose with flaring nostrils. There was a beauty spot above the left corner of her wide mouth. It and a pair of small chickenpox scars on her chin were her only blemishes. Otherwise, her skin was smooth and quite a bit fairer than her suntanned arms and legs.

"Does everything meet with your approval, Mr. Lapid?" she asked.

Her expression was stern, her mouth and jaw set tight. Her eyes were fixed on mine, and there was an unyielding quality to them. This was a woman to be reckoned with.

My brain urged me to feign innocence, but some instinct pushed me to choose a more honest course.

"Indeed it does. You pass muster just fine, Miss Goldman. Keep up the good work."

She laughed, and I realized her sternness had been contrived, that she'd been toying with me. It had been a test of sorts. A minor one, perhaps, but I had passed it.

"You're not too bad yourself, Adam," she said, still grinning. Her examination of me was swift and anything but surreptitious. "And please call me Hannah. I don't like formality in my home. I get too much of it where I work."

"You're a teacher, I understand."

"That's right." She gestured toward the two-seater, and we sat side by side, our knees nearly touching. Mine were hidden behind my trousers; hers were exposed and quite lovely despite an ancient scar on the right one.

"You work at a language school?"

She arched her left eyebrow. She was one of those people who could move one without the other.

"You've been asking about me?"

"I came by here yesterday afternoon, and you weren't here. A neighbor explained where you might be."

"He told you the truth, but not the whole truth, which is important in your line of work, isn't it? I teach schoolchildren in the morning and adults in the afternoon and evening."

"What do you teach?"

"In school: history, geography, and literature. I teach third, fourth, and fifth grades. At the language school, I teach Hebrew to fresh immigrants. Your Hebrew is excellent, by the way, but you weren't born here."

"In Hungary. I learned Hebrew as a boy. My father insisted."

"Smart man."

"Yes. Yes, he was."

She caught the sorrow in my voice. "I'm sorry. I should have assumed he had passed."

That made me smile in bitterness. "That's how it is with Jews from

Europe, isn't it? The assumption is that our family and friends are all dead."

She said nothing to that. She looked into her glass and then drained it. She got up to pour herself another. "Shall I replenish yours?"

My glass was half full. I downed what remained of the water and handed it to her. She returned a minute later with both glasses full.

A sign, I thought, to get the conversation back on its original course.

"I was told you had some sort of relationship with Emmanuel Feldbaum."

"Who blabbed?"

"Two women called Bella and Ruthie."

"Ah. The queen of the gaggle and her loyal lieutenant. That's who Zelda was rushing off to report to, no doubt. They run a regular wire service here. What did they tell you about me?"

I hesitated.

"That I'm unkind, unsocial, that I run around with men, even married men?" she asked, but there was no real question in her voice.

"Just about."

"I suppose you have a pretty low opinion of me, then."

"No, Hannah. I've been at this game too long to take what people say at face value."

"Well, it's true, for the most part. I am unkind to that coven of witches. I find them repellent. I want nothing to do with them. They've made the lives of several people in this neighborhood quite difficult with their whisperings and insinuations and gossip. All because those people don't conform to some societal mold."

"Like you don't?"

"Like I don't," she said, her face turning harder, her tone of voice sharp and combative. "My sins are manifold, Adam. I'm not married, I don't have three or four children to run after, and I don't try to make my difficult circumstances better by comparison by badmouthing similarly unlucky people. But a worse crime is that I'm a 'loose, immoral woman,' to quote Bella. I'm a twenty-eight-year-old woman, who should have been long married and with a herd of small children underfoot. But I'm single by choice. Well, in that case, I should be alone and pious, like a Catholic nun, keeping myself pristine and pure for the future husband who would one day rescue me from my current dismal situation, providing my luck changes. But that's not how I choose to live my life."

She paused and drank half the contents of her glass, but the water didn't seem to cool her down any.

"I have men over when I wish to. At night. It doesn't happen too often, but nor is it as rare as a lunar eclipse. Of course, to hear Bella and her cohorts tell it, there's a line of men outside my door as though this were a brothel. I'm a blight on the neighborhood. I'll bring the morality of the children to ruin if I'm allowed to stick around. They even went as far as going to my headmaster to say I'm unfit for my role as a teacher."

This, it seemed, was the greatest insult of all. A muscle in Hannah's cheek was rippling, and her eyes were a blazing blue, like a fire about to leap out at you. She was a passionate teacher, I could tell. One not merely devoted to her work, but also defined by it. The neighborhood women had known where to strike.

"I'm sorry this happened to you, Hannah."

"Don't worry. It didn't work. My headmaster shut them up before they could get much out. He's a stuffy old sort, but he doesn't care what his teachers do outside the school as long as they can teach. And I'm a damn fine teacher, Adam. And in school, I'm completely professional."

"I believe you."

"But my worst sin is that I'm the sort of ungodly woman who tries to snare every man she sees, and I have a particular craving for married men."

She laughed without humor, setting her glass down. "That's not Bella's fault entirely. I actually feel a little sorry for her. Can you guess what happened?"

I took a moment to think, keenly wishing I could come up with the answer. I wanted Hannah to think highly of me. I pictured Bella from yesterday and compared her with Hannah and ventured a guess: "Bella's husband made advances on you?"

Hannah eyed me with a glitter of appreciation. "You are clever, aren't you? Ami Rapoport chose well. Yes, that's precisely what happened. Though 'made advances' is a sort of genteel way to put it. Her foul brute of a husband came over one day, dressed in his too-tight Sabbath clothes and stinking of cologne, and tried to put his paws on me. I turned him down and didn't bother being gentle about it. He was gobsmacked. He'd heard I was easy. Then he got angry, started calling me names men use for women they lust after but can't have. Finally, he stormed off, saying I'll be sorry."

"Let me guess: he told Bella that *you* tried to seduce *him*."

"And she believed him, the fool. Or pretended to. Sometimes, I suspect that she knows the truth and can't stand it. Which makes her hate me even more. What wife wouldn't hate a woman her husband tried to bed? Since then her opinion of me has become quite toxic, and she poisons the others."

"Why don't you leave?"

"Why should I? I've done nothing wrong. Besides, it's not as if I have enough for a nice apartment by myself. Here, at least I have a garden."

"They can make life difficult for you, can't they?"

"Sure they can, and they do. But I let it be known that one of my lovers is a high-ranking police officer, and that has kept them from doing anything worse than talk." She laughed again, then leaned forward and said in a hushed voice, like one of her pupils would have done when sharing a secret, "It's not true, Adam. I don't even know any policemen. But let them think otherwise. Let them be scared."

She leaned back into the cushions. The movement made the collar of her shirt spread open, exposing a wide triangle of skin pointing down between her breasts. I did my best not to stare. She said, "Am I making a bad impression, Adam? Am I tarnishing my image?"

I shook my head. "Not in the slightest, but I don't know many women who'd be so open about it all."

"I have nothing to be ashamed of. And anyone who disagrees can—"

"Put your door to good use and not come back," I completed.

"That's right. You learn quickly."

Perhaps that assessment was true, because I suddenly thought I had the answer to one question that had been niggling me.

"Did a Sergeant Bilenko talk to you about Emmanuel Feldbaum?" I asked.

"Yes. Two days after the murder. He sat right where you're sitting now."

"Did he ask a lot of questions?"

"Not many. I don't think he spent ten minutes here. I remember thinking he looked to be in a hurry. Wouldn't even take a glass of water."

"Did he write your answers down?"

"No. Why do you ask?"

"I don't suppose you told him you were involved with a high-ranking police officer."

"Of course not."

"Would Bella and Ruthie have done so, you think? They're the ones who told Bilenko about your connection with Feldbaum."

Hannah's lips curled into a smile. "So that's why he was so uncomfortable. I was wondering about that. You know, he wouldn't meet my eyes for more than a split second at a time."

I smiled back. "He was worried you might complain about him to your high-ranking lover. The one who doesn't exist. I imagine Bilenko thought long and hard how to ask you as few questions as possible to satisfy himself you were in the clear, so you wouldn't get upset. He must have been relieved when he left."

"He did let out a big exhalation as he was crossing the threshold. And I spied on him from the window and saw him mopping his brow with a handkerchief before heading off. The poor man."

We both laughed. An unbridled, free sort of laughter. The air seemed to grow lighter with it. I wished it could go on for a good while longer, but like all good things, it died much sooner than it should have.

"About Emmanuel Feldbaum," I said, once we both ceased laughing, "can you tell me what your relationship with him was like?"

Hannah's expression turned grave. Her eyes lost their glitter. No hint remained of either the defiant humor or the righteous anger of before. All I saw was deep sorrow. "It wasn't anything like Bella and Ruthie insinuated. Emmanuel and I weren't lovers or anything of the sort. I'm not sure he was even interested in women."

"What were you to each other, then?"

"Just two people who talked with each other. I initiated it. I'd like to say I did it because I felt sorry for him, because he was lonely and misunderstood and rejected, but that's not the truth. I did it for purely selfish reasons."

"Which were?"

"I wanted him to tell me about Sachsenhausen."

"The concentration camp? How did you even know Emmanuel had been there?"

"Someone told me he and Ami Rapoport had been in the same concentration camp. I knew Ami had been in Sachsenhausen for a short time near the end of the war. I wanted to talk to someone who'd been there before, who'd spent more time there."

"Why?"

Instead of answering, Hannah rose to her feet and walked to the opposite wall, which was festooned with photos of her. She stood for a moment motionless before removing a single photo from its nail and bringing it back with her.

"That's me," Hannah said, pointing to the girl in the picture. She had on a summer dress that was fluttering in the wind. Her hair flapped about her head, and she was laughing at something lost to time. She didn't have glasses back then. "And these are my parents." She pointed at a man and a woman, both middle-aged, he in a well-cut suit and tie, she in a conservative dress that went all the way down to her shoes. The man held a pipe in one hand; the woman a handbag. Both were smiling.

"And this," Hannah continued, her voice tinged with old, yet still keen, sadness, "is my brother, Stanislaw. He's seventeen years old here. I'm fourteen."

"When was this taken?"

"1938. This is just outside Danzig. The Free City of Danzig, as they used to call it."

"In Poland."

"Yes, but back then it was right on Germany's doorstep. On two of its doorsteps actually, sandwiched between East Prussia and the rest of Germany, and first on the list of demands Hitler made to Poland. In the photo, we're celebrating because I'd just gotten an immigration certificate to come to Mandatory Palestine to study here."

"Your family stayed behind?"

"Yes. My father wasn't worried. He said Britain and France wouldn't let Hitler invade Poland. 'They'll sweep the little dictator off his throne so fast, he won't have time to say schnitzel,' he used to joke. But the joke ended up being on him, on my whole family."

"What happened to them?" I asked, guessing the answer and feeling its tragic bite in my gut.

"I don't know everything," Hannah said, and by now her eyes were sparkling for a different reason than before. "I haven't been able to find out all the details. But I know my parents were moved to a ghetto farther east in Poland. From there they were taken to one of the death camps and murdered. It happened in 1942 or '43."

"And your brother?"

"He ended up in Sachsenhausen. He got there in early 1940. And he died there three years later, in the winter of '43. But other than that, I know almost nothing. About what he went through there, I mean."

I gave her a long disbelieving look. "And you actually want to know?"

"Very much so."

"Why would you? You're smart enough to know that nothing good happened there. That he suffered beyond belief. Why do you want to know the particulars?"

She didn't answer. Her eyes were angled down and toward me, and I realized she was staring at my forearm, where my number tattoo was, the tattoo I'd been rubbing without being aware of it.

Raising her eyes to my face, she gave a tiny, helpless shrug. "I can't help it. I have this need to know. I left them behind, you see. I came here and I was spared. I know it wasn't my fault, but still, I want to know all I can."

So you can suffer with them, I thought. *Maybe that's one way of alleviating irrational guilt. But it sure as hell hasn't worked for me.*

"So you asked Emmanuel about your brother?"

"Yes."

"What did he tell you?"

"He was difficult to understand. He would start talking about one thing and then digress to something else entirely and wouldn't remember what he'd been talking about before. But I was patient. You don't find many people who were in Sachsenhausen for a long time and survived. Most of the prisoners there weren't Jews, and that makes contacting them even harder."

"Did Emmanuel know your brother?"

She nodded. "He knew the name. He could describe him. They were assigned to the same detail. The shoe detail."

"What was that?"

"The Nazis wanted a way to test a variety of designs and materials for footwear, and they used some of the prisoners in Sachsenhausen for that. Prisoners would be forced to march or run with full packs on for hours on various surfaces, wearing all sorts of experimental shoes. As you can imagine, this was very difficult and painful. I understand prisoners in that detail died quickly from exhaustion. My brother lasted longer than most. He was a strong boy."

"Did they also test army boots?" I asked, a shiver of horror slithering up all the way from my tailbone to the nape of my neck.

"Yes, they did. They wanted to test boots for their soldiers. And maybe also soften them up before they delivered them to the front. Why did you ask me that, Adam?"

I rubbed a hand over my face as the tragedy of Emmanuel Feldbaum revealed another of its secrets. A most horrific, heartbreaking secret. Sadness filled my chest and squeezed my heart.

"Emmanuel used to walk at night. Did you know that?" I asked.

Hannah shook her head.

"He would get up at night and walk the streets of Tel Aviv for hours on end. Walking in his sleep. I'm not sure exactly where. And he would do so in old army boots with soles worn almost clear off."

"Dear God," Hannah said, her eyes wide and glistening. She'd been like a porcupine earlier, all bristling needles, ready for war. Now she was showing me a softer side. It made her look more vulnerable, and I had the urge to reach out and touch her hand, but didn't.

"Before, I didn't know why he did that," I said. "But now I do. He was reliving his time in Sachsenhausen every night. He would walk in his sleep like he did there, trapped in his nightmares, only partly in the here and now. He was murdered while on one of those walks."

A silence descended. Apparently, neither of us knew what to say next. Then Hannah murmured: "For in that sleep of death what dreams may come."

I looked at her. "What was that?"

She repeated the line. "It's from *Hamlet*. Shakespeare. It's apt, don't you think? Emmanuel was sleepwalking with his dark dreams for company, and it was a sleep of death. One from which he never awoke. He was imprisoned in it when he was killed."

She started crying then, quietly, and I gave her my handkerchief. She squeezed my hand tightly as she dabbed at her eyes, and her touch sent a warm current up my arm and into my chest. Then we sat for a while without speaking, together physically, but each of us alone with our thoughts of the man caught in that sleep of death in which the darkest dreams may come.

15

Hannah Goldman rose to make tea. "I don't have any sugar, but I've got a little honey left. Would that be all right?"

I said it would be fine.

She filled a kettle with water and set it to boil on a little kerosene stove. When the kettle whistled, she poured its steaming cargo into two cups, put in more honey than most people would have done in these trying times, and returned to the sofa with the tea.

I thanked her and said, "I need to ask you about your talks with Emmanuel. Are you up for it?"

She nodded. "Anything I can tell you, I will."

"Did he ever mention the names of people he knew who were probably long dead?"

"Yes. That happened often."

"Any names you remember?"

Her answer mirrored those I'd heard before: Feldbaum's relatives and Menashe Volkoff.

"Did he say anything about Volkoff? Anything at all?"

"A few times he said that he needed to ask Menashe 'where it is,' that Menashe would know."

"Any idea what *it* was?"

"No. Emmanuel was his most confused when he talked about Volkoff. I could understand almost none of it."

I bit back my frustration. The answer was dangling just out of reach, kept away by death and injury and suffering. I wanted it so much I could scream.

"Anything else he said?"

"One time, after saying that Menashe would know where it was, Emmanuel straightened abruptly and said as certainly as I'd ever heard him speak, 'Menashe is here.'"

"Here? Where is here? In Israel?"

"That was how I interpreted it, but who can say? Emmanuel might have believed he himself wasn't in Israel at that moment."

"I understand. Anything else?"

Hannah shook her head.

"What about Yosef Rudinsky? Did Emmanuel ever mention him?"

"No. Never."

"You sure?"

"Beyond a doubt, Adam. Trust me, I listened to every word Emmanuel said to me very closely, hoping I would learn something new about my brother. Who is Yosef Rudinsky?"

I explained that Eli Soffer told me Emmanuel mentioned that name when they talked.

Hannah pursed her lips. "I wish I could ask Emmanuel about him. Maybe Rudinsky was also in Sachsenhausen."

"Or he might have come from the same town in Poland as Emmanuel," I said.

She drank some tea. "Emmanuel was happy that day, you know."

"What day?"

"When he went to talk to Eli Soffer about the job. He said Soffer was very nice, and he thought the store would be a better place for him to work than the construction site."

"Soffer told me Emmanuel was very confused during their interview. I guess Emmanuel himself didn't notice."

"I guess so. He would often not remember things he said shortly before." Hannah sighed. "It's so sad what happened to him."

"Soffer felt bad about the whole business," I said, and asked her if she knew him. She said she'd never met him, but she knew of him, that some of her pupils purchased their school supplies at his store and that Soffer was in the habit of giving discounts to poor customers. I said I wasn't surprised to learn of his generosity, and I told her about Oded, Soffer's employee, and that Soffer felt he couldn't hire Emmanuel, that he wouldn't be dependable.

"I can understand that," she said.

"He feels guilty about it."

"I can understand that, too. I keep thinking I might have done more for Emmanuel, but I'm not sure exactly what."

"It seems like you gave him a lot. You were a friend at a time when he didn't have many."

"Was I really? Like I said, I didn't talk to him for the pleasure of his company. I did it for entirely personal reasons."

"I doubt that it mattered to him why you talked to him, only that you did. That you had the patience to listen to him. Your home was the one place in which he was welcomed, and that must have counted for a great deal."

She looked at me, her eyes like a bright sky that you see through a clean window. There was a resolute toughness in her features, even now when she no longer viewed me as a potential enemy. But her glasses softened her edges, giving her a bookish cast, which made her look both smarter and more attractive.

"Thank you for saying that, Adam."

We drank our tea, and she asked, "How is the investigation going?"

"So far, there's not much to go on. And there's no telling if there ever will be. But I'm nowhere near giving up."

"I'm glad to hear it. But how long will you be able to work on it? Ami can't be paying you much."

I told her about Batya Rapoport being angry at her husband for hiring me, and how I ended up giving back my retainer.

"So you're working on this case for nothing? Why would you do that?"

I pondered how to answer her. A stupid, reckless part of me

wanted to tell her everything, but a more cautious, wiser part prevailed. "Emmanuel Feldbaum deserves justice. And I like Ami Rapoport quite a bit."

"I've only spoken with him once, briefly, but from what Emmanuel told me, he's a good man. Batya, though, is another matter."

"She hated Emmanuel."

"I know she did."

"Do you know her well?"

"Better than I'd like to. She's part of Bella's gang of malicious gossipers."

"She didn't tell me about you when I asked her about Emmanuel."

"She knows I don't like her. Maybe she was worried I would say something bad about her."

"Ami didn't tell me either."

"Maybe he didn't know. Emmanuel might have neglected to tell him about me."

"Wouldn't Batya have told him?"

Hannah flashed a scornful smile. "She might not have wanted to talk about me with her husband. I have a reputation, remember? I hunt husbands down and steal them from their wives."

"Would Batya actually believe such nonsense?"

"She might. That's the strange thing about lies. First you make them up, then you spread them, and finally you start to believe them. Besides, who knows what Batya Rapoport would choose to do? She's a schemer. You can see it in her eyes. Always calculating."

"Do you think she might have done it?"

"Done what? You mean the murder?"

"That's right."

"I never would have thought... I mean, she has a deadly tongue, that's for sure, but to actually kill someone..." She paused to think it over. "I don't know. I want to say it's ridiculous, but I can't bring myself to do it. There's something dark about her. Know what I mean?"

"I think so. I sensed the same thing."

"And she truly despised Emmanuel. She wasn't even at the funeral."

"You were?"

"Yes. I was the only woman there. Ami Rapoport was there, and a handful of men not from the neighborhood. Judging by their dusty clothes, I think they were Ami's co-workers. Ami was distraught, and I thought of going over to say something, but I ended up keeping my distance. I wasn't sure how he'd take my being there."

"So he didn't see you?"

"I don't think so, no."

"Tell me, Hannah, can you think of anyone who might have had motive to kill Emmanuel?"

She said that she couldn't imagine anyone who'd want to do Emmanuel any harm. "What benefit would someone get from killing Emmanuel? It must have been a robbery like the police say."

"Maybe," I said, my stomach souring with my dislike for the idea.

"You don't think so?"

"It's the likeliest option but not the one I favor." I explained why.

"I see," she said. "I don't know which would be worse or that it would make any difference. Dead is dead, isn't it?"

"It is. But it matters if the killer faces justice."

We finished our tea, and she cleared away the cups. When she returned, I asked, "Did Emmanuel ever talk about his father's house?"

"Yes. I remember a few times."

"What did he say about it?"

"Almost nothing. He seemed not to remember anything about it. Not the address or how many rooms it had or any other detail. But he did say you could see the sea from the windows."

Maybe that was why he used to walk on the beach, I thought, like on the night I had seen him with the waves licking his feet. Maybe it was a reminder of his father's lost house. Maybe he had been searching for it.

"It must have been a nice place to live," I said.

"Maybe. Then again, you can see the sea from many of the shacks here in Mahlul, and most people want to leave."

She told me she'd been living in her shack for six years. It was either that or continue living with a roommate, a style of living she abhorred. "Living here is not as bad as most people think. I have my privacy and my little garden and chickens, and I can be in the water in less than two minutes."

I liked hearing her talk. I liked looking at her. I realized I wanted to stay with her a bit more, to learn more about her, and maybe even tell her a bit about myself.

But I had taken too much of her time, and I had done so for a specific reason, and try as I might, I could think of no more pertinent questions to ask her.

So I thanked her for her cooperation and the tea and stood up. She said I was welcome on both counts and walked me to the door.

A step beyond it, I paused and said, "You said you teach fourth graders, right? What should I buy a nine-year-old girl for her birthday?"

She asked me about Reuben's daughter Shoshana, and I told her she was a bright, polite, and shy girl but was forced to admit it had been a while since I last saw her.

Hannah pursed her lips. She glanced at her wristwatch and said, "Tell you what, Adam, I have a class in ninety minutes. There are some stores on the way to work where I'm sure you could find something. I can go with you if you want."

I said I would like that, and she told me to wait a couple of minutes while she changed.

I stood like a sentry with my back to her closed door, trying hard not to imagine her taking off her clothes inside, and doing a pitiful job of it.

When she emerged, her appearance was transformed. The work shirt and trousers had given way to a simple yet elegant blue dress that clung to her waist and bust in an appealing yet demure way. The sandals had been replaced by black shoes with low heels, drawing attention to her fine ankles. She wore a slim necklace. And she'd washed her face and applied a faint touch of color to her lips and cheeks. She'd been pretty before, but now she was beautiful.

My admiration must have been evident because her lips quirked. She said, "Ready to go, Adam?"

It was easier to nod than to form syllables.

We exited Mahlul, crossing Hayarkon Street, not talking for a couple of minutes. Then I asked her whom she was teaching tonight, and she said it was a group of recent immigrants from Poland. Teaching new Israelis the old-new language of their old-new country.

"Which do you prefer? Teaching children or adults?"

"Children. They're more curious and happier. Many of the adults are burdened by their experiences and loss."

Like me, I thought, but said nothing.

"That's not to say I don't like teaching adults. It's important work. I help people become a part of Israel, to rebuild their lives. There's satisfaction in that."

I asked her what languages she spoke.

"Polish, Yiddish, German, Czech, Hebrew, and English," she said. "Danzig is in an area that used to be in Germany, and my family on my father's side had German roots, so I learned the language as a child. My maternal grandmother came from Prague, and I picked up Czech from her. And of course, all Jews spoke Yiddish and Polish, and I learned Hebrew at a Zionist school from an early age. English is the only language I learned as an adult."

I said that I had also learned English later in life, and that I often read American books. She asked me what kind, and I told her about the Westerns I loved. She smiled at that, and the sun reflected off her glasses, hiding her eyes, so I couldn't tell the nature of the smile. Remembering the hefty, serious tomes she had in her shack, I regretted telling her about my less refined taste in literature.

She asked me how I became a private detective, and I told her of my history as a policeman in Hungary. I braced myself for questions regarding the number tattoo on my arm and my ordeal in Auschwitz, but she said nothing about it.

Near the corner of Allenby and Pinsker, we stopped at a toy store. Wooden blocks and toy soldiers shared the display window with dolls of varying sizes, including one of a baby girl inside a small carriage.

"How about that?" I said, pointing at the baby carriage.

"For a nine-year-old?"

Feeling foolish, I shifted my finger to the bigger dolls. "One of those?"

"Why not the toy soldiers?" she asked.

I was about to state the obvious, but something in her eyes forestalled me. Instead, I said, "I'm not sure her parents would approve. Why don't we go inside and see what we can find?"

We went through the shelves together. I found myself enjoying her company, even when she shot down my suggestions with a succession of blunt remarks, dubious looks, and firm shakes of her head. But at the same time I was also aware of an acute awkwardness growing inside me, born of being with this woman I'd just met, doing something that was more suitable for people of longer and deeper acquaintance.

Finally, the store owner recommended a game involving long thin sticks, which she insisted children adored, and Hannah said that she'd seen pupils at her school playing it.

"But you said the girl was smart, so why not a book?" And she plucked one off a nearby shelf and stuck it in my hand. "This one's perfect for her age."

The book cover showed a pair of identical blond girls in white shirts and red skirts holding hands against a rural, distinctly European backdrop. The book's name was *Double Ora*, and the author was Erich Kastner.

"A German author?" I asked with distaste.

"Yes. But Kastner was no fan of the Nazis. In fact, they burned his books in 1933. This translation came out last year, and it's excellent. All references to German locations were removed, and the character names were changed to Hebrew ones."

I weighed the book in one hand, the game in the other, and tried to make up my mind. Seeing my indecision, Hannah asked, "What did you buy her last year?"

I admitted that I hadn't attended Shoshana's previous birthday and had gotten her nothing.

"Then buy both gifts," Hannah said, "and tell her one's for last year."

So I did. And for the first time in many years handed money to the owner of a toy store, and then watched her wrap the presents in brown paper.

The language school was on Rothschild Boulevard, a couple of blocks south of Habima Theater. Hannah pointed at a second-story window. "That's my classroom right there."

We stood for an awkward moment in the street, facing each other with neither of us speaking a word.

Eventually, I said, "Thank you for helping me find the right present. Or presents."

She smiled, and I noticed that the dimple in her right cheek was a tad deeper than the one in her left. "It was my pleasure, Adam."

Again there was silence. A sense of embarrassment pervaded my body. I knew what I wanted to say, but my tongue felt immobilized and my mind unable to string together the right words in the correct order.

After nearly a minute of this torment, the corners of Hannah's mouth gave a little downward twist. She drew a breath and said, "I should get going now. Good luck with the investigation, Adam. And enjoy yourself at the party."

She held out her hand, and I shook it dumbly. Then she began walking toward the building where the language school was. Each step she took caused a tiny pang inside me. She managed four strides before my paralysis broke. I'd been searching for the right way to invite her to dinner or coffee or a movie, but what came out instead was, "How about going with me to the party?"

She paused, turned. A shallow frown creased her brow. "You're asking me to come with you to the birthday party of a nine-year-old girl?"

Feeling like the world's greatest idiot, I nodded. "I have two presents. Might as well bring someone along."

She tilted her head a fraction, giving me a quizzical look, as though she was trying to decide whether I might have a screw loose somewhere.

I could sense the no coming and hastened to backtrack. "Forget about it. It was a stupid idea. You've already done more than enough. I—"

"What time is it?" she said.

My heart gave a thump. "Five o'clock. But like I said, you don't—"

"Okay, Adam. I'll go."

I stared at her. "Yeah?"

The corners of her mouth gave another tiny twist, this time upward. "Yeah. Pick me up where I live. Four thirty. We'll walk together. All right?"

"Yeah. Sure. Great. I'll see you then."

I watched her as she walked toward the building, a part of me hoping she'd turn around to give me another look, another fearing that she would and think me a fool for staring.

In the end, she didn't. Only when she disappeared inside did I uproot myself and walk away.

16

Greta gave me a questioning look. "What are these?"

We were in Greta's Café. It was a quarter to four, and the place was nearly empty. The early afternoon lull, Greta once called it. I liked the café best at such quiet times. Soon the after-work invasion would commence, and the place would be bustling.

I had a little time to kill before I went to talk to Emmanuel Feldbaum's former colleagues, and I had a craving for Greta's coffee.

"Birthday presents," I said.

"Two of them? I thought there was just one birthday party."

"There is. But I didn't buy the girl anything last year, so I thought I'd make up for it."

"You seem awfully cheerful about it."

"Birthdays are a cause for rejoicing, aren't they?"

"Until you reach a certain age. But two presents? That seems extravagant for you."

"You calling me a miser, Greta?"

"As a longtime beneficiary of your largess, Adam, how could I possibly? Still, I can't help but wonder as to the shift in your mood. Earlier, the prospect of going to that birthday party caused you nothing but grief. Now, there's a stupid grin on your face."

"I'm just relieved I was able to find the right presents," I said, enjoying myself immensely. Greta was a curious type, and it was fun seeing her dig for information.

"Hmmm," Greta said. "Something tells me that's not it. Not it at all. What else have you been up to since I last saw you?"

"Working," I said, with deliberate vagueness.

"Admirable. Have you made any breakthroughs in the investigation?"

"Not yet."

"But still, you're smiling. You keep trying to stifle it, but you can't help it. Have you met anyone interesting?"

"A couple of people. There was this guy—"

"Never mind about him. Was one of the interesting people you met a woman, by any chance?"

"Come to think of it, one of them was."

"Aha. And does she happen to be attractive?"

I pretended to give the question serious consideration. "She just happens to be, yes."

"And are you likely to be seeing her again?"

"Have you ever considered a career as a police investigator, Greta? You certainly possess the requisite relentlessness."

"Better answer the question, Adam, or I'll fetch my rubber hose."

I held up my hands. "Okay, okay. No need to get rough. I'll tell you."

And I did. I told her that I'd met a woman by the name of Hannah Goldman and that she would be coming with me to Shoshana's birthday party.

Greta smiled, clapping her hands together. "A dinner or a movie would have been-how shall I put it?—more orthodox, but this is still good news."

"Don't get your hopes up, Greta. I don't know if this will actually lead to anything."

"Maybe it won't, but it's a step in the right direction. That's what counts, moving in the right direction. Can I get you anything to eat?"

I told her I only had time for one cup of coffee. She went to get it, and I lit a cigarette. After the coffee, I headed north, stopping at my apartment on Hamaccabi Street to drop off the presents, before veering toward Gordon Street.

I found Café Silver without trouble. Inside, there were about ten square tables and a counter on the left. On the walls were pictures of shiny American cars and men playing soccer. Otherwise, there was no attempt to fancy up the place.

The proprietor was a potbellied man with a mustache and a big dome of a head. The customers were all male and, judging by their clothes and weathered faces, worked physical jobs. A working man's joint.

A fog of cigarette smoke trailed lazily through the hot air. There were the underlying scents of sweat, dust, dirt, and beer. The talk was loud and rough, rich with gruff laughter and manly teasing.

Three guys from the construction site were already there, seated at a table near the entrance. One of them, a thin guy with curly black hair, saw me and called out, "Here he is, the man who made our day hell."

"How are you all doing?" I asked, suddenly unsure of the reception I was about to get.

"Now that we're done for the day and here with our beers and smokes, we're much better, thank you very much for asking."

"You should be buying the next round after the mess you caused," a second man, this one shorter and thicker around the middle, added. The third man nodded.

"It would be my pleasure," I said. "But first can I know what I've done to deserve this unexpected honor?"

The first man chuckled. "Because of you, Mr. Caspi was seething mad all morning. He's always been quick to anger, but today his fuse was especially short. When he came back from your little private chat, it was like steam was coming out of his ears."

"Way he laid into that poor driver," the second man said. "It was painful to see."

"And hear," the third man, narrow-faced with a fleshy nose, chimed in.

"I'm sorry to hear that," I said. "I had no intention of ruining your day."

The first man drained his glass and smacked his lips. "Buy us a round and all will be forgiven. Won't it, fellas?"

And so I did, parting with some cash and receiving a tray bearing a quartet of beers in return. The beers had a good color. If they'd been watered, it had not been by much.

I set the beers on the table, and each man grabbed a glass. I pulled up a chair and sipped from my own. The beer was cold and went down my throat with a satisfying bite.

The first man asked, "What did you say to Caspi to get him so riled up?"

I took another sip. "I sort of asked him whether he had anything to do with Emmanuel Feldbaum's murder."

The man's eyes bulged. "You didn't!"

The other two laughed. "Can you imagine that, Arik?" one of them said. "I wish I could have seen it."

Arik wasn't laughing. He set down his beer and leaned a forearm on the table. "You don't really think he was involved, do you?"

The question wiped the grins off the faces of his two friends.

"I don't have a particular reason to believe so. I just wanted to see his reaction."

"And what was it?"

"About what you'd expect. He denied it. He didn't appreciate my question, that I can tell you."

"That's not surprising. No wonder he was so steamed."

I drank some more beer, ran a finger along the perspiring side of the glass. I aimed for a casual tone. "You think he would be capable of something like that?"

The question made Arik draw back in his chair, creating more distance between us. The other two froze. All three exchanged glances. An indecipherable message passed between them.

Arik said, "You're asking a sensitive question. Caspi is our boss."

"It's only sensitive if you're not sure the answer is no. Otherwise, it's pretty easy, don't you think?"

Arik drew a long breath through his nose. He shifted his jaw and finally said, "No. I don't think Caspi would be capable of that. Do you, fellas?"

The other two both agreed that their boss couldn't possibly bludgeon a man to death in the middle of the night.

But I wasn't buying it. If they found the idea of their boss committing a violent crime so outlandish, they would have come out and said so immediately. The notion would have filled them with indignation. Instead, it had scared them, made them think. It wasn't beyond the pale.

I decided to change the subject. To get back to it a bit later. I didn't want to scare them off.

"What can you tell me about Emmanuel? What was it like working with him?"

They hesitated; then Arik said, "I hate to say it, given what happened, but he wasn't a good worker. Had no focus, you know? Would get lost in his thoughts, imagination, go off someplace in his head. Sometimes you had to call to him several times to get his attention."

"But he wasn't a bad guy," the second man said.

"Didn't say he was, Gideon. He wasn't lazy or anything, just not entirely there. I don't think he had a bad bone in his body. We all felt sorry for him."

"No one got angry at him for things he did, the mistakes he made on the job?" I asked.

"Some did," Gideon said, and then hurriedly added, "but that doesn't mean they'd want to kill him. Besides, even if someone was mad at him, Emmanuel was no longer working with us when he died, so why kill him?"

It was a good question, and I could not come up with an answer. I was running around blind, trying to find an opening, but I kept bumping into thick walls that let in no light or sound.

"Sounds like Emmanuel shouldn't have lasted two days on the job," I said. "How come it took a week for him to get fired?"

"I think our foreman, Berman, felt sorry for him," Arik said. "And

Ami Rapoport is a good guy, a solid worker. I know Berman hired Emmanuel as a favor to Ami. He must have kept him on as long as he could for the same reason."

"What made him finally decide to let Emmanuel go?"

"I don't know. It surprised me when he did, because there wasn't anything I could point to and say, 'That's the thing Emmanuel did that finally got him canned.' In fact, it looked like he was starting to find his place, sort of. It turned out he was stronger than he looked. Berman had him hauling bricks, unloading trucks, schlepping buckets of paint here and there, and he could outcarry any man on the site, and why should anyone care if he mumbled incoherently while he did so? But I guess in the end, it got to be too much even for Berman. I know that's what he said to Ami."

I nodded understanding but, in the corner of my eye, caught the third man shifting in his chair.

"You got something to add to that?" I asked.

"What?" He blinked, darted a look at his friends, and shook his head. "No. Nothing."

I was sure it wasn't nothing, but feared pushing him might be counterproductive. It would probably make all three of them clam up.

But I would make sure I talked to him again, just the two of us, later.

"Speaking of Ami," I said, "did Caspi say anything to him after he came back from talking to me?"

Arik shook his head.

"But he was looking at him funny," Gideon said.

"Like he wanted to kill him," the third man murmured, then realized what he was saying and rushed to add, "I meant he gave him an angry look. I wasn't implying anything... you know, anything at all."

"I get it," I said with a comforting smile, wanting to keep him at ease. "Don't worry about it."

I drank some more beer and asked, "Did Emmanuel ever mention the names Menashe Volkoff or Yosef Rudinsky?"

"He said a lot of things," Arik said. "Sort of mumbled most of them. I can't remember much of what he said." His tone turned sheepish. "I gotta admit, I stopped listening all that closely after I realized there was something wrong with him, you know, up here." He twirled his fingers by his right temple.

Gideon said he didn't remember hearing either of the names. But the third man said, "I remember him mentioning a guy called Volkoff a couple of times."

"What did he say about him? Any details?"

The guy shrugged. "I don't know. Like Arik said, Emmanuel was difficult to follow."

And like he'd also said, I thought with bitterness, you all stopped trying. All except Hannah Goldman. She was the only person who had hung on Feldbaum's every word. Thinking of her, and of the fact that I was going to see her again, dissipated the bitterness, and what came in its place was the sort of anxiety-tinged anticipation that I had not felt in years.

I shook it off and decided it was time to bring the conversation back to the hot-tempered Caspi. "Did Caspi ever speak with Emmanuel?"

All three men said they had never seen the two talk.

"How often does Caspi visit the site?"

"He comes by at least once a week," Gideon said. "Two or three times is pretty common."

"So he knew who Emmanuel was?"

"Probably. If I had to bet on it, I'd say he did."

"Did you ever hear him comment about Emmanuel, or shoot him an angry look like he did toward Ami Rapoport today?"

The third man opened his mouth to answer, but then Arik looked over my shoulder, sat up straight, and grabbed his forearm. The third man's eyes followed Arik's, and his mouth snapped shut.

I was seated with my back to the door, so I turned to see what had caused their reaction. I had to tilt my head back to look at the face of the man who now loomed over me within striking distance.

It was the burly man from the building site. The one who'd volunteered to throw me out if Caspi so wished. He was glaring down at me, his lips parted crookedly, showing large blocky teeth. I remembered his name was Boris.

He had a large head, a wide nose, and the sort of bulky chin you would likely bust your fingers against if you were dumb enough to punch it. Seeing him from my lower vantage point only added to the impression of size and raw power his body exuded, and there was no mistaking the animosity that wafted off him like a poisonous gas.

It was much more potent than earlier today, and my first thought was to wonder what had caused it. Just because I had made his boss a little mad?

My second thought, which struck me as utterly irrational yet entirely possible, was that he just might decide to attack me right then and there, witnesses be damned, and my instinct was to leap out of my chair, where I was at a disadvantage. But close as he was to me, I wouldn't have made it to my feet before he landed a blow, if indeed he had been meaning to.

But apparently, that wasn't his intention. He made no move against me. Instead, without shifting his gaze from me, he addressed his three co-workers. "What you boys doing? Having a nice chat?"

"Just enjoying a beer, Boris," Arik said, but his stiff tone belied the casualness of his words. "Cooling off after a long day of work."

"Oh yeah? And what about him?" A fat thumb pointed my way. "He's part of our crew now?"

"Man's got a right to be here, same as everyone."

"You been talking to him? Shooting the breeze?"

"Didn't have time to. He just sat down with us a minute ago."

"Is that a fact, Arik? Is that why there are four glasses on this table here? All nearly empty?"

So he was perceptive, I thought. And not stupid. Arik and the others seemed to be at a loss for words, so I said, "I was at the bar and came over with my beer just before you stepped in. I'm glad you're here, Boris. I have a few questions about Emmanuel Feldbaum."

"That's too bad. 'Cause I won't be answering them. And you boys shouldn't either. You know Mr. Caspi wouldn't like it."

"Caspi said any man who wanted to talk to me could do so. You heard him."

"Yeah. I heard him all right. And it didn't take much to know he still wouldn't like it one bit. And that was before you two went off to talk in private and you got him madder than I've ever seen him. I knew you were trouble. He should have let me throw you out right at the start."

"You got no cause to be angry with me, Boris. I'm just trying to find out who killed your former colleague Emmanuel Feldbaum."

"Colleague." He snorted. "He wasn't our colleague. He just worked with us for a week, and he did very little good during it. He was worthless."

"Sounds like you disliked him. Hated him even."

His eyes narrowed to dark slits. His tone turned even more menacing. "You're saying what I think you're saying?"

"I don't know. You tell me."

His jaw tensed, his chest puffed out, and his lips peeled back from his teeth, and I cursed myself for goading him like this. Was I looking for a beating?

In the next half-second, I frantically assessed the situation. I was still seated, and he was standing very close. What would I do if he pounced? Try to kick him in the knee? My position was bad. I didn't have room to swing my foot, so I wouldn't be able to put much force behind the kick. And I didn't think I'd have time to do even that before he was on top of me.

Luckily, Arik chose that moment to speak. "Let's all keep calm, okay? There are people watching."

Boris's dark eyes flitted about, taking in the other patrons of the small café. Arik was right: everyone had quieted and was watching us intently. The proprietor was leaning on the bar, his expression uncompromising. "You two got a problem with each other, you'd best settle it someplace else, you hear?"

"You know me," Boris told him. "He's the problem, not me."

"I don't care who it is. But if either of you makes trouble in my café, you'll have the police to deal with." He reached under the bar and brought up a telephone. He put the receiver to his ear and stuck his forefinger in the rotary dial. "I won't hesitate," he said.

Boris was fuming. Since he was the one standing all coiled up and tense, all eyes were on him. It was difficult for him to back down without losing face. But I didn't care about such things.

"I'll leave," I said, and pushed my chair back, giving me a little more space. "There won't be any trouble from me." I got up, hiding my wariness, knowing that my rising could trigger an attack.

None came.

Boris let out a low breath, and his shoulders unclenched. He sneered at me. "Run away, then. But maybe I'll see you again soon."

"I'll be counting the seconds," I said. I stepped around him and backed to the exit, keeping him in sight till I stepped out the door.

I walked quickly half a block east, then leaned against a wall and fired up a cigarette. My heart was drumming a bouncy rhythm, and my legs felt a bit loose. The smoke going into my chest steadied me, and I looked back toward the café, wondering again as to the reason for Boris's anger. Was it all due to some loyalty to Caspi? Or did Boris have a more personal reason to detest me and my investigation? Could it be that Boris was the man who had lain in wait for Emmanuel Feldbaum and then bashed his skull in?

It certainly seemed like the sort of method he'd choose to kill someone. But why would he want to murder Feldbaum?

Bereft of answers but feeling I now had one more person to check out, and several more questions to answer, I turned and continued east. I didn't make it ten more steps before I heard a voice calling my name.

Turning, I saw it was the third man from the café, the one I'd planned on seeking out later. Now it looked like I wouldn't have to go to the trouble. His face had a light flush, and his breathing was quick. He'd been moving fast. Not quite running, or I'd have heard him coming, but not walking casually either.

"Glad I found you," he said. "Was worried I'd miss you."

I had the pack of cigarettes in my hand, been about to fire up another. "Want one?" He shook his head. I lit up and took a drag. "What's your name?"

"Noah."

"You've got something you want to tell me, Noah? Something you didn't want Arik and Gideon to hear? Something to do with why Berman fired Emmanuel?" I said, remembering Noah fidgeting in his chair when the topic came up.

"It wasn't like Arik said," Noah told me. "Berman hadn't just finally had enough of Emmanuel. That's what he told Ami, but it wasn't true."

"So what really happened?"

"Caspi told Berman to get rid of Emmanuel."

"How do you know?"

"I overheard the two of them talking. It was lunch break, so everyone was off to one side of the site. Caspi and Berman were at the other, talking where no one was supposed to hear them. But I'd forgotten something, so was up on the second floor we were working on, right above them. I wasn't meaning to eavesdrop, but Caspi immediately started talking about Emmanuel. He wasn't loud, but he was boiling mad, so I decided it'd be best to just stay quiet and out of sight."

"What did he say?"

"That he didn't want anyone with mush for brains working for him. Asked Berman how in hell he thought it was a good idea to hire such a man. Berman explained about Ami, said he thought Emmanuel might be useful, even though he often got confused. He said Emmanuel had been in the camps, that he deserved a chance. Caspi didn't care about all that. 'I don't want to see anyone like that on my construction site again, understand?' he said. 'Get rid of him today.'"

"Was that it?"

"Yeah. After that, Caspi stomped off. Then I heard Berman sigh a few times, and then he walked away too. I waited a couple of minutes and got down. No one saw me."

"Why didn't you tell the others about this?"

"Why take the risk? If someone blabbed and it got back to Caspi, I'd be in for it."

"You think the others might tell on you?"

"I'm pretty sure they wouldn't, but it's best to keep quiet, I think."

"Why did Caspi care about not being heard by the others? He's the boss. He can do whatever he wants."

"Caspi is involved in politics, and he's very ambitious. He's a member of the General Zionists. I heard he plans to run for Knesset next election, and he's destined to get a high position on the list of candidates. If the General Zionists win and form a government, he'll end up a minister for sure. Maybe he didn't want people talking about how he fired a camp survivor. Might be bad for his image."

The General Zionists were the second-largest party in the Knesset. The main opposition party. If anyone could take down Prime Minister Ben-Gurion and his party, Mapai, it was the General Zionists.

"Can he trust Berman not to talk?" I asked.

"I think so. He and Berman go back a long time. Besides, if it got out, Caspi would know it was Berman who talked, and that would be his job."

I took a moment to take in what Noah told me. Did it matter at all to my investigation who decided to fire Emmanuel or why? I didn't see how it would since Emmanuel was killed days after he had been fired.

Noah said, "I'm not even sure I should have told you. It's just that you're investigating the murder, so I figured you should know everything."

"You did right, Noah. And don't worry, I won't tell anyone about you. You have my word."

"Okay. Well, I gotta get back or the others will wonder where I've gone. There's only so long a guy can spend in the can."

"Just one minute, Noah. A couple more questions. You ever hear Caspi get so mad before?"

"He gets mad pretty often, but there was something especially nasty about the way he talked about Emmanuel. It wasn't like his usual form of mad. Come to think of it, today was different too."

"Because of me?"

"Yeah. It's like someone threw gasoline on a fire. It had already been burning pretty good, but all of a sudden it's hotter and wilder, and you need to keep a greater distance."

He probably hadn't meant it as a warning, but that was how it sounded to me. Again I thought that Caspi sure had the right temper to commit murder, but did he also have motive? If so, I didn't see it. He'd already gotten rid of Emmanuel, so why would he want him dead?

No idea, and I could see Noah was anxious to get back to his friends, so I switched topics.

"You all seemed pretty scared of Boris back there. What's his story?"

"He's a hothead. And he's strong as a bull. He's also loyal to the bone to Caspi."

"Why is that?"

"No special reason, I think. He's just like that with whoever pays his wages."

"You've worked with him before?"

"Years ago, before World War Two, at a building site up north. Anytime one of the guys grumbled about the owner, Boris would get upset, tell him to shut up or else."

"He ever got violent?"

"A couple of times. Nothing too serious. A punch or two if an argument got heated."

"If he's as strong as you say, one or two punches could do a lot of damage. What happened to the guys he beat up?"

"A black eye. A split lip. Painful as hell, but nothing that would put you in the hospital. I'm sure you've seen worse."

I sure had. I'd seen things so terrible Noah wouldn't have believed me if I described them, but there was no point in telling him that.

"He seemed close to jumping me back in the café," I said. "Even with people around."

"I thought he might, too. He sure was angry."

"All on account of Caspi?"

"Like I told you, Boris is very loyal to him."

"Maybe there was something more to it."

Noah gave me a look. "What do you mean?"

"Boris didn't like Emmanuel, did he?"

"You're not saying that—"

"He's a hothead; he had something against Emmanuel. It's possible, isn't it?"

Noah started shaking his head but stopped mid-shake.

"What is it?" I asked.

"It's stupid. I don't think—"

"Stupid or not, like you said, I'm investigating a murder. I need to know everything."

Noah hesitated for a few seconds, then said, "I think it was two days before Emmanuel got fired. Boris announced a competition to see who could carry a sack of cement and walk with it for longest around the building site. He wanted people to bet on it, but of course no one did, because everyone expected him to win. Like I told you, he's very strong. But—"

"But Emmanuel won," I said, recalling what Arik had said about Emmanuel being able to carry more than any of his colleagues. Like he carried furniture for one of the residents in Mahlul.

"Yeah. Everyone was stunned. You didn't know the guy, but he looked like he wouldn't be able to lift a feather."

Remembering both the living Emmanuel I'd seen on the street, and the dead one I'd seen in Sheinkin Garden and in the autopsy photos, I couldn't help but agree. Emmanuel had not looked capable of feats of strength. But he had survived the torment of Sachsenhausen, and his body had been altered by it. Perhaps it had developed a preternatural strength. Or maybe Emmanuel's ordeal had made it so he hardly felt pain anymore.

"Boris was humiliated, wasn't he?"

Noah nodded. Fear shone in his eyes. "But you don't think... Boris wouldn't... Not for something like—"

"Wouldn't he? After being made a laughingstock by a guy as thin as a rail, and with a ruined brain to boot? A guy he must have disliked even before that, I bet."

Noah was quiet. Way he was looking at me, there was a good chance he was regretting ever speaking with me.

"You should head back," I said. "And thank you, Noah."

He nodded and didn't offer his hand or say another word. He hurried away, probably walking even faster than he had when he came to find me. That's the thing with fear. You run away from the strongest one, even if you're not sure you'd be entirely safe at your destination.

17

On Tuesday, I woke up late, made myself a sandwich for breakfast, and read half a tattered Western paperback with a horse-riding cowboy on the cover. Both the cowboy and horse looked weary to the bone, their heads drooping, hinting at a long and arduous journey with little food and water. From personal experience, I knew how they felt.

Setting the book aside, I went out to do some grocery shopping.

The shopping had two distinct parts—the legal and the illegal. The legal part took place at licensed grocery stores and involved showing your ration card and receiving whatever the government allotted you. This changed from time to time, according to the vagaries of the food market, Israel's foreign currency balance, whatever agricultural calamity was currently running rampant, and maybe also whether the minister or official in charge got up on the wrong side of the bed that morning. None of which did much to inspire confidence among the citizenry.

The illegal part of my shopping took me to a number of establishments, none of which you'd normally expect to sell you food—a hardware store, a radio repair shop, the apartment of two diminutive spinsters who seemed to have more black-market connections than a criminal kingpin. These places did not ask to see your ration card. All you needed to show them was the cash in your wallet, a hefty portion of which would be absent from it by the time you left.

Recalling the newspaper article about flagrant black-market activities in various places in Tel Aviv, I toured Lilienblum Street and ambled among the stalls at Carmel Market. Either the scoundrels had not read the same article I had, or its indignant tone did not pierce the shell of their greed or indifference. I had no trouble locating where the good stuff was being sold.

From Lilienblum I emerged with a small pack of bitter Swiss chocolate, while at Carmel Market I was able to lay my hands on a bag of sugar at what wasn't quite an outrageous price.

On my way back home, the window display of a men's clothing and toiletries store snagged my eye, and I found myself drawn inside, where a dapper little shopkeeper greeted me with the sort of contrived smile common to his trade.

He asked me what I was in the market for, and I, not sure exactly what had pulled me into the store in the first place, mumbled something about needing a new shirt. He eyed the one I was wearing and nodded with his professional smile still firmly attached to his lips. But his nose had developed a wrinkle, perhaps mirroring the ones on the offending shirt.

"This way," he said, leading me to a rack, where he produced a navy-blue shirt with a narrow collar. "This should fit you well, I think."

In a changing booth, I put on the new shirt. The soft fabric felt glorious on my skin. I always shopped for clothes at one of the Ata stores, where you could purchase clothes for ration points, but those items were made on the cheap with a focus on durability, not fashion or sensation. This shirt was altogether different.

The shopkeeper beamed at me as I pulled back the curtain and stepped out of the changing booth. He looked like a proud mother.

"That does look wonderful, sir. Now all you need is the right jacket and pair of shoes and you'll be a changed man, you mark my words."

He already had the jacket in hand, and he presented it to me like a magician pulling a rabbit out of a hat.

The jacket was single-breasted, a darker shade of blue than the shirt, and screamed exorbitance. I touched the sleeve, and the sensation was luxuriantly soft. Some internal craving kicked in, but not enough to silence my brain. I asked how much it was. With the air of a man mentioning a trifle, he stated a price that made my heart skip a beat. I asked him to repeat it just to be sure I hadn't misheard him. He did, and when I simply stared at him, his smile wavered for the first time. "It's from America," he said, as though that was enough to merit the price tag.

When I told him to put the jacket away, he did so with a doleful expression. He did not mention the shoes.

"Will you be taking the shirt, then?" he asked when he returned, and when I asked what it cost, he answered in a voice laced with uncertainty.

It was also too much, but then I caught my reflection in the long mirror, and I couldn't help but accept the fact that the shopkeeper had been right: the shirt did fit me rather well. Still, it was expensive. But in truth, I needed a shirt, it did feel wonderful, and if it saved me a trip to an Ata store...

"I'll take it," I said, partly surprising myself, and his smile regained its former wattage.

He asked me if I'd be wearing it now, and I said that I wouldn't. I returned to the changing booth and put on my regular shirt. He was waiting for me by the register, where he folded the new shirt, wrapped it in thin white paper, and slipped it into a bag.

I was fishing for my wallet when my nose caught the fresh fragrance of massive ancient forests, the likes of which were nowhere to be found in Israel. Looking up, I saw the shopkeeper holding a short fat bottle filled with an amber liquid.

"Exquisite, isn't it?" he said, and pressed the nozzle topping the bottle. Tiny liquid beads sprayed in a fine mist, and the smell intensified yet remained pleasant. "The ladies do adore it, sir. A good number of my customers assure me of that. I'm sure your lady friend would most appreciate it." His smile had acquired an impish twist.

"I don't have a lady friend," I said.

"But soon perhaps, sir? Yes, soon. In which case, this may prove to be even more important, indispensable even, I dare say. After all, early impressions are everything, are they not?"

The crafty little devil. How did he know I was about to meet a woman? A woman who was new in my life? Was there something in my eyes, in the way I carried myself? Could everyone see it? Or maybe it was only detectable by the shopkeeper's professional eye, a skill he had perfected over many years of catering to men.

He'd probably guessed it the moment I stepped into his shop. Even while I was yet ignorant of what had pulled me into it. Even while I agreed to buy an expensive shirt without knowing why I was buying it.

"How much is the perfume?" I asked.

"Not perfume, sir. It's cologne."

"Never mind what it's called. How much is it?"

He named a price, and when a few seconds of silence came and went, cleared his throat and announced that since this was my first visit to his business, he would be glad to offer me a ten-percent discount. "I value you as a customer, sir. I can tell you are a man of sophisticated taste." He said this smoothly but could not keep his gaze from darting to my scuffed shoes, my well-worn trousers.

I should have said no, told him to save his false flattery for someone more gullible. Again he seemed to know my mind, because he said, "Tel Aviv is so hot these days, isn't it? So hot and humid."

He was right. It was still spring, but the days could be scorching, and the air was heavy. The sort of muggy weather that made sweat trickle down your back and pool in your armpits.

"Fine," I said. "I'll take it."

"Splendid, sir." He wrapped the bottle and slid it into a small bag very quickly, perhaps fearing I might have a change of heart. I took the bags—one with the shirt, the other with the cologne—and handed him money in return. I watched it pass from my hand to his with a sort of bewildered detachment, as though I were watching someone else make this irrational transaction, as though I weren't the man exchanging hard-earned cash for a pair of unnecessary extravagances.

"Thank you, sir," he said, putting the money in the register, and sliding it shut with a clang of finality. He placed both hands on the small counter and waited for me to say something. When I didn't—I couldn't decide whether to thank him or curse him—he asked, "Will there be anything else? Perhaps you would care to try on some shoes after all?"

"No," I said quickly, and took a step back from the counter and the wily shopkeeper. "Nothing more."

"Very well. One word of advice, sir. One or two spritzes of the cologne are quite enough to do the trick. I wouldn't overdo it."

I'd already overdone it by buying it, but I didn't say anything. I just nodded and hurried to the door. First I'd decided to investigate Emmanuel Feldbaum's murder for free, and now I spent too much money on things I could very well live without. Was I losing my mind?

"Come back soon," his voice rang out as I pulled the door open and made my escape.

With one hand holding my black-market purchases and the other carrying the shirt and cologne, I walked home, wondering what had come over me.

I didn't need to think long. The answer was right there. The shopkeeper had sensed it, though he would not have been able to name it. But I could. It was Hannah Goldman. Tomorrow I would see her. It was a strange date to be sure—the birthday party of a nine-year-old girl—but it was one nonetheless. And some long-dormant instinct had awakened within me, wanting me not to merely look good for the occasion, but apparently also to smell good.

And now that I had not just the effect but also the cause in mind, I realized I was only half-mad at myself. I was dismayed by my profligacy, but I couldn't help feeling just a little bit excited too.

18

I was at her door at four thirty in the afternoon on the day of the party. I had showered and shaved. I had polished my shoes. I had put on my new shirt and was wearing two spritzes' worth of cologne on my person and wondering whether the scent was even noticeable.

The weather seemed to be mocking me—it had turned cool and pleasant, with an easterly breeze that had pushed the humidity back toward the sea. I had not sweated one bit on the walk over from my apartment.

The two chickens once again ceased their pecking to stare at me. I couldn't guess what was going through their tiny brains, but they did not seem impressed with me.

A prickle running up my spine made me whip my head around to look behind me. There was nobody there, but a curtain shifted in the window of the shack across the untidy path. Zelda watching me. Gathering more gossip material.

When Hannah Goldman opened her door, she was wearing a white dress with thin red lines that intersected to form small rhombuses. I had seen dresses like that before in one of the Ata stores I regularly shopped at. It seemed that Hannah Goldman's brain had not gone on a sabbatical like mine had yesterday.

Sensible black shoes with short flat heels and a thin necklace with a Star of David pendant completed her ensemble. Her hair was once again coiled at the back of her head and held in place with a large clip. She looked elegant and pretty, but it did not seem like she had made a special effort. Standing close to her as she emerged from her home, I did not detect a trace of perfume.

Unabashedly, she ran her eyes up and down my body. If she noted the new shirt, the polished shoes, my partial success in smoothing all the wrinkles out of my newest pair of trousers by spreading them under my mattress overnight, she displayed no sign of appreciation. It was only when she completed her brisk survey that she raised her eyes to mine and smiled.

"It's nice to see you again, Adam."

"It's nice to see you too."

"I see that you remembered to bring the presents."

"I didn't want to have to bring three of them next year."

She laughed. "Shall we go?"

We walked side by side out of Mahlul and then south on Hayarkon Street. She asked me about Reuben Tzanani, and I told her he had saved my life during the War of Independence.

"He's much shorter and lighter than me, but he carried me on his back away from the battlefield to where I could get medical treatment. He's one of the bravest men I've ever met."

"How did you get injured?"

I told her how I had charged an Egyptian machine-gun position, managed to kill two of their soldiers with a grenade, but that a third soldier had shot me twice in the torso before I killed him as well. "I spent a few weeks in the hospital. It was touch and go for a while, but now I'm okay."

"It seems like you're brave as well."

"Or foolish. Sometimes I think the line between the two is vague."

I didn't tell her that I'd had my picture in the paper, had been lauded as a war hero. It might have impressed her, but I didn't feel comfortable talking about whatever fame my wartime exploits had awarded me. I'd always felt that Reuben Tzanani was much more worthy of it than I was.

I asked her about her work as a teacher, and she said it was challenging to teach children who came from so many different countries.

"Those who were born here speak Hebrew fluently, but some of the *olim* are having a hard time learning the language, and of course, all the lessons are in Hebrew. You need to teach all the kids together, to make them all equal members of the same class."

Olim were those who had recently made *aliyah*, the hundreds of thousands of Jewish immigrants who had come to Israel since Independence in 1948.

She asked me how I became a private investigator, and I told her about working as a police detective in Hungary before the Second World War.

"Were there many Jewish policemen there?"

"I never met another."

"Really? You were the only one?"

"There may have been a few others, but I've never heard of any."

"Wasn't it difficult, being the only Jew?"

"Sometimes. There were officers who didn't like me because I'm a Jew, but others didn't care. Or they pretended not to." I recalled how Hungarian police officers had herded me and my family, and many other Jews with us, onto the cattle cars that took us to Auschwitz. Most of the dirty work was done by local cops; the Germans hardly needed to lift a finger.

"Did you like being a police detective?"

"There were bad moments, things I wasn't crazy about, just like with any other job. You get to see the dark underbelly of society— violence, exploitation, drunkenness, all sorts of sordid and nasty things. And you sometimes need to do unpleasant things to deal with criminals, to protect law-abiding citizens. It can weigh on you. But overall, I liked it very much," I said, trying hard to stamp down memories of the day on which I was thrown off the force when Hungary enacted anti-Jewish laws. The shock and humiliation of that moment, my unfathomable stupidity in not recognizing the warning signs of even worse things to come. The fact that I was foolish enough to stay put and not do whatever it took to get my family away before it was too late.

"I read in the papers that Israel has a shortage of experienced policemen," Hannah said, pulling me back from my dark thoughts.

"I'm sure that's true. Before 1948, much of the detective work was done by British investigators, and they're all gone."

"You never considered joining the force here?"

I shook my head. "I never want to have to follow anyone's orders again. I had enough of it during the war."

She nodded thoughtfully, studying me, and I wondered if she knew I was not referring to the War of Independence, but to my time in Auschwitz.

I asked her what made her want to be a teacher, and she said her father had been one. "He would get this light in his eyes when he talked about his pupils. He'd tell me that educating children was a great privilege, a mission worthy of dedicating your life to. I corresponded with someone who was in the ghetto with my parents, and he told me my father continued teaching there. All the way to the end, he kept on teaching."

She was staring forward when she said this, and there was a tightness to her jaw, but I detected no tears. Perhaps she'd shed her fill of them.

I might have told her how sorry I was, but I didn't think I needed to. Besides, there's only so much commiseration a person can take without getting the urge to scream.

Instead, I said, "And teaching adults? How did you get into that?"

"Someone from the Ministry of Education contacted me. They were looking for teachers who speak several languages. The new immigrants need to learn Hebrew, and someone has to teach them. It's important work. I'm not a soldier or a kibbutznik plowing a field near Israel's borders, but I'm doing my part."

As we walked and talked, I kept looking at her, taking in the curve of her jaw, the line of her nose, the delicate shape of her ear. At a certain point, I began picturing how she'd look without her glasses on, with her hair untethered and free, falling on bare shoulders.

She caught me looking, giving me a knowing smile, and it seemed that she had guessed what was going through my mind, or perhaps something even more indecent than that.

My face heating up, desperate to change the subject, I asked her about Emmanuel Feldbaum.

"Did he ever say anything about a man called Boris?"

"Who's he?"

"A guy who worked with him on the construction site."

"No. I'm pretty sure he didn't. Why?"

I told her about my unpleasant encounter with Boris the day before yesterday. About learning that Emmanuel had humiliated him in a contest of strength at work.

"Is that enough to kill a man these days?"

"You wouldn't believe the reasons people have for killing each other. Sometimes, they're so petty and pitiful you can hardly grasp them." I paused as we passed by a trio of middle-aged ladies chattering in Yiddish. "And this Boris fellow certainly has the right temperament. And the murder method fits. If he were to kill someone, bashing his head in would be just his style."

"Is he your prime suspect?"

"He's a possibility. Another man with a temper is the owner of the construction company, Benjamin Caspi. I don't see a reason for him to kill Emmanuel, but he didn't like my nosing around his site, talking to his men."

"Is he also the sort who'd kill someone by hitting them on the head?"

I had to think about that and admitted I wasn't sure.

"What about Batya Rapoport?" she asked.

"You know her better than I do. If she wanted to kill someone, would she take a hammer or another blunt instrument and smash his head in? What do you think?"

"I don't know," she said.

We stopped before crossing a street, waiting for a bus to trundle past. On the opposite sidewalk, a couple was walking side by side. The man said something that made the woman throw her head back and laugh. I felt like an idiot.

"I'm sorry, Hannah."

"Whatever for?"

"For asking about Emmanuel. For talking about my investigation. Murder is not a suitable topic for a"—I was about to say date, but the word felt uncertain on my lips—"for a little girl's birthday party."

"We're not at the party yet, Adam," she said with a small smile. "Maybe it's good that we're getting all the death and misery out of our systems before we get there."

We entered Kerem Hateymanim, the Yemenites' Vineyard, a neighborhood established in 1906, three years before the establishment of Tel Aviv, and which was later absorbed into the city. The neighborhood, from its inception, was inhabited by many Yemenite Jews, including part of Reuben Tzanani's family.

"Reuben's great-grandparents immigrated here from Yemen in 1882," I told Hannah. "They first went to Jerusalem and later settled here. Reuben told me that in the beginning, the houses were built of wood, tin, whatever the poor residents could lay their hands on."

"Like Mahlul," Hannah said. "But things seem to be changing here."

It was still very different from the newer neighborhoods of Tel Aviv. There were no curving Bauhaus balconies, no elegant European facades, no multistory apartment houses built partly on pillars to allow airflow and shaded communal spaces. In Kerem Hateymanim, the houses were low, one or two stories, flat-roofed, and crowded close together, many touching sides with their neighbors. Narrow alleyways meandered here and there, and despite the neighborhood's relatively small area, you got the feeling you could get lost in them.

Some of the houses showed signs of having been altered and patched over the years. Here, a room had been added on a roof, its bricks not yet plastered over. There, a small balcony jutted like a baby's first tooth from a second story, its slanted roof made of scraps of metal. There, a house shone white with a new coat of paint. But elsewhere there was a pervasive sense of time that had passed, a place that, in part at least, had been left behind.

As we neared Reuben's home, we began to hear sounds of jubilation. Loud chatter, laughter, children squealing happily.

"Here we are," I said a moment later, an awkward feeling coming over me as we stood before Reuben's door. It had been a while since I'd been here. Reuben had often invited me, but almost always I had offered some excuse and stayed away. Beyond that door were parents and siblings, a wife and children, a family birthday party. All the things I'd once had and lost. Just thinking about it kicked open a door inside me that I fought to keep locked and bolted, and from the black room beyond it flooded in sad memories and cloying guilt.

"Are you all right, Adam?" Hannah asked.

"What? Yes, of course," I said, putting on a smile. "Sure I am." I handed her one of the presents. "Here, you take one." Then I gritted my teeth, slamming that door inside me shut, hammering imaginary lengths of wood across its frame.

Then I reached for the door handle to Reuben's home. But before I had the chance to grasp it, the door whipped open, and a pair of furious dark eyes bored into mine.

19

"It's about time you showed up."

The voice was edged with anger. The speaker was a pretty girl with pigtails, her eyebrows knitted, her lower lip jutting out.

I checked my watch. It was two minutes before five. "Happy birthday, Shoshana. Your father told me the party starts at five. We're two minutes early."

"That's not what I meant, Adam," she said, waving an admonitory finger up at me, her tone reminding me of a schoolteacher I once had who was invariably disappointed with me. "You haven't been here in years."

"It hasn't been that long." Which was technically true, but hardly absolving. I hadn't seen Shoshana for over a year, and for a girl her age, that was a lifetime. She had changed in the interim. She had shot up in height, shed part of her younger chubbiness, and become far more assertive than I remembered her.

I said, "Thank you for inviting me to your birthday party. I hope it's all right I brought company. Shoshana, this is Hannah Goldman. Hannah, this is Miss Shoshana Tzanani, the girl of the hour. You look lovely today, Shoshana. I like your dress."

Shoshana's expression did not thaw. "Don't think flattering me will get you off the hook, Adam. I'm still mad at you for not coming last year."

I went down on one knee, bringing my face about even with hers. I looked into her large brown eyes and said, "I'm so sorry, Shoshana. I truly am. Please accept my apology." And as I said this, a bubble of emotion, difficult to define, filled my chest and made my voice quaver. It was intensely moving that this girl, who knew me more from stories than from actual meetings, wanted my company so much that she was insulted by my absence.

Shoshana wasn't quick to offer forgiveness. She examined my face for a few long seconds, probing me like a judge trying to determine whether a criminal's claim of contrition was genuine.

At length, she let out a breath and passed her sentence: "I'll accept your apology on one condition, Adam, that you'll promise to come to my birthday next year."

I laid a hand over my heart, which was beating quite hard and fast. "I give you my solemn word."

"Very well." She smiled. "You can get up now." She turned to Hannah and stuck out her hand. "It's nice to meet you."

"Nice to meet you too," Hannah said, and I could tell by her tone that she was impressed with this child.

"Here," I said. "This is for you." I handed Shoshana the present I was holding, the book.

"And this as well," Hannah said.

Shoshana thanked us for the presents. She pointed at a back door standing open at the far end of the kitchen, past the stove, where a large pot was simmering. "The party is over there."

Shoshana went to the living room to put the presents away. Hannah and I crossed the kitchen, Hannah leaning close to my ear and whispering, "I thought you said she was a shy girl."

"She used to be. Not anymore. For a second there, I thought she might jump me."

Hannah stifled a laugh. "I'm not sure who would have won if she had."

We passed through the back door into an inner courtyard, where about forty people had already gathered. They ranged from infants to the elderly, all Yemenite Jews, dark-skinned and black-haired. Most of the men wore modern clothing, but a few of the older ones still had on traditional garments—a *kuftan*, a loose white dress that went past their knees, and a *kwafti*, a round black hat made of felt. The women were encased in dresses that covered them from their necks to their ankles, and some wore head coverings that hid every strand of their hair.

Two tables laden with dishes stood to one side. The aromas wafting from them were exotic and unfamiliar.

"Adam, am I glad to see you."

"Hello, Gila," I said.

Gila Tzanani was short, wide-hipped, and had the sort of smile that could light an underground cavern. She wore a white dress that ballooned over her pregnant belly.

"Have you seen Shoshana? The girl has been yammering about you all day."

"She met us at the door."

"Good. Because I think she was plotting fiery retribution if you didn't come."

"I can believe it. This is Hannah."

The two women exchanged pleasantries, and Gila ushered us toward the table. "With times being what they are, it's not much, but we make do with what there is, same as everyone."

Reuben and Gila Tzanani were two of those rare righteous souls who did not partake of the black market.

"It smells wonderful," Hannah said. "What are all these dishes called?"

There was soup, but one stripped of its main elements by rationing. Gila said, "It's supposed to contain meat—either chicken or lamb—but these days we make do with just potatoes."

Gila began pointing out the other dishes, all clustered close together on the two long tables. There was *lahuh*, a thin, airy bread dotted with small round indentations. There was *malawah*, a round bread made of puff pastry. *Hilbe*, a brown dip. *Zhug,* a green hot sauce.

Jahnun, a thick pastry made of layers of thin dough, and next to it a bowl of tomato sauce.

"We usually eat *jahnun* only on the Sabbath," Gila said. "But Shoshana loves it, so I decided to make an exception, especially since she helped me make it. It takes more than eight hours to bake it right, you know. In better times we would serve it with eggs or sugar, but these days..."

"It looks incredible," Hannah said, and Gila plucked a roll of *jahnun* off the heaping pile, dipped it in the tomato sauce, and handed it to Hannah, who took a bite and closed her eyes, her mouth smiling as she chewed.

"Some people also dip it in *zhug*," Gila said.

"Don't," I said quickly. "That stuff is like fire. It'll feel like there's an inferno in your mouth."

"Not everyone is as sensitive as you, Adam," Gila said, proceeding to tell Hannah about the time, nearly three years before, when I tried the dreadful stuff, not knowing how potent it was.

"The poor fellow turned beet red, and sweat popped on his brow. I swear I thought he might burst into flame." Gila started laughing and only barely managed to deliver the punchline: "Then he grabbed the nearest glass and gulped it down. Only it contained a particularly strong *arak*, so it was literally like throwing alcohol on a fire."

The two women burst out laughing, each bent over, grabbing the other's shoulder for support. I, feeling a need to save face, said, "I couldn't see anything the way my eyes were watering from the damn *zhug*. I thought it was water."

This only made them laugh harder. Some of the other guests were looking at us, grinning. I nodded amiably, giving them the only smile I could muster, a tight-lipped one.

"What's so funny?" A voice came from behind me, and I turned to see a beaming Reuben Tzanani dressed in pressed black trousers and a white buttoned shirt. It had been a while since I'd seen him out of uniform. I liked him better this way. He looked freer, looser, and very happy.

"Your wife is sharing wild tales," I said.

"Oh, which one?"

Gila, her laughter largely under control, retold the story of my encounter with the *zhug*. Reuben smiled, but to his credit, he did not laugh.

"Let's not make fun of our guest. He's a brave one for daring to come here again." He clapped me on the shoulder. "I'm glad you're here, Adam," he said, casting a curious look at Hannah.

I made the introductions, and I could tell Reuben was surprised that I'd brought a date, but was pleased as well.

After a few moments of pleasant conversation, Reuben asked if he could steal me away for a minute. He walked with me back into the house and then into a bedroom with two child beds and a pile of mattresses that would be spread out come nightfall. Reuben and Gila slept on the foldout sofa in the living room. Reuben shut the door.

"What is it?" I asked. "You've got something for me?"

He nodded. "Yes. Yes, I sure do."

20

"Menashe Volkoff," Reuben said. "He did not die in Europe."

The chatter of guests from the courtyard infiltrated through the closed window. Laughter too. Upbeat and joyful. But Reuben's face bore no remnant of the happiness it had displayed a minute ago.

Finally, a good lead, maybe the opening I needed to find out the truth. "He's here, in Israel? Where does he live?"

"That's just it. I don't know. No one does."

"What do you mean?"

"Menashe Volkoff got to Mandatory Palestine in July 1939. He entered the region legally, disembarking in the port of Haifa. I don't know how he got an immigration certificate; it was difficult in those days, with the British limiting Jewish immigration; but he somehow managed it. I saw his name on the registry of new immigrants. All legal and official."

"And?"

"Upon arrival, Volkoff rented a room in a boardinghouse in Haifa. When he didn't show up a few nights in a row, and didn't send anyone to pick up his belongings, his landlady reported him missing. It was less than a week after he arrived."

"He disappeared?"

Reuben nodded. "No one has seen him since."

I lowered my head, closing my eyes and taking a few deep breaths. Like a steel door clanging shut, the opening I thought I had stumbled upon winked out.

"Any leads?"

"There's not much in the report. He went out one morning and didn't come back. No evidence that he was abducted or worse. Nothing at all."

"Surely there were some theories."

"The usual, general sort. Nothing concrete. Nothing to go on."

"In thirteen years, there've been no reports, no sightings, nothing whatsoever?" There was a strident edge to my voice now, frustration giving it an unpleasant crease.

"The last time the file was updated was three weeks after Volkoff was reported missing. Just a line or two on how the case remained open, but that there were no leads at the moment."

I rubbed a hand across my jaw. "It's odd, isn't it, Reuben, that Emmanuel Feldbaum is murdered in the heart of Tel Aviv, and that the man Feldbaum mentioned most often in his ramblings has disappeared without a trace?"

"I thought you might say that."

"You don't agree?"

He shrugged. "It could be nothing, Adam. Nearly thirteen years have passed. The world has changed dramatically. A world war started and ended. Israel did not exist back then and now does. You and I did not know each other, and now you're here in my home." He looked toward the window, which was still letting in festive sounds, and his lips twitched. "I was a teenager in 1939, and now I'm a married man, and my eldest is celebrating her ninth birthday."

And I'd had a family back then, and now I had nothing but nightmares and sad memories. Reuben was right. Thirteen years was a long time. What was one murder and a single distant disappearance compared to all that had happened in that time period? Most likely, there was no connection. But still...

"You think the officer who investigated Volkoff's disappearance might be interested to learn about Feldbaum's murder?" I asked.

"Would you be in his shoes?"

Probably not. Not without a definite new lead. A piece of evidence that linked the two cases. The confused mutterings of a brain-damaged murder victim thirteen years after Volkoff's disappearance would not suffice.

"Have you discovered anything in your investigation of Feldbaum's murder that might shed light on what happened to Menashe Volkoff?"

I shook my head.

"You can't even be sure the Menashe Volkoff who disappeared thirteen years ago is the same man Feldbaum was looking for."

I could feel my jaw tighten. "It's him."

My tone was a bit harsh, shaped less by my conviction that it was true than by my desire for it to be so.

Reuben did not seem offended. "The officer in charge was British. He's long gone. He did have a Jewish officer as an assistant. He may still be on the force, but I don't think anyone will reopen Volkoff's case. What would be the point?"

"Maybe Sergeant Bilenko would like to know about it."

Reuben nodded thoughtfully. "Maybe he would."

"Unless he's too busy to do anything about it."

"You can be as sarcastic as you want, Adam, but from what I know about Bilenko, he takes his work seriously."

So seriously, I thought, that he decided to omit Hannah from his report just because he thought it might upset some unnamed high-ranking officer he was led to believe was her lover.

But would I have acted differently in his place? I wasn't sure. Why should Bilenko have taken the risk of getting on a superior's bad side for no good reason?

Perhaps the right thing to do would be to go to Bilenko with the information. Maybe he would take another look. But if he did, he would probably tell me to steer clear of the investigation. And I didn't want that. Not yet.

I said, "I don't think Bilenko could do anything with what I have so far. You're right, Volkoff's disappearance might be entirely unconnected to Feldbaum's murder. I'm sure Bilenko has other cases on his plate."

"Quite a few."

"Then I don't see the point in taking up his precious time."

"All right. If you'd like to read the report on Volkoff's disappearance, come to the station tomorrow morning."

"Okay, Reuben. Thank you."

He waved a hand. "It's nothing. Now can you put that frown away for a couple of hours and try on a smile instead? It's a birthday party. There's a lot to be happy about."

He turned to the door, and I started to follow. But then something occurred to me, and I said, "What about Yosef Rudinsky? Any word about him?"

Reuben shook his head. "Nothing yet. But the old records aren't too orderly. Something may come up. I'll let you know if it does."

Then he opened the door, and we went back to Shoshana's party.

21

Hannah said, "I haven't eaten this well, or this much, in a long while."

We were ambling north, our pace leisurely. With my belly full of good Yemenite food, I doubted I could have gone any faster.

"Reuben and Gila are always generous hosts," I said.

"They sure have a big family."

"That wasn't half of them. At least three of Reuben's siblings live in the south and couldn't make it. And Gila also has family that wasn't there. Reuben says they're more like a tribe than a family."

"Must be nice."

I turned my head to look at her. Her profile was quite beautiful in the fickle dimness of an urban evening, alternately illuminated by streetlights and masked by the advancing darkness.

"Did it bother you?" I asked.

"What?"

"That there were so many of them. That Reuben and Gila have so many relatives."

"Why would it bother me?"

"Because... well, because you don't have... because of what happened to your family."

She gave me a long look, not saying anything for a moment. Her eyes were murky shapes behind the windowpanes of her glasses, impossible to read.

"Is that why you didn't go to Shoshana's previous birthday? Why you didn't go to that house for so long?"

"How do you know how long it's been since I was last there?"

"Gila told me."

"When?"

"When Reuben pulled you aside to talk."

"You two certainly hit it off quick."

"I like her. She's very nice. Very easy to talk to."

"What else did she tell you about me?"

Hannah flashed a mischievous smile. "Worried she might have shared some sordid secret?"

The way she said this, I wasn't sure whether that would have been a good thing or not, so I kept silent.

"Don't worry, Adam. Everything Gila said about you was good. Apart from the fact that it's been a while since she last saw you. I gather this was not for lack of them inviting you to their home. Do you find it difficult to be there?"

I didn't answer. She didn't push me. I considered how best to explain myself, my feelings. Would she understand me? I had thought she would, but then she said Reuben's big family didn't bother her as it did me.

After a few moments, she said, "You lost more than I did, didn't you?" And her voice was as gentle as a feather's touch, as a flower petal brushing your cheek as it flutters past on a cool breeze.

"It's not a competition."

"I know. But still. You were married, weren't you?"

"Is it written on my face?"

"A lot is, maybe more than you know, but not that specifically. But it's a safe bet. Most men your age are married. Or were. And you're not bad looking, so I don't think you'd have had any trouble finding a wife."

Not bad looking. Was that a compliment? If so, it was a tepid one.

"Maybe I never wanted to be married," I said. "Like you don't."

"Maybe that's the way you are now, I don't know. But I don't think that's how you used to be. Before the war in Europe. Before you went to Auschwitz. You and people you loved."

She had seen the number on my arm. That would have told her about Auschwitz. It was the only camp where prisoners were tattooed that way. But how did she know about my family?

"Did Gila tell you about my family?"

"No. And I didn't ask."

"But you're asking now."

"You don't have to tell me if you don't want to, Adam." The tenderness in her voice nearly broke something inside me, though I could not imagine why it would do so.

There was something hard stuck at the base of my throat. A jagged-edged clot of old emotions and new. And it wasn't still. It pulsed and pricked, tiny thorns stabbing their sharp tips into me. I had to cough twice and then swallow hard and painfully to clear my throat.

"I was married and had two daughters," I said, noticing the distance in my tone, as though commenting on some stranger, worried how Hannah might interpret it and not daring to look at her. "They came with me to Auschwitz. As did my four sisters and my mother. None of them survived. The only one of our family spared that wretched place was my father, and only because he died before the war. Sometimes death is an escape."

She didn't say she was sorry for my loss, just as I hadn't expressed my sorrow for hers when she told me about her parents and brother. Either she knew instinctively that it would not help one bit, or she had learned that lesson from being too often on the receiving end of such condolences.

"I don't have any family left," I said. "No uncles or aunts, no nephews or nieces, no cousins."

"And Reuben has all that."

"Multiples of it. And he has Gila. Gila and their children."

"So when you go there..."

"It makes the loss harder, sharper. It slaps me across the face, saying 'Here. Here is all that you no longer have. All that you lost because you were stupid and blind.'"

"Stupid and blind?"

"For not seeing what was coming. For not taking action when there was time."

"Like my father," Hannah said, and now I did look at her and found her looking right back at me. "But I don't blame him for that. And you shouldn't blame yourself either."

I knew what she was doing, and I was grateful, but I was nowhere near forgiving myself. I could find no justification for what I had failed to do. "I should have taken them away. Left Hungary and come here."

"It wasn't so easy, Adam. The British were letting very few Jews in."

"Then we could have gone somewhere else. Another country."

"It might not have helped. In my class, there's a boy, ten years old. His parents were German Jews. They left Germany after Hitler came to power and moved to Holland, where they thought they'd be safe. And for a time they were. But then Germany conquered Holland, and they weren't safe anymore. Sometimes, even when you take action, it doesn't help. You can't peer into the future and see exactly what it holds."

I looked away, blotted my damp eyes with my fingertips. I had to draw a few deep breaths to fight back the onslaught of tears.

"How did he survive? The boy in your class."

"Shlomo? When he was six months old, his parents gave him to a Dutch couple who agreed to pretend he was their baby. Then his parents and two older sisters were sent east. Only his mother returned. She also has a number on her arm. He was three when she returned to Holland and took him back."

More moments of silence. There were plenty of them between us. My fault again. This was supposed to be a pleasant evening, a few carefree hours of laughter and easy conversation with this intriguing, attractive woman, but I kept bringing up death and tragedy, like opening a window for darkness to slither through and snuff out all light.

"How is he now? This boy, I mean. Shlomo, you said his name was?"

"Yes. He's fine. A happy child. Smart too. But not as smart as Shoshana. Now that's a sharp girl."

I smiled, remembering Shoshana castigating me for missing her previous birthday. "She's something special, that one."

"And her brothers and sisters are too. I was quite impressed."

"As they were with you. They admire you for being a teacher."

"Which, I don't mind telling you, isn't always the case with parents. But education is important to Reuben and Gila."

"Shoshana liked her presents, didn't she? Especially the book."

"You made good choices."

"Me? You're the one who told me what to buy."

"But you had the good sense to listen. Which isn't common in men."

I laughed, and the pall of dark memories and guilt dissipated.

We were on Hayarkon Street by now, a few minutes from her home. Worry gnawed at me. Hannah had enjoyed herself, it seemed, but was my company part of it? It felt as though all I had brought into the evening was pain, sadness, and guilt, and why would any woman want to spend more time with a man like me?

I glanced at my watch. It was nearly eight thirty. Dark already, but not too late. As long as you're having a good time, that is.

I said, "There's a café on Allenby I like to spend time in. It serves the best coffee in Tel Aviv. Want to join me?"

Hannah shook her head. "I have to get up early tomorrow. I'm teaching."

She didn't say she'd be glad to join me some other time. She didn't say anything encouraging whatsoever. I nodded understanding but said nothing.

We entered Mahlul, walking in yet another silence. This one felt final, a point of no return.

When we were outside her shack, she said, "Thank you for walking me home, Adam."

"Don't mention it." I stuck my hands in my pockets. "And thank you for coming with me to the party. And for helping me with the presents. You have a good night." And I turned and started walking away.

Her voice stopped me. "Adam, come back here."

I did. She was standing quite still with a curious expression on her face.

"That's not the way I want you to wish me goodnight."

I frowned, unsure of her meaning. She rolled her eyes, let out a little sigh, took a step forward, and grabbed me by the shirtfront, pulling me down toward her.

Our mouths met. There was nothing shy or tentative about the way she kissed. My head filled with the sensation of her. The cool softness of her lips, the clean smell of her skin, the heat of her against my chest. My hands emerged from my pockets and curled around her narrow waist, pressing her closer to me. A small moan escaped her mouth, a satisfied sound that vibrated against my lips, sending a tingle along my jaw and cheeks.

The first kiss gave birth to others, and for a stitch of time we flowed with them. When we stopped, it was at her initiative. She broke contact and pulled back, leaving behind an acute absence of touch, the way a body reacts when a blanket is whipped off it.

In the gloom of Mahlul, her eyes were in shadow, but her teeth shone bright as she smiled.

"You not only listen well, but you're also a good kisser. Another thing in which you're unlike most men."

My face was hot. My heart was thudding. Bewildered by how the night had taken such an unexpected turn, it took me a moment to say, "I'm glad you approve."

Her smile widened. "I'd like to see you again."

I was surprised by her directness. Most women would have waited for the man to initiate a second date. Some men would have been taken aback by her forwardness, but I was simply glad that I would get to spend more time in her company.

"I'd like to see you too," I said.

"Will you take me out Saturday night?"

"I'd be happy to."

"Good. That's very good."

"I'll pick you up. Seven o'clock?"

"I'll be here." Then her eyes went over my shoulder, and she called, "Goodnight, Zelda." And I turned in time to see Zelda's face vanish from the window of her shack. How much did she see? I realized that I didn't care.

Turning back to Hannah, I said, "Now they'll really talk."

"Let them."

We looked at each other for a few long seconds. She smiled, and I smiled back. I wanted to kiss her again, was about to move in and do so, but she retreated a step.

"Goodnight, Adam."

"Goodnight, Hannah."

I turned to go, but again she stopped me.

"Adam?"

"Yes?"

"You smell nice. Whatever you're wearing, it's good."

I stared at her. Then I nearly burst out laughing, but I managed to hold it down to a smile. The little dandy salesman at the clothing store. A manipulative devil to be sure, but he knew what he was talking about. I felt like shaking his hand, maybe slipping him a banknote as a gratuity.

I said, "I'll be sure to wear it again on Saturday."

My steps were light when I walked out of Mahlul. Passersby saw me and smiled, and I realized there was a stupid grin on my face.

It was still there when I turned onto Hamaccabi Street. I was just outside my building when a cat saved my life.

22

It was a black cat. I know they're supposed to be bad luck, but I sure was lucky it was there.

I was also lucky it was black. If the cat had been any other color, I'd have seen it and shooed it away. Instead, I stepped on the tip of its tail, and when I did, it jumped with a screech and swept its paws at my leg.

Startled, I leaped away, and a heavy brick plunged inches from my face, right where I'd been standing a second earlier. It smashed into the ground with a cracking thud, splitting into two uneven pieces.

The cat screeched again, streaking away with a flick of its tail. I whipped my head up and saw a silhouetted figure on the roof, peering down at me.

"Hey!" I yelled, and the figure drew back and disappeared from sight.

I ran into the building and pounded up three flights of stairs. A metal ladder set into the wall of the third-floor landing led up to an open roof door. I paused there, knowing that I'd be vulnerable when I climbed it, that whoever was up there could choose that moment to drop another brick on my head, or maybe pounce on me when I emerged from the door.

Should I go into my apartment and get a weapon? My door was right there, on the third floor. It wouldn't take me more than a minute.

No. I needed to move as quickly as possible, before he had time to get ready for me. I grabbed the ladder and flung myself up its rungs. I didn't pause at the top to peek around but hurled myself over the rim of the opening and onto the roof, rolling to my feet and coming up with clenched fists.

There was nobody there. The roof was empty.

Where could he have gone? Could he have jumped to another building? I didn't think so. The distance between my building to its neighbors was more than twelve feet, and there was a high stone railing that would prevent him from having a running start.

Still, I swept my eyes over the roofs of the neighboring buildings, peering into the shadows.

Nothing.

Then I heard it. The unmistakable pop of a branch snapping.

The tree!

Swearing, I sprinted to the back of the building, where the heavy top of a tree reached, just one foot below the level of the roof.

Not an escape route I would choose gladly, but if I was eager to get off the roof and I couldn't use the usual exit...

Leaning over the railing, I peered down three stories and saw the figure finish his descent and drop to the ground from a low branch. He landed awkwardly, sprawling in the dirt with a muffled grunt, then began to slowly push himself up.

At that distance, in the gloom, half obscured by branches and leaves, I couldn't make out his exact build or height, but I was pretty sure it was a man. Certainly not Batya Rapoport with her bloated belly.

"Stop right there! Don't move!" I shouted, and his head wrenched upward. I couldn't see his face, but from the way his body jerked, I

JONATHAN DUNSKY

could tell I'd startled him. He jumped to his feet and began running toward the front of the building.

I rushed back to the roof door, threw myself down the wall ladder, and hurtled down the stairs at a dangerous speed, losing my footing once and bouncing hard against the wall of the stairwell, not quite managing to stifle a grunt of pain.

I burst out of the building and scanned in all directions.

There was no one.

The man had a head start, and Hamaccabi Street wasn't long, so he could have reached a corner and turned onto another street. But I didn't know which way he'd run.

The corner of King George was closer, so I hurried that way. At the corner, I stopped to look all around me.

I didn't see anyone running. I didn't see anyone with leaves stuck to his shirt, or his trousers torn from getting snagged on tree branches, but maybe the bastard had escaped being marked that way. What I did see was plenty of people; King George was crowded on this warm night. My assailant might be strolling casually, hiding in plain sight among passersby, and I would not be able to detect him. He also could have ducked into a store or a café, and I'd be none the wiser. Maybe, at that moment, he was getting ready to order a drink, the murderous scum.

I asked a few people if they'd seen a man running a couple of minutes ago, someone who looked agitated, someone with torn clothes or scratches. I got a couple of head shakes, a few noes, a handful of wary or bemused looks.

"Dammit," I hissed, then walked back home, frustrated, and circled to the rear of my building to where the tree stood. I got down on my haunches and examined the ground, thinking the man might have dropped something that could identify him when he took that final tumble.

There was nothing. Some footprints, but I couldn't make out the treads in the dark, and I doubted I'd ever find myself in a position in which it would matter if I could. The size of the footprints supported

168

my initial impression that it was a man who'd tried to kill me with the brick. But it didn't tell me anything more than that.

The broken brick was still where it had landed, directly under where my head had been when I was about to enter my building. The man's aim had been good. If the cat hadn't made me jump, I'd be lying there with my skull busted open and my brains spilled out.

Just like Emmanuel Feldbaum.

Was the man on the roof Feldbaum's killer? Had my questioning made him nervous, and he decided the best thing to do was to get rid of me? It was a likely possibility and one that did not displease me. For if Feldbaum's murderer had targeted me for death, it meant that Feldbaum had not been killed by some random robber. He had been killed deliberately, for some personal motive. And it also meant that I had come into contact with the killer. This still left a lot of potential suspects—including all of Feldbaum's co-workers on the construction site and all the Rapoports' neighbors—but the main thing was that I'd come close to the killer, and I could do so again.

Of course, the man on the roof didn't have to be Feldbaum's killer. Maybe he was Boris, out to get me for my perceived sins against Caspi, or as payback for that scene in Café Silver. Hardly good reasons to murder someone, but like I'd told Hannah earlier, you wouldn't believe the reasons people have for killing each other.

Did the murky figure I'd seen at the bottom of the tree fit Boris's physique? I closed my eyes and tried to sharpen my memory, but it was no use. I could not be certain.

I opened my eyes and looked down at the busted brick by my feet. It was a large gray chunk, now split unevenly into two pieces with jagged edges like eroded clifftops. Something tightened in my stomach as I thought of how close that brick had come to smashing into my head. Then something occurred to me, and I crouched down for a closer look at the instrument of my near destruction.

I'd seen other bricks just like it not too long ago. I'd seen them in Caspi's construction site. Some had been piled to one side, but there had been a few that were scattered around. I lifted the bigger of the two pieces and turned it in my hands. Its surface was pocked and rough to the touch, the sort of roughness that could scrape your fingers raw if you mishandled it.

It was also heavy. And if you added the weight of the other piece, the one still on the ground, it would be heavier still. Not a comfortable weight to schlep around for long.

My assailant hadn't come here by car; there were none parked on Hamaccabi Street that were unfamiliar to me. But he might have taken a taxi, and there was a bus stop not too far off on King George.

But if he had come in a taxi, he wouldn't have told the driver to drop him off right outside my building. Not unless he was very stupid. So either he got dropped off a few buildings away, possibly at one of the corners of Hamaccabi Street, or he had come by bus, which meant a similar walking distance. He also could have ridden a bicycle, but I did not recall seeing any about when I arrived at my building earlier.

I shook my head. I was letting my mind drag me in pointless directions. It didn't matter how the man had come to kill me. What mattered was that he had lugged the brick a certain distance and then up three flights of stairs. Could any man have done that? Boris certainly could. He was particularly strong. But what about other men?

Well, Emmanuel Feldbaum could have done it, but he was dead. But if they wanted to, or needed to badly enough, most men could have hefted this brick for a good distance. I certainly would have been able to. I'd done harder things when I had no other choice. Much harder things.

I sighed. So the weight of the brick did not narrow the possibilities to the brawny Boris. I had no idea who my assailant was.

I picked up both pieces of brick and put them near the large trash can in the street. I didn't see the point of keeping them. Then a soft mewling sound reached my ears. I followed it, and there, beneath some shrubs near the fence, was the black cat.

It was a she. I could tell by the two kittens huddled behind her. They were tiny little things, and she was scrawny herself. I kept my distance this time, crouching down slowly so as not to alarm her. Her gold-green eyes glittered as she appraised me, her whiskers shifting like antennae.

"Thank you," I said.

Her only reply was opening her mouth, showing sharp fangs, and then rolling her tongue across her lips. She mewled again, a plaintive sound, or maybe that was just the way I interpreted it.

"Wait here. Be back in a moment."

In my apartment, I emptied my milk bottle into a large bowl and reached into the cupboard for my last two cans of sardines. The sardines had come from a shrewd old lady who'd turned part of her apartment into a storeroom of black-market delicacies and charged through the nose for them. I opened the cans and dumped their contents onto a plate.

I carried the milk and fish down the stairs and across the yard and set both on the ground a few feet from the cat, then retreated a distance that felt safe to me, as I hoped it would be to her.

She eyed me for a long moment with the wary suspicion common to those who had experienced many shattered hopes and bitter disappointments. Add to that the burdens of new motherhood, and I could well understand her caution.

"For you," I said softly, retreating another step and sitting on the ground. "Eat. Please."

The cat mewled again, tilting her head to study me further, from a new angle. Finally satisfied that I posed her no threat, or perhaps goaded by hunger, she approached the food slowly, her eyes twitching from it to me.

She lapped at the milk, found it good, and called to her young ones. All three ate hungrily while I watched, ready to jump to their aid if some other street creature dared try to rob them of their meal.

When they'd finished, the mother cat eyed me again and let out another mewl. An appeal for more?

"I'm sorry," I said. "I don't have any more. That was everything."

She approached me slowly, rubbed her side against my knee and allowed me to caress her back.

"If only you could talk," I said, "you'd tell me who the man was, wouldn't you? You wouldn't keep secrets from me."

She responded with another mewl, looking right at me, and if I hadn't known better, I'd have sworn she'd understood me, that she had answered my question in her feline tongue.

"Sorry about stepping on your tail," I said, and she hunched her shoulder, as though in a shrug, saying, *Don't worry about it. It's no big deal.* Then she turned and walked away toward her offspring, pausing midway to give her fur one long cleansing lick of her tongue, then peering at me motionless with those curious eyes unique to her species, and finally turning and disappearing with her kittens into the shadows of the shrubbery.

I took the empty bowl and plate upstairs and put them in the kitchen sink. I opened the faucet and started rinsing them, noticing that there was stone dust on my hands, left there by my handling the broken brick. Oddly, I hadn't noticed it earlier, so intent I was on bringing my savior her milk and sardines.

I washed my hands, then thought that while most men could have hauled the brick from the corner of Hamaccabi Street and up the stairs to the roof, they wouldn't have held it in their hands. For one thing, it would dirty up their hands and clothes. For another, the brick was too large and of the wrong shape for a man to be able to hold it in one hand. He would need two of them. But he would also need at least one free hand to hoist himself up the ladder to the roof. Most importantly, my assailant wouldn't want to be seen walking around with a heavy brick. Not when he planned on dropping it on my head. Someone might remember him.

I stepped out of my apartment, climbed the wall ladder again, and walked to the front edge of the roof, to where the man had stood when he'd launched the brick at me.

There it was, what I expected to see, a bag, empty and discarded, lying near the stone railing.

I picked it up and carried it with me back to my apartment, where there was more light.

The bag had the sort of long handles you could hold in your hand or hang over your shoulder. A bag for carrying groceries or other shopping, certainly not designed to hold heavy bricks with murderous intent.

It was white, made of thick, rough cloth, stained here and there, but I wasn't sure by what. It wasn't old; there was almost no fraying. Nothing was written on it. No indication as to who made it or used it. It was empty inside—well, almost empty. Stuck in a fold at the bottom was a small piece of paper, torn off a bigger one.

It was twice as large as the pad of my thumb and scratchy to the touch. It was the color of dry mud except for a printed line of black along one edge. The line was cut off at both ends, and I couldn't begin to guess what it was. Nor did I have any clue as to what the piece of paper was. Part of a product of some kind or some packing material?

I simply didn't know.

I put the piece of paper in my wallet. Maybe it would prove useful one day. Or maybe, like most things in life, it would end up meaning nothing at all.

23

The next morning, a little after eight o'clock, I was at the police station on Yehuda Halevi Street. I was sitting in Reuben's office, the file of Menashe Volkoff's disappearance open on the desk before me.

"It's not much, is it?" Reuben said.

That was an understatement. The file was flimsy. And what little there was did not amount to much.

"So, is he the Menashe Volkoff you're looking for?"

"It's him," I said, though the contents of the file did not make that certain.

What they did show was that Menashe Volkoff had arrived at the port of Haifa on Friday, July 21, 1939, disembarking a ship that had sailed from Athens. He had come alone. He reported having no family in Israel, and presumably no one was awaiting his arrival. He had come from Poland, but the file did not say from what town or city. I was sure it was Mastarnia, the hometown of Emmanuel Feldbaum. That was why Feldbaum told Ami Rapoport that Menashe was here. He meant here in Israel. He had remembered that Volkoff had left Mastarnia with an immigration certificate in his pocket. But the memory had become jumbled in his broken mind. All that remained were fragments and slivers, nothing that could be articulated. But what had remained whole was the need to find Volkoff. Because Volkoff had information that Feldbaum was desperate to have. As Feldbaum had told Ami Rapoport, Volkoff knew where *it* was. Whatever *it* might be.

On July 26, five days after Volkoff's arrival in Haifa, a woman by the name of Dita Steinberg reported to the local police that one of her tenants, Menashe Volkoff, was missing. He had rented a room in her boardinghouse the day he arrived in Haifa and had slept there for two nights. But then three more nights had come and gone without him showing his face. This despite him paying for a week in advance, including meals. This made alarm bells ring in Mrs. Steinberg's head. New immigrants of modest means tended to be cautious with their money.

In addition, Volkoff's single suitcase was still in his room, as were his toiletries and most of his clothes. "The only clothes missing are those that he had on when he went out the morning he vanished," Mrs. Steinberg told the officer who took down her statement.

She had no idea where Volkoff had been going that day. The other three boarders she had at the time all said the same thing when they were later interviewed by police.

There was a list of Volkoff's belongings in the report. The aforementioned clothes and toiletries. A novel in Yiddish. Another in Hebrew. A map of Mandatory Palestine. An unopened pack of cigarettes. A slim album with photographs showing Volkoff in the company of people the police assumed were his family.

All dead now. As, in all likelihood, was Menashe Volkoff himself. Thirteen years is a long time to be missing without a trace if you're still breathing.

I chose a single photograph, the one showing Volkoff's face most clearly, and slipped it into my pocket.

The report detailed the police effort to locate Volkoff. If such a short and desultory series of actions could be termed an effort.

After interviewing Mrs. Steinberg and her remaining boarders, and canvassing the surrounding streets for any sightings of Volkoff, the police in Haifa sent copies of Volkoff's picture to other stations.

The report also said that an appeal was made in the press for any information.

The results left much to be desired. A shopkeeper on the corner of Mrs. Steinberg's street reported seeing a man fitting Volkoff's description pass by his shop window at about the time Mrs. Steinberg said Volkoff had left her home.

A seventy-three-year-old woman claimed that Volkoff had boarded the same bus she had traveled on, an inner-city line that originated in the Port of Haifa and climbed a circuitous route up the slope of Mount Carmel. The line had a stop not far from Mrs. Steinberg's home, and the shortest route to it would have taken Volkoff past the shopkeeper's window.

Volkoff, the woman from the bus said, had sat a few rows ahead of her and did not talk with anyone. She had disembarked before he had, so she did not know his destination, but it had to be one of the line's last two stops because she had gotten off one stop before that. The bus had been nearly empty by then, unfortunately, and she did not know any of the other passengers by name. The bus driver did not recall Volkoff, but he said that if he indeed had been on the bus, he'd gotten off at the next-to-last stop; the driver said he tended to notice the passengers that got off on the last stop and that Volkoff had not been among them.

A canvass of buildings near the next-to-last stop yielded no sightings of the missing man, raising doubt as to the veracity of the old woman's report. Or perhaps that doubt was simply due to the general mistrust some young cops tend to feel toward elderly witnesses.

The report stated that over the next week further sightings were claimed in disparate locations such as Tel Aviv, Jerusalem, Nahariya, and a number of smaller communities across the land. But none of these seemed reliable. Whenever you appeal to the public, you need to separate a lot of chaff from very little, or sometimes no, wheat.

No one knew where Volkoff had been heading that day. No one knew whether he was going to meet someone. If he was, that person never came forward. If he was, the person he set out to meet most likely murdered him.

24

The bus to Haifa was half full and hot. But it ran better than many other busses in Israel; the straining of its engine did not reach worrying levels.

I stared out the window at the rapidly changing landscape—rolling dunes followed by low shrubs and sparse copses and then the wooded slopes of Mount Carmel, getting ever bigger as we approached our destination.

Several times during the ride, my hand dipped into my pocket and touched the folding knife I had tucked into it before leaving home. A precaution against further attacks.

I had gotten the knife in Germany after the Second World War and before I had come to Israel. Its previous owner had been a Nazi. I had killed him and taken the knife as a keepsake. It was mine now, but its provenance showed in the symbol stamped into its handle. It was the greatest symbol of evil the world had ever known: the swastika. If people could really roll over in their grave, that Nazi bastard must have been tossing and turning constantly at the thought of his knife being in the hands of a Jew.

I normally kept the knife in a secret compartment I'd installed in my bedroom closet, alongside other mementos of my Nazi-hunting days. I only took it out when I felt the need for it.

After last night, that was exactly how I felt.

I also had a revolver I'd gotten not too long ago. A Smith & Wesson that held six rounds. But a knife is quieter than a gun and easier to explain if found on your person, even with the swastika.

I did not think I'd need it in Haifa, but this case was developing in unpredictable ways, so it was better to have protection.

At the central bus station in Haifa, I inquired how to get to Mrs. Steinberg's boardinghouse. I was told I could either wait for another bus or take a taxi. I opted for the bus. With the nothing I was earning on this case, I could not afford to splurge.

The shop that Menashe Volkoff might have walked past on the morning of his disappearance was still there, its window full of pots, pans, sieves, and all sorts of kitchen utensils. But the shopkeeper was not the man who'd reported seeing Volkoff through the display window on that fateful day.

"That must have been my father," the shopkeeper told me. "He opened this store in 1928 and ran it for twenty years. He passed away in 1948, just two days after independence."

Dita Steinberg had not passed away. In fact, she lived at the same address and still rented out rooms in her large house.

"My husband and I bought this house when we came to Haifa in 1934," she told me. "We ran a boardinghouse in Germany, so we decided to do the same thing here. He died in 1937 of a heart attack, and I've been running the place by myself ever since."

There was something of the stork about her, with her tall, thin body, spindly limbs, long neck, beady gray eyes, and sharp nose. On the tip of said nose perched a pair of glasses, secured further with a cord that encircled her neck, and she peered at me alternately through them and over their rim.

"It must be difficult to do everything by yourself," I said.

"I have a girl who helps now that I'm getting a bit on in years, but for a long time that's exactly what I did. And you're right, it's not easy, but one does what one must. More tea, Mr. Lapid?"

The tea was hot and bitter—sugar wasn't easy to come by in Israel, and there was never enough of it even if you did manage to lay your hands on some—but I nodded my head and held out my cup just the same. I didn't want to risk offending her.

We were sitting in a cozy living room—she on a small couch, me on a hard chair—with the teapot between us on a coffee table. The room was well lighted with sunlight pouring through a large window, and a bunch of flowers in a vase gave off a pleasant scent. Everything was in perfect order. Mrs. Steinberg ran a neat house.

"I'll do my best not to take too much of your precious time," I said, taking a tiny sip and putting the cup on the table.

"Don't concern yourself with that, Mr. Lapid. Menashe Volkoff disappeared while he was a guest under my roof. Most of my counterparts would think nothing of it, but I feel a measure of responsibility for all my boarders, even those who stay with me but for a short time. But I can't help but wonder why, thirteen years after the fact, you find yourself interested in his disappearance."

"I'm working a case in Tel Aviv. It concerns a man who recently died. I believe he knew Volkoff and was trying to find him before his death."

"Why did this man want to find him?"

"That's unclear. The man who died was not well. A brain injury he suffered a few years back made him difficult to understand. But he was quite keen on locating Volkoff. I believe they came from the same town in Poland."

"Mastarnia?"

I stared at her in surprise. "How do you know that?"

"How do you think? Like any other guest, when Mr. Volkoff arrived at my door, I inquired where he'd come from, and that's the name he gave me."

So he was the right Menashe Volkoff after all. I'd managed to trace him to this house in Haifa. But did it matter? How would learning where Volkoff had been thirteen years ago help me catch Emmanuel Feldbaum's killer?

"I'm surprised you remember it so clearly after so many years," I said.

"Normally, I probably wouldn't. Especially with someone who only spent a few nights here. But some guests stick in your mind. Usually, they're the bad ones, and I've had the misfortune of having quite a few. There were some drunks. A couple of petty thieves. One disturbed young man who heard voices in his head and was in the habit of shouting at them to pipe down at all hours of the day and night. I even had a young woman who snuck men into her room, something that I strictly forbid. Them I remember quite distinctly. Mr. Volkoff gave me no trouble; it's the fact of his disappearance that has kept him firmly in my mind."

She paused to sip her tea, then stared into her cup for a few good seconds before speaking again.

"In eighteen years of running this place, and in the decade my husband and I had our former boardinghouse in Germany, no guest of mine has ever died under my roof or while being my boarder. There's no certainty Mr. Volkoff is dead, but I suppose he must be." She raised her eyes to mine. "He didn't simply disappear, did he?"

"I don't believe so, no."

She gave a small nod. "Neither do I. For a while after he vanished, I kept hoping he'd turn up somewhere. Each time I opened a paper, I searched for news about him. But I suppose I knew even back then that something awful must have happened to him. Do you believe he was murdered?"

"That's my working assumption."

"And the killer buried him somewhere. What other option is there? If he had an accident, someone would have found his body, wouldn't they?"

"In all likelihood."

She gave a small sigh, took another sip of her tea, and placed her cup next to mine on the coffee table. Her eyes were glistening.

"That's why I remember him better than I do most of the others. He has stayed in my mind for a long while after he was gone, after the police took away all his things and not a trace of him remained here.

And once I came to terms with the fact that he was dead, I told myself that maybe one day someone would come asking about him. Someone from his hometown. From Mastarnia. And here you are, even though you're not from Mastarnia."

"It's remarkable that you care so much about him, Mrs. Steinberg. Can you tell me what he was like?"

"I should be able to, shouldn't I? With how I talk about him. But in truth, I hardly knew him, had barely time to form an impression. He was here for just two nights, a day and a half in total, and I did not expect him to be anything other than an ordinary guest. There was nothing impressive about him physically, and in the short time he stayed here, he did not make any trouble or noise."

"I read in the police report that he arrived here on July 21."

"Yes. That was the date. In late afternoon. He had one suitcase. He came straight from the ship that had brought him here."

"What made him choose your boardinghouse?"

"I don't know. Perhaps one of the workmen at the port suggested it. I have a good reputation, Mr. Lapid."

"I'm sure you do."

"And I speak Yiddish, so Volkoff and I could converse."

"Did he tell you anything about himself?"

"Almost nothing. We didn't have time for a proper talk. But I do know he had family back in Poland. I know because he wrote them a letter and asked me to mail it for him. It's a service I provide for my boarders. They can leave their letters on a small table by the front door, and I take them all and mail them together. I mailed his letter on the morning he disappeared, though, of course, at the time, I did not imagine he would never come back."

"I don't suppose you know what he wrote in his letter?" I asked, guessing the answer, but hoping against hope that I was wrong.

"Certainly not. The letter was in a sealed envelope, and I did not open it." For a second, I thought my question might have offended her, but she gave no such indication. Instead, she looked at me thoughtfully for a few seconds and then said, "But I still have the letter they sent him."

Again she'd managed to surprise me. "What letter?"

"The letter that Mr. Volkoff's family sent him in reply to the one I mailed for him."

"There was no mention of such a letter in the police report."

"That's hardly my fault. I informed the police when the letter arrived."

"And?"

"And the officer who was working the case—the Jewish one, not the British—he came over, but he found nothing in the letter that could further the investigation."

"And he left it with you?"

"At first, he wanted to take it, but I asked to keep it. I had the feeling that it would be safer here with me than at some police storage unit. I thought that when—if—Mr. Volkoff was ever found, he would want to see this letter. Back then, I still harbored hope that he was alive. And later, after the passage of time had extinguished that hope, I thought maybe one day one of Mr. Volkoff's relatives might come calling, so I kept the letter safe in a drawer."

"May I see it?"

She didn't hesitate. She'd been waiting so long to share that letter with someone who cared about Volkoff that she was eager to let me see it.

"Wait here. I'll go fetch it."

She went through a door into another room and returned a minute later with a wrinkled envelope in her hand. She gave it to me.

The envelope crinkled in my grip. On its front someone had written Mrs. Steinberg's address in large, masculine letters. On the back was the return address—Mastarnia, Poland—and a name: Misha Volkoff. Menashe Volkoff's father? His brother?

I pictured the person who'd sent this letter walking with it through the streets of Mastarnia to the post office. He must have been overjoyed to have received the letter Menashe Volkoff had sent from Haifa. He thought Volkoff was safe and sound in the Land of Israel, at the end of a long journey from Poland. He did not know, would not have imagined, that Volkoff was at that moment missing and likely dead.

My fingers trailed across the envelope, found its slitted opening, slipped inside, and drew out a single sheet of paper folded into thirds and very dry to the touch. I unfolded it and saw a date in the top left corner: August 26, 1939. Less than a week before the outbreak of the Second World War. I imagined the letter fleeing Poland just before German tanks rolled across the border, moments before Luftwaffe bombers began raining hellish fire on Polish towns and cities. The writer of the letter had not been as fortunate. He had not fled in time.

"When did the letter arrive here?" I asked Mrs. Steinberg.

"Early October. I don't remember the exact date."

"And Volkoff wrote his letter on July 21 or 22?"

"Or early on the morning of July 23. That's when I mailed it, the morning of Sunday, July 23. The day he went missing."

That letter had traveled across the Mediterranean to the south of Europe and then northward over land into Poland, finally arriving at Mastarnia about a month later. And the return letter had traveled a similar route in reverse, only this time a bit longer and with the clamor of war at its back.

I looked down at the letter. Both sides were covered with rows of text in straight, rigid handwriting. The letters were Hebrew, but the language was Yiddish. I could pick out several singular words, a short phrase or two, but I wasn't fluent in the language. I said as much to Mrs. Steinberg and asked if she could read the letter for me.

She took it from my hand and held it at arm's length from her eyes. She began reading, and I looked at her as she spoke, this middle-aged woman who, due to an exaggerated loyalty to her guests, had kept this letter for thirteen years and would likely keep it for the rest of her days, waiting for someone to come and claim it.

The letter had been written by Menashe Volkoff's father. It began with an expression of happiness and relief that Volkoff had made it safely to the Land of Israel, and there were several questions about how the land was—the weather, the people, the food. And also about how Volkoff felt to be standing in the "land of our forebears," as

Volkoff's father put it. Obviously, this was a cause for jubilation. Volkoff's father did not know that lamentation was more appropriate to his son's reality.

The letter proceeded with information about Mastarnia and Volkoff's family. He had a brother and a sister, both younger than him, and both were well. His grandmother was doing better, the doctor having prescribed a new medicine, but there was no indication as to what ailed her. Volkoff had obviously known.

I don't suppose it mattered very much in the long run. The ailing grandmother and the healthy siblings, and Volkoff's father too, had all met a similar fate after the Germans invaded.

There was no mention of Volkoff's mother. Perhaps she had passed away earlier. Perhaps, like my father, who had also died before the Nazi storm swooped in to eradicate us, a natural death had spared her the unnatural horrors to come.

Upon reaching the bottom of one side of the letter, Mrs. Steinberg paused and asked, "Anything so far?"

I shook my head. Nothing that she'd read to this point had shed any light on Menashe Volkoff's final days or the cause of his disappearance.

She turned the page over and continued reading.

Volkoff's father told his son that tensions were high with the Germans, but he expressed confidence that war would not break. "Poland has an alliance with France and Britain. Hitler wouldn't dare start a war with us." He mentioned plans to travel to Krakow in December for Hanukkah—Volkoff's uncle lived there—and griped about the price of train tickets, which had risen recently. Volkoff's father needn't have worried about that, I thought. That journey never took place. Not unless he and his family had been shipped to the Krakow Ghetto.

Then Volkoff's father wrote a few questions to his son. "So tell me, Menashe: How is the place? Is it as you imagined? Is the sea as blue and warm as they say? Everyone is excited to know more. Mr. Persky and some of the others asked that you send over some photographs so we can see for ourselves. We've included some money for a camera or a photographer, and I've added a little for yourself."

I could feel more pieces of paper inside the envelope. They were banknotes. Old Polish currency in varied denominations. Dead money belonging to dead Jews.

I looked at Mrs. Steinberg in astonishment. "You've kept the money for all this time?"

"Of course. It's not mine to spend."

"I'm surprised the police officer let you keep it."

"I removed the money before he came over to see the letter."

"But he would have known there should have been money when he read it."

Her thin lips curled into a mischievous smile. "The man knew not a word of Yiddish. He had me read the letter to him. I simply omitted the sentence about the enclosed money."

I grinned at her. "You keep surprising me, Mrs. Steinberg. I would not have believed you to be so wily."

"I do what I must, Mr. Lapid, as I've told you. Don't get me wrong: I have the utmost respect for the police, but I did not think it wise to tempt any officer with loose cash."

"You did the right thing. And the noble thing."

She accepted my compliment with a small nod, but I could see that I'd pleased her.

All that remained of the letter were words of farewell, reserved expressions of warmth and love, as a father would feel comfortable sharing in a letter with his son, and an exhortation to write again soon. And that was the end of it.

A sad quiet permeated the room. Both of us were silent, the ancient words of a dead father to his dead son lingering invisible in the air around us.

My thoughts turned once more to the letter. What place had Volkoff's father referred to? I asked Mrs. Steinberg what she thought, and she said she'd always assumed Volkoff's father was talking about Haifa and perhaps the boardinghouse itself.

I considered this. It was eminently plausible, likely even. But something felt off about it, though I could not put my finger on what.

"Who is this Mr. Persky the letter mentions?" I asked.

"I have no idea. Mr. Volkoff never said the name to me."

"And 'the others' Volkoff's father wrote about—who do you suppose they were?" I did not really expect her to know. I was simply voicing aloud the questions I was asking myself.

"I've always assumed they were neighbors," she said. "Perhaps Mr. Persky was as well?"

Perhaps so. But again, there was that sense of wrongness, of something not aligning properly, like a door that had warped and no longer fitted its frame.

"'The others' is an odd way to refer to neighbors, isn't it?" I said. "And why mention Mr. Persky specifically just before that? It makes me think of a group, with Mr. Persky being a prominent member. A group other than simply a collection of neighbors."

Mrs. Steinberg pursed her lips. "I never thought of it that way. I think you're right. It does seem a bit strange."

But not impossible, I thought. "The others" could have been nothing more than neighbors, all eager to learn more about life in the Land of Israel. And Mr. Persky might have been someone important, like a rich merchant or the headmaster of the local Jewish school. It could be interpreted that way.

But my instincts told me differently.

I drew a deep breath and gazed out the window toward the street outside, my mind turning the matter over, looking for an opening and finding none. It felt as though I were holding one of those cleverly constructed jewelry boxes that can only be opened by some trick. But the nature of that trick kept eluding me, masked by the smoke of thirteen years and a bunch of dead Jews.

"This case is important to you, isn't it?" Mrs. Steinberg's voice drew me out of my thoughts.

"Very much."

"Why?"

I thought about sharing the desolate nighttime streets of Tel Aviv with Emmanuel Feldbaum, about the strange kinship I felt with him, about seeing him lying dead with his skull busted open and his blood seeping into the earth around him. I could tell her none of this, of course. This was another piece of darkness that I could reveal to no one, that I had to keep solely to myself. Like too many others that darkened my soul.

"I feel something for the man who died in Tel Aviv. It's difficult to explain why."

"Who was he?"

I told her a little about Feldbaum, his ordeal in Europe, his final weeks here in Israel, the way he used to talk about Menashe Volkoff. She listened attentively, her expression growing ever more somber.

"How awful. To die like that." Her eyes suddenly widened, and she pushed her glasses up her nose and peered at me through them, as though to see me with greater clarity. "Do you think there's a connection between that murder and whatever happened to Mr. Volkoff?"

"I don't know. It's possible." I didn't tell her that a part of me hoped it was so. That in such a case, Feldbaum's murder would not be the result of a random robbery gone wrong, that it might provide me with the opening I needed to catch Feldbaum's killer. And Menashe Volkoff's killer too.

She folded her arms around herself, as though a sudden chill had cut through her. "If this is true, then the same killer murdered them both."

"Yes."

"Shouldn't we alert the police?"

"I may end up looking for the officer who worked the case, but I doubt he'd do anything about it. I used to be a police detective myself; I know how the police operate. Volkoff's case is too old, Feldbaum's looks too much like a robbery, and the connection between them is too flimsy and vague. There's no actual evidence that connects the two cases. The police won't dedicate resources to such a baseless investigation. Not with their workload."

"So what will you do?" she asked me.

I didn't hesitate. "I'm going to catch the killer myself."

25

Mrs. Steinberg refilled her cup with tea. She did not offer to refill mine.

"I could tell you didn't like the tea much," she said with a small smile.

"You should have been a detective."

"I don't think it would have suited me. I wouldn't want to spend my time around criminals and murderers. And I don't like to even think about violence and death. Perhaps that's why it took me so long to come to terms with the idea that Mr. Volkoff was murdered."

"Most people try to avoid thinking about such things. It feels better to ignore the existence of evil."

"You don't approve, I take it."

"I understand it," I said. "It's just that it's been my experience that ignoring evil doesn't make it disappear or pass you by. Sometimes, it makes you blind to the danger it poses until it's too late."

Her eyes dropped a little, and, following her gaze, I saw that I was unconsciously rubbing the number tattoo on my left forearm. I stopped and curled my hand around it, hiding it from view.

Eager to change the subject, I said: "If the place Volkoff was supposed to photograph wasn't your house or Haifa in general, can you think of what it might be?"

"I'm afraid I can't."

"And you have no idea where he was going the day he disappeared?"

"Not the slightest."

I told her about the old woman on the bus and her possible sighting of Volkoff. "Do you know that bus line?"

She did and told me where the next-to-last stop was.

"Can you guess what Volkoff might have been looking for there?"

Again she claimed ignorance.

I could think of nothing more to ask her. She had told me all she knew, which was very little. But my visit to her had proved fruitful nonetheless. I had learned that Menashe Volkoff had existed, and that he had indeed come from Mastarnia. And I knew of the letter his father had sent him. Maybe there was a clue in it. Maybe one day I'd be able to identify it.

Mrs. Steinberg invited me to lunch, but despite being hungry, I declined. I had found a lead, however tenuous, and I was keen to pursue it and see where it led me.

"Are you sure?" she asked. "It's almost noon."

"Yes. Thank you for the invitation and for your time."

She said she'd fix me a sandwich, and wouldn't take no for an answer. She put the sandwich in a paper bag and handed it to me. At her door, she gave my hand a squeeze. "Thank you for investigating this case, Mr. Lapid."

"Thank you for your time, Mrs. Steinberg. And for caring more than most people would."

The sandwich was delicious. I wolfed it down on the way to the bus stop where Menashe Volkoff had boarded the bus on the morning he disappeared—if indeed the old lady's eyes, or her memory, hadn't played tricks on her.

I smoked a cigarette as I waited for the bus to arrive, and looked around as though in search of a sign of Volkoff. I often did this in places where a crime had been committed, or just somewhere the victim had been. I hardly ever found anything tangible, but I kept on looking all the same. Maybe I was hoping to establish a link with the victim. Maybe it made me feel closer to him.

This time I felt nothing. Maybe because I didn't know for sure that Volkoff had indeed been here on the day he vanished. Or maybe because he truly hadn't been.

The bus groaned up Mount Carmel, and soon I could see the sea spread out below and to the west like an infinite promise. It shimmered and sparkled in blue glory under the spring sun, and I wondered if Menashe Volkoff had seen it about the same way as I did now. Did his heart fill with awe at the sight of it? Had he wished he had a camera on him at that moment, to snap some photos to send back to his doomed family in Mastarnia?

I wondered if this was the same bus that Volkoff had traveled on thirteen years ago. By its appearance, the bus was of the right age. Was the seat I now occupied the same one Menashe Volkoff had sat in on his last bus ride? Or perhaps he had simply claimed the same position on another bus?

I chided myself for filling my brain with these frivolous questions. Even if I could unearth the answers, what good would they do me?

Unbidden, my mind turned to Hannah Goldman, and the next instant I could feel the phantom pressure of her lips on mine. I smiled to myself, running in my mind that moment in which she'd seized my shirt and pulled me down into a kiss. Then I shook my head and wondered what was wrong with me. Why couldn't I stay focused on what I was doing, on the case?

The driver was much too young to be the one who'd driven the bus that Volkoff might have taken. And even if he had been the same driver, I couldn't see the point of speaking with him. The driver hadn't remembered seeing Volkoff when the police interviewed him a few days after his disappearance. His memory wouldn't be sharper thirteen years later.

And what of the old woman who claimed to have seen Volkoff on the bus? I had copied her name and address in my notebook when I'd read the police report. Would it do any good to talk to her?

I couldn't see how it would. Like the driver, her memory was unlikely to produce anything new after so long.

If she had really seen Volkoff to begin with.

Looking out the window again, this time at low houses with laden clotheslines swinging in the breeze, I decided that she had. There was no reason behind this decision, no justification other than my preference. I simply chose to believe that it was so. And the reason was simple: it was the only lead I had. If it was true, I had a slim chance. If not, I had nothing to go on.

I got off the bus at the same stop Volkoff had, where I'd decided he had. It was in the middle of Pevzner Street. Three- and four-story apartment buildings lined both sides of the road, with small businesses occupying the ground floors.

I stood there for a minute, just looking around. There was a bicycle repair shop, a barbershop, a grocery store, a radio and gramophone store, a wine shop, a seamstress, a cobbler. Small businesses with their windows displaying wares, and a slow flow of people going in and out of them.

Why had Menashe Volkoff come here? Where was he going? To one of these businesses, or those that had occupied these spaces thirteen years ago? Or maybe to one of the many apartments above them? It was a long street; plenty of possibilities. And nothing with which I could begin to winnow them down.

I thought of the letter. Was there anything in it to indicate why Volkoff had come to this street?

Nothing came to mind.

After getting off the bus, Volkoff might have gone in either direction. I chose my right and started there. I entered one business after another, questioning whoever worked there.

The barber remembered being questioned by the police on the matter thirteen years ago. His story had not changed in the interval: he hadn't seen Volkoff. The seamstress was equally unhelpful, and the cobbler had been on a summer vacation that long-ago July. The owner of the wine shop shook his head morosely. The woman behind the counter of the bookstore said she was sorry, but she couldn't help me.

Some of the businesses were new, including the one right across the street from the bus stop. It was a law firm, with five desks, and it smelled of paper and ink and pencil shavings. The man whose name was on the door had started his practice fifteen years ago and moved into this space four years later, two years after Volkoff disappeared.

"Before us, there was a travel agency here, but it went out of business. I don't think it lasted two years. And before that some other business, I don't remember what it was, and it also went belly up. Some would think the space was cursed, you know?" He laughed a little, showing that he was a sophisticated modern man and not prone to superstition. "But we've only grown since."

The bicycle repair shop next door was also new. The owner laid down a wheel he'd been about to attach to an overturned frame and wiped his hands on a rag.

"I remember that. I was still in school then, the tenth grade, so there was another business here. But I live just a few doors down, and I remember the cops coming to our apartment, asking about the missing man. He still hasn't been found, eh? What makes you think you can find him after so long?"

I didn't have a good answer to his question, just like he didn't have any good answers to mine. I asked him how long he'd had his store, and what business had occupied the space before it.

"I've been here eight and a half years. It started out slow, and there are always ups and downs, and during the war, I closed up entirely and joined the army. But now things are improving a little. There are a lot of new people in Haifa, and bicycles are relatively cheap. Before I opened this place, there was a guy who fixed watches and clocks. Sold them too. A Mr. Gruntman. Had the place for ages. Nice enough man."

"Know where I can find him?" I asked.

"You can't. Not to talk to. He got sick and died. That's why the space became vacant and I moved in."

It went on like that. Some of the business owners vaguely remembered being questioned about Volkoff thirteen years earlier, but said they'd never laid eyes on him. The others hadn't heard of him at all.

All that remained of Volkoff was a wisp—an undefined, barely discernible trace of his existence. You only noticed it if someone called your attention to it, and even then, it barely registered. It had not been that way for Emmanuel Feldbaum, but he was dead. The only people for whom Volkoff continued to hold any importance whatsoever were Mrs. Steinberg and now me.

No, that was wrong. There was another person who might still think of him.

Volkoff's murderer.

26

After visiting all the businesses within two blocks of the bus stop, I leaned against the side of a building and smoked a cigarette. I'd been walking and talking for over ninety minutes, and I had nothing to show for it but aching feet and a dry throat.

I was also hungry again, and I partially regretted having declined Mrs. Steinberg's lunch invitation. Judging by the sandwich she'd made me, I'd missed out on a good and filling meal.

There was a small café just a few doors up the street. I'd visited it earlier, and it looked good enough for a bite. But my lack of results made me choose to ignore my hunger pangs and carry on with my canvassing. I took a last drag and tossed what remained of the cigarette into the street.

I needed to start visiting apartments. There were so many more of them than businesses that I knew it would take me hours to visit them all. Still, it was something that needed doing, and thinking about how long and tedious it would be wouldn't make a difference.

I trudged up staircases and lumbered down them. I rang doorbells where there were some installed, and rapped on doors where there weren't. Some of my rings and knocks went unanswered while others resulted in opened doors and conversations of varied lengths.

I met people who'd moved to Pevzner Street after Volkoff disappeared, and spoke with them only as long as it took to establish this fact. There were also people who had been living there in the summer of 1939, and with them I talked a bit longer. Some of them remembered being interviewed by police at the time, and others were utterly free of such memories. Some expressed sadness that Volkoff had yet to be found. Others assumed an out-of-place, almost cheerful cast, and in an elevated, optimistic tone said baseless things like: "You'll probably find him soon," and "I'm sure he's perfectly all right." Some people don't like facing the grimness of life.

A fat stubby man, upon hearing my mission, expressed both surprise and bitterness. "After thirteen years? I wish the government or the army worked as hard to locate our missing soldiers. My cousin went missing fighting the Egyptians in the Negev. His body hasn't been found. His parents can't even give him a proper burial. Maybe the army should hire detectives like you to find him."

I agreed that it would be a good idea and moved on to the next apartment.

A thin woman, eager to help, started rattling off names of neighbors who'd lived on the street in 1939 but had since moved. "Maybe they'll remember something," she said. But when I asked her for current addresses, she spread her hands and said she had none. "I haven't kept in touch with any of them. What would we do, send each other letters? Who has time for that?" But maybe some of the other neighbors could give me the addresses.

I thanked her and headed up the stairs to the next floor and the next apartment.

Another woman, this one plump and in her sixties, after telling me she hadn't seen Volkoff the day he disappeared, asked me if any of the other people I spoke with remembered seeing him.

"No," I said. "None so far."

She asked how many people I'd spoken with, and was stunned to hear the answer.

"So many? No wonder you look so worn out. You must be about to fall off your feet." She invited me in and poured me a cool glass of water, which I gratefully gulped down. Then she offered me cookies that she'd baked herself that morning, and I ate three of them in quick succession and was about to grab a fourth when I stopped mid-reach and looked at her sheepishly. "I'm sorry. I'm gobbling your cookies like an animal."

She laughed. She had a kind face with motherly eyes, and her laugh was tinkly. "Go ahead, have some more. The more you eat, the less there'll be for me, which might not be a bad thing." She patted her ample stomach and winked.

"Okay," I said, grabbing three more before she could change her mind. "But now you owe me a favor."

She laughed again.

I had two more cookies, making eight total, and my stomach was feeling quite good about itself and had ceased rumbling.

"My, my, you were hungry."

"The only thing I had to eat since breakfast is a sandwich. Which, come to think of it, I got from another woman in Haifa I met for the first time today. Are all Haifa women this nice?"

"I'm afraid not. You should count yourself lucky to have stumbled upon two on the same day."

"I don't feel so lucky."

"Oh? The sandwich wasn't good?"

"It was excellent."

"And my cookies?"

"Even better, I assure you." I cast a glance toward the jar. "In fact, I wouldn't mind another one, a bit later."

She grinned, showing a gold tooth on the left side of her mouth. "Consider it yours, Adam. May I call you Adam?"

I told her she could, and she asked me to call her Ingrid.

She told me she had come to Haifa in 1927 and had moved into her current apartment in 1938.

"It was a different city back then, before the War of Independence. There were plenty of Arabs, most of them living in the lower neighborhoods, closer to the sea. But they fled during the war, after some intense fighting. The mayor begged them to stay, but most refused.

Do you think the man you're looking for—this Volkoff—do you think he might have been killed by an Arab?"

"Why would I think that?"

"It was a perilous time, 1939. The Arab revolt that started in '36 was winding down, but it was still dangerous here."

When is it not? I thought.

"I didn't dare go into the Arab neighborhoods back then," Ingrid said. "Certainly not by myself."

"This isn't an Arab neighborhood. Nor was it in 1939."

"Maybe Volkoff didn't really come here that day. Maybe he went down to one of the Arab streets and that was the end of him."

"There's no evidence to indicate that he went anywhere but here."

"Of course not. No Arab would have told on another. Not when the victim was Jewish. They hated us with a passion. Still do. Maybe even more today after we beat them in the war and established our country."

"I don't believe Volkoff was killed by an Arab," I said.

"But you do believe he visited this street on the day he disappeared?"

"Sounds like you don't."

"No one saw him, did they? None of my friends—I know because I talked with them about it at the time—and none of the people you spoke with today. What does that tell you?"

Nothing that I wanted to acknowledge. But that didn't make it untrue.

She must have read my feelings on my face. "I don't mean to discourage you, Adam. Maybe I should keep quiet."

"No, that's all right, Ingrid. I'm a big boy."

"It's just that I've been living here for a long time. I know this street. It was July. There would have been people outside. Children playing. He couldn't have walked on this street for a minute without being seen by half a dozen people at least."

An unexpected thought suddenly struck me, and I studied her with greater care than I'd done so far. Why was she trying so hard to convince me I was wasting my time? Was she aiming to get me to look elsewhere, and if so, why? Did she have something to do with Volkoff's disappearance? Was this why she'd been so hospitable to me?

She had gray hair that reached her shoulders and the sort of wrinkles a person gets when they smile a lot. Her eyes were brown, and in them I detected nothing but kindness and the shallow sort of worry you feel toward a stranger who somehow touched your heart.

"Where did you live before you came to Haifa?" I asked.

"Holland," she said, and I watched her closely as she said it. Her face was open and frank, no sign of deceit. "Why did you suddenly ask that?"

"No reason," I said, and smiled blandly. "I was just curious." Which was a lie. The reason I'd asked her about her former home was in order to know if she happened to come from Poland, had maybe known Volkoff and Feldbaum. With a name like Ingrid, it was possible though unlikely.

My gut told me she was being truthful. She was guilty of nothing but hospitality and an innate desire to be helpful, even when help was not requested. I let out a low breath. This case was getting to me; my lack of leads and mounting desperation were making me overly suspicious.

I asked, "Were any of your neighbors from Poland?"

"A few of them."

"From a town called Mastarnia?"

She shook her head. "I've never heard that name before. Is that where Volkoff came from?"

"Yes."

"I see you still believe he came here. It's funny, you believe it more than the officers who came to talk to me in 1939."

Maybe I was a bigger fool, then. For Ingrid had a point. It was a lively street. If Volkoff had truly come here the day he disappeared, why had no one seen him?

27

The police station was in a square building that had been built to last, not to please the eyes of passersby. It seemed to have done its job well, judging by the way its facade was pocked with bullet holes and shrapnel. Maybe there hadn't been money to fix it since the War of Independence ended. Or maybe someone with a devious mind decided to let the building keep its scars, to better put fear into those brought in for questioning.

Inside, it reeked of bad coffee, sweat, and fear—common odors of police stations worldwide.

I had not planned on coming here. When I'd set out for Haifa that morning, I thought I had all the information the police possessed, but now I wasn't sure anymore.

The police report made no mention of the letter Volkoff's family had sent him. Maybe other pieces of information had been omitted from it as well.

There was a line at the desk, and I had to wait a while until the gentleman ahead of me finished making a complaint about a break-in at his office. A little money was taken, and a big mess left for him to discover that morning. The desk cop promised they'd send someone around soon.

When it was my turn, I asked for David Goren, the Jewish officer who'd worked the Volkoff case in 1939. I didn't know what rank he was. He'd been a constable then, but maybe he'd been promoted since.

The guy at the desk narrowed a pair of dark eyes at me. "Goren? What you need him for?"

"I'm a private investigator from Tel Aviv. I'd like to talk to him about a case he worked."

"What case?"

I looked at him. Something was amiss. His tone was suspicious and belligerent, his face hard.

"It's a missing-person case. A guy called Menashe Volkoff disappeared in Haifa thirteen years ago. Goren worked the case with a British officer called Morrison."

The cop grunted. "I remember that son of a bitch. I used to wish the Irgun would kill him. But he made it all the way to May '48, when he and the rest of the Brits got on the ship that took them back to England. Good riddance."

"Yeah," I said. "Anyway, is Goren around?"

The cop shifted his jaw; then he shook his head. "You're out of luck, buddy. Or maybe I should say it's Goren who's the unlucky one. He got killed in '48, in the Battle of Haifa. An Arab shot him in the head, the son of a bitch."

I closed my eyes and took a deep breath. Another dead Jew. Another dead end.

The voice of the desk cop made me open my eyes. "It's funny, you know."

"What is?"

"You asking about Goren and that missing guy, Volkoff."

"What's funny about it?"

"It's just that you usually don't see anyone interested in a case that old. But you're the second guy who came here to ask about that case."

I stared at him. "Someone else was here to ask Goren about Volkoff? You sure?"

"Wouldn't have said so if I wasn't. It's not like people are coming to look for Goren in general, you know. The man's been dead four years now. And he was just a regular constable."

"Was the guy called Feldbaum?"

"I don't remember his name."

"When did he come here?"

The cop pursed his lips, shifting his head side to side as he worked things out in his head. "Ten months ago or so, maybe a bit more."

So it wasn't Feldbaum. Because Feldbaum hadn't been in Israel that long ago. It was someone else. Someone who'd been seeking Volkoff out, had learned of his disappearance, and had come here to talk to Constable Goren in the hopes of learning more.

And he had done so for a reason. What that reason was, I couldn't say, but I had a feeling it was the same reason Feldbaum had been eager to find Volkoff. Because Volkoff had information both Feldbaum and the mystery man wanted. Volkoff knew where *it* was.

"Was the man's name Yosef Rudinsky, by any chance?" I asked the desk cop.

"I told you, I don't remember the guy's name," he said, and I could feel another dead end forming, a brick wall blocking off another lead, but then he added, "But maybe Sergeant Karni knows."

"Who's Sergeant Karni?" I asked.

Karni turned out to be the sergeant the mystery man had talked to when he'd come looking for Goren. A stocky little man with a wide square face, a head of tight brown curls, and short, thick arms.

"Me and Goren joined the force together," he told me. "Grew up on the same street here in Haifa, three buildings from one another. So I knew him well. He was a great guy."

"I'm sure he was. I heard he died in the war."

"Yeah. Last day of the fighting here. Right before the Hagannah took complete control of the city. Bad luck. But I guess that's the difference between dying in a war and surviving one."

I agreed that was the nature of things, and we were both silent for a moment, replaying bloody scenes in our heads. We were sitting in an office with four desks, but only his was occupied. He had a cigarette going, and a glass on his table with the muddy remnants of cheap coffee. He took a drag, blew out smoke, and said, "I gotta wonder why two guys come here asking questions about a thirteen-year-old case."

"I would wonder too, in your place."

"Maybe you can satisfy my curiosity."

"I can as far as I'm concerned. I don't know anything about the other guy. What was his name, by the way?"

Karni gave a little smile. "Why don't you tell me your interest first?"

I nodded. So it wasn't going to be that easy. I would have to give something in order to get something in return. A little information, and perhaps something more besides.

"I'm investigating a murder that happened in Tel Aviv. The victim's name is Emmanuel Feldbaum. Does it ring a bell?"

Karni shook his head. "When did this happen? Why are you on it and not the police in Tel Aviv?"

I explained the situation. He had some questions, and I answered them with a level of truthfulness that fell far short of the one required in a courtroom. I did not tell him about my prior connection with Feldbaum or how someone had tried to murder me with a brick. I also didn't tell him I was working for free and did my best to act as though the case held no personal importance to me whatsoever. I wanted him to think my interest was solely monetary. Anything else would make him suspicious of not only my motives, but of me in general.

"At first," I said, "I was mainly going through the motions, thinking the cops had it right, that it was a robbery that escalated to murder. But then I learned that Menashe Volkoff had disappeared without a trace, and it got me curious."

"I understand. But I don't see a connection between whatever happened to Volkoff and Feldbaum's murder. For one thing, thirteen years separate the two events. For another, one happened in Tel Aviv, the other here in Haifa. You have any indication that Feldbaum ever visited here?"

"The ship that brought him to Israel docked in Haifa."

"And there it would have been met by immigration officials, right on the docks, who would have taken Feldbaum straight to the *ma'abara* in Afula. That's how it works. I know because I've been there on duty more times than I like to think about. If he had family here or someone willing to house him, it would have been different. But he didn't, you say."

"Not at first, no. Not until he came to Tel Aviv and ran into my client."

"So effectively, Feldbaum was never in Haifa. Apart from the docks. And Volkoff was never in Tel Aviv. He arrived in Haifa and never left the city. So if they were targeted by the same killer, how did the killer know about both Volkoff and Feldbaum?"

"Volkoff might have gone to Tel Aviv on the day he disappeared," I said.

"But you said you believe otherwise. You told me you believe that old woman who said she saw him on the bus here in Haifa. And no one saw him in Tel Aviv or on the way there. Whether he took the bus or the train, it's a long journey. Someone would have remembered him."

What Karni said wasn't certain, but I had to admit it made sense.

"But both of them were murdered," I said, not ready to surrender the argument.

"Maybe. Even probably. But it's not one hundred percent. There's a chance Volkoff is alive and well somewhere, that he had personal reasons to disappear. It's a slim chance, I grant you, after thirteen years with no sightings, but so is the chance that two murders thirteen years apart in two different cities, with no apparent connection between the victims, are related."

"But there is a connection between them. They both came from the same town."

"But how would the killer have known that? Known about them both? That's the connection that's missing, Adam. That's the way I see it as a cop."

"I see what you mean," I said reluctantly. "I used to be a cop myself."

"Really?"

"In Hungary. I was a cop in Hungary before the Second World War."

"I never met anyone who was a cop in another country. Well, apart from the British bastards who used to lord over us. I meant I never met a Jewish one."

"There weren't many of us," I said, thinking that if there had been any Jewish cops in other European countries, they were most likely dead.

"As a former cop, you must know I'm right. But maybe you see things differently as a private detective, eh?" Karni said, and there was more than a hint of slyness in his voice. He was intimating that because I was paid for working the case, maybe by the day or week, it was in my interest to stretch out my investigation by making connections that weren't there.

You son of a bitch, I thought, and was about to put it into words, but I managed to corral the impulse. Karni still had information I wanted; I needed to stay on his good side.

I smiled, as though sharing a private joke. "I'm more than happy to share, Sergeant."

He said nothing when I pulled out my wallet, and remained silent when I took out three lira notes and slid them across the table toward him. I lifted my hand from the bills, and his hand descended upon them instead, and then he pulled them toward him and stuck them in his pocket without comment.

"What was the name of the man who asked about Menashe Volkoff?" I asked, figuring that my end of the bargain had been completed, and now it was Karni's turn.

"Shimon Suskind."

So it wasn't Yosef Rudinsky after all. I had yet to pick up his scent. "You seem very sure."

"I have a good memory for names."

"So you'll know whether Suskind mentioned Emmanuel Feldbaum."

"He didn't."

"What about Yosef Rudinsky?"

"No. Who's he?"

"Another guy Feldbaum wanted to find."

"Suskind didn't say one word about him."

"What did he talk about?"

"Volkoff. He wanted to know what had happened to him. He wanted to talk to the investigating officer, which was Goren. But Goren was dead, so he talked to me instead. And, as you know, I had basically nothing to tell him."

"How did he take it?"

"I can't really say. He had one of those faces that didn't show much. But I could tell it got him thinking."

"Thinking?"

"Yeah. I could see it in his eyes. You've taken part in interrogations, you know what I mean: when a guy's mind is racing, but he's trying to pretend he's indifferent, you can often tell by the way his eyes shift about."

"Any idea what he was thinking about?"

Karni's answer was a shrug and a spread of his hands.

"What did he care about Volkoff?" I asked.

"Said he knew him. From back in Europe."

"He came from the same town? From Mastarnia?"

"He didn't tell me where he came from. Just said he knew Volkoff."

"They were friends?"

"Could be. Or maybe just acquaintances. Like I told you, Suskind wasn't easy to read."

And you didn't bother asking, I thought.

"What did he ask about Volkoff?"

"Not much. He wanted to know what we knew."

"He didn't go to the boardinghouse where Volkoff had stayed."

"Oh? You've been there, I take it?"

"Earlier today."

"You wasted your time, then, didn't you? As the investigation report says, no one who was there at the time knows anything about Volkoff's disappearance."

The report didn't mention the letter that came from Volkoff's father, I thought, but maybe that didn't change the overall picture. Because if there had been anything in it to shed light on Volkoff's vanishing, I didn't spot it.

Karni said, "I guess Suskind didn't see the point in going there after I showed him the report."

"You let him see it?"

"Some of it. His Hebrew wasn't perfect, so I had to read parts of it to him. I skipped most of it, just told him enough so he'd have a general idea of where things stood. He was a civilian, and he wasn't family, so I really shouldn't have shown him any of it. But he insisted, and I could tell he wouldn't give up easily, so I fed him enough so he'd go away without complaining."

Enough so he wouldn't think it worth his while to visit the boardinghouse, apparently. Which was a shame because Suskind might have seen something in that letter that I did not. Too bad Suskind wasn't a detective, or he wouldn't have skipped the boardinghouse no matter what Karni had told him.

But maybe it wasn't really an oversight. Maybe there was a different reason why Suskind didn't bother.

"Did Suskind think Volkoff was alive?" I asked.

"Why would he think that, after thirteen years?"

"You said yourself there's a chance Volkoff isn't dead."

"That doesn't mean I believe that's the case," Karni said. "Sure I think he's dead, just like you do, like everyone else would. All of a sudden you think different?"

"I'm just wondering what Suskind thought."

"I didn't think to ask him. Would you have?"

Probably not. But now I would have loved to.

"Ever hear from him again?"

"Suskind?" Karni shook his head. "Never."

"Did he leave an address or a number for you to contact him in case anything new turned up?"

"No. But why would he expect that? The case is as dead as Volkoff, probably."

"Did Suskind think that?"

"He'd be a fool to think otherwise, wouldn't he?"

"Did he seem despondent or sad when he left?"

Karni didn't answer straight away. For a couple of minutes now, I'd had the distinct feeling that he was getting tired of me, that his answers were thrown out automatically and with dwindling patience. But now he looked thoughtful.

"No. I don't think he was sad at all," he said at length. "At least, no more than he'd been when he got here."

"But something else was different about him?"

"Yeah. He seemed... determined. Yes, that's the word. Determined. And angry as well. Like I said, he didn't show much during most of our talk, and by the end of it, I just wanted him gone. But now that I think about it, that's how he looked."

"Angry at whom?"

"Whoever killed Volkoff, I guess."

"Or at Volkoff himself," I said.

"Huh?"

"Maybe he thought Volkoff was alive and hiding somewhere. Maybe Volkoff had something he wanted. Maybe he was determined to get it back."

28

I thought of asking Karni to search police records for any mention of Shimon Suskind, but I knew my three liras had bought all they were going to. Karni wouldn't lift a finger to help a private investigator dig into a cold case that had no tangible new leads. But that was all right. Reuben would do it for me.

I called him from a café near the central bus station. I gave him Suskind's name and asked him to see what he could find.

"All right, Adam. By the way, Shoshana loved her presents."

"I'm glad to hear that."

"And she was also quite taken by Hannah. As was Gila."

"I'm glad to hear that as well."

"Are you likely to be seeing her again?"

"Shoshana or Gila?"

Reuben sighed. "I meant neither of them, Adam, as you very well know."

"Are you asking for Gila?"

"How did you guess?"

"Women tend to be more curious about such things than men."

"Should I be worried that I find myself a bit curious as well?"

I smiled. "No. I don't think there's any cause for alarm. Tell Gila that I'll indeed be seeing Hannah again, but that this will be my last report until further notice."

"I'll pass on the word. Have a safe trip back to Tel Aviv."

I had a soda and a sandwich at the café, and while I nursed the first and nibbled the second, I wrote down in my notebook all that I'd learned from Sergeant Karni, including the description of Shimon Suskind that his sharp memory had furnished. Two minutes after I'd finished my summary, I boarded the bus to Tel Aviv. On the way, I pondered the things I'd learned on my trip to Haifa.

There was the letter that Volkoff had received from his father back in 1939, the one Mrs. Steinberg had held onto for all these years. I'd had high hopes for it, but if the contents held any clues, I was blind to them.

But the letter had proved useful nonetheless. Without it, I would not have gone to the police station in search of other potential items that might have been missing from the police report of the Volkoff case. I would not have spoken to Sergeant Karni. I would not have learned of the existence of Shimon Suskind. I would have been three liras richer, but a lot poorer in information.

Suskind was still an enigma. I knew next to nothing about him. I did not know his exact age, where he was born, or how he came to know Menashe Volkoff. Most importantly, I had no idea why he had sought Volkoff out.

It was possible he had been a close friend of Volkoff's, but I did not think so. A friend would have gone to the boardinghouse; not to glean information that potentially could lead to discovering Volkoff's whereabouts, but for purely emotional reasons: to know as much as he could about Volkoff's final days.

So Suskind's interest was different. But what it was, I could not say. Perhaps when I found him—if I found him—I would know.

Back at the police station, I had raised the possibility that Suskind had been mad at Volkoff, that he'd thought Volkoff had done a vanishing act. If this was true, and if Feldbaum's murder was not random, then Volkoff was now a suspect. Because Feldbaum had been looking for him, and Volkoff might have viewed that as a threat.

Here's how it might have been:

Volkoff left Mastarnia early in the summer of 1939. He arrived in the Land of Israel and promptly vanished off the face of the earth.

Volkoff had something. The mysterious *it* Feldbaum had muttered about, the thing that only Volkoff knew its location. It had to be valuable. A large sum of money or some other treasure.

And it didn't belong solely to Volkoff. Perhaps making off with it was the real reason Volkoff had made *aliyah*.

So Volkoff got to Haifa, spent a couple of nights at the boarding-house, just enough to make it seem like he was a regular immigrant finding his feet in a new land, and then decided it was high time to disappear. His motive: to keep everything to himself. To not have to share when people who knew him and what he possessed came searching for him, for *it*.

And the letter he sent?

A ruse. A trick. A way to add verisimilitude to his disappearance. To allay any suspicion that might arise that he had staged the whole business.

If so, then Volkoff was a cold bastard. For he had not only attempted to fool Suskind and Feldbaum, and whoever else knew what he had in his possession, he had also deceived his father and the rest of his family.

When he'd made his plans, he would have known how they would feel when no second letter came from him. How at first they would be worried, then scared, and finally overcome by grief when news of his disappearance made it to them. But he didn't care.

As it turned out, they were spared that ordeal because they became victims of a much harsher one. Before they could begin to worry about Volkoff, the Germans had invaded Poland, their world was shattered, and they found themselves in a struggle for survival—a struggle they lost.

How did Volkoff feel when news of the Holocaust made it to wherever he had hidden himself? Did his conscience clench in pain and guilt? Or did he feel relief that he was in the clear, that the people who knew his secret were now dead?

Only some of them weren't.

Shimon Suskind, for one; Emmanuel Feldbaum, for another.

Feldbaum, with his damaged mind, could not hold onto that knowledge fully. It kept slipping away. But Suskind was another matter.

That would explain his anger and determination. He would have been angry at Volkoff for disappearing. He would have been determined to find him.

All this depended on Volkoff being a culprit rather than a victim. On him being alive rather than dead.

I had gone to Haifa to find answers. But all I got were more questions.

29

The next day was Friday. A little before noon, I headed to Mr. Soffer's store.

He was there with a client. The client was pointing at a high shelf. Soffer looked even more doleful than the first time I saw him, and his forehead was shiny with perspiration. His assistant, Oded, was not present.

Soffer noticed me and smiled. "Just in time, Mr. Lapid. Could you do me a favor? Mrs. Cohen wants that book up there. I can't reach it. But with your height, you probably could."

I couldn't. The shelf was near the ceiling. I had to use a stepladder. I handed the book to Soffer. He thanked me, put the book and a large pile of other items in a bag, rang up the sale, and handed the bag to Mrs. Cohen.

When she had gone, he mopped his forehead with a handkerchief and said, "I shouldn't complain, but she had me running all over the store and into the storeroom as well. And in this heat!" It was indeed warm, but not unseasonably so. Soffer would cool down plenty if he shaved his beard and mustache, but naturally, I didn't tell him so. Given his faith, it might offend him.

Soffer folded his handkerchief and put it back in his pocket. He laced his fingers atop the counter and asked how I was doing.

"I'm fine, thank you. And yourself?"

He made a little motion with his thin shoulders that seemed to signify a weary acceptance of a cruel and unjust world. "As well as can be expected."

Which obviously wasn't much. I wondered what had caused him to develop his overall morose manner—a series of sunken hopes and failed endeavors, no doubt—but did not ask. I had other tragedies on my mind.

"I have another question for you."

"I hope I have the answer."

"I was wondering if, when you were interviewing Feldbaum, he mentioned the name Shimon Suskind."

Soffer narrowed his eyes in contemplation, running his fingers through his unruly beard. He shook his head. "No, I'm pretty sure he didn't. I'm positive I never heard the name before just now. Who's he?"

"Someone who came up in my investigation."

"You're making progress, then? Good. That's very good."

"Some," I allowed. I couldn't say I was disappointed that Feldbaum hadn't mentioned Suskind to Soffer. I'd assumed as much. Still, I'd needed to make sure.

"I'm sorry I couldn't be of more help," he told me.

"That's okay," I said. "I'll find out who and where he is."

"You sound very confident."

"That's because I am," I said, and I meant it. Suskind wasn't the only one who could be determined. From the beginning, I had been eager to solve Feldbaum's murder, but that initial desire had strengthened many times over when I'd learned of Volkoff's disappearance. Whether the disappearance was genuine or fake, I now knew that what I was facing was graver than a single murder, regardless of how grisly. It was something far more sinister and evil. Something rotten that had begun in pre-WWII Poland but that had since spread its poisonous tentacles to Israel. "I don't know how long it will take me, but I am going to get to the bottom of this case."

30

Ami Rapoport was fixing a chair outside his shack. When he saw me approach, he stole a quick glance over his shoulder in the direction of the door. His wife was home, then.

"I heard there was a little trouble with Boris the other day," he said.

Maybe not so little, I thought. *Not if he was the guy who dropped the brick on me.*

"I understand he didn't like Emmanuel. That Emmanuel humiliated him in a show of strength at work. Why didn't you tell me about it?"

"I didn't think it was that big a deal."

"I don't think that's how Boris saw it."

"But that's not a reason to kill someone, surely."

"From what I understand, Boris has a short fuse."

Rapoport rubbed his jaw. "Yeah, he can get angry quick."

"And he's not averse to using his fists, to hurting people."

"I never saw him do that."

"Someone who worked with him in a former outfit told me about it. And he's also very loyal to Caspi."

"Why does that matter?"

"Did you know it was Caspi who made Berman fire Emmanuel?"

His eyebrows shot up. "Did Berman tell you that?"

"No. He covered up for the big boss. One of your co-workers told me. Caspi didn't like having Emmanuel around because of how he acted, the way his mind was damaged."

"That's the first I've heard of it."

"And Caspi didn't like my sniffing around. I think he's hiding something, but I don't know what."

"You don't think Mr. Caspi had—"

"I don't know, Ami. Did he talk to you about me? Try to find out if you're my client?"

"No. But I think he knows. Or at least suspects. The day you two talked, he kept giving me these looks." He exhaled hard, looked at the door to his shack, and started wringing his hands. In a voice not much louder than a whisper, he said, "What if he decides to fire me, Adam? I can't lose my job. Not with the baby coming."

"I don't think he'll do that," I said. "He's hiding something, I tell you, and he knows I'm digging around. He wouldn't want to make me even more suspicious of him."

Rapoport licked his lips. "I hope you're right."

"Just keep doing your job, and it will be okay. Maybe Caspi had nothing to do with it. Besides, there's a chance I'll have some answers soon. I've been doing some work, learned a few things."

He studied my face. "I get the sense that they're not good."

"You could say that. I found Menashe Volkoff. Or, more accurately, I picked up his trail."

"Really? He's here? In Israel?"

"Yeah. Probably," I said, and went on to explain what I'd learned about Volkoff—his arrival in Haifa and his subsequent disappearance.

His face darkened. "What does it mean, Adam?"

"I don't know."

"What do you think happened to Volkoff?"

"Either he was murdered too, or he faked his disappearance."

"But why?"

"I don't know that either, regardless of whether Volkoff is dead or alive somewhere. But that's not why I'm here, Ami. I'm going to tell you two names, and I need you to think long and hard whether Emmanuel ever mentioned them. The first is Yosef Rudinsky. The second is Shimon Suskind."

"No," he said after a moment. "He never talked about either of them. At least not to me."

"You think Batya might have a different answer?"

He winced at the mention of her name, started shaking his head, but the creak of the door stopped him. In the doorway stood his bloated, surly wife, shooting poisoned darts at the pair of us through her slitted eyes.

"I thought I heard voices," she said. And to her husband: "If you're done with the chair, Ami, I need you to go to the store. Mrs. Raskin said she was going to get some sugar today and promised to hold some for me."

The chair wasn't done, as Batya could plainly see by the fact that one of its legs had yet to be attached. Rapoport hesitated, looking from his wife to me and back again. "Go on," she said. "And you can leave too, Mr. Lapid."

"I have some questions for you, Mrs. Rapoport."

"I thought I made it clear I did not wish to speak with you again."

"It's important."

I could see Rapoport growing tense. Batya saw it too. Perhaps that changed her mind. Or maybe it was the fear of missing out on the promised sugar.

"All right. Come in. But only for a few minutes." And to her husband: "Don't dawdle, Ami. Or do you prefer sugarless tea? Because I sure don't."

I gave Rapoport a reassuring nod, and he hurried away with what seemed like a mixture of reluctance and relief. I followed Batya inside, where she lowered herself heavily onto the armchair.

"I'm very tired, Mr. Lapid. So be quick with your questions and leave."

"All right. First, I want to know why you didn't tell your husband about Hannah Goldman."

"Because she's a loose, immoral woman, and I don't want my husband anywhere near her."

"Why would he go near her?"

"Because she used to meet with Emmanuel. I don't know what they did together. Some of the other women think that they were sleeping together, but I can't imagine any woman wanting him. But then again, this is Hannah Goldman we're talking about, so I guess nothing is beyond the pale."

"So you thought... what? That Ami, wanting to know more about Emmanuel, would go see her and she'd seduce him?"

"I'd put nothing past that woman."

My voice turned hard. "You can inform your friends that nothing like what they imagine happened between Hannah and Emmanuel. They just talked."

Her lips spread into a sneer. "Is that all you and Hannah do as well? Talk?"

I could feel my cheeks heating up. With embarrassment, sure, but also with fury. "You know the answer already. I'm sure Zelda was quick to tell you everything."

"She did. And you're a damn fool for getting involved with that woman. But that's what she does with men. She turns their brains to mush."

"You don't know anything about her."

Her sneer widened. "I know her better than you do. Any other questions?"

"Yes. Did Emmanuel ever talk about a Yosef Rudinsky or a Shimon Suskind?"

"He jabbered about so many people; how can I remember?"

"Think. Try to recall. Just do that, and I'll be out of your hair."

She sighed. "What were the names again?"

"Shimon Suskind and Yosef Rudinsky."

It didn't take her more than a second to answer in the negative.

"But like I said, with all his mumbling and muttering, he could have talked about David Ben-Gurion, and I wouldn't have noticed."

"Too bad he didn't talk about money. I bet you would have noticed then."

She barked out a laugh. "Money? Emmanuel? He didn't have a lira and had no way of getting any, the lazy lunatic."

"That's where you're wrong, Batya," I said, leaning a bit forward and giving her a smile. "Somewhere in his muddled brain, Emmanuel held knowledge of something very valuable. Something that came from his hometown in Poland. Money, or something that's worth a great deal of it. That's why he was looking for Menashe Volkoff, because Volkoff had it or knew where it was. I don't know what it is yet, but I'm going to find out. If you'd paid more attention, if you'd listened to Emmanuel a little more closely, you might have heard him talk about it in one of his ramblings. You might have been able to find it. And, being who he was and how little he needed, he probably would have given you all or most of it."

Her expression had developed an almost frozen quality. Nothing moved apart from a small muscle at the side of her jaw that kept twitching. For the first time, her eyes lost their narrowness. She looked shell-shocked.

"It probably would have been enough for an apartment," I said. "Hell, it might have been enough for a house with a garden." I did not know this, of course, but I wanted to jab this wicked woman where it would hurt her most.

"You're lying," she said, her voice quavering.

I shook my head. "No. No, I'm not. All you needed to do was open your ears a little. But for that you would have needed to open your heart a little, too. And I'm not sure you're capable of that. It was your big chance, and you blew it, Batya. You blew it."

Her face tightened all over, like a clenched fist about to be rammed into someone's mouth. She didn't hit me, but she did the next best thing. She grabbed a cup that was standing on a small end table by her armchair and hurled it at my head. I ducked, and it flew past my ear, spraying me with cold droplets of something before smashing into pieces against the wall.

"Get out!" she screamed. "Get out of here! And next time you show your face around here, I won't miss. You understand me, damn you? Next time I'll get you right in the head."

31

I thought about dropping by Hannah's shack, to ask her about Shimon Suskind, but I figured it could wait. I was going to see her tomorrow anyway. It was close enough.

Instead, I went to Greta's Café. I needed some idle time, and I craved a cup of her excellent coffee.

The place was buzzing, so Greta poured me a cup, gave me a smile, and left me to myself. I got my chessboard from behind the counter, set up the pieces, and played for a while, letting my mind drift about without thinking much of anything.

After a while, the place emptied a bit, and Greta came over and sat at my table.

"Okay, spill," she said.

"The coffee?"

"No. Not the coffee, Adam. You know what I want to hear about."

"Why is everyone so interested in my private life all of a sudden?"

"I'm not the only one?"

"Not hardly. Reuben and Gila, the parents of the birthday girl, were fishing for information earlier."

"That must mean they liked this Hannah Goldman."

"That's the impression I got."

"That's good, isn't it?"

"I suppose so."

"So why the long face?"

"It's just that I can't help but wonder why everyone seems so keen to know about my first date with a woman."

"Can't the people who care about you be curious?"

"Is that all it is? Just idle curiosity? Or is there more to all the questions, the need to know?"

She didn't answer. Just stared at me with her warm eyes. Her fleshy, wrinkled face was not easy to read, but I thought I detected a trace of sadness in it. Someone called to her from another table, and, without moving her eyes from mine, she called back, "In a minute, Yoram." But still she did not reply to me.

"Are you worried about me, Greta?" I asked after a few more seconds of silence.

Her lips gave a tiny twitch, she took a deep breath, and her large shoulders rose a bit and then fell back into place.

"Why? I'm all right," I said.

"I know. I know." But doubt rang deep in her voice, like the faint echo of a distant tolling church bell.

"You don't sound too sure about it."

"Oh, I know you're tough and strong and determined. I know you can handle great adversity and land on your feet. I've known you to take on great challenges and overcome them, face difficult mysteries and solve them; I've even seen you injured badly and recover fully—"

"With your help," I said.

She waved a hand. "But I don't think I've ever seen you truly happy. Not in all the years since you first walked in the door of my café."

I was struck dumb by surprise. Happy? The word seemed alien, an indecipherable sound in my ear. A new term I had to survey from multiple angles, to weigh in my mind, in order to perhaps achieve true insight as to its meaning.

Happy. I knew what the word meant. I could define it as well as any dictionary. I could explain it to a child. But still it felt foreign. Like a faded photograph of some ancient event. Known yet unfamiliar.

When was the last time I felt happy? Truly happy, as Greta had put it. I cast my mind back in search of that moment. Was it in November 1947 when the United Nations adopted the partition plan that called for the establishment of a Jewish state? Other Jews danced in the streets that night, overcome by joy. But I did not dance, nor did my mood match theirs. I knew that war was coming, and that I would take part in it.

Prior to that, perhaps?

How about the moment American troops liberated us from Buchenwald, or a short while later when Nazi Germany surrendered to the Allies? No. Neither of those moments brought true happiness. There was relief, yes, satisfaction at the fall of an enemy, but not happiness. Because for me the war had not ended. In some ways, it had just begun. I had Nazis to hunt down and kill.

Earlier still?

Before my time in Auschwitz, for certain, before I lost my wife and daughters. And before the Germans invaded Hungary. And earlier than that, before the Second World War started, before Hungary enacted anti-Jewish laws and I was thrown off the police force. When I was still Hungarian and not, in essence if not formally, a stateless Jew.

But that had been in 1938. Fourteen years before. Those years stretched like a black ocean of time so large that there was nothing on the horizon but more darkness.

But I'd had a life before then. Before those long, dark years. Like a man digging for treasure in a lightless tunnel, I began dredging my distant memory for a truly happy moment.

It was like digging through sticky sludge, through gooey mud. It took an effort to hack through the bad times, to reach back to what now felt like another life, a life that belonged to a man who bore my name and likeness, with whom I shared a birthday and parents, but who felt like another man entirely, not the same man as I.

And then I saw it. A faraway memory, glittering like a diamond. I reached for it, and it expanded and grew clearer. An image spread out in all its colorful glory in my mind.

We were all together. My wife, my daughters, and I. We were sitting at the table, plates and cups before us in homey disarray.

My elder daughter, a spoon held in her tiny hand, food smeared across her face and on the napkin my wife had tied around her neck, was singing a children's song. Her high-pitched, trilling voice rang out across the room. She sang wildly off-key, and every third word or so was mispronounced, and some of the mispronunciations changed the words to others, some with a meaning far beyond her years. It was hilarious, and what made it more so was her earnestness. She sang as seriously as a professional performer.

My wife and I exchanged looks, barely able to hold our laughter in check. We both joined in for the final chorus, all of us singing together. When the song was over, I doubled over in laughter. On the other side of the table, my wife did the same. When I straightened, I saw her eyes glistening with joy, and I felt mine were wet for the same reason.

True happiness.

"Are you okay, Adam?" Greta's voice seemed to come from very far away.

I blinked, slightly dazed. "What?"

"Are you all right? You have tears in your eyes."

So I did. I hadn't felt them until she called my attention to them. But now they stung like a dreadful loss. I dried my eyes with my hands and nodded. "Yes, Greta. I'm fine. Don't worry about it."

"You were mumbling something."

"I was?"

"It was a song, I think. I couldn't understand the words."

The song. The children's song. The last chorus. That was what I'd mumbled. I hadn't noticed while I was doing so.

"It's a Hungarian children's song. I just remembered how my daughter sang it once, a long time ago."

Greta said nothing, just laid a hand on mine. Her fingers were warm. Yoram called to her again, and again she told him to wait. I clenched my teeth and ordered away the tears that threatened once more to invade my eyes.

"I just want you to be happy," Greta said. "Truly happy. It's no sin, you know."

Wasn't it? If I became, as Greta put it, truly happy, what would that say about all those I had lost? Wasn't it an abandonment?

"You are alive, Adam," Greta said, as though reading my mind. "You are alive, and you're entitled to live your life fully. To enjoy it fully. Do you see that?"

I didn't answer, and she gave my hand a squeeze. "Adam, do you understand what I'm telling you?"

I looked at her, knowing what she wanted to hear, and decided to say it. Partly for her sake, and largely to spare myself more of this conversation. "Yes. Yes, I understand, Greta."

She said nothing. Just probed my face. By her expression, I could tell that she did not believe me. Yoram called to her again, impatiently. Greta gave my hand a final squeeze and rose to her feet.

"Just think about it, Adam. Just give yourself a chance." And with that she was gone from the table, leaving me alone with my thoughts.

32

A little later, I went to Rothschild Boulevard. I was going to buy some butter from a diminutive mother of five who seemed to have an endless supply of the stuff. I was walking past the window of a café when I saw him.

Benjamin Caspi, sitting at a corner table with a sixty-something man who looked familiar but whose name eluded me. When he turned his face so I could see him fully, I recognized him. It was Peretz Bernstein, leader of the General Zionists, head of the opposition in the Knesset.

I knew that Caspi was meant for greatness in the General Zionists, and here he was, deep in conversation with the party's head guy.

Apparently, I was spying on the end of their little chat because a minute later Bernstein and Caspi both rose with smiles on their faces and shook hands. Bernstein turned toward the exit. Caspi sat back down with a satisfied look on his face, sipped from his cup, and signaled the waiter for a refill.

By the time Bernstein had exited the café, and I had walked inside, Caspi was engrossed in a newspaper. He didn't notice me until I sat down in the chair Bernstein had vacated.

"Nice to see you again, Mr. Caspi."

His surprise quickly morphed to anger. He folded the newspaper messily and thumped it on the table.

"What the hell are you doing here?"

"I was just passing by when I saw you through the window. I thought it would be a good time to continue our talk from the other day."

"There's nothing to continue." His upper lip had acquired a disdainful curl. "Now go away."

"I saw you with Peretz Bernstein. That's impressive. I guess the rumors are true: you're headed for the Knesset next elections."

"You're rude, did anyone ever tell you that? First, you sit at my table without asking. Then, you stick around even after I told you to leave. You're starting to get on my nerves, Mr. Lapid."

"Really? I wouldn't want that. From what I hear, making you angry can be risky."

His cheeks became suffused with blood and his jaw clenched. He leaned forward and was about to let me have it, when the waiter approached with a coffee pot.

"Shall I pour, sir?"

Caspi leaned back and nodded curtly. The waiter filled his cup.

"Shall I bring another cup?" the waiter asked.

Caspi opened his mouth to answer, but I beat him to it.

"Yes. Thank you," I said, flashing the waiter a smile. From the corner of my eye, I could see Caspi's mouth shifting as he ground his teeth.

When the waiter went away, Caspi hissed at me, "I told you to leave, didn't I? So leave! Get lost!"

I wagged a finger at him. "Is that any way for a politician to talk to a citizen? Don't you want my vote?"

"I don't want anything to do with you," he said in a low, grating voice. He made his body relax as the waiter came over with a cup for me and filled it. He was breathing heavily through his nose, keeping a lid on his fury but just barely. If he wanted to kill someone, would he choose to drop a brick on his head? His face was free of scratches, but his arms might have had some. He was wearing a jacket, so I couldn't tell. And the man who'd thrown the brick might have managed to climb down the tree by my building without being marked.

I took a slow sip of the coffee, keeping my eyes on his face.

"I heard it was you who decided to fire Emmanuel Feldbaum." And when his eyes flashed, I added, "I know what you're thinking, but it wasn't Berman. He wouldn't tell on you; he lied to keep you out of it. One of your other workers overheard you telling Berman to fire Emmanuel."

"Who?"

I ignored his question. "Which made me wonder why you'd want to keep this a secret? It's not like you didn't have legitimate cause to fire Emmanuel. He was unstable, unreliable. And besides, it's your company; you can do whatever you want."

"I don't fire workers at Feldbaum's level. That's one of the reasons I have Berman."

"Don't want any unpleasantness, eh? Do you usually get other people to do your dirty work for you?"

"Are you suggesting something, Mr. Lapid?"

"I just might be, Mr. Caspi. Want to guess what it is?"

There was a dangerous look in his eyes now. If we hadn't been in a public place, I'm not sure what he would have done.

But angry as he was, he was not without control. He wasn't the sort to burst out in violent rage. He could bide his time. He could plan things.

"I did not kill Emmanuel Feldbaum," he said.

"Did I say you did?"

"Nor did I have him killed by proxy."

"If you say so."

"I had nothing to do with it, I'm telling you. Why can't you understand that?"

"What I understand is that you didn't like my asking questions about Emmanuel."

"I told my men they could talk to you, didn't I?"

"You don't own your workers, Mr. Caspi. You don't get to tell them whom they can talk to after hours. Or are you used to your workers doing your bidding beyond their regular work duties?"

"What are you saying now? You think I had one of my workers kill Feldbaum? I run a construction business, not a crime outfit. Can't you get it through your thick head? I had nothing to do with Feldbaum's murder."

"So why didn't you like my poking around?"

"Like I said, I run a business. I want my workers to be focused on their work. I need them to think about bricks and mortar and plaster, not about one of their colleagues getting his skull bashed in."

I didn't believe him. I took another drink of coffee, set my cup back on its saucer, and rotated it a quarter circle.

"Mr. Caspi, if you're going to become a politician, you'll have to learn to lie more convincingly."

Now there was fire in his eyes. "You lay off me, you hear? I don't have to talk to you. You're not the police."

"No, I'm not. And I notice you haven't threatened to file a complaint with them against me. You don't want them nosing around any more than you want me to do it."

"I don't need the police to handle you."

"Oh? You've got another idea?"

He smiled without parting his lips. Some of the tension drained from his body, but his dislike for me hadn't dimmed one bit.

"How much is Ami Rapoport paying you to work this case?"

"My client isn't Ami Rapoport."

He snorted. "You're the one who needs to work on your lying skills. Whatever it is, it can't be much. I know where Rapoport lives. He doesn't have much."

"Do you know where all your workers live?"

He looked taken aback by the question. "Why? What does it matter?"

"It's just that whoever killed Feldbaum must have known about his habit of taking long nighttime walks. And for that, he would need to know where he lived. And he lived with Rapoport."

His mouth tightened with exasperation. "Are you still on about that? I've already told you I did not kill Feldbaum. I'm trying to talk to you about something else."

"All right. What?"

He drew a breath and let it out slowly and evenly. There was a feral sort of intelligence in his eyes. I could tell what was coming, and he didn't disappoint me.

"Like I said, Rapoport can't be paying you much. But I can. What will it take for me to hire you?"

"Hire me to do what?"

"To quit badgering me. To quit this case. It's not like you're making progress if you keep on harassing me with your stupid questions."

"You want to buy me off? How much?"

He smiled, and his shoulders loosened. I was speaking his language now. "How does three hundred liras sound?"

"Not as good as five would."

"Okay, five. But I don't carry that much on me. We can go to the bank right now and I'll give it to you."

I downed what remained of my coffee, but I didn't rise. After putting the empty cup back on its saucer, I gave him a steady look and slowly shook my head.

His eyebrows shot up and his lips parted. "You said five. You said it. Now you want more? Well, five is plenty. Five is all you're going to get. Five hundred, not a lira more, you understand? Now, do we have a deal or not?"

I allowed a moment to pass before answering, then said, "No. No deal."

He let out a sigh. "Be reasonable, Mr. Lapid. It's more than you make in six months, I bet."

"Oh, it's a lot of money. More than enough to buy someone off. But I can't be bought by you. Not for five hundred and not for five thousand. Not for all the money in the world. Not where this case is concerned. You need to understand something. I am going to solve this case. I am going to figure out exactly what happened. And not just to Emmanuel Feldbaum but to Menashe Volkoff too."

He drew back a little. "Who the hell is Menashe Volkoff?" he asked.

I smiled a little smile, pushed my chair back, and stood. "I want to thank you for our little conversation, Mr. Caspi. It was most enlightening. I learned a lot. Including one thing that's very important. Want to know what it is?"

He didn't answer, but I didn't need him to. I was going to tell him anyway.

"I learned that whatever it is you're hiding, whatever it is you don't want me to find out, is worth a great deal to you. At least five hundred liras. Which makes me even more determined to learn what it is. Good day to you, Mr. Caspi. I'm sure we'll talk again very soon."

33

I wore a different shirt this time and another pair of trousers. With an iron I'd borrowed from one of my neighbors, and using my dining table as an ironing board, I'd banished nearly all the wrinkles from both.

I took a shower and did three passes with my razor, leaving my face smooth and slightly tender. A look in the mirror left me largely satisfied. Despite the faint lines that age and bad experiences had sliced into the corners of my eyes and my forehead. Despite the purplish tinge to the skin under my eyes. Years of bad sleep left their mark.

Two spritzes of the overpriced cologne, and I was as ready as I was ever going to be.

Again she seemed to have made less of an effort than I had done. She did not wear perfume, and her dress was the same as the one she'd worn to Shoshana's birthday party. But the smile she gave me was new. A woman treats you differently after you've kissed her. Or, in this case, after she's kissed you.

"Hello, Adam," she said.

"Good evening, Hannah."

We stood for a moment simply looking at each other. There was a slight awkwardness between us, or maybe I alone felt it. As though we weren't quite sure what to do with each other. Should we kiss again? Did she want to?

Finally, she said, "Where are you taking me?"

"A movie, I thought. Do you like movies?"

"Doesn't everyone?"

I guessed there were some who did not enjoy what was likely the national pastime, but they were very rare indeed. Israelis thronged cinemas, and their taste did not appear to be particularly discerning. One would find sold-out shows of musicals, historical dramas, crime movies—anything really. As long as it had images that flickered on a taut screen, it would more than pass muster.

"And later we'll have a drink somewhere. Or a late bite if you'd like."

We started walking. We did not hold hands or touch. She asked me what movie we were going to see, and I suggested one that was playing at Esther Cinema. I had alternatives lined up in case she'd already seen that one or did not find it appealing; earlier, I'd gone over the movie listings in that day's newspaper, so I was prepared. But in the end, I needn't have gone to the trouble. She said my pick sounded good.

I needed to ask her about Shimon Suskind, but I wasn't sure when to do it. A part of me did not want to inject my case into this date, but there was no way of avoiding it. Best to do it now and get it over with?

She made my decision for me by asking how the investigation was going.

"It's developing into something I wasn't expecting. I don't know into what exactly, but there's more to it than what it seemed at first."

"Oh?"

"Remember Menashe Volkoff? He did make it to Israel after all. Thirteen years ago, in the summer of '39. He was in Haifa for two days and then he vanished. There's been no trace of him since." I explained the circumstances of Volkoff's disappearance.

Hannah was quiet for a few good seconds. Then she said, "What do you think happened to him?"

"One possibility is that he's dead. Murdered. Because if he died in an accident, his body would have turned up."

"And the other possibility?"

"That Volkoff faked his own disappearance. That he thought people would come looking for him, people from Poland, and he didn't want to be found."

"Why?"

"Because he had something valuable. Something that didn't belong to him. Or not solely to him. And he wanted it all to himself."

"The thing Emmanuel was looking for?"

I nodded.

"What could it be?"

"I don't know. A large sum of money. Or something that's worth a lot."

"Jewelry, perhaps?"

"Could be, yes."

"It would have to be something small, wouldn't it? Because you said Volkoff left his suitcase in the boardinghouse."

"He might have stashed it somewhere else and picked it up the day he did his little vanishing act," I said.

"Would you have done so in his place? Put something so valuable where you couldn't see it? He was here for only two days before he disappeared. He wouldn't have been able to find a secure place. And if he planned on stealing it, he wouldn't have trusted anyone to hold it for him."

I thought about it and nodded. "You're right. It was something small enough to carry it on him. If he did indeed fake his disappearance."

"Even if he didn't. Because whether he was a victim or a villain, Volkoff still had whatever *it* was."

I smiled at her. "If you ever decide teaching's not for you, Hannah, I'd recommend becoming a detective."

"I doubt I'd get many clients. It's not a woman's job, is it?"

Her tone had an edge, and I saw her jaw was set. I recalled her asking me why I would choose a doll for a young girl instead of a toy soldier. She was the sort of woman who bridled at the limitations society placed on her. When I'd been younger, before the war, I might have found this unappealing. But I was no longer the man I'd once been. I'd been changed by incidents and experiences so extreme that they'd altered the very fibers of my beliefs and preconceptions. That had made me into a different man.

I viewed some of these changes as positive and some as not. And there were many that were somewhere in between, in the gray zone that now colored the way I looked at the world.

Hannah was right. She wouldn't get many clients. Perhaps none. Most people wouldn't think my profession was suitable for a woman, regardless of her skills. Now that I'd been made to think of it, I recognized the injustice there.

"Perhaps one day it will be," I said, and I could tell by the flare of her eyes that my answer had surprised her. She smiled at me. "When that day comes, will you teach me the ropes, Adam?"

"I'm sure you'll pick up all my tricks and secrets in no time," I said, and her smile got bigger.

We crossed the road, walked past a closed grocery store with a sign in the window stating quite firmly that no meat had been delivered this week. The sign advised the hungry masses to complain to the government, not the hapless shopkeeper.

"If Menashe Volkoff didn't fake his disappearance..." she said.

"Then he was murdered. And the killer got rid of his body."

"The same killer who murdered Emmanuel?"

"The police detective I spoke with in Haifa thinks that the chances of that are negligible."

"But you think otherwise?"

"I don't know what I think," I said, then stopped walking, and when she stopped as well and looked at me, I continued, "That's not exactly true. I think he's right, logically. But I also think he's wrong. Or maybe it would be more accurate to say that I feel he's wrong."

"And this worries you?"

"That I feel it instead of think it? A bit. But a good part of detective work is instinct and hunches. At least that's the way it's always been for me."

"Do your hunches always prove correct?"

"Not even close. I make my share of mistakes. More than my share, actually. It's quite likely that Emmanuel was killed by a robber, or by someone he met recently, but I can't ignore what I feel. And what I feel is that there's a good chance that the death or disappearance of Volkoff and Emmanuel's murder are connected." I looked at her and saw her somber expression. Inside, I groaned. *There you go again, Adam.* "Maybe we should talk about something else, Hannah. It's not the most pleasant topic of conversation, is it?"

"I'm not some faint-hearted woman, Adam."

"I know that."

"In fact, most women aren't that kind. We're stronger than what you men believe."

"I know that too. It's just that this isn't the most fitting subject for a night on the town, is it?"

"I don't recall ever discussing something as interesting with any man I've gone out with. Let me tell you a secret, Adam. Most men are quite dull. Their favorite thing to talk about is themselves, and usually without good reason. Their work is boring, and they're not as smart as they think they are. I like hearing about your investigation. And I like how you don't make yourself out to be something you're not. That's another failing of most men."

"In that case, I have a question for you: have you ever heard of Shimon Suskind? Did Emmanuel ever talk about him?"

She shook her head and asked who Suskind was. I told her how I'd learned of his existence when I'd visited the police station in Haifa.

"He was keen on finding Volkoff," I said. "Probably for the same reason Emmanuel was. I was hoping Emmanuel mentioned him, but it seems he hadn't. Not to anyone. I think it's due to timing. Volkoff left Poland in 1939, right before the war, so Emmanuel assumed he was alive—at least some part of his damaged brain did. But Suskind was still in Poland when the Germans invaded. So Emmanuel would have assumed he was dead. And he would not have known that Suskind had come to Israel."

We started walking again, rounded a corner, and now we could see the cinema ahead of us, people milling about the entrance.

Hannah said, "Do you know where Suskind is now?"

I shook my head. "I asked Reuben to send out a query on him. Suskind must appear in some official record. When I find him, I'll get my answers."

34

The movie hall was packed. We sat two rows from the back, but our view of the screen was uninhibited.

Preceding the movie was a newsreel. From all the chatter as it was playing, I doubted most people were paying it much attention. Israelis came to movies to forget about their reality, to be taken to places outside the borders of their tiny country, not to be reminded of the many challenges it faced.

Still, some joker was attentive enough to boo when Ben-Gurion appeared on the screen. A woman laughed in response. A man yelled at them both to shut up.

The movie was pretty good, but at first I was unable to focus on it. Partly, it was the case that kept intruding on my thoughts, but mainly it was the sensation of Hannah in the seat beside mine, our arms sharing the same armrest, lightly touching.

Was she enjoying herself? I wondered, and, as though reading my mind, she turned, saw me looking, and gave me a smile. "Watch the movie, Adam," she whispered. "You'll get to see enough of me later."

After the curtains closed, we joined the crowd that spilled out of the cinema and onto Dizengoff Square. The night was warm, but there was a breeze that kept the humidity at bay.

"Did you like the movie?" Hannah asked.

I said that I did.

"Me too. You said something about going to another place? I could use some coffee."

I told her I knew just the place.

Greta's Café was nearly full. But my table at the rear was vacant. Greta saw us come in, and a smile as wide as Rothschild Boulevard spread on her face.

"Hannah, this is Greta, the owner of this fine establishment. Greta, this is Hannah Goldman."

The two women shook hands, and Greta looked so delighted that for a second I was worried she might pull Hannah into a tight embrace. Luckily, this didn't happen, though Greta did hold onto Hannah's hand a bit longer than was warranted.

"Can you get us some coffee, Greta?"

Greta assured me she could, and I led Hannah to my table.

When we sat down, Hannah said, "She sure seemed happy to see you, Adam."

It's you she was happy to see, I thought, but instead I said, "I come here often. Almost every day."

"You're her best customer, then?"

I laughed. "The worst, probably. At least financially." And I told her how I had helped Greta deal with the thug who had squeezed her for protection money.

"Instead of paying me, Greta and I came to an arrangement: I'd eat and drink my fee."

Hannah notched her head, her lips quirking. "Why do I get the sense that you've long since collected what was owed you?"

"Because it's true. For a long while, Greta wouldn't accept any money from me. And not for lack of my trying. I think she feels safer with me around, and I never abused the privilege she granted me. But finally I insisted we change the terms of our arrangement, and I started paying for my meals. But she's been undercharging me. She doesn't know it, but I've been keeping tabs and waiting for the right moment to tell her it's time to settle my debt."

"She must like you very much, and I can tell you like her."

I looked over at Greta, who was setting our cups on a tray at the counter. "She's an exceptional woman, and I owe her a lot."

Greta brought the coffee over, and Hannah remarked on the delicious aroma wafting from our cups.

Greta beamed. Her smile was so broad that it verged on the maniacal, and I worried that it might have been a mistake to bring Hannah here. She might begin to question Greta's sanity.

"Just wait till you taste it," Greta said, and she stood there, holding the tray to her bosom with both hands, waiting for Hannah to pass her verdict.

Hannah blew on her cup, drew on it cautiously, and gave a slow smile. "Exceptional. I don't think I've tasted its equal since before the war. What's your secret?"

Greta winked. "A lady never tells."

"I'm a lady," Hannah replied, "and I often do."

She and Greta burst out in laughter. Greta, still smiling, asked if we wanted anything to eat. Both of us shook our heads, and Greta said we should feel free to change our minds at any time. Then she went away, but I had to give her a hard look to get her to stop staring at us from her perch behind the counter.

Hannah took another sip of her coffee. I drank a little of mine. I was feeling a bit nervous, searching for something to say. Preferably something unrelated to murder and death.

Again, she came to my rescue. "You were right to bring me here, Adam. It's so homey. And not as pretentious as some of the more popular cafés with their bow-tied waiters."

"Some people like those places. They remind them of cafés and restaurants they used to go to in Europe."

"I can understand that. But I like this place better. It's Israeli, is what it is. Something new. Something that's still being formed." She looked at me. "Do you feel Israeli, Adam?"

The question took me by surprise. "What else should I feel?"

"Hungarian, I suppose. You haven't been in this country long. I know people who arrived here nearly twenty years ago, and they still

JONATHAN DUNSKY

feel German or Russian or Polish."

"Do you feel Polish?"

She considered it. "Sometimes. Not very often. Not as much as I used to. But I've been here longer than you."

"I don't feel one bit Hungarian. And I haven't for some years." *Not since May 1944*, I thought, *when Hungarian policemen pushed me and my family into the cattle cars that took us to Auschwitz.* "I used to," I said, "but that was a mistake. Because I was never Hungarian. Not as far as other Hungarians were concerned. They viewed me as a Jew, a creature apart from them."

A man at a nearby table turned his head to look at me, and I realized that I had raised my voice without noticing. I took a deep breath, cursing inwardly, oddly enough doing so in Hungarian, and said, "I'm sorry, Hannah."

"What for?"

"For getting a little loud."

"I teach third-graders, Adam. I'm immune to loud voices."

I tried to explain: "I can get carried away sometimes, thinking about my former life."

She reached over and put her hand on mine. She had long slender fingers with short nails. They were cool and pleasant to the touch. It was the first time we really touched that evening, and I could feel my skin responding to hers.

"You don't need to apologize. I understand." She gave me a smile before changing the subject. "You said you read Westerns. I've never read one. What are they like?"

I told her about Zane Grey and Max Brand and Clarence Mulford, some of the writers I liked. I told her about rugged cowboys riding across wild terrain, mountains and deserts and endless plains. Self-reliant men, tough, resilient, quick to violence when it was called for, with codes of honor and justice that belonged on the fringes of civilization. I told her about Indians and outlaws, about train robberies and gunfights. About adventure, and how a single man often took on great odds and emerged triumphant. Battered and bruised but not beaten.

240

She listened attentively, not interrupting me. There was a tiny smile on her lips, and again I recalled the serious books that crowded her shelves.

"I guess they don't sound like quality reading material, do they?" I said.

"What they sound like is a lot of fun. Will you lend me one?"

She sounded sincere, and I was happy because her request meant that she wanted to see me again.

"Sure," I said. "And maybe you can lend me something more substantial?"

"I know just the thing," she replied, and there was a twinkle in her eye.

I asked her about her garden, and she said it was a lot of hard work cultivating it on the infertile land of Mahlul.

"The sea winds don't help. The salty air doesn't either. Still, I enjoy it, even though a good many of my plantings fail to produce much of anything."

"Do people steal from gardens?" I asked. "I imagine a lot of people in Mahlul don't have full iceboxes."

"That's another benefit of having a pretend lover in the police," she said, with an impish raise of one eyebrow. "But most people in Mahlul are honest. Just because people are poor, it doesn't mean they'd steal."

"Believe me, I know. Some of the biggest criminals I've had the displeasure to meet were quite well off." I thought about Caspi and wondered if he belonged to that group.

"You've got interesting stories to tell, don't you?" Hannah said.

I shrugged in false modesty, but I was enjoying being the subject of her interest.

She said, "Why don't you get us more coffee and tell me some of them?"

So I did. Over the next hour or so, I told her about some of my investigations as a policeman in Hungary, and to my surprise, I found a measure of pleasure both in the telling and in the recollection.

It's not often that I think of those days with fondness. Usually, I shy away from them because they inevitably bring with them memories of loved ones who are now dead, their ashes scattered across Polish fields and rivers. But this time was different.

I told her about my early days on the force, about chasing criminals on the streets of Budapest, about an older cop who taught me how the real world worked.

"They teach you how to be a cop before they put you in a uniform, but that's just a tiny part of the education you need to have. You learn on the streets, hopefully with someone with experience and the patience to teach you. And you quickly learn that the world is not black and white but an infinite range of gray."

"Gray?"

I nodded. "You start out thinking police work is pure as snow, but it's really like how snow looks a few days after it's come down. All dirty and sludgy and messy. You sometimes need to let a criminal go in order to get information, or you learn that some small crimes are not worth wasting your time on. And that sometimes the law isn't the solution to everything."

"Like with the thug who was bothering Greta?"

"Exactly."

"I was wondering why she came to you instead of the police."

"Because the police are overworked, underpaid, and they often work slowly. They have procedures, protocols, and they need proof to put someone away. The guy who was squeezing Greta needed to be dealt with quickly, firmly, and given a message he would never forget in a language he would understand."

"Violence?"

"That's right."

"Do you often get violent in your work?"

"Only when I have to, and never more than is necessary."

She studied my face, a small frown etched on her forehead, and again I berated myself for saying things I shouldn't have. Here was this attractive woman, and we seemed to be hitting it off, but I kept raising inappropriate topics. First I dumped a load of death and grief on her, and now I just came out and told her I habitually used violence. No wonder she was frowning. She was probably thinking of how best to get away from me without incurring my dangerous, potentially violent wrath.

But then she surprised me by giving me a slow smile. "You're just full of surprises, Adam."

"I am?"

"Yes. You don't go out with women often, do you?"

"How could you tell?"

"You seem refreshingly out of practice. You talk about things other men would keep to themselves."

"Maybe I simply lack self-control."

"No, I don't think that's true. In fact, if I had to guess, I'd say you're very disciplined. But you do talk about things and then regret doing so."

"I don't want you to think my life is all gloom and death and violence."

"I don't think so. But all those things are a part of it, aren't they?"

"Yes," I admitted.

"Well, that's all right. Life isn't meant to be all blue skies and sunshine. A few clouds and a little rain are fine."

How about more than a few? I thought. *And not a little rain, but a torrent of it? An earth-rattling storm? Because that's what my life is like sometimes, Hannah.*

I said none of this. Nor did I tell her about my bloodier cases, the men I'd killed, or how violence sometimes soothed my turbulent soul. She was a strong woman, and apparently, she did not scare easily, but a glimpse into the dark corners of my life was all I dared show her. I doubted she could handle more.

A while later, we left Greta's Café and ambled toward Mahlul, with an unspoken understanding that I would walk her home.

She said, "I wonder why Emmanuel mentioned Yosef Rudinsky only to Mr. Soffer."

"He might have done so to other people as well. People I didn't speak with."

"But he didn't to me or to Ami and Batya Rapoport, and he was with us more than with others. But he did say it to Soffer, when was it —a week or so before he died?"

"Yeah, you're right. It's strange."

"Do you think something happened before he saw Soffer that made Emmanuel think of Rudinsky?"

"Maybe so," I said, a few possibilities coming to mind. Did Emmanuel see something shortly before meeting Soffer that reminded him of Yosef Rudinsky? Maybe he saw Rudinsky himself? Did the two of them speak? I simply didn't know. Yet another item on the long and frustrating list of things in this case that were stubbornly obscure, opaque, or completely hidden from me.

Hearing her chuckle softly brought me back to the moment.

"What?"

"I'm sorry, Adam, but you've got such an intense expression when you're thinking deeply about something."

"A funny expression?"

"No. Well, maybe just a little. Because it is quite intense indeed. I don't think I've ever seen anything like it. But it's mostly attractive. I like a man who can think deeply."

We were close to the beach by then. We could hear the waves beating ineffectually against the shore. We stopped on the corner of Hayarkon and Allenby and looked at each other. Hannah was standing so that the streetlamp illuminated only half of her face, leaving the other half in nightly shadows. It made her look otherworldly and so very beautiful.

She was breathing deeply, and her breasts rose and fell alluringly. Her lips were slightly parted, her chin raised a little as she gazed up at me.

I had been nervous and tentative most of the evening, but now all hesitancy fell away. I took a decisive step toward her, curled a hand around the small of her back, and drew her to me with a powerful pull of my arm. A surprised gasp escaped her lungs as our bodies met. I kissed her hard, pressing her tight against me, the heat of her body seeping through my clothes as the taste of her filled my mouth.

She made a small purring sound, and her hands went into my

hair. My eyes were closed, and for a spell, there was only the sensation of her.

A shrill whistle followed by a burst of adolescent female laughter made us break contact. On the other side of the street stood a trio of teenagers, two girls and a boy, and all were grinning at us.

"Long live love!" the boy, fifteen or sixteen, cried out with a flamboyant raise of his arms. The girls laughed again.

My cheeks turned hot, but Hannah was not embarrassed in the slightest. She stepped to the edge of the curb and called to the boy: "Let this be a lesson to you, young man. This is how you kiss a woman."

The boy fell silent, struck dumb either by Hannah's words or the fact that she had said them. Women did not tend to be so outspoken on such matters. I was speechless myself, as were the boy's two companions.

Hannah wasn't finished. "It's very important that you remember what you just saw. You won't forget, will you?"

I could see the boy gulp from across the road. He shook his head as though under the effects of severe shock.

"Because we can give you a repeat demonstration if you feel your memory is shaky, can't we, Adam?" She was looking at me now, and I slowly nodded my head. She turned back to the boy. "Well? Will that be necessary?"

The boy's face was as red as a tomato now. In a tremulous voice that barely reached our ears, he said, "No, ma'am."

Hannah wasn't finished. "What about you, young ladies? You shouldn't forget this either. Women deserve to be kissed properly, just like they deserve to be treated well in all aspects of life. Are you in need of further examples?"

One of the girls actually started to nod, but her friend smacked her on the arm and gave her a warning look. "No, ma'am. We're sorry for laughing."

"That's all right," Hannah said. "We weren't offended. Besides, we were rapidly running out of air, so you may have done us a favor. Now run along. There's school tomorrow, so make sure you go straight to bed, you hear?"

In chastened voices, all three promised they would. Then they made a quick getaway. We watched them flee until they disappeared around the nearest corner. Then Hannah turned to me with a smile that quickly gave way to a quizzical look.

"What?"

"Is this how you are as a teacher?" I asked.

"I don't kiss men in class, Adam."

I laughed. "That's not what I meant."

"Good. Because I wouldn't want you to think I have no boundaries whatsoever. And no, that's not the way I teach. I'm much softer and nicer and more patient. But I felt a different approach was in order with those three."

"You certainly got your point across. I doubt they'll ever forget you."

She smiled. "I always aim to leave a lasting impression, Adam."

We arrived at her door. The scent of wet wood traveled on the faint breeze. Somewhere close by, a cat mewled.

"Come inside," Hannah said. "I'll give you the book I was talking about."

She lit two lamps. The amber, rural light they cast chased the shadows away into the corners of the shack.

From the bookcase, she removed a thick volume and handed it to me. By the creases on its spine and the curling of its pages, I could tell this was a book that had been read many times.

"*Jane Eyre*?" I read the title, then studied the front cover. It showed a woman reclining on a sofa. By her clothes, I could tell she lived somewhere in Europe at least a century ago. "Doesn't look very thrilling."

"It is. Incredibly so. But not in the same way your Westerns are."

I wasn't convinced. "Isn't this a book for women?"

Hannah's lips compressed in admonishment. "It's a book for everyone, Adam."

I opened the book at a random spot. The tiny, densely typed

words looked like an army of ants marching across the page. What had I gotten myself into?

"All right," I said. "I'll read it."

Hannah smiled. There were two pins in her hair, and now she removed them. Her hair fell free around her face.

"Good. But not right now," she said. "Right now, I want your undivided attention on me." And with that, she drew her dress higher up her legs, gathered the hem, and whipped the entire garment off her body.

She did not break eye contact throughout her disrobement, apart from when the dress went over her head. Now she stood before me in underwear and brassiere, the skin on her stomach and chest and thighs a creamy white, contrasting sharply with the woodsy tan on her forearms and calves.

She was not voluptuous, not endowed with the sort of figure that would feature in the dirty dreams of men. And her face was not one that sculptors would seek to immortalize in clay or marble. Yet I found her incredibly beautiful at that moment. And seductive. So much so that my mouth went dry, my heart revved up, and my fingers involuntarily lost their hold on the book.

It fell to the floor with a thud, making me jump. Hannah laughed. "Don't look so stunned, Adam. I told you earlier you'd be seeing much more of me tonight."

35

She was the second woman I had been with since the death of my wife in Auschwitz seven years before. The first had been Sima Vaaknin, a high-end prostitute I had met on a previous case, and with whom I'd had an intermittent relationship whose nature I could not define, a relationship that had ended bitterly a few months ago.

Hannah and Sima were nothing alike. Sima was the embodiment of the male fantasy, her every line and curve perfectly shaped to arouse, entice, and excite. Hannah's beauty was not as immediate and physical.

Sima was an enigma. She hid more than she showed, an accomplished actress who presented herself in whatever form would most please her client. Hannah was outspoken, forthright, candid, showing more of herself, her thoughts, her unorthodox beliefs than most women did. Sima was a shapeshifter; Hannah was what she was, and if that didn't suit you, it was your problem.

But the main difference was in how they made love.

Sima was a consummate professional, the perfect courtesan. She had an uncanny sense of what you wanted in bed, and she gave it to you. Hannah was the other way around. Sima gave, but Hannah took.

Hannah did not give you what you wanted. She took what *she* wanted from *you.*

She took control, bluntly and without apology. She wasn't with you to please you. She was with you because she desired you, and to get pleasure herself. And she wasn't shy about doing things the way she liked or saying what she wanted.

And in so doing, in focusing on deriving pleasure from me, and not the other way around, she made me feel bigger, better, more attractive and capable. In enjoying me, in using me in a way, I enjoyed her all the more.

Later, when we lay spent on the rumpled sheets, she asked me about my scars. I knew the questions were coming. How could she miss them? Whether by sight or touch, they were prominent.

I was silent, looking up at the dark ceiling. As always, when I thought of my scars, I felt a mixture of pride and shame. There were the scars I'd gotten in the War of Independence, when I was a soldier fighting for my country; these gave me nothing but pride. But they were but a short note compared to the ugly, strident symphony of agony that was the mass of scars on my back.

"You don't have to tell me if you don't want to, Adam," she said.

I turned to look at her. She was propped on one elbow, her skin still glistening with the sweat of our exertions. Her hair was mussed, her lips puffy from my kisses.

She gave me a slow smile and notched her left eyebrow. "We don't have to talk at all, you know." And she reached for me.

After that, she said, "Don't take this the wrong way, Adam, but—"

"You'd like me to leave."

"Not really. But I have to teach early in the morning, and if you stay here, well..."

"I understand," I said, and pushed myself to a sitting position.

"Please tell me you're not offended."

I smiled at her and ran a hand from the swell of her hip, up her flank, and cupped the side of her neck, rubbing a thumb on her cheek. I leaned in closer and kissed her. "I'm not. Not in the slightest."

In truth, I was relieved, though of course I did not tell her that. I did not want to sleep next to her. Not tonight. I feared the nightmares would come, and that I would wake up screaming. I didn't want her to see me that way. I didn't want to have to explain my terror.

I got into my clothes and picked up the copy of *Jane Eyre* from where it lay on the floor. I looked at it dubiously.

"It's really very good," Hannah said from behind me. She had climbed into a shift that hung to her thighs. I could make out all the wonderful contours of her body through the thin fabric.

"I'll take your word for it."

"And you were very good, too," she said.

"I'll take your word for that as well."

We kissed a bit more at her door, where anyone passing by could see us. But no one did. Not even Zelda. The windows of her shack were dark.

After we parted, I lit a cigarette and walked away, contemplating the night and its wonderful activities. But I did not go home despite it being well past midnight. Instead, I headed north, leaving Mahlul behind me, and then went down to the beach, where I stood gazing at the water. I was all alone with the waves and my thoughts.

And they were turning dark, as I'd expected them to. My wife, my dead wife, Deborah, was the subject of my thoughts. I missed her still, terribly, seven years after her death in the gas chambers at Auschwitz. For a long while after, any romantic involvement I had with a woman brought with it an intense sense of guilt toward Deborah, the love of my life who was no more.

And that guilt was still present. Like a stone in my gut and a closed fist around my heart. There were tears in my eyes and a catch in my breath. All familiar feelings. I'd known them with Sima Vaaknin, and with other women I had begun to get close to but in the end didn't.

But these sensations, this burden of emotions, felt like a prison cell that was contracting around me, the bars closing in, shutting out light and air and freedom.

"I just want you to be happy, Adam," Greta had told me. "Truly happy. It's no sin, you know."

Did I really believe that? Was I capable of believing it? Did I even want to? Or was it my wish to remain imprisoned by my guilt?

Now the tears began to flow in earnest, cutting down my cheeks and pooling at the corners of my mouth, on the lips that had kissed Hannah Goldman just a short while ago. I buried my face in my hands, quaking.

Past the tears, past my shuttered eyes, projected on the screen of my haunted mind, I saw an image of Deborah. There was a frown on her forehead and a mournful smile on her lips.

"She's right, Adam," she whispered to me. *"It is no sin, no crime. You deserve to be happy. I want you to. And so do the girls. You're alive, Adam. So live! Don't forget us, but live."*

A shattered cry of pain erupted from my throat, and I fell to my knees.

Which was a good thing. Because I'd have been dead otherwise.

36

As I dropped to my knees, I felt the air split above and behind me, just where my head had been an instant before, and I could sense the sweep of something powerful missing me by a hair.

"Look out, Adam!" Deborah screamed in my head, and then she was gone, and what flooded into my consciousness was the sharp awareness of mortal danger and the need to take action.

So I shifted my motion, and instead of ending up on my knees, I let the movement carry me forward into a roll.

I rolled on the soft sand and jerked to a crouch in an instant, ready for war. My cheeks were wet, my eyes still blurry, but I could make out the shape of the large man now standing a couple of meters before me. A sweep of my forearm across my eyes dried my tears and brought the man into sharp relief.

Boris.

He had crept up on me while I was crying, deaf to his approach, and it was only by luck that I was not lying dead at his feet.

He was armed with a large wrench. Its gray metal gleamed in the faint moonlight. He must have swung it hard, and that was lucky for me, because his uneven stance told me the movement had taken him off balance. He'd needed to stabilize himself, or he would have jumped me even as I was rolling.

Just like with the brick, I had barely escaped having my head bashed in.

I rose to full height. "How did you find me, you bastard?"

Boris grinned. It was the sort of grin that showed you a lot of teeth and no mercy whatsoever.

"Followed you from Allenby. You were so keen on that broad, you didn't notice. Don't know what you see in her. She looks stuck up, that one, and I don't like women with glasses. But I guess she's the sort of woman who spreads her legs for just about anyone, so maybe that's why you went with her."

"Shut your dirty mouth!" I said, and had to restrain myself from going at him then and there.

He barked out a gruff laugh, flexing the muscles in his hands and arms, and shifting onto the balls of his feet and back again. Like a boxer looking for an opening.

"She's not my type, but I still might go have a taste of her after I'm done with you, you crybaby. She'll like that, I'm sure."

"I don't think she goes for gorillas," I said.

His face twisted in fury. "You have some mouth on you. But soon you won't be saying anything. You won't be breathing either."

We were alone on the dark beach. The closest lights of Tel Aviv were more than fifty meters away. Normally, a yell would carry that far, but the waves were pounding the shore, and the wind had picked up and was blowing toward the sea. I didn't think anyone would hear me if I yelled, or would be able to tell where the sound had come from if they did. Not that it mattered because I didn't want anyone to come. I didn't want anyone to see. I wanted to end this right here on this deserted stretch of sand with no witnesses around.

"You didn't get me the first time, remember?" I said. Because now I knew he was the man who had dropped the brick on me. He had gotten it from the building site and carried it up to the roof of my building. Why he hadn't waited for me on the roof, I didn't know.

Maybe he feared I was going to call the cops. Or maybe he didn't have a weapon and wanted better odds some other time. "And you won't this time either."

"You got lucky once," he said, confirming my suspicion. "But you won't a second time." He was moving side to side and closing in inch by inch, feinting with the wrench.

"Why? Because of your boss? Is he the one who told you to kill me?"

He went stone still, and his mouth fell open, and I knew I'd called it right. Caspi had sent him. Caspi wanted me dead, and he'd told Boris to do it. Boris who had a violent side and was unnaturally loyal to his boss. Boris who hated Feldbaum for besting him in that contest of strength, who wouldn't have needed much goading to get revenge.

"He said you were too smart for your own good," Boris said in a low voice. "But that's not gonna last. I'm gonna brain you like I almost did the first time."

I wanted to ask him why Caspi had told him to kill Feldbaum, but I didn't have the chance. The time for talking was over. I could see it in how he shifted his weight forward, ready to lunge at me.

He had some advantages on me. He had size and strength and that heavy wrench. But he didn't know I had a weapon too. The knife. I dipped my hand into my pocket in search of it.

And found nothing.

The knife wasn't there. Had it somehow dropped from my pocket at Hannah's?

There was no time to ponder the question because here was Boris, coming at me with his face warped into a barbaric mask, and the wrench was streaking toward my head.

Which was a mistake. He should have done what they'd taught us in the army when we were learning how to shoot a rifle.

"Aim for the center of the body," the sergeant had instructed us. You had a greater chance of hitting something that way, and a blow from that wrench would have been debilitating even if it got me in the arm.

But Boris had gone for the head, and he wasn't the quickest guy in the world, so I managed to duck under his swing and move in while his torso was exposed, punching him in the belly.

It was a good blow, and it landed right where I wanted, but it didn't affect him much. He grunted but didn't even fold. He had one of those hard, slightly bloated bellies, and his abdominal muscles had absorbed my punch without it hurting him.

I stepped back quickly, guessing what was coming, and barely avoided the reverse swing of the wrench. As it passed in a blur before my eyes, I aimed a kick at Boris's knee, but my shoe glanced off his calf, making him wince but no more than that.

I retreated again as he cursed me, and I stepped on something hard. My eyes flicked down, and there was my knife lying partially submerged in beach sand. It had fallen from my pocket as I was rolling away from Boris.

I wanted to grab it; I needed it because I didn't think I'd be able to beat Boris without it. But if I went for it, I was a dead man. Before I had it in my hand and got the blade open, Boris would smash the wrench into my skull.

He had the wrench over his head now, gripped in both hands, and brought it down with a ferocious growl. I caught his wrists and just barely managed to arrest his movement. Dammit, he was strong, the force of his swing drove me onto one knee, and it was all I could do to maintain my hold on his wrists.

He was above me now, jerking his arms violently side to side, trying to wrest his wrists free. His face was a fearsome grimace of hate and bloodlust—teeth bared, eyes flashing baleful fire, the tendons in his neck standing out. He was growling constantly, and spittle flew from his lips and onto my face. I was holding on for dear life because I knew that once his hands were free, the wrench would come down, and this time there'd be no escape.

My hands were clammy, my fingers aching in spasms as they struggled to keep their grip. I could feel them slipping, losing their purchase. I gritted my teeth and tightened my hold, but it was no use.

Boris was too strong, and my position was too weak. In a few seconds he would break free.

The knife. It was next to my right shoe, lying there like an unclaimed treasure, so close yet impossibly distant. I couldn't reach it. Not even if I let go with one hand.

So I switched tactics. Instead of simply holding his wrists, I yanked Boris toward me, adding to the momentum by falling backward, pulling him down with me.

The move took him by surprise. He fell forward, landing on my chest, and all the air was pushed out of my lungs. For a second, I was suffocating, and my vision blurred at the edges, but then I gulped a lungful of air, and I was seeing properly again.

Boris pushed himself off me and onto his knees. He hadn't lost hold of the wrench.

"You're dead," he screamed as he raised it over his head, ready to bring it down for a decisive, bone-shattering blow.

As the wrench was moving upward, I scrabbled for the knife. For a panicked instant, I felt only sand, but then my fingertips touched polished wood. The wrench reached its zenith over Boris's head, held aloft like an executioner's ax, the metal glinting a promise of imminent death.

He was just beginning to bring it down when I flicked open the blade and drove the knife into his chest all the way to the hilt.

His eyes went huge as the blade sank in, and a choked exhalation squeaked from his mouth. The wrench dropped from his hands, bouncing painfully but harmlessly on my left shoulder before ending its fall on the sand at my side.

Boris's hands clutched my right shoulder, and he looked at me with a stunned and hurt expression, as though he were shocked that I would even think of doing him harm. He let out another labored breath, loosened his hold on me, and slipped onto his back on the sand.

"Why did Caspi tell you to kill Emmanuel Feldbaum?" I asked him, grabbing him by both shoulders and looking into his open, erratically blinking eyes. I was desperate for answers, knowing that time was running out, that he was dying rapidly. "Come on, Boris, tell me. Why did he want Emmanuel dead?"

He opened his mouth, but what came out was not words but bubbles of blood. I must have stabbed him in a lung.

He let out a tormented strangled sound from deep in his throat as his body yearned for air. His hands twitched at his sides. His mouth stretched wide, gasping, and more blood came out.

I could see the light deserting his eyes and knew that life was abandoning his body.

"Why?" I asked again, but I no longer expected an answer. Boris wasn't capable of giving me one.

A few seconds later, he was gone. His eyes stared glassily at the dark sky, his lips and chin spattered red, and his expression still that of total surprise that the night had taken such an unexpected final turn.

With the scents of death and blood and sea mingling into a rotting wreath around my head, I made a circular sweep with my eyes. There was no one. No witnesses. No one to point the finger at me. No one to support a claim of self-defense either.

I went through the dead man's pockets, finding a wallet fat with bills. More than three hundred liras in fifties and tens. I left ten liras in the wallet and stuffed the rest in my pocket. Then, using my handkerchief, I wiped my fingerprints off the wallet, pressed Boris's fingers onto the leather here and there so the cops wouldn't know the wallet had been cleaned, and stuck it back in his pocket.

My knife was still wedged in the dead man's chest. The handle was bloodied, the swastika emblazoned on it as red as the flag of destruction and death it had once adorned.

I pulled the knife out and wiped the blade on Boris's shirt. Then I crouched down at the water's edge and let the seawater wash the rest of the blood away. I wrapped the wet weapon in my handkerchief and put it in my pocket.

It was time to go. A final look at Boris's dead form, and then I was walking briskly north along the water, much like Feldbaum had done. But while he had been heading toward death, I was moving away from it.

After half a kilometer or so, I cut east into the city, then navigated the nighttime streets toward home. As I walked, I thought about how my beloved Deborah had saved my life. And how, in a way, Hannah Goldman had done so as well.

37

At nine o'clock in the morning, I called Reuben from Levinson's Drugstore on the corner of Hamaccabi and King George. He picked up after eight rings.

"It takes you eight rings to answer your phone?" I chided him playfully. "You can cross your office in about two steps."

"It's four steps for those of us not blessed with your height, Adam. For your information, I was at the end of the hall when the phone started ringing, though I see no reason why I should explain myself to you. Not unless you decide to join the force. In which case, I might revise my statement."

Reuben periodically broached the possibility of my becoming a cop in Israel. He was proud of his work and, knowing my history, saw no reason why I shouldn't wish to return to my old profession.

"I'll remain a mere citizen if you don't mind."

"As long as it's a law-abiding one, Adam."

"I shall do my best," I said, the image of dead Boris lying on the beach with his shirt drenched in blood rising in my mind. I blinked it away. "Have you found out anything about Shimon Suskind or Yosef Rudinsky?"

He told me he hadn't, and suggested I call him tomorrow. I went to Greta's and sat with my chessboard at my table. Greta came over, her face full of curiosity.

"It went fine, Greta," I said, anticipating her questions. "Though for a moment there, I was worried you might ruin it for me."

"Me?" she said, laying a hand on her chest, looking horrified.

"The way you were smiling at Hannah, or maybe you didn't notice."

"What's so bad about smiling?"

"When the smile in question could get you committed to an insane asylum, it can be very bad indeed."

"Oh dear. Was it really that terrible?"

I nodded and then, seeing how mortified she was, gave her a comforting smile. "Don't worry about it. Like I told you, it went fine."

She sighed in relief. "I'm glad. Because I like her a lot."

"You barely exchanged a dozen words with her."

"It was slightly more than that. Enough to get an impression. And that impression was very positive indeed. I take it you like her too."

"I do."

"And the evening went well, you say, so why do you look troubled?"

"I look troubled?"

"Uh-huh. Is it the case?"

"Yeah." I cast a quick look around at the patrons at nearby tables. "Let's just say I got some answers, but there are still some important open questions."

I was going to have to answer some questions myself once the police figured out who Boris was. So it was no surprise when, about ninety minutes after lunch, a couple of tough-looking officers walked in and found their way to my table.

"You're Adam Lapid?"

"Yeah," I said, making sure to look both surprised and puzzled to see them. "What's this about?"

"We need you to come with us to the station. You'll find out there."

As we walked out, I gave Greta a surreptitious wink. I'd told her earlier that police officers might pay me a visit later in the day and that she shouldn't worry. Now she pressed her lips tight and gave me a *I hope you know what you're doing* look.

The station was the one Reuben worked in, on Yehuda Halevi 6. The room they put me in wasn't bad as far as interrogation rooms go; it was clean and didn't stink of desperation and fear. But it still had some of the common characteristics: the uncomfortable chair for the interviewee, the naked walls with degraded paintwork, the uninspiring bare metal table. The lack of an ashtray did not deter me from lighting a cigarette. A little ash on the floor wouldn't make much difference to the overall atmosphere.

I knew the cops would come for me after they identified the body and spoke to Boris's colleagues. The three guys I'd spoken with at Café Silver would have told the police about the near-fight I'd had with Boris there. In truth, the cops had worked faster than I'd expected. Maybe they were becoming more efficient.

The two constables put me in a chair and told me to sit tight. This I did for about forty minutes, during which time I smoked a few cigarettes and replayed vivid memories of the time I'd spent in Hannah Goldman's bed. If the cops had intended for me to stew in my own juices and thereby become less resistant to what they wanted to pin on me, their plan couldn't have gone more wrong. I could have waited there for hours with no problem whatsoever.

The officer who ended my wait had a mustache on his lip and sergeant stripes on his shirtsleeves. He was average height and a little stocky, with thinning brown hair and a nose that dominated his pudgy face. He looked tired and jaded—a common look among cops with a few years on the job.

He sat down opposite me and put a thin file on the table.

"Mr. Lapid?"

I nodded.

"I'm Sergeant Bilenko." He gave me a tight-lipped smile. "I see you're familiar with my name."

"Sure," I said, recovering from my surprise. Though I should have seen it coming. When the police had learned of my friction with Boris, they also had learned of my case. It stood to reason that they would alert the police officer in charge of that case, and that he would take a personal interest in the private investigator who was poaching on his turf.

"I take it you know why you're here," he said.

It was a neat little trap he was laying for me, because Boris's death had not been publicized yet. If I answered in the affirmative, it would be almost as good as a confession.

"No idea, I'm afraid. But I suppose it has something to do with the murder of Emmanuel Feldbaum."

"No, it doesn't. Though we'll get to that case in due course, don't you worry about it. The reason you're here is because of another murder. You know the one I'm talking about."

It was a question modulated to sound like a statement. Another trick. Trying to make me feel like he already knew everything, so I might as well come clean. But I knew what was really going on. He was fishing, hoping to get a lucky bite. But I wasn't going to take the bait.

"Another murder? Who died? When?"

Bilenko kept his eyes on my face for a silent moment, then opened the file before him and looked down at it thoughtfully. He'd angled the file so I would not be able to see what it contained. Yet another trick. Again trying to get me to believe he knew more than he did. I almost smiled at the act.

He looked up from the file and gave me a probing stare. When he spoke next, his voice was harder than before. "Do you know a Boris Melvitzki?"

"Is he the one who was murdered?"

"Do you know him or not?"

"I know someone called Boris. I don't know his last name."

"Who is this Boris you know?" he asked, closing the file and leaning forward with his forearms on the table.

"He's a guy who used to work with Emmanuel Feldbaum."

"Used to?" Bilenko asked with emphasis, thinking he'd caught me speaking of Boris in the past tense, as only someone who knew he was dead would do.

"Yeah. Until Feldbaum got fired."

Bilenko's shoulders dropped a little. My answer was entirely logical. I had not given myself away.

"I understand you and he knocked heads."

"Yeah. I think he was close to taking a swing at me. I heard he has a short temper. Don't tell me he killed someone."

Bilenko pushed out his lower lip and tapped his fingers on the table. He notched his head and perused my face, looking for some tell I wasn't about to display. He let the silence linger, and I responded by taking out my pack of cigarettes and offering him one.

"Put that away, Mr. Lapid," he said, with a touch of annoyance.

I raised my eyebrows in mock surprise, then shrugged and put the cigarettes back in my pocket.

"Why did you and Boris Melvitzki get into a fight?" he asked.

"We didn't."

"But you came close, you said. Why?"

"I don't know. It's something I've been wondering about." I paused, deciding it was time I stopped acting dumb. "Someone killed him?"

Bilenko considered whether to answer me, and finally did. "On the beach. Last night."

"How?" I asked. Because I felt I needed to show curiosity.

"He was stabbed to death. Know anything about that, Mr. Lapid?"

"No. Any idea who did it?"

"We're pursuing several leads."

"So you've got nothing."

Bilenko lifted his eyebrows.

"I used to be a cop. I know what 'pursuing several leads' means."

"And now you're a private investigator, and you're investigating my case."

"From what I understand, you're not working it any longer."

He flushed a little. "The case is still open."

"That doesn't mean anything. A case can stay open for decades without anyone putting in any actual work."

His face went hard. "Are you suggesting something, Mr. Lapid?"

"No. Nothing."

"Are you insinuating that I'm negligent in my work?"

"Not in the slightest, I can assure you."

His expression did not soften, and I worried he might start shouting at me or worse. But he controlled his anger and brought the questioning back to its original course. "Where were you last night?"

"With a woman."

"What's her name?"

"Hannah Goldman. You've met her, remember?"

He did, and I could tell the recollection made him uncomfortable. My knowing Hannah Goldman meant I also knew that he had omitted her from his report. Which might not rise to the level of negligence, but it was certainly not doing things by the book.

He rubbed a finger across his mustache, attempting to hide his discomfort, recovered his poise, and said, "What were you doing together? Where were you?"

"Depends on the hour," I said, and told him about going to a movie, then drinking coffee, and finally walking Hannah home.

"And you stayed there with her?"

"Yes."

"For how long?"

"A couple of hours."

The implication was clear. I didn't need to explain what Hannah and I did during those two hours. I couldn't tell what he thought of that, and I found that I didn't care one bit. Hannah would have approved of that.

"So you didn't stay the night?"

"No."

"When did you leave?"

"Around two o'clock."

"Miss Goldman would corroborate this?"

"Sure," I said, thinking that Hannah would not be embarrassed in the slightest to confirm that I had been with her in her shack, notwithstanding what Bilenko might think of her character. But would this make her rethink her involvement with me? I hoped it wouldn't, but it was out of my hands.

"Where did you go after you parted with Miss Goldman?"

"Home. I live on Hamaccabi Street, but you know that already."

"You went straight home?"

"Yes."

"You didn't stop at the beach?"

"No."

"What route did you take?"

I fed him a direct route from Mahlul to my apartment. I knew that part of the city well, and it was easy to rattle off the right street names.

"What were you wearing?"

"The same clothes I have on now." I gave him a small smile. "I changed my socks and underwear."

"Stand up."

"Why?"

"Because I told you to, that's why. And move to the side of the table where I can see you."

He commenced a sweep of my clothes with his eyes. I wasn't worried. I'd checked them for blood when I got home last night and found not a single drop. And I'd brushed away every single grain of sand that clung to the fabric.

"Are these the same shoes you had on last night?"

When I confirmed that they were, he told me to prop my right foot on the table and studied the sole. Looking for beach sand in the treads.

He found none. Not in the right shoe, and not in the left one either. I'd scrubbed the treads clean when I got home, then wandered about the city before going to Greta's Café this morning in order to dirty them up again, even making sure to get some sandstone in the treads, as there would have to be since I'd visited Mahlul the night before.

His face showed resigned disappointment. A common sentiment among police detectives the world over. He had no evidence, no witnesses, nothing tangible. But then someone had told him about me, and he hoped he would be able to close the case without much

265

effort. I almost patted him on the shoulder and told him I knew how he felt.

He told me to sit down, then spent the next minute pursing his lips, moving his jaw about, thinking deep thoughts whose nature I could not guess. Then he looked at me with naked suspicion and went for the direct approach. "Did you kill Boris Melvitzki?"

"Of course not. Why would I want to kill him?"

"Maybe it was self-defense. He tried to kill you last night on the beach, and you protected yourself. The judge would understand that."

"I wasn't there, I told you."

"He came at you with a wrench. That's what happened, right? No one can blame you for that. But you need to tell the truth."

"You're barking up the wrong tree, Sergeant. I did not kill this man."

"Why did he want to hit you in Café Silver? And don't tell me again you don't know. I don't believe that."

"I wasn't lying. I don't know exactly. But I do know he didn't like my investigating Feldbaum's murder."

"You think he had something to do with it?"

"I don't have any evidence. What I do know is that he hated Feldbaum." I told him about the contest of strength that Feldbaum had won, thereby casting Boris in an uncomplimentary light.

"Doesn't sound like a reason to kill someone."

I agreed that it didn't. I could have told him about Caspi, but I held off. What would be the point? There was no evidence that pointed at Caspi, and he had no motive to kill Feldbaum. And Caspi was a successful and respected businessman with political connections. I doubted I could make Bilenko believe he had arranged the murder of a lowly, scramble-brained former employee.

"I take it you don't think Feldbaum was killed in the course of a robbery," he said.

"No."

"Why?"

"Because of Menashe Volkoff," I said, and told him what I'd learned in Haifa.

He listened attentively, his chin sinking toward his chest while his eyes stayed glued to my face. But he didn't write anything down.

I was expecting him to ask some questions, tell me I'm crazy, say something related to what I'd just told him. But what he said instead was, "I want you to stop your investigation, Mr. Lapid."

"What? Why?"

"Because since you started working on it, a man with whom you had a run-in was knifed on the beach."

"I told you I had nothing to do with it."

"I'm not convinced that's true. But I also don't think I'll be able to prove it one way or the other. Luckily for you. But I don't need proof to tell you to stay away from my case."

"Without me, you wouldn't know about Volkoff."

"And what does that change? A minute ago, you suggested Boris Melvitzki was the one who murdered Feldbaum, and now you bring up a disappearance that happened thirteen years ago. Is there any connection between Melvitzki and Volkoff?"

"No, but—"

"There you have it. Not that it matters much to me. Because I still think Feldbaum was killed by a robber."

"There's something more to this case, Sergeant."

He leaned back in his chair, folding his arms. "I'll look into it, Mr. Lapid. When I'm good and ready. When I've exhausted all other avenues of investigation."

"You have no other avenues," I said, beginning to get mad. I had inadvertently offended Bilenko's professional pride, and now the stupid man was paying me back.

"What I have is a badge and the authority that goes with it. And I'm telling you to stay off the case. Have I made myself clear?"

I had the urge to clobber him or shout at his face that he was being dumb and obstinate and was letting a killer stay free. But I couldn't see how either of those actions would benefit me. He would either use the information I gave him, or he wouldn't. It would be his decision alone. The more I tried to convince him, the more stubborn he'd be.

"Yes," I said. "Crystal clear. Are we done?"

On my way out, I ran into Reuben.

"Adam? How did you know to come here?"

It took a few seconds for his words to penetrate the cloud of fury that enveloped me. Then I said, "You found something."

He nodded. His expression was grim.

"It's bad news, isn't it?"

"I'm afraid so," he said.

38

"Shimon Suskind was found dead ten months ago on the outskirts of Tel Aviv," Reuben said.

"Murdered?"

"Yeah. Someone bashed his head in and buried his body in a copse of pines."

It was a shallow grave. Otherwise, the dog wouldn't have caught the scent of the corpse.

The dog belonged to a man called Max Schumer, who lived in the city of Holon, a few kilometers south of Tel Aviv. Schumer was an avid collector of butterflies. His hobby often took him out of the city and into nature, where those lovely creatures abounded. And when he ventured out, he took his dog—a German shepherd called Igor —with him.

On this particular trek, as they were cutting through a copse of pines toward a wild field where Schumer hoped to find more butter-flies for his collection, Igor paused near a bump in the earth and began barking madly.

"He wouldn't budge," Schumer later told the police. "Not when I called him, nor when I pulled on his collar. He started circling this bump, barking loudly and digging at the earth with his paws. I figured he'd found something, and the earth looked freshly turned over, so, with a flat piece of rock I found lying nearby, I helped him dig."

Inside the hole, just a foot below soil level, were the clothed remains of a man. The body had not been in the ground long. Decomposition was in its early odoriferous stages, which was how Igor the dog got interested in the first place.

"The smell was awful, like nothing I'd ever experienced," Schumer said to the cops, from which I deduced he'd never had the misfortune of being incarcerated in a Nazi death camp. "I could barely keep my lunch down. Anyway, when I saw it was a body, I covered it up again so no animal could get to it, and called you guys."

It was lucky that no animal had done so regardless, I thought, before Schumer and Igor had come upon the body. Otherwise, I might never have found myself reading this report.

I was sitting in Reuben's office, one floor above the room where Bilenko had interviewed me. Bilenko who had ordered me off the case. But I had no intention of obeying.

I hadn't told Reuben this, and I felt guilty about it. But I wanted to read the report first. I'd earned the right to read it. I had worked this case better than Sergeant Bilenko and any other cop. I had nearly died because of it. I deserved to see it through, and it was clear to me now that if I didn't solve this case, no one ever would.

After getting the call from Max Schumer, the cops dug up the body, and in a trouser pocket they found a wallet with identification papers. The photo therein matched the corpse's face, which was still recognizable. It was Shimon Suskind.

He had arrived in Israel less than two weeks before his death, which was estimated to have occurred two or three days before his body turned up. The medical examiner didn't take long to determine the cause of death. Suskind's skull was busted open. The murder weapon had likely been made of metal—a hammer or a pipe, the report suggested. *Or a wrench,* I thought, remembering how I nearly got brained with one yesterday. Did Boris kill Suskind too? Did Caspi tell him to do it?

Suskind had emigrated from Poland. He had no family in Israel and had stayed in a furnished room in Jaffa. His landlord wasn't as caring as Mrs. Steinberg was. He hadn't bothered notifying the police that Suskind was missing. He hadn't even noticed his tenant was gone.

"He still had two days left before he needed to pay rent again," the landlord told the cops. "As long as they pay, I leave 'em alone. I give 'em privacy, is what I do."

The landlord said that Suskind had stayed with him for three days. They had never spoken beyond the necessary bare minimum. He did not know where Suskind had come from, what his plans were, or where he'd been going the day he ended up dead.

In Suskind's room, the cops discovered the meager belongings befitting an indigent immigrant to a new land. There was an old suitcase that had done its share of traveling, clothes that had been worn to within a thread of their life, some toiletries, a couple of old books, a new map of Israel, and a copy of the *Palestine Gazette* that had been published in September 1939.

"Ever heard of the *Palestine Gazette*?" I asked Reuben.

He frowned. "I should know this... oh, yes. It was the official newspaper of the British. I mean the local government of the British Mandate. Before independence."

"What sort of things did they publish there?"

"Never read the thing in my life. Official stuff, I guess. Nothing that I'd find interesting. Why?"

"Suskind had an edition of the *Gazette* in his suitcase. An old one. Why would he have it?"

Reuben spread his hands. "I don't know, Adam."

I frowned at the report. September 1939. A terrible month. On the first of that month, Germany had started World War II by invading Poland. And two days later, Britain had declared war on Germany because of that invasion. But that couldn't have been related to why Suskind had hunted down an old copy of the *Gazette* thirteen years after it was published. If he had wanted to read news about the war, the regular dailies would have served him much better. He must have had another reason.

Volkoff had vanished in July 1939. Had Suskind searched for clues of his whereabouts in an official government gazette that came out two months later? It seemed unlikely, but I would need to hunt down a copy of that magazine to see for myself.

At the bottom of Suskind's suitcase, the cops found a small box of the sort you keep jewelry in. But this one contained a treasure of a different kind. Inside the box was a medal comprised of a piece of green cloth with two vertical black lines set wide apart, and a gold-plated Greek cross hanging off a ring at its bottom. There were various words and images inscribed on the cross. Some cop who knew Polish supplied the translation.

In the center of the cross on the obverse side was a tiny image of an eagle. The horizontal arms bore the inscription "For Poland, Liberty, and People."

The reverse side carried the horizontal inscription "To Partisans," and two years were also inscribed: 1939, at the tip of the top vertical bar, and 1945, at the end of the bottom one. The two years marked the beginning and end of the Nazi occupation of Poland.

Someone, perhaps the same cop who wrote the translation, identified the item as a Partisan Cross, a medal awarded to Polish partisans at the end of World War II. Shimon Suskind had not merely survived the Nazis; he had taken up arms against them. He had been a partisan. He had skirted death for six years of struggle in Poland, had managed to elude its icy claws, and finally had made his way to his new-old homeland of Israel. And here he met the violent end that he had evaded for so long.

Here. In the land of the Jews. At the hand of a fellow Jew.

Just like Emmanuel Feldbaum, Shimon Suskind should not have died this way.

But who had killed him?

One possibility was that Boris had done it at Caspi's behest, just like he had killed Feldbaum. Or was it Menashe Volkoff, covering his tracks? Or was Volkoff also lying dead in a hole somewhere? A deeper one that hadn't been dug up.

I rubbed my forehead in a futile attempt to banish the dull ache that had started in my head. So many questions, too many of them, and very few answers.

In addition to the partisan medal, and in stark contrast to it, the suitcase held another military insignia. A round metal pin showing two wicked lightning bolts on a black background. I didn't need the police report to know what it was. An SS pin. One of the marks of the Nazi evil.

Spoils of war? A memento stripped from the body of an SS officer Suskind had dispatched as a partisan? That was my initial guess. Until I saw the photograph.

It was lying inside a book of Polish poetry that Suskind had left on the small bedside table next to his rented bed. It showed the dead man dressed in a black coat with the collar turned up and his hands stuck in the pockets. He had dark hair, narrow shoulders, and the sort of hollow-cheeked ascetic face that seemed incapable of smiling. His expression could have been interpreted as combative, or perhaps merely determined. A man on a mission.

Behind him stretched a long street with piles of rubble on one side and bombed-out buildings with gaping holes instead of walls on the other. I turned the picture over. Someone, perhaps Suskind himself, had jotted a place and time on the picture's back.

Hamburg, March 1946.

Hamburg was a German city that was in the British occupation zone after Germany surrendered to the Allies. Perhaps Suskind had been in one of the displaced persons camps in the area, and the picture had been taken on a trip to the devastated German city.

But something in Suskind's expression, in the flat harshness of his deep eyes, made me think he was not a mere refugee recovering from the travails of war. Seeing his picture and knowing when and where it was snapped, combined with his history as a partisan and the SS pin he had obtained, made me suspect that for him the war had not ended in May 1945. In some ways, it had just begun.

I couldn't know for sure, but I would have bet good money that Suskind had acquired that SS pin not in Poland before May '45, but in Germany afterward. And that he had done so not as a partisan but as a Nazi hunter.

Like I had been.

He had gotten that pin the same way I had gotten my knife, from a Nazi he had executed in Germany after the war. For all his dead relatives. For all the murdered Jews. For revenge, and for justice.

I closed my eyes and said a silent prayer over this man whom I had never met yet felt a connection with. He and I had never worn the same uniform, never fought side by side, yet we were brothers-in-arms. Fellow soldiers in the same tiny, hopeless, unwinnable war that had followed the end of the bigger one. A war conducted by a scattered handful of survivors, trying to even the score just a little by hunting down Nazi war criminals and dispensing immediate and ultimate justice.

Like Feldbaum, Suskind was a stranger to me, but I felt a closeness to him. Closeness and a duty to see that his death was avenged.

Bilenko wouldn't do it. But I would.

39

Since the British were gone and the *Palestine Gazette* no longer existed, it wasn't easy to track down copies of it. I went to two public libraries, but neither had any issues. I finally found a couple in a dusty used bookstore on Ben-Yehuda Street, but neither had been published before 1945. I browsed through them anyway and found nothing of interest.

They contained announcements of new government appointments; open positions members of the public could apply for; statistics of various kinds; a list of people who had legally changed their names; a registry of every kind of permit imaginable; government surveys across the land; lists of newly registered trademarks; all manner of decrees, laws, and regulations; changes in the status of villages and towns and other communities; municipal bylaws and ordinances; various announcements by corporations; a variety of notices to the public by the British authorities; and more items in that vein.

All quite dull, dry, and yawn-inducing. Nothing I could imagine Suskind would find interesting in the slightest. So why did he have a copy in his possession? And why one so old?

The owner of the bookstore, who seemed as dusty as his wares, told me the Israeli government also published an official newspaper, a continuation of the British one. "They probably have all the old copies of the *Gazette*. They have an office in Jerusalem."

On a public telephone, I asked the operator for the number of that office. But by then it was well past office hours, and no one picked up.

In the morning, I boarded another bus to Haifa. The cops had traced Suskind's movements all the way back to the port of that city, where he had entered Israel shortly before his death. During his first week in the country, he'd stayed at a cheap boardinghouse near the sea, and by ten o'clock I was talking to the landlady, a Miss Glickson.

She was a plump woman with kind brown eyes, an incipient double chin, and round, rosy cheeks. She remembered Suskind quite well.

"The police talked to me about ten months ago. They said someone killed him."

"That's right. Can you tell me what he was like?"

"Morose and taciturn. A lot of them are like that. With what they went through over there in Europe, it's hardly surprising. But he was quieter than most and didn't show much emotion. He was polite, and he never failed to eat everything I put on the table. A lot of them are like that too."

"Maybe you're just a good cook," I said, hoping to get on her good side.

"I don't get many complaints," she said modestly, "but there's a difference in how people eat. Those who've experienced starvation eat differently than those who haven't. Suskind belonged to the first group."

I did too, and I knew for a fact it had changed the way I viewed food. But I hoped I wasn't as obvious about it as Suskind had been.

"Did he ever talk about his life in Europe?"

She shook her head.

"He didn't even say what town he came from?"

"Yes, he did. I asked because I'm also from Poland, even though I came here when I was twelve." She squinted in concentration. "I don't remember the name of the town, but I never heard of it before. Something beginning with an *M*, I think."

"Mastarnia?"

She snapped her fingers. "That's it."

So there it was. That sealed it. Suskind had come from the same town as Volkoff and Feldbaum, and of the three men, at least two had been murdered. The third either had met the same fate or was the culprit. And it all had to do with something valuable. Something that Volkoff had. Feldbaum had wanted it, and Suskind had too. That was why he had gone to the police station after learning that Volkoff had vanished. That was why he had been killed.

And what about Yosef Rudinsky? Was he also from Mastarnia? Was he another victim, yet to be found?

"Did Suskind mention anyone he was hoping to meet here in Israel?" I asked.

"I don't think so."

"Anything else? Any plans for the future?"

She started shaking her head, but then stopped and said, "I remember that, shortly after he arrived, he asked me about a place called Tel Zion."

"Tel Zion? Where's that?"

"That's just it. I'd never heard the name before, and I told him so. He said it was somewhere between Haifa and Netanya, right on the beach, and I told him I traveled that road from time to time and had never come across a community by that name." She paused, clasping her hands in her lap. "When I said this, he got quite agitated. Told me I must be mistaken and asked if I had a map of Israel. I did. A new one I got when I took a vacation the year before. I spread it out on the dining table over there, and we looked at it together."

She looked at the dining table now, as though watching that scene that had long since passed.

"'See?' I said to him. 'There's no such place as Tel Zion. What made you think there was?' He didn't answer. He just looked at me, and his eyes were suddenly fierce and angry, like I'd just slapped him across the face. I don't mind telling you that for a moment there I was quite scared of him. It was like he had a dark side that he kept hidden, and now I was getting a glimpse of it. But then he lowered his head and took a deep breath, and when he looked at me again, he no longer looked scary, just sad, so very sad."

We were quiet for a moment, she with her memories and I with a mind churning with new questions.

"He didn't say what he was looking for in Tel Zion? Or who?"

"He was quiet for a while, and I could tell he was thinking unpleasant thoughts by how his jaw was clenched. He was no longer merely sad but angry too. But for some reason, I was no longer scared of him. I was sure he wasn't angry with me. I didn't know with whom, but I was sure I didn't have anything to worry about. And then he asked me how I would go about finding a man."

"A man? Did he give his name?"

She shook her head. "I asked, but he wouldn't say. And not only that, but his face closed off, do you know what I mean?"

"I think so," I said, remembering that Suskind had lived in the underground for years. He had learned to be mistrustful and secretive.

"I told him that if he wanted to find someone, he should try the police. They would have a list of residents."

And he did, I thought. The first time resulted in him discovering that Volkoff had gone missing; the second time was the conversation he'd had with Sergeant Karni of the Haifa Police, in which Suskind tried to find out what the police knew about the disappearance. They didn't know anything of worth, but Suskind must have discovered something, or he wouldn't have been murdered. His death was evidence of him getting very close to the killer.

"Did you tell the police about this?"

"No. Do you think I should have?"

I shook my head. "It wouldn't have done any good. Not without a name. Is there anything else you remember?"

"I... well, no, never mind."

"What is it?"

She hesitated. "I'm sure it's nothing. I don't know why I thought of it at all."

I smiled in encouragement. "Maybe it's nothing and maybe it's something. Either way, it would do no harm if you told me."

She signified her agreement with my logic with a short nod. "A day or two after the conversation I told you about, he asked me how to get to Pevzner Street."

It was the street where Volkoff had reportedly stepped off the bus on the day of his disappearance. So Suskind had gone there in search of some clue as to where Volkoff might be or what had happened to him. I had gone there as well and found nothing.

"Did he go there?"

"I think so. He left right after I told him which bus to take, and when he returned a few hours later, he was different."

"Different? How?"

"There was that fierce look in his eyes again. And everything about him was tense. His face, the set of his shoulders. He looked... I don't know exactly how to put it."

"Determined?" I suggested, echoing the word Sergeant Karni had used to describe Suskind.

"Yes. That's it. That's it precisely. Determined. Like he had something important to do that would suffer no delay. And an hour later he was gone."

"He left?"

She nodded. "He went straight to his room, packed his suitcase, and left. He had paid in advance for three more days, and I offered to refund him that, but he refused. I don't know why. I doubt he had much money, judging by his clothes, and, well, I keep a neat house, but people with money generally don't stay here."

"For him this house would have seemed palatial compared to other places he slept in during the war in Europe."

The remark made her examine my face, for what I'm not sure, but finally she offered a small smile of appreciation. "That's nice of you to say. Thank you."

"Do you know where he was going?"

"He didn't say. I asked him what was the matter; the way he was acting, his sudden departure—naturally, I was worried."

"What did he say?"

"He gave me this long look, and his eyes were full of sorrow. And then something compelled him to speak more openly to me than he had ever done before. He said I shouldn't worry, that now he knew why he had survived the war when so many others hadn't. That his purpose was now known to him.

"I asked him what that purpose was, and why he looked so bleak. And he smiled. I think it was the first time I'd seen him smile, and I wish I hadn't. Because it was an awful smile. There was nothing joyful about it. And then he said: 'I thought I was done with this sort of thing, but I guess it was fated. I guess that's why I survived.'"

"Those were his exact words? Are you sure?"

She nodded. "I doubt I'll ever forget them. When the police detective came here, I told him what Suskind had said. He listened and wrote it down, but I could tell he didn't know what it meant. I don't know either." She paused and peered into my eyes. "But you do, don't you?"

"Yes," I said. "I think I do."

"Will you tell me?"

"I don't think I should. It wouldn't do you any good to know. Only the opposite."

She accepted this without argument. Perhaps she only half wanted to know and was relieved when I absolved her of the burden of knowing.

"Did he intend to do something wrong? Just tell me that wasn't it."

"It was the exact opposite," I said. "He was aiming to set things right."

"And he was killed while trying?" There were tears in her eyes now. "Is that what happened?"

"Yes. I think that's it precisely."

She started crying in earnest then and kept at it for a couple of minutes. Finally, the tears subsided, and I offered her my handkerchief, which she used to dry her eyes.

"Are you going to catch the person who killed him, Mr. Lapid?"

"Yes, Miss Glickson. One way or another, I will see that justice is done."

40

I called the office of the government newspaper, and this time the phone was picked up. A lethargic clerk told me they had all the back copies of the *Palestine Gazette* in storage, but he didn't seem enthusiastic about the prospect of having to dig through them.

I'd anticipated this, which was why, at the beginning of the call, I'd identified myself as Inspector Meyerson, Tel Aviv Police. I doubted I would get any sort of real cooperation any other way.

"It's important," I said.

"What could be important about a thirteen-year-old newspaper?" the clerk in Jerusalem asked. His voice held a tinge of annoyance now. I was proving to be the bane of his bureaucratic existence; I was asking him to perform an actual helpful task. This was going to require some persuasion.

"It may contain information related to an open case. A serious crime. Very serious indeed."

"What sort of crime?" he asked. Was there a hint of interest in his voice? I couldn't be certain.

"I'm not at liberty to say. Your swift cooperation will be much appreciated. I'll be sure to put in a good word with your superior—if you can locate a copy of the magazine today and send it to me."

The promise also carried a threat. If he failed to accommodate me, the good word could easily be replaced with a bad one. That might disrupt his tranquil routine even more than a trip to the archives.

Still, he attempted to stall: "I have a lot of work to do. I'm not sure I could get to it today."

It didn't require much acting to sound angry. "Listen to me now, you lazy bastard, and listen good, because I'm not going to tell you a second time. I need that magazine, and you're going to get it for me. And you're going to do it today. Right now in fact. If I have to come to Jerusalem to get it myself, I'll do more than talk to your boss. I'll stop by your office, and I'll be bringing my nightstick and handcuffs with me. I'll charge you with interfering with a police officer in the performance of his duties. And when I do, you can forget about your cushy government job. You'll be lucky if they hire you to pick up street litter. Do I make myself clear?"

There was a stunned silence, and I worried that I might have overdone it. If he was the sort of person who didn't take kindly to threats, or if he had a semi-functioning brain and saw through my bluster, I might have just blown my best chance of getting a copy of that newspaper.

But after a moment in which the only sounds I heard were his heavy breathing and the faint crackle of the telephone line, he spoke again, and his tone was that of a chastened child—timid and eager to placate.

"I'll get right to it, Inspector. You can count on me."

"I'm glad to hear it," I said, adopting a tone of mollified authority, like a father about to pat his wayward son on the head after the boy had apologized for misbehaving. I decided to press my advantage: "Is there a car coming to Tel Aviv later today?"

"A car?"

"A government car. A vehicle carrying documents, or an official coming over for a meeting."

"Not from our department."

"But from another one?"

The clerk was hesitant. "I suppose so. I mean, I don't know for sure, but—"

"But you can find out, right? You can do that for me?"

"I guess so," he said, sounding petulant. But then he cleared his throat and added, "Yes. I can do that. I want to help any way I can." He was trying to stay on my good side now. Afraid I might get angry again. "You want me to send the magazine to you, Inspector? Where is your office?"

Greta's Café? I thought. But naturally, I couldn't tell him that. It had to be an official building. A police station. Could I wait for the car outside of one? No, that might arouse suspicion, and I had no way of knowing at what time the car would arrive.

I scoured my brain for an answer, cursing myself for not planning ahead. I didn't have time to come up with the perfect solution. I could see only one feasible option. I didn't like it much, but it would have to do.

"Here's what you do," I said. "When you find that magazine, put it in an envelope and address it to Reuben Tzanani. He's a cop who works at the station on Yehuda Halevi 6, Tel Aviv. You got that?"

He read the name and address back to me, no mistakes. It appeared my threats had sharpened his mind. Perhaps that was why he asked a most logical question, "Why not address it to you, Inspector Meyerson?"

I injected a dose of impatience into my voice. "Reuben Tzanani is my subordinate. He handles the case material. Do I really need to explain to you the way I run an investigation?"

"No, no. I didn't mean to... I'll do as you say, Inspector."

"See that you do," I said, and was about to hang up, when another thing occurred to me. "One more thing: this is an ongoing investigation. It's vital that no one knows about my getting this magazine from you. So tell no one about our talk. Absolutely no one. You understand me?"

"Yes," he said. "I understand."

"Good. Now get to it." And I ended the call.

I picked up the receiver again and gave the operator Reuben's number. When he answered, I told him that an envelope addressed to him would be coming by official car from Jerusalem later that day.

"What's in the envelope?"

"A copy of the *Palestine Gazette*, the September '39 issue."

"The one Shimon Suskind had?"

"Yes." I explained about the government department that published the Israeli official magazine and how they had copies of old *Gazette* issues.

"You just spoke to them now?"

"A few minutes ago."

"And they're sending it today? That's fast."

I lit a cigarette and took a bracing drag. I did not relish explaining myself to Reuben, but there was no avoiding it.

"I sort of gave the clerk I spoke with the impression that I was a cop."

"You did what?"

"I told him I was Inspector Meyerson of the Tel Aviv Police."

Another stunned silence. It seemed like I was having that effect on people today.

"It was the only way to get him to cooperate, Reuben. Otherwise, I don't think he would have gotten the magazine for me in the near future."

Reuben sighed. "Instead of pretending to be a police officer—which is illegal, by the way—you could have asked me to call him, Adam. Didn't that occur to you?"

"I didn't want to involve you." Another drag on the cigarette. "You see, I'm not supposed to be working the case anymore."

"Why not?"

"Sergeant Bilenko told me to stop."

"What? When did this happen?"

I studied the smoking tip of my cigarette. Another drag wouldn't make this easier. "Yesterday."

A short pause while Reuben's fine mind added two and two together. "Before I showed you the report of Suskind's murder? That's why you were at the station? You had a talk with Bilenko?"

"Yes," I said, shutting my eyes. Just like numerous criminals had done when I'd been a police officer and they were about to confess. I opened them, disgusted with myself. "I'm sorry, Reuben. I should have told you."

"That's right. You should have. Why did Bilenko order you off the case?"

"He felt upstaged. Like I didn't respect his professionalism. He doesn't want me to work the case, but he's not going to be putting in much effort either. Not in the foreseeable future, and maybe never. He still thinks the murder was random, and he doesn't want to be proven wrong."

I didn't want to tell him the other part, but I feared he would hear about it somehow. "There's another reason. One of the guys I interviewed during my investigation has wound up dead. Someone knifed him on the beach in Tel Aviv."

"And?"

A final drag and I tossed the cigarette away. "Bilenko brought me in for questioning about it. The dead guy and I had exchanged heated words."

"Bilenko thought you killed the guy?"

"Yeah. Or at least he wanted to rule me out."

"You convinced him, I hope."

"Unfortunately, I couldn't. I don't have an alibi."

Reuben was quiet for a long moment, and with each passing second, my unease increased. Could he tell that I was hiding the truth? Should I come clean and rely on our friendship? Or would that be an abuse of it?

I did not regret killing Boris. It was self-defense and he deserved it. But I wasn't sure how Reuben would take it. He would wonder why I hadn't called the police, why I had lied to Bilenko. I could tell him I didn't want to risk not being believed, that there had been no witnesses to back my claim of self-defense. But Reuben was a dedicated cop. He wouldn't like my having left the scene without notifying the authorities. And I had done more than that. I'd taken money from Boris's wallet. That was a crime.

Not for the first time, I wondered what the nature of our friendship really was that I would keep such things from him. And what if he ended up suspecting the worst?

"Reuben," I said, unsure of my words until they left my lips, "the dead guy was a violent man. A few days ago, he tried to kill me by dropping a brick on my head."

There was a sharp intake of breath. "What?"

I told him how Boris had taken up position on my roof and tried to kill me with a brick.

"You didn't call us? You didn't file a complaint?"

"No."

"Why not?"

"No proof. And at the time, I wasn't sure it was him."

"That's what we're here for, Adam, to find out who commits crimes. Do you have so little trust in the police?"

"In my investigation of the murder of Emmanuel Feldbaum, I learned more in less time than Bilenko did."

Apparently, Reuben had no answer to this. He was silent for a while, and then he said, "What happened on the beach with the dead guy, do you know?"

I let out a low breath. I thought I understood what Reuben was doing, but I wasn't entirely sure. It sounded as though he was putting distance between me and Boris's killing, keeping things vague. He wanted to know what had happened, and was assuming I was involved, but he didn't want to ask me outright to confirm or deny it.

All right, Reuben. I'll follow your lead.

I said, "Bilenko told me the cops found a wrench by the dead man's body. He thinks that the man attacked someone with the wrench and got knifed in self-defense. Remember that Feldbaum was killed with a blunt object, possibly a wrench, though Bilenko doesn't believe the dead man had any involvement with Feldbaum's murder."

"I see," said Reuben slowly. "Did Bilenko have any idea why the guy who defended himself with the knife didn't call the cops?"

"He didn't share it with me if he did. I suppose it was because there were no witnesses. There was no one to back a claim of self-defense. And think of how it would be interpreted: a knife versus a wrench. Not so easy to make a case for self-defense, is it?"

"No. I see what you mean," Reuben said, and I could almost hear him think it over, trying to reconcile his friendship with me and his innate sense of justice on one side, with his duties as a cop on the other.

I could imagine him pinching the bridge of his nose, or rubbing the center of his forehead, or closing his eyes with his lips pressed tightly together. All gestures I'd seen him do many times over the course of our friendship.

"I know I should have told you all of this yesterday," I said, "but I needed to read Suskind's file, and I figured it would be better for you if you didn't know about Bilenko ordering me off the case. And about the other stuff as well. Suskind came from the same town as Feldbaum. And so did Volkoff. Two of them have been murdered, maybe all three, maybe Yosef Rudinsky too, and if I don't find out who did it, no one will. Not Bilenko, that's for sure."

I stopped talking. I had said all I could. Now it was up to Reuben to determine the cost of my deception.

It took him less than a minute to make his decision, but it felt much longer than that. Time does that when your fate hangs in the balance: it stretches and curves and changes shape.

"You shouldn't have done it, Adam. Not that, and not the other stuff as well. But I understand why you did. Are you close to catching this killer?"

I knew Boris had killed Feldbaum, and I knew Caspi had told him to do it. It was likely the two of them were also responsible for Suskind's death. But I had no motive, no proof. I needed both.

"I think so."

"And Bilenko can't be persuaded to carry on with the case with what you've found out so far?"

"No. He's too stubborn. Maybe he'll come around at some point, but I don't want to wait."

"Okay. But don't ever do that to me again, Adam. You may not want to be a cop, but I want to stay one."

"You have my word."

"Okay. Any idea at what time this envelope would be arriving?"

"No. It will be a few hours."

"I'll hold onto it for you. Oh wait, it wouldn't be wise for you to come here to take it, would it?"

I hadn't thought of that. Bilenko worked at that station. I couldn't risk going there. Not until the case was done.

"Can you drop it off at Greta's Café?" I asked. "Greta will keep it safe."

After we ended the call, I stood at the phone, pondering if I was worthy of Reuben's friendship and fearing I wasn't. I might have sunk deeper into this bleak frame of mind if a pudgy man in suspenders hadn't tapped my shoulder and inquired if I was through with the telephone. I smiled at him and confirmed that I was.

41

I lit another cigarette and considered my next step. Suskind had left Miss Glickson's boardinghouse immediately after he had visited Pevzner Street. This meant that he had found something there. I'd failed to do so on my previous visit to that street, but since I was in Haifa and could think of nothing better to do, I decided to go there again.

As I walked to the bus stop, I thought back to the hours I'd spent on Pevzner Street. What had I missed? Where did I fail to ask the right questions or recognize the significance of a piece of information?

And why did no one see Menashe Volkoff after he got off the bus there?

More questions. And not a single answer.

As the bus chugged up Mount Carmel, I looked out the window at the people and buildings streaming by. The glass reflected a translucent, wavering image of my face. I looked insubstantial and lost, like a ghost barely clinging to the mortal world. I turned my eyes away from the sight.

I kept on asking myself what I had done wrong on my previous visit to Pevzner Street, but by the time the bus dropped me off there, I was no smarter.

I stood at the bus stop and took a slow, sweeping look at the street around me. Shops, trees, a couple of benches, sheets and clothes flapping on clotheslines, a noticeboard laden with overlapping notices, a bicycle leaning against the side of a building, a few cars parked at the curb or rumbling down the road, people on the sidewalk or standing at balcony railings. Nothing out of the ordinary. I tried seeing everything from a fresh angle, in a new light, but nothing caught my eye and screamed *"Here I am. You missed me last time."*

My gaze stopped on the building where I'd spoken with Ingrid, the woman who doubted that Volkoff had been here the day he disappeared. There were too many people on this street, she'd told me. Someone would have seen and remembered him.

Looking around me now, I couldn't fault her logic. This street wasn't as crowded as Allenby or Dizengoff or Ben Yehuda Street, but there were plenty of people around. Mostly women, but some men too. In three or four minutes, I counted more than three dozen people.

It was later in the day now than when Volkoff had come here, and a different time of the year, but would the street had been emptier then? I couldn't say. But if so, it wouldn't have been by much.

Someone should have seen him.

But everyone I'd spoken with claimed they hadn't.

What did I miss? What question did I fail to ask?

Or maybe I was thinking about this all wrong. Maybe I should be asking myself what I knew now that I didn't then, on my previous visit to this street.

I knew one thing. I knew about Shimon Suskind. Not just who he was and how his life came to an end, I also knew he had come here, to this street. And I knew that he had found something here. Otherwise, he wouldn't have left Haifa right after. And he wouldn't have told his landlady that he knew why he had survived. Those were the words of a man on a mission, and somewhere on this street, Suskind had learned something that was to help him fulfill it.

So search for Suskind, and that might lead me to Volkoff.

I went right, just like I had on my previous canvass. The business owners remembered me. I showed them Suskind's photo from Hamburg, told them when he had come to this street, and said he might also have asked about Menashe Volkoff.

The barber was as unhelpful as last time. So was the seamstress. The cobbler wasn't any better, nor was the owner of the wine shop. And the woman working in the bookstore apologized once more for her inability to help me.

And with each negative answer or shake of the head, I grew a bit more despondent, sensing despair closing in around me. I did my best to shake it off. I was going to find out why Suskind had come here, and what he'd discovered. I would not give up until I had some answers.

I visited a few more businesses with equally dismal results, then crossed the street and entered the law firm I had visited the last time. The only person present was a short, fifty-something woman tapping away on a typewriter. She had not been here the last time.

She had gray hair and equally gray eyes, which she raised to meet mine, ceasing her tapping.

"Hello, can I help you?"

I looked around at the empty desks. She answered my question without my having to vocalize it.

"They've gone out to lunch. I'm holding the fort in their absence."

I gave her a smile. "Something tells me you do that even when they're around."

She chuckled. "You're a perceptive man. Are you here for legal advice? The lawyers should be back in twenty minutes at the most. There's a chair there and a couple of newspapers to read, and I can make you coffee if you like."

I shook my head. "That's not why I'm here. My name is Adam Lapid. I'm a private investigator. I'm working a case that involves a man who may have come here ten months ago."

"That's sort of vague."

"The man I'm interested in came from Poland. He may have been asking about a guy called Menashe Volkoff. Here's his photo."

The woman nodded without hesitation. "I remember him."

"You do?" I asked, barely able to believe my ears.

"Quite clearly. He was standing right where you are now."

I looked down at my feet dumbly, as though I'd be able to see Suskind's footprints and they might lead me somewhere.

"And he asked about Volkoff?"

"Not at first. Just before he left. I told him I'd never heard the name before."

Of course she didn't. The first time I'd been in this law firm, the owner told me they had moved to this location eleven years ago, two years after Volkoff disappeared. If this secretary had been here on my previous visit, I would have gotten my answers then. I had been unlucky, but it seemed my luck was improving.

"What did he ask about? Why did he come here?"

"He was looking for a business that used to be here before us."

"The travel agency?" I asked, remembering that was the business that had been here before.

"The one before that. The construction company."

"Construction company?"

"Yes. They had their offices here."

A tingle spread all over my arms and chest. Caspi owned a construction company.

"Was the company's name Hebrew Builders?"

"No. That wasn't it. The name of the company was Zion Construction."

"You seem very sure about that."

"I very well should be. I live a couple of streets from here, and I've been doing my shopping on this street for over fifteen years. I must have passed by this storefront a few hundred times before I started working here. Zion Construction. That was the name."

I wasn't disappointed that the name didn't match Caspi's company's name. Because business names can be changed. You fill out a form, pay a fee, and some government official makes the change for you.

Nothing too complicated or difficult.

And just the sort of thing that would be listed in an official government newspaper like the *Palestine Gazette*.

I looked out the front window. A blue Ford was parked right outside. And beyond it, just across the road, was the bus stop.

"Was that bus stop always there?" I asked.

"The bus stop?" Her eyes traveled to the window as though to assure herself it was still there now. "Yes. Yes, it was. Why do you ask?"

I thought of Ingrid telling me that someone would have seen Volkoff on the street. She had given me a clue without her realizing it, and without me recognizing it for what it was. I should have known that the only way no one would have seen Volkoff was if he went straight to a building that was very close to the bus stop. Like directly across the street from it. All he would have to do was walk across the road and into the same office I was in now. How long would that take? Ten seconds? Fifteen at the outside? Short enough that he might have gone unnoticed by anyone on the street.

And once he was here? There were two options. Either he was killed here, soon after he crossed the threshold, or he was escorted to a car parked outside, right where the Ford was parked now.

And if I had been smarter, I would have figured it out on the spot and paid all the businesses that were close to the bus stop a second visit. I would have had the information then.

Would that have made a difference in the grand scheme of things? I couldn't see how. Maybe Boris would still have been alive. But I couldn't say that his death saddened me one bit.

It irked me that I'd failed to figure it out immediately, but no matter. I had the answer now. I had succeeded.

"What is it, Mr. Lapid?" The woman was eying me curiously. "All of a sudden you look happy."

Because I was. Because in an instant all the despondency I had gathered that morning, and in some ways throughout this case, fell away from my body. And in its place, a warm glow of triumph spread through me.

"Not happy," I said. "Just satisfied. Do you happen to remember the name of the owner of Zion Construction?"

"I never knew it. I never walked in that door until I started working here."

That wasn't cause for disappointment either. Because I knew who that owner was. Benjamin Caspi.

She said, "But a few years ago someone told me the company no longer operated in Haifa. They'd moved to Tel Aviv."

Yes, they did, I thought. *And now I knew why.*

42

It took a few phone calls from a nearby café. Again I was Inspector Meyerson, only this time I didn't have to use threats, and I never once got angry. My luck had indeed changed: all the clerks I spoke with seemed to go out of their way to assist me.

I had two simple questions to answer: Had Hebrew Builders ever operated under a different name? And if so, what was it, and when had the name been changed?

At the end of those phone calls, I had my confirmation. I learned that Hebrew Builders had indeed been previously called Zion Construction, and that the name had been changed in August 1939.

The month after Menashe Volkoff disappeared.

And given the fact that the *Palestine Gazette* had been a monthly paper, the name change would have been listed the following month, in the September '39 issue, the one Suskind had in his possession. That was how he'd found out about the name change. That was another step in the journey that had led him to the killer and his own death.

I almost laughed. I had bullied that indolent clerk in Jerusalem for no purpose. I didn't need that magazine anymore. I knew all its secrets now.

Another phone call, and I had the address of a house in Tel Aviv. I was going to pay it a visit later tonight.

I returned to Tel Aviv, went home, ate a quick lunch, showered, and stretched out on my bed to rest.

My plan was to take a nap, but I wasn't the least bit sleepy. So, with more than a little reluctance, I picked up the copy of *Jane Eyre* Hannah had lent me and started reading.

I had expected to be bored stiff, but when I pulled my nose out of the book, I discovered that more than three hours had passed without my noticing.

I looked at the book in bewilderment, wondering how a story about the life of a girl in England during the reign of George III had ensnared me so. There were no shootouts, no chases on horseback, no swashbuckling adventure; it should have been decidedly dull. But it was riveting. Somehow, I had become involved in Jane's life. I grew to care about her. I mourned her setbacks, rejoiced in her triumphs, and, above all, longed to discover what happened to her next.

Remembering my reaction when Hannah had presented me with the book, I couldn't help but smile at my foolishness. I made myself a cup of tea and opened the book again.

It was well past dark when I came up for air. I had read more than half of the novel and found it difficult to set it aside. I felt a powerful longing to continue reading to the last page, to see how Jane's story would end, but I had business to attend to tonight, a story of my own to finish.

But first a little food; after all this reading, I was hungry.

I whipped up an omelet from two eggs I got on the black market and ate them with two pieces of toast. For dessert, I toasted a third slice and spread a generous portion of the jam Greta had given me.

After dinner, I went to my closet and took out my revolver. I checked that the cylinder was full and put the weapon in my pocket. I might need to do some persuading today.

Then I opened the door and went out to see a murderer.

43

He lived in a two-story house not too far from Rothschild Boulevard. A good part of the city. The house must have cost him a pretty penny, but he wasn't short on cash. I didn't know how much he'd made from his scam, but it had to be a great deal.

There were lights in the windows and a shiny black car parked right outside the door. A new model. That only made me angrier.

I studied the windows for a while. The curtains were pulled back, so I could see into the house.

There he was, standing in the kitchen with a glass of red wine in his hand, then a cigar curling bluish-gray smoke. I watched for twenty minutes and saw no one else.

He was alone. My good luck was holding.

I knocked on the door and heard footsteps approaching. Confident footfalls. The walk of a man who has made his mark on the world. And on people.

His face registered surprise when he saw me. His expression was in the process of shifting to outrage when I gave him a hard shove and stepped inside.

"Hey," he protested, teetering back from my push before bracing himself against a wall.

"Shut up!" I told him, and swung the door shut. "Let's go sit down. I want to talk to you. I know everything. Everything you've worked so hard to hide."

His face lost a little color. He swallowed hard and said nothing. There was the look of the cornered quarry in his eyes.

We went into the living room—spacious, nicely appointed, good art on the walls—and he dropped down onto a sofa. He bowed his head for a moment, and when he raised it, his eyes were deep and gray as a foreboding winter sky. His facial muscles were taut with tension, but he wasn't panicking. He wasn't even sweating. He had been close to disaster a few times before, and he'd emerged unscathed. He was already planning how to do it again.

"Why are you here, Mr. Lapid?"

"To talk, like I told you."

"So talk. Tell me what you want."

"There are things I want to know."

"I thought you said you knew everything."

"Almost everything. I know the general picture. But there are still some details you need to fill in for me."

He frowned in apparent puzzlement. He had good control of his expression. "I'm not sure I know what you're talking about."

"I'm talking about Emmanuel Feldbaum, about Menashe Volkoff, about Shimon Suskind. I know about them all. And I know about the land fraud."

"The land fraud?" A small gap had formed between his lips. It took him a few seconds to speak again. "I'm sorry, but I simply have no clue what you're getting at. And I've never heard those names you just said. Well, apart from Feldbaum, of course."

He sounded genuinely baffled. I had to admire his acting skills. But every confidence man is a talented actor. It's a necessary tool of his trade.

I gave him a smile that was one hundred percent contempt and zero percent warmth.

"It won't work, Caspi. You can't con yourself out of this. It's the end of the line for you."

"I really don't—"

"How about I tell you what I know, and then you can stop this charade and fill in the gaps, okay?"

He didn't answer, just stared at me. I kept a distance of six feet between us and put my hand in my jacket pocket over the gun. I didn't want to threaten him openly just yet, but if he made a move, a bullet would get to him before he got to me.

"It didn't start with Emmanuel Feldbaum," I said. "But it did for me, so I'll talk about him first.

"He used to ramble about his father's new house. I thought he was confused, that the house had been new when the Nazis invaded Poland, but that wasn't the case. Then there was the newspaper he kept in his suitcase. An old newspaper from 1938 from his hometown in Poland. From Mastarnia. You know Mastarnia, don't you?"

"I've never heard of that town," Caspi said. He was sitting straighter now, looking more confident. He had recovered from the initial shock of my coming to his house and claiming to know everything. He wasn't going to crumble and confess. I was going to have to break him, and it wasn't going to be easy. In truth, I wasn't sure I'd be able to do it at all.

"At first," I said, "I thought Feldbaum had this newspaper because his father had run an ad in it. His father was dead, as you very well know, along with most of the other Jews of Mastarnia, and I figured the newspaper was a way for Feldbaum to feel connected to his father. But I was wrong.

"The real reason Feldbaum had this paper was because of an article in it. An article about plans to build a new Hebrew city somewhere between Haifa and Netanya. The people of Mastarnia could buy land there, the paper said. That was a nice touch, a new Hebrew city. The whole Jewish world knew about Tel Aviv, the first Hebrew city. It would spark their imagination, make them eager to buy land there. How many of them did you scam?"

Caspi shrugged his wide shoulders and spread his hands. There was a crooked little smile on his face. He let out an awkward chuckle. "Like I said, I have no idea about any of this."

I felt like ramming that chuckle back down his throat. But the best way to break someone is with information, not force. I wanted him to confess and tell me all I didn't know. Where Volkoff's body was. Whether he had also killed Yosef Rudinsky. And if there were more victims I didn't know about.

"You went to Mastarnia in August 1938," I said. "You held an event there. A sales event. And what the good Jews of Mastarnia could buy there were plots of land on which your company would build houses. It would be a new Hebrew coastal city. Its name would be Tel Zion.

"If enough of them bought land there, they could one day make *aliyah* as a community, live next to their neighbors. It wouldn't have been a hard sell. Not if you got them to trust you. There was just one problem: the British were limiting the number of Jews they were letting in. Immigration certificates were hard to come by. The British did this in an attempt to mollify local Arabs, who at the time were in open revolt against British rule.

"The Jews of Mastarnia would have known this, but perhaps you led them to believe this was a temporary measure. And besides, the new city of Tel Zion wouldn't be built in a day. There was time for British policy to change."

I paused, swept a hand across my chin and jaw. I thought of all those dead Jews hoping to build a new home here in Israel. Caspi had swindled them all.

"It was a devilishly beautiful scheme; I'll grant you that. Sell land to Polish Jews, knowing they wouldn't be able to come claim that land any time soon. Perhaps not for years.

"But then one of those Jews showed up. Menashe Volkoff. He had somehow obtained an immigration certificate. And he had come to Haifa to meet with you, wanting to see the land his father and their neighbors had bought. To see what work had been done on it.

"But nothing had been done. Tel Zion was a fiction. A lie. It had never been real. And Volkoff couldn't be allowed to know that, or the game would be up and you'd be in trouble."

I stopped and looked down at him. "How did you kill him? What did you do with his body?"

Caspi grinned at me. "So now you're accusing me of not just one murder, but two?"

"Three," I said. "At the very least. And one attempted murder."

"Oh, that too? Whom did I attempt to kill?"

"Me. Don't try to deny it. Boris told me you'd sent him."

All the humor drained from his face. "Boris? Boris who worked for me?"

"He tried to kill me the other night. But he was the one who ended up dead. He said he attacked me on your request."

"That's a lie," he shouted. But then he quickly subsided, and fear entered his eyes. "You... you killed Boris?"

I nodded. "But before he died, he confirmed that his boss—you-was the one who told him to kill me."

Caspi opened his mouth as though to issue further denials, but he uttered no sound. His eyes did a frantic dance, and when he spoke, his voice had a fearful edge: "His boss? He said his boss sent him?"

"Yes. And don't bother denying it. Boris had no reason to lie. He thought he was about to finish me off. But it didn't work out that way. Just like the previous time he tried to kill me when he dropped a brick on my head."

Caspi looked incredulous, and this time I wasn't sure he was faking it. "He didn't tell you about it, did he? Was probably embarrassed to admit that he ran away."

I told him about my narrow escape from the brick, how I ran up to the roof to discover Boris had fled down the tree. How I failed to catch him on the street.

"I guess he figured next time he needed to get close and personal. And it nearly worked. But nearly is not enough."

I stopped, waiting for him to again claim innocence, but he kept quiet. There was a look of shock on his face. As though he'd been hit by a couple of blows he hadn't seen coming. A good sign. I was making faster progress than I'd expected. Perhaps I could break him still.

"I see you're not denying it," I said. He gave me a look that was surprisingly low on hatred but high on despair. Another good sign. "What did you do with Volkoff's body? Where is it?"

He didn't shake his head or say I was crazy or claim ignorance of what I was talking about. All he said was, "Tell me the rest of it."

"The police couldn't find Volkoff. He had disappeared without a trace. But before his death, he sent a letter back home to Mastarnia. You probably didn't know that. And I'm sure you don't know about the letter his father had sent him, just a few days before Germany invaded Poland.

"Volkoff never got to read it. By the time it arrived, he was already dead. But the woman who ran the boardinghouse where Volkoff had stayed before he died had kept it, and she let me read it. In the letter, Volkoff's father asked his son about 'the place,' and about the sea. It was possible 'the place' was the boardinghouse Volkoff had been staying in or the city of Haifa itself—either made sense given that Haifa is a coastal city. But Volkoff's father was asking about a different coastal city altogether. Tel Zion. And he wasn't asking just for himself. He was asking on behalf of other people in Mastarnia too. People like Feldbaum's father and Shimon Suskind or someone in his family. All the dead Jews of Mastarnia. All the people you swindled."

Again, I paused to let him protest, but he remained quiet. I noticed he had folded in on himself a little, was sitting a bit hunched over with his shoulders curled inward and his gaze aimed at the floor. Like a man under an attack he doesn't know how to ward off.

"I don't know where you buried Volkoff's body, but no one has found him since. You got away with his murder, but you were rattled. If Volkoff had come, other Jews from Mastarnia might follow. So you closed your office in Haifa and changed your company's name from Zion Construction to Hebrew Builders. And you moved your operation to Tel Aviv.

"And then Germany invaded Poland, and Polish Jews were herded into ghettos and later exterminated. Including the Jews of Mastarnia. I wonder how you felt when you read this. Were you shocked and saddened like other Jews? Or did you secretly rejoice in the knowledge that all the people you'd swindled were now dead?"

I hurled the last question at him like a javelin. He didn't even flinch, the heartless bastard.

"This turned out to be not true," I said. "For there were a handful of survivors. Shimon Suskind was one. Emmanuel Feldbaum was another. They knew your dark secret. You could not allow them to live."

I let out a sigh and rubbed my face hard, back and forth, until my skin felt on the verge of splitting open. I was suddenly tired to the bone. Tired and disgusted with myself for all the mistakes I had made.

I had misjudged so much. I'd felt a connection with Feldbaum, but I had failed to read the true meaning of his ramblings. Like what he'd said about Volkoff.

I said to Caspi, "When Feldbaum used to ramble about Menashe Volkoff, he'd say that Volkoff knew where *it* was. He wasn't able to say what he meant; the knowledge of what Volkoff knew had been lost in the ruins of Feldbaum's brain. Initially, I assumed that it was a valuable physical object that Volkoff had brought with him from Poland: money, jewelry, a piece of art, a gemstone. It had to be small or Volkoff wouldn't have been able to carry it on him the day he disappeared.

"But it was as large as a city and easy to carry on one's person. It was knowledge. Stored inside Volkoff's head and always with him.

"Feldbaum had been a teenager when you sold the poor Jews of Mastarnia land in the fictional city of Tel Zion. Then the war came, and he was separated from his father. And after the war, he returned to Poland and suffered a head injury that made a mess of his brain.

"Feldbaum's injury made it difficult for him to remember things clearly. He said to Ami Rapoport he had gone back to Poland to get his father's new house. I think he really went back to see if any of his family survived and to find the ownership papers of the land his father bought from you. He didn't find any.

"He didn't remember the details, but he knew on some level that here in Israel there was supposed to be land his father had bought to build a new house on, and that the land was by the sea. Sometimes he got confused and talked as though the house had already been built. He also remembered that one man from his town had escaped Poland before the Germans invaded, that he had gone to the Land of Israel, and that this man's family had also bought land here, right where Feldbaum's father did.

"His name was Menashe Volkoff. He would know where the land was. Find Volkoff, and Feldbaum would also find his father's land. His father's new house."

Caspi was utterly silent and motionless. It didn't look like he was listening to me. But I knew he was hearing me. And besides, by now, I was talking for my own benefit as much as his.

"Fate had been cruel to Feldbaum several times during his life," I said. "It placed him in the clutches of the Nazis. It led him to a Polish jail. It steered him to a situation that resulted in a severe brain injury from which he never recovered. And, as a finale, it played a sick joke on him.

"It guided him here, to Israel, where he should have found solace and shelter. But then it brought him to the attention of the one man in Israel he needed to avoid. The man who had defrauded the Jews of Mastarnia. Who had killed two men who knew of his fraud. The man who would not hesitate to murder anyone who knew of his crime.

"You!"

Caspi shifted then. He lifted his head slowly and looked at me. I thought I saw sorrow in his eyes. Sorrow and remorse. I was getting close. Just a few more pushes and I would topple him.

"That's why you told Berman to fire Feldbaum. You needed him off your building site. As far away from you as possible. It's also why you didn't fire him yourself. You didn't want to talk to him; you were worried he might recognize you. And a short while later, you sent Boris to kill him. And so another Jew from Mastarnia found his death."

I lit a cigarette, pulled on it, and blew smoke that curled lazily toward the ceiling like hazy distant memories.

"But before Feldbaum, there was Shimon Suskind. He was not brain-damaged. He remembered everything. He came to Israel ten months ago after surviving the war as a partisan. He came looking for Tel Zion, for the house his family had bought. By now, it should have been built. But he soon learned there was no Tel Zion. And he understood that something had gone wrong. He figured Volkoff could tell him what. But when he learned that Volkoff had vanished, he realized what had truly happened.

"He could have talked to the cops. He should have done so. But Suskind had been a partisan and later a Nazi hunter. He was accustomed to dispensing justice himself. So he went after you. I think he wanted to kill you. But somehow you managed to catch him off guard, bashed his head in, and buried him in a copse of pines outside Holon."

And was I that different from Suskind? I was also used to dispensing justice myself. Wasn't that part of the reason why I had a loaded gun in my pocket?

I pushed the thought away and continued, "But his body, unlike Volkoff's, was found. Because you buried him in a shallow grave. That was idiotic of you, you know that? Careless and utterly idiotic."

He winced at that. At being reminded of how stupid he'd been. His head drooped once more.

"What do you want?" he asked me. His voice was that of a vanquished man. I knew I had him.

"I want to know if you also killed Yosef Rudinsky."

He didn't answer. I kicked him in the foot. "Yosef Rudinsky. Feldbaum had talked about him too. Did you also murder him?"

Slowly, tentatively, still wavering between denial and confession, he said, "I've never heard that name in my life."

I believed him. He was an adept liar, but he had no reason to lie about this. Not anymore.

"And Volkoff? What did you do with his body? Where did you bury him?"

Again, he answered slowly. "I didn't bury him anywhere. I took him out to sea, weighted him down, and cast him into the water."

"Why didn't you do the same with Suskind?"

"I used to own a boat back in '39. But I haven't had it for years."

"How many people in Mastarnia did you swindle? How much money did you steal?"

"Enough!" he said, surprising me with his vehemence. He rose without a word, went to a side table, and picked up a photograph framed in silver. The photograph showed a younger Caspi sitting on a park bench beside a beautiful blonde. Both of them were smiling at the camera. By Caspi's appearance, I judged the photo to be at least fifteen years old.

He looked at the image intently for a long moment, unmoving. Then he laid the photograph flat on its front, hiding it from view. He turned to face me. "Take me to the police station and I'll confess to everything. But I'm not going to say another word to you."

44

"I just can't believe it," Rapoport said.

We were standing not far from the building site, from which no sound of labor was coming. Caspi's arrest had not been publicized yet, but word had reached his employees, who were now discussing the news instead of doing any work. They did not have the whole picture, only that Caspi was in custody for murder. I didn't share the details with them. They weren't my client.

"It's a lot to take in," I said. "Completely unexpected, isn't it?"

"You can say that again. It's hard enough to believe Caspi had Emmanuel killed, but you say he's responsible for three murders."

"That's right."

"And he defrauded many people."

"An unknown number. But I guess dozens of people bought land from him. If you count their family members among the victims, it comes to hundreds."

"Unbelievable."

Rapoport looked stunned by the news, which was understandable. Good people find it difficult to accept that evil can manifest in such large and sophisticated forms. Despite the many times history has shown us that evil knows no bounds. That there is no boundary of morality that it will not cross.

"So when Emmanuel was talking about his father's new house, he wasn't being crazy."

"No. He just couldn't articulate it correctly. His head injury made that impossible."

"He came here to find his home, but that home never existed."

"That's true. But he found another home. The one you gave him."

His eyes welled up. "I was about to throw him out, Adam. Dear God, I was about to kick him out into the street." He let out an anguished sob, covering his face with a large hand.

I clasped his shoulder. "You did more than most men would have. You gave him a home for as long as you could. And you were a true friend to him. Both in life and after his death. You cared enough to take him in, and you cared enough to hire me. You have nothing to feel guilty about."

He lowered his hand and looked at me. "And you cared too. You cared enough to investigate his death for no money. Why did you do it? You didn't even know him."

"I knew enough," I said. "Enough for him to matter to me."

"Thank you. Thank you so much," he said, and before I could react, he pulled me into a bear hug.

He smelled of physical labor and old clothes. The scent of an honest, hardworking man who owns few tangible possessions, but has a sense of honor and humanity so great that it couldn't fit in a palace.

At the first instant, I was taken aback by his embrace, but then my arms curled around him and tightened, and I closed my eyes and thought of Emmanuel Feldbaum and all the dead Jews of his hometown, and then I was crying too.

After a minute or two, we released each other. We dried our tears and did not make eye contact until the awkwardness of our embrace had faded. Rapoport looked at the fence of the building site, and his brow creased. "Am I out of a job now?"

"I doubt it. Maybe you'll get a couple of days off. But if there's one thing in this country that doesn't get stopped for long, no matter what, it's construction."

"But who will run things?"

"Someone from the government, probably. Until they find another contractor to take over."

"I hope you're right," he said, then shook his head in self-disgust. "Listen to me. I shouldn't be thinking of such things right now. I don't know what's wrong with me."

"Don't be too hard on yourself. You have every right to worry. You have a wife and a baby on the way. What happened to Emmanuel doesn't change that."

He accepted this with a short nod. We were quiet for a moment, and then he said, "It's hard to believe about Boris, too."

I didn't tell him about the money I'd found in Boris's wallet. He didn't need to know about that.

I said, "He hated Emmanuel, and he was loyal to Caspi. Too loyal."

I'd worried Caspi would tell the cops I'd killed Boris. I would have denied it, of course, and there was nothing to prove I'd killed him, but it would have been a hassle nonetheless. But Caspi had said nothing about it.

As for Sergeant Bilenko, his anger that I'd ignored his command to stay off the case quickly evaporated when he understood what I was handing him on a platter. He would be able to close not just one murder but three. And I sweetened the deal by saying that he could take all the credit; I wanted none of it, and no publicity too. There was a good chance Bilenko would end up with a promotion. And he wasn't the sort to turn it down because he had done nothing to earn it. So he was pleased, and so was I.

I hoped that somewhere Emmanuel Feldbaum, Menashe Volkoff, and Shimon Suskind were pleased as well.

45

I walked in the door, said hello to Greta, and asked if I could get a cup of coffee and something to eat.

"Of course," she said, put a tray on the counter, and filled a cup from a coffee pot. "You had a telephone call yesterday afternoon. From Reuben Tzanani."

"Did he leave a message?"

"Yes. He said the clerk in Jerusalem was sorry, but he found the magazine too late to send it to you yesterday. He said the clerk was effusive in his apologies. Why are you smiling?"

"Oh, it's nothing."

"It's enough to put a silly grin on your face. Anyway, the clerk swore on his mother's life he would send it first thing today. What is so important that someone would swear on their mother's life?"

"A government job," I said. "With a pension fund and a two-week annual vacation in a mid-level hotel in Netanya. It's not that important, actually. Just tying up a loose end in the case."

"A loose end? Does that mean you solved it?"

"Yes, I did. It will probably make the news later today. Well, most of it, at any rate. I'll tell you all about it when we have a private moment."

"Later tonight, after everyone has gone?"

"I'm meeting Hannah tonight, so I can't."

"I can wait. Where are you taking her?"

"She told me she'll decide where we go tonight."

Greta smiled. "A woman with her own mind. I'm liking her more and more."

I was still in the café when Reuben came in. He dropped a large envelope on the table. "Here it is, Adam. Though from what I hear, you don't need it anymore, do you?"

"No. But thank you for bringing it."

"It was no bother. I wanted to see you anyway. Congratulations on solving the case."

"It's Bilenko's case, not mine."

Reuben made a face. "Don't I know it. He's strutting around the station like he's a Jewish Sherlock Holmes." He paused, running a fingertip along the edge of the table. "I still feel uncomfortable about what we discussed yesterday."

"I know. I'm sorry."

"But I want you to know that I'm not angry with you. I'm proud of you. I'm proud to be your friend."

I could feel my mouth stretching in a huge smile. "Thank you, Reuben. It means a lot."

He studied his hands for a moment, and a vertical crease appeared between his eyebrows. He said, "What we talked about yesterday. What we sort of talked about. That wasn't the only time you've done such a thing, was it?"

"No."

He nodded without making eye contact. "And it was always necessary? There was no other way?"

"Yes, it was. And no, there wasn't."

Another nod. He drew a breath, looked to his left for a moment, then lowered his gaze once more to his hands.

"What we talked about and the way Bilenko so naturally took the credit for something he hadn't done, they make me wonder whether I'm right for this line of work, or if I'm too straight and naive." His eyes met mine. "Do you think I am, Adam? Am I too straight and naive?"

I considered my words. "I don't think you'll get far in the department, Reuben. Which is a shame. Because you're a credit to the badge. I wish all cops, all men, were like you. The world would be a better place if they were."

We drank coffee together and talked of this and that. With the shift to lighter topics, Reuben's mood brightened, and he told me about funny and stupendous things his children had been doing, and for some reason, I did not find it as difficult to hear as I would have expected.

We parted with him inviting me to come over for dinner at his house next week, and unlike what I normally would have done, with me not begging off on the basis of some contrived excuse.

"You can invite Hannah too," he said.

"We'll see, Reuben," I answered. "We'll see."

Hannah took me to a place on Ben-Yehuda Street with a small stage on which four musicians crowded. Three violins and a cello. They played waltzes, and couples thronged the dance floor, moving about in elegant coordination.

I told her about Caspi. I told her about the entire case, leaving out only how I initially met Feldbaum and the parts having to do with Boris.

She listened with rapt attention and seemed to be holding her breath at certain points, and when I was done, she gave me a long evaluating look.

"What?" I asked.

"You don't see it, do you? Incredible."

"See what?"

"Yourself. And all that you've accomplished on this case. How remarkable it is that you solved it."

"I made many mistakes. Like what I assumed about Feldbaum's newspaper and the first time I went to Pevzner Street, and I—"

"Yes, I know. You're not omniscient. You can't see back in time, and you can't read the minds of murder victims you've never met. You're not perfect, and there's no reason why you should be. But somehow, despite all these faults—as you seem to think they are—you got to the truth. And what's even more remarkable is that you're not boastful to the point of obnoxiousness."

I smiled. "Did you expect me to be?"

"I haven't known you long enough to be sure what to expect, but most other men would be bragging incessantly. They wouldn't dwell on their mistakes, only on their success." She took my hand. "You are remarkable, Adam."

"And you're very beautiful," I said. And she was. The dim lighting of the café and the glow of the candle on our table combined to bathe her features in a soft, warm illumination that created the illusion that she was shining from within.

"Keep talking like that, mister, and who knows where the night may take you," she said with a wink.

She sipped the wine in her glass. "Why did Caspi confess? You couldn't actually prove anything, could you?"

"I couldn't, but Caspi didn't know that. And people don't always confess just because their backs are against the wall, because they'll go to jail regardless. Sometimes, they confess because of guilt or the sheer fatigue that comes from having to hide their crimes for so long. And sometimes criminals confess because they're looking for fame, and it's the only way to get it."

"Caspi wasn't looking for fame, was he?"

"No."

"Do you think he was tired of hiding his sins?"

I shook my head.

"That leaves guilt. Did he look to be burdened by it?"

I thought about it. I ran my conversation with Caspi through my mind, remembering the points at which his resistance fell apart.

"Yes," I said. "Yes, he did. He didn't show it at first, but it became more apparent the more I told him what I knew."

"I wouldn't think a man like that could feel guilt at all."

"Guilt is a beast no one can understand, Hannah."

After a while, she said, "Batya Rapoport must be relieved."

"Why's that?"

"It turned out that Emmanuel didn't have knowledge of a valuable object or a large sum of money. She didn't miss out on anything because she was mean to him."

"That's true," I said, smiling at the memory. "But it sure was nice to make her think so."

We finished the main course, and I said, "About *Jane Eyre*..."

"Yes?"

"I'd like to keep it for a while longer if that's all right."

"You started it?"

"I finished it. I stayed up half the night and read it."

"So why..." She paused and smiled. "Oh, I see. You liked it, didn't you? You want to read it again."

"It's a great book."

"Not just for women?"

"For everyone who's human, I think."

"I think so too. Adam?"

"What?"

"I think you're going to learn that truly great things are better when you experience them again and again."

We had some coffee, and then she said, "Nice music, isn't it?"

"Very nice."

"Want to dance?"

I looked at her and then away. "I'm not much of a dancer."

"That's all right. I'm not much of one either." She held out a hand for me to take.

"No, really. I have two left feet. I'll step on your toes or trip you or something."

"Well then," she said, rising from her chair with her hand still stretched in invitation, "I guess you'll have to follow my lead."

Later, she led me to her shack and to her bed, and we made love with the sound of the waves for a soundtrack. I found out she was right. Truly great things are better when you experience them again and again.

We lay in our afterglow for a while, not speaking. Then I got the urge for a cigarette and asked her if she wanted one. She declined, and I went to my clothes in search of pack and lighter.

The lighter was in the same pocket as my wallet, and as I pulled it out, the wallet did a somersault onto the wooden floor of the shack, coming open in mid-flight and ending its journey with a messy thud.

I crouched to pick it up, and jutting out of one of the pockets like the raised hand of an ignored pupil was the piece of paper I'd found in the sack Boris had carried the brick in. The brick he'd launched at my head.

I still didn't know where that piece of paper had come from, but did it matter anymore? The case was done. The big questions had been answered. Answering this one small, inconsequential question wouldn't make an iota of difference.

"What is that?" Hannah asked. She'd risen from the bed to get a drink of water, and was now standing next to me, holding a glass in her hand.

"Just a torn piece of paper. But I don't know from what."

"Let me see." She lit a lamp and held the piece of paper to the light and rubbed her thumb over the scratchy surface. "I know what this is."

"You do?"

"It would be embarrassing if I didn't. I see this type of paper every day. More times than I can count."

"Are you going to keep me in suspense or tell me what it is?"

She flashed me a smile and brandished the piece of paper in triumph.

"This, my darling detective, was torn off a school notebook cover."

She handed it back to me, and I looked at it and then at her. "Are you sure about this, Hannah?"

She gave me a mildly disappointed look. "Trust me, Adam. I know a piece of notebook when I see it. That brown color and scratchy texture are unmistakable. And see this cut-off black line here? It's the top of a letter. I can't tell you which, but it's part of the word 'notebook.' All my pupils have them. Where did you get this?"

I didn't answer. Her look of curiosity morphed into one of concern. "What's wrong?"

I shut my eyes, thinking about this piece of paper and the sack it came in. And then I thought of the brick that had been in that same sack. And then I thought of Boris and my conversation with him on the beach. Boris with the wrench in his hand and murder on his mind, and a little later, him lying on the beach with dead eyes and a blood-drenched shirt.

"Adam, are you all right? You look like you're about to be sick."

I opened my eyes. Hannah was peering at me, worry etched on her face. Her hand clasped mine, and I curled my fingers through hers and said, "I'm not sure. But I think I made a huge mistake."

46

The magazine lay where I'd left it, on my dining table, still in its envelope. I hadn't bothered opening it. I hadn't thought I needed to. I was lucky I hadn't tossed it in the trash.

I tore the envelope open and pulled out the magazine. I scanned each page quickly, looking for an obvious clue.

Nothing caught my eye, and I once again turned to the first page. There was no avoiding it. I was going to have to read the whole dull thing.

This turned out to be untrue. I found what I was looking for about three-quarters of the way through. It was a single line in a list of them. Just four words in total. But they made my heart skip a beat and then begin to thump furiously.

There was no question about it. I had made a mistake. But I still didn't know the full picture.

It took me until late afternoon to connect all the dots. All through the day, I was on the phone, spending good money to call government clerks in myriad departments, having to cajole, persuade, wheedle, and occasionally threaten to get them to cooperate. But finally, I had all the information I needed.

At nine o'clock I left my apartment, armed like the night before with a gun.

But this time my destination wasn't a private home on an affluent street. It was a humbler residence.

A weary voice answered my knock. "Who is it?"

"Adam Lapid," I said. "I need to talk to you."

I felt, or perhaps imagined, a hesitation, but then I heard the snick of a bolt, and the door swung open.

"Good evening," he said.

"Good evening, Mr. Soffer. Can I come in?"

He moved aside, and I stepped past him, and he shut the door behind me.

He wore slippers and black trousers and a white shirt, open at the neck. His *kippah* was on a side table by the door, and he snatched it up and set it on his head.

"Shall we go sit down? Then you can tell me what brought you to my home at this hour."

The living room was small and modest and tidy. Like the store. Like the man himself. There was a sofa and some chairs. There was a coffee table. There was a radio next to a shelf with religious texts. Their spines were free of creases.

The room had a sad air about it. Again, like its owner. Soffer's expression was even more sorrowful tonight. Like a man who'd gotten his share of bad news and was expecting even worse at any moment.

"You heard the news, I gather?" I asked.

"The news?"

"About Benjamin Caspi."

"I haven't listened to the radio today. Who's Benjamin Caspi?"

"Caspi was Feldbaum's boss at the construction firm. He confessed to killing Feldbaum."

"Oh? So your case is over, then."

"Almost."

"Almost?"

"Yes. Because Caspi didn't do it."

"I thought you said he confessed."

"It was a false confession. He's protecting someone. Is Oded Caspi here, by the way?"

"No, he's..." Soffer's voice trailed off. He didn't bother trying to cover up his slip. He scratched his face through his beard and lowered himself to the sofa like a man twenty years his senior. "How did you find out?"

"By mistake. Oded used a bag to carry a brick to the roof of my building. A brick he tried to murder me with. When he missed, he escaped, leaving the bag behind. Inside the bag was this." I showed him the small piece of brown paper. "I didn't know what it was at first, but last night I found out. It's part of a notebook cover. The kind schoolchildren use. The kind you sell in your store."

"Oded's a good boy," Soffer said. "A very good boy. And loyal."

He was speaking softly, like a father trying to put an infant to sleep, but then his gaze shifted to somewhere behind me, and I heard a footfall, and it was all the warning I needed. I jerked to the side and the hammer swept past my head in a violent arc.

I turned, and there was Oded, flush-faced and wild-eyed, the hammer gripped in both hands.

He had swung it too hard, and his hands and the hammer they gripped had dropped to the height of his knees. His face was exposed, and I took advantage. I jabbed at his nose with my left hand and hooked his jaw with my right.

He crumpled without a sound, out cold, his nose a bloody mess. I turned quickly to face off with Soffer and saw that he had risen from the sofa. I almost decked him, but he wasn't coming at me. He knelt beside Oded, crying fat tears over his unconscious form.

"He's dead. You killed him," he said breathlessly.

I grabbed him by the arm, pulled him away, and pushed him back onto the sofa. "He's alive. Unconscious but alive. Now stay there and don't move, or I'll really hurt him."

The windows had curtains, and I pulled them down and tore them into strips, which I used to tie Oded's hands behind his back and tether his feet together. There were a couple of cloth napkins on the table, and I jammed one of them into Oded's mouth. When he came to, I didn't want him to make any noise.

"Now," I said, turning back to Soffer and rubbing some comfort into my aching knuckles. "I think it's time you told me everything, don't you?"

He was quiet for more than a minute. Then he reached up and removed the *kippah* from his head. He folded it in two and dropped it beside him onto the sofa, as though he were discarding an object that had outgrown its use.

"I don't believe in God," he said, a transient mirthless smile passing over his lips. "I tried to for many years, but I could never convince myself that He existed. I wore this for another reason."

"It's part of your disguise," I said. "Like the mustache and beard. I should have known there was something off about them. They're the only things about you that aren't neat."

"Ah, yes, the beard." He scratched through it again, this time with furious twists of his fingers that had to cause him some pain. "It's not only my disguise but part of my penance. Christian monks used to wear hairshirts, you know, to suffer for their sins. This beard, the way it irritates my face, is my own little torment."

"A part of your penance? What are the other parts?"

"I live very modestly, as you can see."

"Many Israelis live in far worse conditions."

"That's true. But they don't have the wherewithal to change that. I do."

"The money you stole from the people of Mastarnia."

"Yes. The money I stole."

"Is Oded part of your penance too?" I asked.

Soffer looked at the fallen, tied-up man on the floor with sorrow and affection. "At first, he was. But it's no longer that way. I love him like a son, Mr. Lapid. He is my son, no matter who sired him. How did you learn Caspi is his father?"

"If not for that piece of notebook cover, I never would have. But I should have seen it straightaway. They share certain physical attributes. They have a similar build, they have dark gray eyes, and both have notched chins. That's not so common, a notched chin. Does he know about his father?"

"No," Soffer said.

"You told me you were a friend of his family. That you knew his mother. But that wasn't the whole truth. You know Caspi too."

"Benjamin Caspi and I have known each other for many years."

"You sold him your company, Zion Construction."

"Yes."

"With the condition that he change the company's name?"

"That was part of the deal. He didn't mind. I sold him the company for a pittance. He jumped at the chance."

"It doesn't sound like you like him much."

"I don't. He's not a good man, and he neglected his son. I was fonder of his wife, Oded's mother."

"You said she was one of the first customers in your store."

"She was. I opened the store after I sold the company. But I knew her from before. From Haifa. She was a good woman, a wonderful mother. But then she got sick. Cancer. And when she lost hope, she came to me and asked me to take Oded in. His father didn't want anything to do with him."

"Was she blonde? Blonde and beautiful?"

"How do you know?"

"I saw a picture of her with Caspi at his house. I think he loved her very much."

"He did. But he didn't love his son. He couldn't stand the sight of him. He was going to put him away in some institution. His mother didn't want that, so she came to me."

That was why Caspi had wanted Feldbaum gone from his building site. Why he had talked so crudely about him. Feldbaum had reminded Caspi of his son.

And as for getting Berman to do it instead of firing Feldbaum himself, I thought it was because of Caspi's political aspirations. He didn't want to be seen as callous, as uncharitable to a Holocaust survivor trying to build a new life in Israel.

Those aspirations were also the reason he didn't like me sniffing around. He was hiding something, all right, but it wasn't an involvement in Feldbaum's murder. It was the existence of his son, Oded. The son he had deserted. That was something that could sink him politically. His party would repudiate him. He could forget about the Knesset and being a minister.

"I was very surprised to learn that Caspi confessed," Soffer said. "I can't imagine why he did so."

"Because of Oded," I said. "You're wrong about Caspi. He does love his son. He doesn't want to see him or be reminded of him, but he loves him enough to sacrifice himself to protect him. I talked with Caspi last night. I was sure he was guilty, and I had everything sorted out in my mind. I told him what I believed, and he of course knew it was nonsense. But he realized something from what I told him. He realized that it was Oded who had tried to kill me with the brick and that it was Oded who had buried Shimon Suskind. I told him that burying Suskind in a shallow grave had been an idiotic act, and he winced, like the word 'idiotic' caused him pain. I think it really did. Because he knew that Oded had done it. Did Oded also kill Suskind?"

"Yes," Soffer said. "He did it to protect me. Suskind came to this apartment. He had found me somehow. He wasn't interested in money. He couldn't be bought." He paused and looked at me without much hope. "You can't be bought either, can you?"

I shook my head.

"Are you sure? I have a little over six thousand liras here. All cash."

"No. Get on with the story."

Soffer shrugged his thin shoulders. He did not seem disappointed by my refusal. "Suskind wanted revenge. He intended to kill me. Oded surprised him from behind. Like he almost surprised you."

"Why did you let Oded bury him alone?"

Soffer leaned back and pulled the tail of his shirt from his waistband. He exposed a stretch of pale belly, and I saw an ugly red scar running from his navel to his ribs.

"Suskind had a knife. He sliced me. I was in no condition to drag a body or dig a grave or even walk. It was all I could do to drive Oded and the body to somewhere remote. I told Oded what to do, but he didn't dig deep enough, and the body was found."

"Caspi understood that. He knew you wouldn't have made such a mistake. That's why he confessed. Because he knew that Oded was involved."

Oded stirred then, and his breathing changed. He opened his eyes, blinked a few times, and then started to panic when he couldn't move his arms. He struggled against his restraints, issuing frantic muffled sounds from behind the gag.

"Tell him to calm down," I told Soffer. "Tell him to stay quiet."

Soffer went to Oded, cupped his cheek, and spoke softly to him. Oded relaxed, though he still stared at me with frightened, child-like eyes. Soffer sat on the floor beside him, a hand on Oded's shoulder.

I said, "But I can't figure out how Caspi knew Oded was the one who tried to kill me with a brick. I told him it was Boris, and I think I know why he didn't believe it. Boris wouldn't have run away by climbing down a tree. He would have stayed to fight me on the roof. And it wasn't Boris's style, to kill someone by throwing a brick at him. He was the sort who'd do it up close and personal, like the way he tried to kill me with a wrench the other night." I told him about my fight with Boris on the beach.

"Boris had told me I'd been lucky to escape him once but that I wouldn't a second time. I thought he meant the brick throwing, but he was talking about his initial swing with the wrench. Boris also told me his boss had sent him to kill me. Naturally, I thought it was Caspi, especially as I already suspected he was hiding something. But it was you. You were his boss, too. He used to work for you."

"Years ago. In Haifa."

"You also had a worker called Noah, right?" I described the third man from Café Silver, the one who had overheard Caspi telling Berman to fire Feldbaum.

"Yes."

"He told me he and Boris worked together for another company up north. That Boris was always very loyal to the boss. I guess that loyalty persisted. Though I'm sure it helped that you slipped him some money."

"Three hundred liras. And it didn't require much persuasion. He hated you."

"So Caspi, knowing Boris, didn't believe he was the one who had dropped a brick on me. But why was he sure it was Oded? Why couldn't it be you?"

"I suffer from acute acrophobia," Soffer said.

"You're afraid of heights?"

"Extremely so. There's no way I'd be able to look down from a rooftop and aim a brick at someone below."

I recalled Soffer perspiring and looking anxious the last time I saw him, when a customer wanted him to get something from a high shelf.

"That's why you asked me to bring that book down?" I asked. "You can't even stand on a stepladder?"

"I can. If I absolutely must. But it fills me with apprehension. Like I said, my condition is acute."

"And Caspi knew that about you. That's how he knew it was Oded who had thrown the brick at me."

Soffer caressed Oded's brow, brushing his fingers gently through his hair. "May I remove the gag? Oded won't make a sound."

"All right. But if he shouts or screams, I'll knock him out again."

Oded didn't scream. He said something in a low frightened voice to Soffer, who replied, "It's all right, Oded. Don't worry. Everything is going to be fine."

"Tell me how it started," I said. "The whole dirty scam."

"I was born in Mastarnia," Soffer said. "My family had lived there for generations. But by the time I was born, only my parents remained there. I was an only child, and from a young age, I wanted to come here, to the Land of Israel. In 1931, I got off the boat in Haifa."

"And you went into construction."

"Yes. My parents had given me a little money, and I went to a bank and was able to borrow more." A half-smile of reminiscence. "The bank should never have approved the loan; I had no collateral. But I was always good with words and was able to get the bank manager to throw caution to the wind."

"You conned him."

"I did nothing illegal, but I played him all right."

"What did you do with the money?"

"Bought land, built houses, tried to sell them. At first, the business was going well. But then my luck soured, and I got to the point where I had to beg for loan extensions, put off paying suppliers, and postpone paying my workers their wages. I was on the brink of bankruptcy, and there was a good chance I'd end up in prison. There was no way out for me."

"And then you thought of Mastarnia."

"Yes. Then the idea came to me. By that time, both my parents were dead, but people there knew me. They trusted me. And many of them were Zionists. I didn't have to work hard to convince them to buy land in the city I planned on building."

"Tel Zion."

"I chose the name carefully. *Tel* to make them think of Tel Aviv, and *Zion*, well, we all know what Zion is. I spent what little money I had on good clothes, so I'd look successful, and I had made detailed plans of the city to show them. It was perfect."

There was a creepy undertone of pride in his voice. He heard it himself and gave me an awkward shrug of contrition. "I know that sounds terrible, but it's the truth. I made no mistakes. And without much hesitation, they handed me their money in return for fake documents giving them ownership of nonexistent lots of land."

"How many people did you cheat?"

"Fifty-three."

"Fifty-three individuals or families?"

"Families. How many people they represented, I don't know."

At least five per family on average, I thought. So over two hundred and fifty people all told.

"That must have been a huge sum of money," I said.

"I did not keep all of it. Most of it went to pay my debts, my suppliers, everyone I owed."

"What did you do with the rest?"

"At first, I planned to build Tel Zion. I was hoping to make everything right, you see. But I didn't have enough money left, and the banks wouldn't give me more loans, so I had to put the plan aside."

"Weren't you worried that someone from Mastarnia would come looking for you?"

"With how the British were clamping down on Jewish immigration, I figured it was unlikely anyone would show up any time soon. By the time they did, I hoped to have started on the project. That would have made it all right."

"But then Menashe Volkoff showed up."

"Yes. I did not expect it. He came to my office in Haifa. Walked in the door unannounced one day and wanted to see the work that was done on Tel Zion."

"But nothing had been done."

"Nothing. I hadn't even bought the land. I could have offered excuses, I suppose, tried to explain the delay. But I was worried Volkoff would see through it; he was an intelligent guy. And even if he bought it, he would surely write his family about it, and then people might start to get antsy."

"So you decided to get rid of him."

"I didn't feel I had any other choice. I got him into my car, told him I'd drive him to the site. On the way, I said I wanted to show him something. A new piece of land I wanted to buy. There was an old abandoned farmhouse off the main road, surrounded by trees, so you couldn't even see it. You had to know it was there. I let Volkoff walk ahead of me, picked up a rock, and slammed it into the back of his head."

Oded let out a whimper. Silent tears slithered from the corners of his eyes and down his cheeks. Soffer shushed him, again promising that all would be well.

"What did you do with the body?"

"I buried him there. And I dug deep enough so no one found him."

Caspi had told me he'd dumped Volkoff's body in the sea. That's because he had no choice. Because I was certain of Caspi's guilt, and because I tried to get him to confess, I'd told him practically the whole thing, everything I thought had happened. And Caspi had listened closely, so he knew everything I did. But I didn't know where Volkoff's body was. When I asked Caspi where he'd buried it, Caspi had a problem. He needed a place that couldn't be checked, or his confession would fall apart, and then he couldn't protect Oded. So he chose the sea and then lied about not having his boat anymore so he couldn't dump Suskind in the sea as well.

An obvious lie, and I had bought it like a fool.

"That was when you decided to sell the company," I said, hiding my disgust with myself.

He nodded. "I was afraid someone else from Mastarnia would show up. So I sold the company to Caspi, under the condition that he change its name and move it out of Haifa. Then I moved to Tel Aviv."

"And changed your name."

"Yes."

"That's how Suskind found you. When the British ruled here, they published a government magazine called the *Palestine Gazette*. It listed all sorts of things, including all name changes. Yours appeared in the September 1939 issue. Your original name was Mendel Barshavski."

Soffer twisted his lips. "I should have known about that." He sounded vaguely disappointed with himself.

"It must have been a shock, to be found after all those years. Especially since you believed all the Jews of Mastarnia had died in the Holocaust. How did it make you feel, by the way? Knowing what the Germans did to them? Did it make you happy?"

For the first time, I saw anger on his face. "Of course not. I was devastated. Shattered. Those were people I knew."

"You knew them when you defrauded them."

"But I didn't want them dead. I was just desperate. I needed a lot of money from somewhere, and I couldn't think of another way."

"You killed Volkoff," I reminded him.

"Because I was afraid. I didn't want to be found out. I'd have been jailed." He started crying then, and so did Oded, though the latter cried like a child of three—big, breathless sobs that grated on my ears.

"It's okay, Oded. It's all right, my boy," Soffer said to Oded through his tears, putting on a fake smile. He caressed Oded's cheeks and dried his eyes, and gradually, Oded stopped bawling.

"After I knew what had happened in Europe, my world changed. I knew I would have to repent for my sins. So I took Oded in, and I give free school supplies to poor kids, and I live very modestly."

"But you kept the money."

"That's also part of my penance. To have it and not use it. A little extra suffering."

Looking at him, I did not doubt that he was being truthful. But he could have turned himself in at any time. His remorse, whatever it was, was not enough to compel him to do that.

"Who killed Feldbaum?" I asked. "You or Oded?"

Soffer took a few seconds to answer. "When he walked in the store, I nearly had a heart attack. I had not expected to see anyone from Mastarnia ever again, and I recognized him instantly. He'd been a teenager when I'd gone to Mastarnia in 1938. His father was one of the men who bought land from me. But very quickly I relaxed. I realized he didn't recognize me, that something was wrong with his memory, with his brain. Briefly, I contemplated letting him live, but then he started asking me about his father's new house and Menashe Volkoff, and I feared that one day his brain would improve, and he would be able to tell someone about Tel Zion."

"So you decided to kill him."

"I had to. If it were just about me, I might have taken my chances. But it's not just about me. I have a responsibility." He paused and looked down at Oded. "You are a good boy. You are a very good boy, and I love you." He looked at me. "If I were found out, Oded would be in trouble for killing Suskind."

"Who did the actual killing?"

"Oded. Because of my injury, I'm in no condition to do it myself."

"How did you know where Feldbaum would be going that night?"

"I followed him a few nights. He used to walk in his sleep. He didn't seem to notice anything around him. And every night, he would cross Sheinkin Garden. It was the perfect spot. Quiet and secluded. There would be no witnesses. I told Oded where to wait and what to do. When Feldbaum went into Sheinkin Garden that night, Oded hit him from behind."

"And you told him to take Feldbaum's wallet."

"To make it look like a robbery. To make the police think whoever killed Feldbaum didn't know him. And it worked, didn't it? Until you showed up."

There was no rancor in his voice, no bitterness. Just a resigned acceptance of his fate.

"After you came to my store the first time, Oded decided on his own to kill you. I didn't think it was necessary. I didn't think you'd get far in the investigation. It was clever on his part, don't you think? The attempt with the brick? I understand it almost worked." He sounded like the proud father of a precocious child. Only this child's sole talent lay in killing people.

"Almost. Where did he get the brick?"

"There's a building site two blocks from here. It's easy to get in. Anyway, when Oded returned, all shook up and frightened, and told me what he'd done, I realized I had to eliminate you to protect him."

"So you hired Boris to do it."

"Yes. Boris was a violent man. He'd served time for assault many years ago, and I knew he wouldn't refuse me. When he worked for me, he offered to beat up people on my behalf. And he hinted at doing worse. So I knew he'd do it, especially if I slipped him a little money. But I didn't expect him to be so eager. He was chomping at the bit to kill you."

I remembered the look in Boris's eyes when we faced each other on the beach. The bloodlust. My gut cramped as I recalled how close I'd come to being killed that night.

"Why didn't you come after me again, once you realized Boris had failed?"

I could see him weighing his words before he spoke them. "I

didn't know anyone I could hire to do it, and I was afraid to send Oded after you. It took a few days to find out where I could buy a gun. I just got it today. It's in the middle desk drawer over there."

It was a snub-nosed revolver. Five shots. I emptied the cylinder and put the gun and bullets in my pocket.

"Were there any other victims?" I asked. "Anyone else you killed?"

"No."

"What about Yosef Rudinsky?"

"He lived in Mastarnia. I imagine that he died in one of the camps. I told you his name to try to make things difficult for you. To send you off on the wrong track."

That was why Reuben hadn't found a trace of Rudinsky. He had never set foot in Israel.

We were quiet for a while. Then Soffer said, "What happens now?"

"Now we call the cops, and you make a full confession. Enough people have suffered. It must end. You won't know peace until you come clean."

"What will happen to Oded? He won't survive prison."

Oded stared with partial comprehension from me to the man who became his father.

"They won't put him in prison," I said. "He can't be held responsible for his actions. They'll send him to an institution somewhere. For his sake, and so he won't hurt others."

"He'll be all alone in the world," Soffer said, and his voice broke.

"His father will be there for him. I think he'll be ready to do that now. He wouldn't have confessed to murder to protect Oded if he wasn't."

47

Someone had closed off the entrance to the building site, and there was a notice on the fence promising that work would resume soon. None of the workers were there.

I went to Mahlul. I wanted to tell Rapoport the news before word got to him some other way.

It was early in the morning the day after Soffer made his confession. I was feeling more refreshed than I had in weeks. The night before, I hadn't stayed at the police station for the duration of what had to be a lengthy interview. I explained everything to Bilenko, congratulated him on solving the case a second time, and went home to bed, sleeping the whole night through without a single nightmare for company.

Nearing Rapoport's shack, I heard noises coming from within that I would not have associated with that unhappy home. Female and male laughter.

I knocked on the door. The laughter died like it had been turned off with a switch. Soft voices mumbled words I could not make out, and then Batya's voice, shrill and sharp, sliced through the door. "Go away. Come back later."

"I need to see Ami," I called back. "It's urgent."

"Go away, I said. Ami isn't here."

Something was off, so I pushed down the handle and opened the door.

There was a man there I didn't know. Black hair, dark eyes, thick mustache, handsome in a rough sort of way. And there was Batya, sitting in her chair, wearing a brown dress. A flush tinted her cheeks, and her hair was mussed. I expected her to start shouting at me, but when she spoke, it was at a normal volume. "Mr. Lapid, what are you doing here?"

"I came to see Ami," I said, looking at the man, who stood awkwardly to the side.

"He's not here. He's working."

"I went to the building site. There's nobody there."

"He's doing a day's work for some other outfit in Jaffa. Why do you want to see him?"

"I need to tell him something important." I was still staring at the man. He wouldn't meet my eyes.

Batya cleared her throat and said, "Thank you for dropping by to check on me, Gilad. Give Bella my regards."

"Sure thing, Batya. Sure thing," the man said, flicking me a quick sideways glance. "I'll see you later." And he slapped his hat on his head and was out the door like a flash.

"He's Bella's husband?" I asked.

"Yes," Batya said. "Not that it's any business of yours." She seemed to have regained some of her natural acerbity now that the man was no longer present.

"What was he doing here?"

"That's none of your business either," she snapped, but then she had a change of heart and added, "He came to ask me if I wanted something from the store. He offered to do my shopping for me. In my condition, it's better that I don't exert myself."

"Does Bella know he's here?" I said, a horrible suspicion beginning to take shape in my mind.

"I suppose so. What difference does it make?"

"I was just thinking that she might not like her husband to spend time with another woman alone behind closed doors, especially as he's the sort of guy women throw themselves at."

Batya said nothing.

"Come now. You must know what I'm talking about. I'm sure you and your gossipy friends talked about it quite a bit. Hannah Goldman tried to seduce him, right? At least, that's the story he told his wife. But we both know that isn't true, don't we, Batya?"

"I know nothing of the sort. Hannah Goldman is an immoral woman."

"Hannah isn't married. You are."

She gave me a venomous look through her slitted eyes. "I won't tolerate these disgusting insinuations, Mr. Lapid. Not in my home."

"It's Ami's home too. Or perhaps you've forgotten."

"You'd better not tell Ami any lies about me, you hear?"

"What was Bella's husband really doing here?"

"I told you that already. He offered to go to the store for me. It's what good neighbors do for each other."

"Is that why your cheeks were flushed when I came in? Why your hair is mussed?"

Her hand jerked involuntarily to smooth her hair. As guilty a gesture as she could have made. And she realized it almost instantly and yanked her hand down.

"I'm hot; it's part of being pregnant. And I haven't had time to brush my hair this morning."

"His fly was undone, you know that? And his shirt was tucked in crookedly."

I was lying, but she didn't know that. Her eyes swung toward the door. Another sign of guilt. Now it wasn't a suspicion anymore. It was a dreadful certainty.

"How long has this been going on?"

She was not yet ready to admit it. "There's nothing going on. It's just what I told you. He—"

"Stop lying!" I shouted at her. "Or do you want me to go find Gilad and get the truth out of him? And then I'll tell Bella about it."

She didn't answer. She might have been scared speechless. An animal caught in the headlights of a speeding truck.

"Have it your way," I said, starting for the door.

My fingers were on the handle when she spoke. "Don't. Please."

She hardly sounded like herself. She hardly looked like herself either. Something had broken inside her. She seemed smaller despite her huge belly.

"How long?" I asked.

"A few weeks."

"You're lying. Last chance."

"A year." She spat the words at me, leaning forward like a snake looking to bite. "It's been a year, all right? Damn you, you nosy, irritating man."

That had the ring of truth. And it gave birth to another truth. One much more terrible than what she had just confessed to. Getting hit with it was like being gut-punched with a battering ram. For a moment, I couldn't breathe.

I looked at the door Gilad had fled through, then at the unfaithful woman in her chair, then inward at my memory, recalling what Rapoport had told me about his first marriage and how he and Batya had failed to conceive for a few years.

"It's not Ami's baby, is it?" I said, my voice barely recognizable to my ears.

"What?" Batya said. "What are you saying? Of course it is." She attempted a snort of derision, but it ended up sounding like a dying breath.

"It's not. Ami and his first wife did not have any children. She never got pregnant. And you didn't either until recently. It's not Ami's baby. It's Gilad's."

Batya's shoulders started trembling. She began shaking her head as though she could deny away my presence, her treachery, the awful secret she was carrying in her womb. She hugged her pregnant belly like it was a slippery treasure that threatened to defy her grip and be forever lost to her.

"You don't know that. You can't know it." Her voice had risen in pitch, thinning to a scalpel's edge of desperation.

"No. But you know it," I said, my head pierced by a memory, another thing I'd missed. "When I first met you, you said you wanted to live somewhere better. 'For me, for Ami, and for my baby,' you said. Not *our baby*, yours and Ami's, but *my baby*, yours alone."

"You can't tell Ami. Please, Mr. Lapid. You can't tell him." And if I hadn't seen her utter the words, I would have found it hard to believe she had said them. I never would have thought I'd hear her beg.

Without a word, I turned the handle and opened the door.

"Don't tell him," she shouted after me as I stepped into the sunlight. "Don't do it, or you'll break his heart."

48

It took me a few hours to find him. He had found work in Jaffa, on a building site not far from the sea. He was in the middle of a water break when he saw me approaching. He put down his canteen and came toward me, a perplexed look on his face.

"Adam, what are you doing here?"

"I came to find you. Can we talk somewhere private?"

He told his foreman that he was taking a short break, and we walked west along a dirt path toward the sea. Along the way, he told me he'd gotten his hammer back.

"A redheaded boy returned it yesterday. Apparently, he took it on a stupid dare from his friends. I was angry at first, but he was so ashamed and remorseful that I couldn't stay mad."

"I know who he is," I said, remembering the boy who'd felt bad about ridiculing Feldbaum. "I talked with him about Emmanuel. He's a good kid, but he's easily influenced by his friends."

We went down to the beach and stood squinting at each other in the glaring sun while seagulls squawked above us.

"Have you heard the news about Caspi and Soffer?"

"No. What news?"

"That's why I'm here. I wanted to tell you personally. I thought it would be best if you heard it from me."

And I told him. I explained why Caspi had confessed to murders he hadn't committed, and about Soffer and Oded.

"I can't believe it," he said when I finished. "I've already come to terms with Caspi being guilty and now Soffer..." He shook his head. "He was the nicest guy. A generous man."

"That was part of his penance. I don't think he enjoyed the fruits of his crimes. Or maybe he did for a short while, but mostly he felt guilty and remorseful. But he was too scared to come clean. He didn't want to pay the full price for what he'd done. He wanted to control the extent of his penance."

"I see. And he wasn't even religious?"

"Not in the slightest. That was just a way to make it difficult to recognize him in case he happened to run into someone from Mastarnia."

Rapoport gazed toward the sea, at a distant boat rising and falling on the waves. He looked pensive and didn't talk for a minute.

"It's strange," he said at length. "I've already mourned for Emmanuel after he died, and I started grieving for him all over again after Caspi confessed. And now I feel like I'm about to start the whole process yet again." He looked at me. "There's no chance this is another mistake? Soffer is really guilty?"

"He really is, Ami. There's no mistake. You don't have to worry about that."

He blew out some air. "I'm glad. Because I don't think I could have handled having my reality upended yet again."

He gave me an abashed smile and didn't notice when I didn't reciprocate. There was a cold rock in the pit of my stomach. Because I knew that the core of his life was false.

After a minute, he said, "So Caspi is out."

"Yes."

"You think he'll keep me on the job? I was the one who hired you. If not for me, he wouldn't have been arrested in the first place."

"I don't think you need to worry about that at the moment. Not for a while."

He frowned at me. "Why not?"

I reached into my inside pocket and took out the thick envelope I had brought him. "This is yours."

His frown deepened as he took the envelope from my hand. He peered inside and his mouth dropped open and he gave me a startled look.

"There's six thousand three hundred and twenty-eight liras in there," I said.

"I don't understand."

"Soffer kept this money in his apartment. Another form of penance, he said. Money he had at hand but did not allow himself to spend. Or maybe he wanted a stash so he could make a quick getaway if he needed to. Either way, I took it last night before I called the police. I told Soffer I would give it to you. Because as far as I'm concerned, it's Emmanuel's money. It's the money his father gave to Soffer for the house he never built. And since you're the closest thing Emmanuel had to a family, you should have it."

Rapoport wore an expression of utter astonishment. He looked at the money and shook his head.

"I can't take this."

I reached over and closed his fingers around the envelope. "Yes, you can. It's enough to buy a small apartment. Or put down a payment on a bigger one. Emmanuel would have wanted you to have it. It's tax-free. No one knows about it. Soffer swore he wouldn't tell the cops. I think the thought that you'll be getting this money made him feel like he was atoning in some small way for all his sins."

He looked at the money again, then at me. "You should have some of this, Adam."

I shook my head.

"It's only right. I didn't pay you a lira for working the case."

"That's okay," I said, thinking of the money I had taken from Boris's wallet. "I made out all right. This is all yours."

Again he looked at the money, and then he let out a short laugh. "Wait till Batya hears about this. She'll be so happy."

He was grinning now, happier than I could have imagined him, and I felt like running away without another word. Because now I had a decision to make. He had hired me to discover one awful truth, and along the way, I'd discovered another.

I could either keep him ignorant and happy and living a lie, or I could shatter his world by telling him the truth.

49

It was evening when I returned to Mahlul.

Hannah and I were to meet the following night, but I needed to see her now. I wanted to tell her everything. And I wanted to kiss her and smell her and forget about the real, awful world for a while.

The sky was cloudless and purplish black. A faint sliver of moon shone like a fickle promise that the darkness would soon come to an end and that there would be light again. From the sea came a wind that brought with it the scent of salt and algae and foreign shores. A dog barked somewhere far off to my left, and another responded from an unseen place to my right. Perhaps they too had experienced weighty days. Perhaps they too needed to share their troubles with someone.

I was twenty feet from Hannah's shack when I saw her through the window. She wore a bright blue dress that made her look like a princess of the sea. Her profile was sharply defined in the lamplight, as though it had been stamped into the face of an ancient coin.

My heart lifted at the sight of her, and the weight on my shoulders did as well. My step lightened, the song of the blood flowing in my veins changed from a dirge to a festival, and the skin on my fingers tingled with anticipation. It would soon feel Hannah's skin.

For the first time that day, I felt my lips curl into a smile, the movement strange and tentative, like atrophied muscles relearning forgotten movements.

Hannah tucked a strand of hair behind her ear. Her mouth moved as she spoke unheard words, and her hands gesticulated to accompany her speech.

I had just formulated the question in my head, *Who is she talking to?* when the answer appeared through the glass.

It was a man. Mid-thirties. Blond hair combed back from a high forehead. Clean-shaven. Lean build. Dressed in a gray suit jacket. He was talking too. A watch glinted silver at his wrist.

I stood there, frowning at the scene, when the man moved in closer. In a quick, certain movement, his left arm curled around Hannah's waist while his right hand cupped the back of her head. And then he was kissing her, his mouth pressed tightly on hers, his passion unmistakable and fierce.

With a shock, I whirled around, turning my back on the dreadful scene. I shut my eyes, but it was too late. I had already seen it, and now it was engraved in my memory. Indelible like a scar.

A blade of jealousy and anger cut through my abdomen. I felt like screaming. I wanted to smash my fist through something. I had the urge to curse Hannah, myself, the world at large. But I did nothing but stand there as my pulse hammered in my temples.

"I could have told you she was cheap," came a woman's voice.

I opened my eyes, and there was Zelda. She was standing outside her door, wearing a frumpy dress on her dumpy body and a nasty smile on her lumpy face.

"You thought you were the only one, huh? That she was faithful. You should have known that a woman who'll take you to bed so quickly couldn't be trusted."

My face was hot, my heartbeat uneven and painful.

"She cast a spell on you. She's nothing but a cheap whore. A promiscuous, immoral whore. She has no honor, no self-respect. She uses men and lets them use her."

I had the urge to tell her to shut up. To not talk about Hannah that way. But I'd seen the proof with my very eyes, hadn't I?

"She likes to laugh at me," Zelda said, her upper lip curled like a bow about to unleash a poisoned arrow. "She looks down her nose at all of us, thinking she's so special. But she's not. She's indecent, filthy, and deceitful. She deceived you."

A part of me didn't want to believe it. Didn't want to believe what I'd just seen. Perhaps I wasn't willing to accept it. I started to turn for another look, but Zelda's voice stopped me: "Don't! Don't look! Not unless you want to see him slipping her dress off, kissing her and fondling her breasts."

I didn't want to see it. Just hearing her describe it made my stomach clench.

"You can do better than her," Zelda said. "She belongs in a gutter, in a sewer. You can find someone better. Go away and don't come back. And don't look. She's caused you enough pain already."

I didn't want to listen to her anymore. I didn't want to hear another word. But she was right. What I mostly didn't want was to be anywhere near Hannah. I wanted to be as far away as I could. I took a step forward, and then another, and with each one, my pace quickened until I was running. Without looking back, I put Hannah and her lover farther behind me, but knew I would carry the sight of them kissing in my head for a very long time.

50

That night the nightmares were back in full force. They drove me from my bed and out of my apartment and into the empty nocturnal streets. I found myself walking for hours. Down empty roads and up deserted boulevards, trying to sweat out the poison that had collected in my body over the past few days, and especially the sight of Hannah and the blond man kissing.

I walked aimlessly, or so I believed, but at some point I found myself close to Sheinkin Garden. I veered into it, treading the same ground Emmanuel had on his final night. I stopped where I'd found him dead and looked at the naked patch of ground that had swallowed his blood.

Later I wound up at the beach, where I had stuck my knife in Boris's chest. There was no trace of him left on the golden sand. Most deaths leave only transient traces. Like most lives do as well.

My walk took me past Soffer's store, now closed and dark. It had also died, and soon it would be gone, and I doubted many people would remember it a few years from now.

Caspi's building site was still closed off, and someone had torn a piece of the notice promising its imminent revival. I wondered what would happen to Caspi. I doubted his political aspirations would survive the scandal. I hoped he would be a good father to Oded.

I did my best not to think of Hannah, and in this, I failed completely. With each step, I tried to stomp her out of my system, but she wouldn't be erased. Hannah Goldman was the sort of woman who made an impression that did not fade easily.

I considered the possibility that I was overreacting. Hannah and I weren't married. We'd known each other but for a short time. She and I had made no commitments to each other. But not once had she hinted that she was seeing anyone else, and it was obvious that I was not involved with any other woman, so I felt deceived.

Perhaps I was unsophisticated. Perhaps I was old-fashioned. Perhaps I was a damn fool. But I knew truth from lies.

Hannah had hidden her lover from me, suspecting that I would not be willing to see her if I knew of his existence. And she was right. She had invited me to get close to her under false pretenses. This was not a deceit as huge as the one Batya Rapoport had committed, but it was one nonetheless.

My mood remained sour throughout the day. I tried getting some sleep but could manage nothing more than fitful dozes. I was supposed to pick Hannah up at her shack that evening, but I didn't go and did not bother letting her know I would not be showing up.

That night, I again awoke from a nightmare and prowled the city streets in search of solace. I failed to find any.

At one point, I began wondering whether I was on the road to becoming a sort of Emmanuel Feldbaum. Was I destined to spend my nights plodding along gloomy streets in a futile attempt to satisfy some nameless instinct that was driving me to ruin? Perhaps I was doomed. Perhaps I deserved to be, given how I had failed my family.

Perhaps this had always been my destiny: to fall into mental decay, be secluded from the world, become ensnared ever more hopelessly in my memories of better and worse times.

I spent the bulk of the day in my apartment, reading a Western I had picked up shortly before I began working the Feldbaum case. I read it cover to cover, and when I turned the last page, I realized that I recalled none of the plot. Where my mind had been, I couldn't say, but the moment I set the book aside, I thought of Hannah.

Her copy of *Jane Eyre* lay on the bedside table, a reminder of her and the broken promises I had seen in her. I had wanted to read the book again, but now I could not imagine doing so. In fact, I wanted to throw it in the trash, but I couldn't bring myself to do it.

I'd return it tomorrow. I'd go in the morning when she was at school and leave it by her door. But for now, I put it in the closet under my winter blanket so I would not have to look at it.

When evening came, I decided I was being ridiculous. Why should I let a woman I barely knew turn me into a prisoner in my own home?

I cursed her as I'd failed to do when I saw her kissing the man in her shack, but this did not make me feel any better. More due to stubbornness than any real desire for company, I went to Greta's Café.

The moment I went in the door, Greta's eyes widened in concern. "What's wrong, Adam?"

"Why do you think there's anything wrong?"

"Your face, that's why. Have you looked at yourself in the mirror? You look like you haven't slept in weeks."

"I've had a lot on my mind."

"The case? I heard on the news that one man confessed, but then another one turned himself in."

"That's right."

"I know you had something to do with the first one. What about the second?"

"I was the one who got him to give himself up. The first guy confessed to protect someone else."

"I see," Greta said slowly. "Well, actually, I don't. I kept expecting you to come in yesterday to tell me all about it, but you didn't."

I wasn't in the mood to explain anything. In fact, I felt like leaving. But that might offend her. "Can I get some coffee, Greta?"

"Sure," she said. "Give me a minute."

I spent that minute taking my chessboard to my table and setting up the pieces. Greta came over with a cup and set it beside the board. Then she sat down across from me.

"If you solved the case, why are you so glum?"

"Who says I am?"

"You can't fool me, Adam. I've known you too long."

"It's not the case, Greta."

"Then what is it?" she asked, and then realization dawned on her face like a surprise morning attack. "It's Hannah, isn't it?"

"I don't want to talk about it."

"Did you two have a fight?"

"I said I don't want to talk about it, Greta."

My voice was harsh, and heads turned my way from other tables. I waited until they stopped looking and said, "Hannah and I are over, Greta."

Greta said nothing. I could tell the news saddened her deeply.

"Are you sure?" she asked.

"Yes."

"Will you tell me what happened?"

"I don't want to."

"It will do you good to talk, Adam."

"I don't think so. I'm pretty sure it won't. All I want to do now is drink some coffee and play some chess. Alone."

I regretted it the moment I said it, but I made no apologies. Greta looked at me sternly, and she might have been about to remark on my rudeness, but she was a smart woman, smarter than me, and she overcame the impulse. With a sigh, she rose from her seat. Her eyes were full of hurt but also compassion. "I'll be here if you need me, Adam. When you need me." And then she went away, and I got my wish: I was alone. But it only made me feel worse.

I played with unaccustomed ferocity, preferring to kill off pieces rather than employ sound strategy. On either side of the chessboard, fallen white and black pieces littered the tabletop. It looked as though an explosion had taken place on the board, flinging the pieces in all directions.

Game after game, white and black pummeled each other, as

violent as the emotions coursing through me. I did not pay attention to which side was winning, nor did I take time to reflect on the outcome of a game before I rapidly reset the board for another battle.

In this dismal way, I passed a few mindless hours. Drinking coffee, smoking cigarettes, killing off pieces without restraint.

I was in the middle of another war when a shadow fell over my table. I lifted my gaze and there she was.

Hannah Goldman.

She had on a white-and-red checkered dress that made me think of a blood-spattered chessboard. She took in my table: the crowded ashtray, the chessboard, me the solitary player. A frown drew faint lines on her forehead. Without asking or waiting for an invitation, she sat down.

"I expected you last night, Adam," she said. She was reproachful, but not very. She could sense my overall mood, but she did not know the cause of it.

"I was busy," I said, putting the white queen on the wrong square and then sliding it angrily to its rightful place.

"Doing something important, I hope."

"Very."

"Care to share what it was? Because I don't appreciate being stood up."

"I'm sure you didn't lack for company."

"What is that supposed to mean?" Her tone was angrier now, and her eyes were blazing. I set another two pieces on the board, and when she touched my hand to stop me, I jerked it away.

"It's not going to work, Hannah," I said, looking straight into her blue eyes, seeing a blend of confusion and pain in them.

"You don't want to see me anymore?"

"No."

"Why?"

"It's not going to work."

"You said that already. I want to know why."

"Does it matter?"

"Yes, dammit, it most certainly does. Things were going pretty well, I thought, and then you stand me up and don't even bother apologizing for it, and now you're acting distant and cold, and you look like you hate me, and I want to know why."

"Because I saw you," I said, the words coming out in a hoarse growl of accusation. "I went to see you two nights ago. I had solved the case, for real this time, and I wanted to tell you. I needed to. But when I got close to your shack, I saw you. I saw you kissing the blond man."

Hannah sat frozen for a moment. Her frown deepened for a second, but then her forehead smoothed out, and she leaned toward me, putting both forearms on the table.

"Did you also see me slap his face, or did you happen to miss that?"

Now it was my turn to frown.

"You didn't, did you?"

"Why would you slap him?" I asked.

"Because the bastard kissed me against my will, that's why. It was either that or kick him in a sensitive place."

"You didn't want to kiss him?" I asked slowly, feeling slightly dazed.

"No, I most certainly didn't." She drew in a big breath and then let it out in an exasperated huff. "Here's what happened, Adam. Here's the truth, and you can do with it whatever you want. The man you saw in my shack was a lover of mine until recently. Two nights ago, he came to my shack, hoping to spend time with me, but I told him he and I were through. He didn't much care for the idea. He tried to change my mind. And when his words failed, he grabbed me and kissed me. Maybe he thought he was such a great kisser that I would immediately want to go to bed with him. Instead, I pulled away as soon as I could and landed a slap that must have been heard as far away as Jerusalem."

With a mounting sense of unease, I said, "Zelda told me he undressed you, that he touched your breasts."

"Zelda told you? How did you end up talking to that witch?"

"She was there, in the doorway of her shack. She saw me standing there right after you kissed—I mean right after the man kissed you. She told me he proceeded to take your dress off."

"And touch my breasts, yes, I understand. But why did you need Zelda to tell you this? Couldn't you see for yourself?"

I could barely look her in the eye. "No, I couldn't. Because the moment I saw the man kissing you, I turned away. And when I was about to look again, Zelda warned me not to, saying—well, what I told you she said."

"Huh," Hannah said, shaking her head. "I must say I've underestimated her. She's more devious than I thought."

"She lied to hurt you," I said, and all the anger I'd felt over the past two days evaporated in an instant.

"And you too, I imagine, though I was certainly the primary target."

"She said pretty nasty things about you."

"I can well imagine."

And I believed them, I thought. *I believed them all.* I ran a hand over my face, a powerful sense of shame coming over me.

"I'm so sorry, Hannah. I was a fool. A stupid fool." *And I've ruined it all. I've driven her away.*

"A fool is usually stupid, Adam," she said, but her tone was light, not berating. "And I accept your apology. You jumped to conclusions, but you had cause. It really hurt you to see him kiss me, didn't it?"

I shifted in my seat. "Maybe there's no reason why it should have. I have no claim to you."

"That's right, you don't. No man does. The last one who thought he did got his face slapped, but you know that already. Adam, do you know why I told this man he and I were through? It's because of you. Because I like you. I find you interesting and attractive and brave and honorable, and I want to get to know you better. I'm not ready to wear your ring or bear your children or have you over every night of the week, and maybe I'll never be. But for now, I don't wish to see any other man but you."

A pleasant heat formed in my chest, and I could feel a silly grin forming. I looked across the table and saw that Hannah was grinning too.

"Does this mean we're all right, Adam?"

I nodded, still grinning, and took her hand. "Yes. We're all right, Hannah."

"Good. Now why don't you get me a cup of that excellent coffee? What do you say?"

I didn't have to be told twice. I caught Greta's eye—it wasn't difficult, she hadn't looked away from us since Hannah had sat down across from me—and raised two fingers in the universal sign of victory, and the Greta's Café sign of two coffees, please.

Greta actually clapped, and there again was the borderline maniacal grin she'd worn when I'd introduced her to Hannah. Only this time, I didn't mind it at all.

After Greta brought us the coffee and we each took a sip, Hannah said, "Have you heard about Ami and Batya Rapoport?"

"No."

"He left her. He just left her. And she's pregnant. Why don't you look surprised?"

"Because I'm not," I said, and told her about Batya's betrayal.

"Unbelievable," she said when I was done. "You're not kidding, are you? Bella's husband had an affair with Batya?"

"And got her pregnant."

"And all the while, she was part of that gaggle of gossipers who said terrible things about me."

"People often castigate others for their own sins."

"How did Ami react when you told him the baby wasn't his?"

"Like the world had come to an end."

"Poor man."

"Yes."

"It must have been difficult for you as well, to see him like that."

"It was. He's a good man; he does not deserve to feel such pain. Up until the moment I told him, I wasn't sure I was going to."

"What made you finally decide?"

"Two reasons. One, before I told him, I handed him an envelope with over six thousand liras in it."

Hannah's eyes became massive pools of blue. "Where did the money come from?"

"Mr. Soffer. He's the one who killed Emmanuel. Well, he arranged for him to be killed. He's the one who committed the land fraud, not Caspi. It's Emmanuel's money. At least that's how I see it." I saw her perplexity and added, "It's a long story."

"I can't wait to hear it."

"I'll be happy to tell it to you a little later. Anyway, Ami was the closest thing to a family that Emmanuel had, so I felt he should have the money. When I gave it to him, he said how happy Batya would be to have it. It's enough for an apartment, which is what Batya wants most in the world. I didn't feel it would be right for her to benefit from Emmanuel's death in any way. Not after the way she treated him."

I finished my coffee. "You see, I know now that Batya didn't want Emmanuel gone just because he was costing her money. It was also because while he was there, she couldn't meet with her lover."

"Dear God," Hannah said.

"So she doesn't deserve the money. That's how I feel. But ultimately, I left it for Ami to decide."

"What's the second reason you told him?"

"Much simpler than the first. I just thought he deserved to know the truth, to make an informed decision about his life. I'd be robbing him of too much if I kept him in the dark."

She thought about it and nodded. "You did right, Adam."

I hoped she was right because I remembered how Ami had looked when I told him. How angry denial gave way to agonized acceptance. How he collapsed to his knees in tears. And how he ran away, richer in money and truth but poorer in how he saw his life.

"Now, how did you end up realizing Soffer was the killer and not Caspi?" Hannah asked.

"It's a pretty remarkable story."

"I'm all ears."

"Want another cup of coffee while I tell it?"

"Why not?"

I made eye contact with Greta and signaled her for more coffee. But instead of raising two fingers, I raised three.

Because Greta should hear the story too.

AFTERWORD

Dear reader,

Thank you for reading *In That Sleep of Death*. I hope you enjoyed it. If you did, I'd be grateful if you took a minute to write a review on whatever website you use to buy or review books. Thank you. I appreciate it.

I thought you might like to know more on how I came to write this novel. It was born from the research I do into the Holocaust and the history of the State of Israel and the Jewish Yishuv that preceded it.

I am always on the hunt for interesting facts about those times and events. Often these facts help to enrich my writing, but sometimes they become ideas from which whole books are born.

In the case of *In That Sleep of Death*, the story came from a combination of a few different facts that caught my attention.

The first was the shoe detail in Sachsenhausen. I don't recall how I learned of it initially, but it made a distinct impression on me. From that came the vision of a man sleepwalking through Tel Aviv in the dead of night, wearing army boots, reliving the nightmare of the shoe detail in Sachsenhausen. That man became Emmanuel Feldbaum, though at the time I knew next to nothing about him.

The second was the fascinating story of Reuven Schenzvit, a man of many exploits and schemes, who in the 1930s devised an elaborate land fraud in the Land of Israel. Schenzvit bought land not far from Tel Aviv and marketed it as the location of a new city, which he called Tel Nof. Schenzvit had no intention of building the city; his only goal was to profit from the sale of his land. Among the people he targeted were Polish Jews.

The third fact that helped bring this story to life was my introduction to the *Palestine Gazette*. This was a real government magazine, and it did include lists of people who changed their names. This not only gave me the idea that the villain of this book had changed his name, but also the means by which Adam Lapid would discover this.

An interesting fact is that the *Palestine Gazette* did not merely list people's original and newly acquired names, it also indicated their nationality as Palestinian. This included Jewish people. In those days, everyone who lived in the region was viewed as Palestinian.

Naturally, these three facts were only the initial spark of the novel. Much was left to be discovered in the course of the writing. As always, I did not plan the book in advance, so I found myself surprised by where the narrative took me. I hope you found the journey as rewarding and intriguing as I did.

I'd like to thank Liz Clare, Jeannie Blau, and Sandy Dobres for their generous assistance in the editing of this novel.

In That Sleep of Death is book 8 of the Adam Lapid series. You can find an updated list of all the books in the series here: JonathanDunsky.com/books

Adam's story is far from complete. I am already thinking of the next book. It may continue Adam's life in Tel Aviv, or it may be set in Europe before Adam immigrated to the Land of Israel.

As always, I'd welcome any questions or feedback that you may have, dear reader. You can email me at Jonathan@JonathanDunsky.com.

I invite you to join my author's page at https://Facebook.com/JonathanDunskyBooks or to visit my personal website at https://JonathanDunsky.com.

Thank you for reading my work. I hope to see you in the next book.

Jonathan Dunsky,

Israel, December 2023.

BOOK CLUB DISCUSSION
QUESTIONS

1. Discuss Adam and Emmanuel Feldbaum's encounters on the nighttime streets of Tel Aviv. How did you feel when you read that first chapter?

2. Adam agrees to investigate the murder of Emmanuel Feldbaum even though he thinks he shouldn't. What does it say about him that he decides to proceed with the case?

3. Discuss the character of Ami Rapoport and his relationship with his wife, Batya.

4. Hannah Goldman is described as an outsider among the women of Mahlul. What do you think of her character and her attitude toward the other women?

5. Adam is reluctant to visit Reuben Tzanani's home so he wouldn't be confronted with his family. What do you think of this decision?

6. What do you think of Emmanuel Feldbaum? How did the way his character was described make you feel?

7. Eli Soffer did a wrong when he defrauded the Jews of Mastarnia. Then he compounded that wrong by becoming a killer. Discuss the way in which one wrong can lead to other and bigger wrongs.

8. Benjamen Caspi is ashamed of his son, but he still loves him on

some deep level. What sort of love can we have for blood relatives of whom we are ashamed?

9. Adam finds it difficult to start a relationship with Hannah because he feels as though this would be an abandonment of his dead wife. Discuss the way in which a person can find love again after the loss of a spouse and do so in a healthy and guiltless way.

10. Adam feels a kinship with two of the victims. With Feldbaum because of their similar trauma; with Suskind because of their actions after the war. In what way are these two feelings similar? How are they different?

<<<<>>>>

BOOKS BY JONATHAN DUNSKY

The Adam Lapid Series

Ten Years Gone

The Dead Sister

The Auschwitz Violinist

A Debt of Death

A Deadly Act

The Auschwitz Detective

A Death in Jerusalem

In That Sleep of Death

The Unlucky Woman (short story)

Standalone Novels

The Payback Girl

The above list is accurate at the time of the publication of this book.

For a continuously updated list, visit:

JonathanDunsky.com/reading-order

ABOUT THE AUTHOR

Jonathan Dunsky lives in Israel with his wife and two sons. He enjoys reading, writing, and goofing around with his kids. He began writing in his teens, then took a break for close to twenty years, during which he worked an assortment of jobs. He is the author of the Adam Lapid mystery series and the standalone thriller The Payback Girl.

Printed in Great Britain
by Amazon